A perfect world begins with

X^n

by
Clint Townsend

$$X^n$$

Xⁿ

X to the Nth

Clint Townsend

ELM HILL

A Division of
HarperCollins Christian Publishing

www.elmhillbooks.com

X^n
X to the Nth

Published in Nashville, Tennessee, by Elm Hill, an imprint of Thomas Nelson. Elm Hill and Thomas Nelson are registered trademarks of HarperCollins Christian Publishing, Inc.

Elm Hill titles may be purchased in bulk for educational, business, fund-raising, or sales promotional use. For information, please e-mail SpecialMarkets@ ThomasNelson.com.

Library of Congress Cataloging-in-Publication Data

Library Congress Control Number: 2018956335

ISBN 978-1-595558992 (Paperback)
ISBN 978-1-595559241 (Ebook)

For my sister Kim - with all my love, admiration,
gratitude, and deepest respect.

TABLE OF CONTENTS

CHAPTER 1

ADAM

Lubbock, Texas, 1986.

"All right, boys, what'll it be for last call?" asked the waitress as she placed the beers on the table.

The five young men clapped and whistled as they reached for the cold bottles of Shiner Bock.

"Who's behind the bar tonight?" Evan inquired and wrapped his arm around her hips.

"Ricky and Blake," she replied seductively, laying her hand on his shoulder.

"Excellent!" he stated, looking up at her shimmering eyes. "First, we're gonna have a repeat on the cocktails."

"All of you? All five?" she asked astonishingly.

"Yes, ma'am!" the quintet answered in jovial unison.

"Three Jacks, a Crown, and a Bacardi?"

"You got it," Evan confirmed.

"All right, I'll get these out in a few minutes." she replied, turning to walk away.

"WHOA!" the men erupted.

"Hold on, hold on! We're not done." Ron said, reaching for the young girls' arm.

"You just got five beers, you're about to get another round of cocktails, and you want to order more?"

The barmaid snuck a peek at her watch, shook her head, and lamented, "I don't know if y'all will have enough time to finish everything before the bell."

"Oh, we'll finish in time!" John declared confidently.

"Tell Ricky we want another shot," Evan instructed the girl, "But I don't wanna know what he's making. He can fix us Coconut Kamikazes, Fruit of the Looms, or DeLoreans; I don't care, just surprise us."

"Oh, he's gonna love y'all for this one!"

With a sigh and roll of her eyes, the waitress turned to deliver the lengthy drink order.

Evan and his brood lunged to the middle of table to clink the necks of their beers in a celebratory toast.

"You gotta be kidding me!" Ricky complained loudly as he read the ticket request.

"To Ricky!" the five men cheered, turning to face the bar. Although flustered, the mixologist managed to let a smile cross his face as he scurried to fill the drink requests before the bell.

"All right, gentlemen, now we come to the real reason I've called you here this evening," Evan abruptly stated.

"Here it comes," Ken whined.

"Hold on now," Ron interjected. "Let's see what kind of evidence the prosecution presents before we make a plea bargain."

"He always does this!" Greg complained. "He's got something to tell us, but instead of just saying what he's gotta say, he's gonna drag it out and make a show of it!"

"Patience, Greg, patience," Evan patronized. "A good attorney waits to hear all arguments before he reveals his plan of attack."

"Thank you for the lecture, professor," Greg snapped back.

Evan reached into the breast pocket of his jacket and slowly pulled out a certified envelope. He deliberately took his time as he looked over the front of the letter, ever so slightly nodding his head.

"Come on!" John demanded, "Just say it and quit jackin' around!"

Evan casually tossed the envelope on the table and reached for his beer. The quartet made a mad grab for the letter, but it was Ron who was successful and held the prize in his hand.

"So what was your score on the MBE?" Ken asked Evan as Ron removed the letter and began to read.

"I don't even wanna know!" Greg commented drolly.

"You know he's gonna milk it just to see us squirm," John followed.

"Oh my goodness!" Ron exclaimed, smiling.

"One fifty-nine," Evan calmly answered Ken.

"What is it?" Greg asked Ron.

"Nice!" Ron stated, nodding his head as well, "Does Shelly know about this?"

"Know about what?" Greg anxiously piped up.

"Not just yet," Evan replied mysteriously.

"Just say it and get on with the conversation!" John demanded.

Tired of getting the runaround, Ken leaned over the table and snatched the letter from Ron's hand.

"If you two Chatty Cathys are done wasting our time...," John quipped.

"You fine lobotomized morons are speaking with the newest member of the staff fortunate enough to be in the employ of...Christian and Connor," Evan proudly stated.

"Houston?" Ken asked in bewilderment as he scanned the content of the communique.

"Yes, sir!" Evan quickly answered.

"What're you gonna be doing?" Greg inquired, yanking the paper from Ken.

"I'll be leading a team dealing primarily with international contracts, intellectual property, and acquisitions," Evan informed his cohorts.

"When did this happen?" Greg asked.

"While you guys were cliff jumping at the lake, I was in Austin having a meeting with Mr. Connor to discuss salary and benefits," Evan explained.

Just then, the waitress appeared and hurriedly called out the drinks as she placed them on the table.

"Three Jacks, a Crown, and a Bacardi," she spewed. "And you guys are gonna hafta slam the shooters, 'cause…."

Before she could warn Evan about the time, Ricky yanked the rope on the bar bell and began yelling, "Drink 'em up!"

He rang the bell loudly and quickly, all the while smiling and staring at Evan.

"He can't do that!" John declared.

"Well, actually he can," said the waitress.

"Don't argue, just drink!" Ron ordered.

"What do we have here?" Ken asked as she gave each of them their shots.

"Coconut Kamikazes," she hotly answered. "Hurry, y'all! He's gonna have me start clearing tables! It's two o'clock right now!"

"To Ricky!" Greg toasted.

The five buddies stood quickly, turned to face the bar, and held up their glasses.

"What a man!" John stated before they slammed back the potent concoctions.

"Oh, c'mon!" the waitress griped, removing the bottles and empty glasses, then added "You're messin' around and he's gonna have me pull your drinks."

"No one's gonna nothing," Greg comforted as they rushed to finish their cocktails.

"To Evan and new beginnings," Ron announced, holding his glass high.

"To Evan," they echoed.

"Hey!" Ricky shouted from behind the bar, "It's after two! Pull the drinks! Now!"

"I'm trying!" the waitress yelled back, exasperated, as she hovered beside Evan, just itching to take the glasses from their hands.

The intoxicated men turned away from the impatient barmaid, making it virtually impossible for her to reach the glasses.

"C'mon y'all, I don't have time for this!" she complained loudly, "I still gotta do my cash out and break down my section."

All five men slurped the last of their highballs in near perfect unison and handed them off to the waitress.

"Thanks Evan," she grumbled as she handed him the check, "You don't have to leave just yet, but if you would pay out that would be great."

Every man began reaching for his billfold, but Evan spoke up, "Not tonight, gentlemen. This one's on me."

"Wow!" Ken commented, "That must have been some salary negotiation."

"Something like that," Evan answered, then added, "Oh! I almost forgot. I knew there was something else I was supposed to talk to y'all about."

Evan pulled a large wad of cash from his pocket and held it high in the air.

"Aren't you gonna count that?" John asked, looking confused.

"Nah!" Evan scoffed, "No need."

The waitress saw Evan holding the check and cash, darted to the table, and plucked the money from his clenched hand. She silently scurried away as Evan continued.

"Along with the new career and change of address, there's gonna be one major additional change."

John looked over Evan's shoulder at the waitress in the corner of the bar.

"I need to get your opinions on something...," Evan began as he leaned back and dug down into his pants pocket.

While the other men watched Evan, John kept his eyes on the waitress. She pulled out her ticket book and the last check and cash from Evan. John could see her as she counted out the bills in front of Ricky.

"But I also want y'all to be the first to know," Evan finished saying as he slowly pulled his hand out of his pocket and placed a small, dark purple, crushed velvet box in the middle of the table.

Ron leaned back in his chair and once again said "Oh, my goodness!"

John watched Ricky and the waitress shake their heads as they counted and recounted the cash Evan had given her.

"Does she know this is coming?" Ken asked as Ron reached for the box.

"We talked about it a few months ago," Evan replied, locking eyes with Ron.

Ricky and the waitress turned their attention to the five friends.

"When are you gonna ask her?" Greg asked as he leaned over to see what was in the jewelry box.

Ricky and the waitress held up the cash and pointed at the ticket as if to ask, *Does he know how much he gave her?*

"Oh, my goodness!" Ron declared for the third time that evening. He stared in amazement as he gingerly removed the two-and-a-half carat, white gold and platinum, rectangular-cut diamond ring from the cushioned jewelry box.

John nodded his head to Ricky and the waitress, confirming, "Yes, he meant to give you that much," and motioned them away.

The waitress held her hand over her mouth and jogged in place with excitement over receiving such a large gratuity.

"I'm going to meet her on Sunday in Amarillo. She went to visit her parents for the weekend and I thought I'd propose after they got outta church," Evan informed his entourage.

"Wow!" "Nice!" and "Sweet!" seemed to be to be the only words the flabbergasted men could muster.

"Do you like her parents?" Ken inquired as the men stood to leave.

"Sure; they're pretty nice," Evan commented. "Her dad is kind of quiet, but if you start talking football or get him to play dominoes, he'll be nonstop conversation."

"Why not go to church with all of 'em and then ask her dad?" John asked.

"Ah," Evan began with a shrug, "I'm not much into that hocus-pocus kinda thing."

"All I can say is 'Wow!'" Ron admitted, gazing at the ring.

Grasping Evan's shoulder, Ron handed him the ring and continued, "My best friend…getting married, graduating, moving, getting a new job. Ever since I knew you when we was kids, I knew good things were gonna be coming your way."

"Whadya mean 'coming his way'?" Greg complained as they swaggered down the staircase.

"He's had nothing but good things happen to him his whole life," Ken declared.

"Yeah!" John agreed, "Who got the attendance records for junior high and high school."

"Evan," the quartet hollered.

"Who never got sick in school?" Ron asked.

"Evan," they again bellowed.

"Oh, I got one," Ken said as he exited the bar, "Who was the high school valedictorian and graduated from the Tech School of Law at the top of the class?"

Once more the men triumphantly cried out "Evan!"

"I think y'all are blowing this way out of proportion," Evan commented.

"Yeah? Well, proportion this," John stated and punched Evan in his arm.

"Oh!" Evan grunted, trying in vain to laugh off the hurt, "You are such a 'tard!"

"To Evan!" the remaining three shouted and proceeded to punch Evan's arms.

"I'm never gonna buy y'all another drink!" Evan threatened his comrades as he fought back.

After the slugfest subsided, Evan rubbed his biceps and stated "Take one last, long, good look, my brothers."

The quintet turned to face the lighted restaurant sign.

"Good ol' Gardski's," Ken moaned.

"We sure had some great times, didn't we?" Ron asked sorrowfully.

"It's nights like these that remind me of nights I've forgotten," Greg added.

"A lot of good times," Evan confirmed.

"All right!" John jumped in, "I'm getting outta here before you sissies start huggin' and cryin.'"

With that comment, John once again punched Evan in his arm and abruptly turned to walk away. Greg and Ken blindsided Evan and landed one more solid jab each on Evan's shoulders, then quickly caught up with John.

"Be sure to send us an invitation!" John hollered over his shoulder.

"Man!" Evan grunted, wincing in pain.

"Oh, c'mon," Ron chimed in, "You know you love it."

Ron landed one more mighty wallop to Evan's already sore and tender bicep. Evan fell to the ground from the force of the hit.

"You too?" he shouted with a chuckle of disbelief.

"Nothing's too good for my best friend," Ron declared as he extended his hand to Evan.

"Man, you're killing me!" Evan complained as he rose to his feet.

The lifelong buddies began walking down Broadway towards the main entrance to the campus of Texas Tech University, reminiscing about their boyhood and their future plans.

"I'm telling you right now," Evan began, "I'm not gonna miss the flatlands or the panhandle wind."

"Well, you know what my cousin Mike says about Lubbock, don't you?"

"No, what does your cousin Mike say about Lubbock?"

"He says Lubbock is so flat you can watch your dog run away for three days!"

Evan and Ron were still laughing at the joke as they crossed the intersection of Broadway and Avenue W, just one block away from the Tech campus.

From out of nowhere, a beat up Oldsmobile came racing around the corner. Evan gave Ron a mighty shove and both men fell headlong into the curbside. Ron let out a moan of discomfort as he landed, whereas Evan gave a shrill scream of pain and agony.

"What's wrong? Are you hurt?"

"No, you idiot! I scream all the time just for kicks when I've almost been run over! Yes, I'm hurt!"

"All right, let's take a look," Ron said as gingerly tried to roll Evan over on to his back. "Where does it hurt?"

"Ah, Holy Mackerel, that hurts like crap!"

"Oh, my God!"

"What? What is it? Tell me!"

"We need to get you to the hospital! Now!"

Protruding from the underside of Evan's ribcage was a large shard of glass from a broken beer bottle. The bright red blood poured swiftly from the massive entrance wound just below the last rib on Evan's right side.

"Is it bad?" Evan asked with a sense of panic in his voice.

Ron began to remove his shirt and soothingly said, "You're gonna be fine."

Evan stared up at the clear, summer night sky. He tried to focus on the sound of his friend's voice as he surveyed the glistening stars and carefully reached for his ribs. Ron pressed his shirt around the wound, trying desperately to slow down the bleeding. Evan felt the jagged point of glass sticking out from his gut and barked "Oh, crap! Oh, crap! Oh, crap!"

"Ah, c'mon, quit your belly achin'! Or I'll bust you one in the other arm."

"Ow! You bonehead! Don't make me laugh!"

"I'll make it to where you'll forget all about your little tummy ache!"

"Hit me again and you won't be my best man AND I'll never buy you another drink."

"Okay, truce. First, we got to get you up. We'll go on three."

"Let me count it off," Evan offered, then took a series of long, deep breaths.

"Okay, I'm ready. Here we go," he said as he wrapped his left arm around Ron's neck.

"One, two…." Ron jumped the gun on the count and shot skyward with a powerful burst of energy and brought Evan to his feet.

"Three!" Ron exclaimed.

"Augh! You freaking idiot!" Evan shrieked in horrific agony, "I said I'll count it off! You're killing me!"

"You're up, ain't ya? What does it matter?" Ron remarked smartly, "Let's get you to the car and over to the hospital."

***

"I need to ask you a few questions," said the rotund nurse.

She leaned over Evan's face and spoke loudly, as if having sustained an injury makes one's hearing immediately diminish.

"That's fine," Evan replied smoothly.

"You mind telling me once more how this happened?" asked the doctor.

"Well," Evan began, "we had just left Gardski's and were crossing Avenue W when all of a sudden this car came around the corner from behind us. It was turning off of Broadway on to W."

"Ever been hospitalized?" the nurse interrupted.

"No, ma'am," Evan answered, "So the car came from behind us to my right; I heard the tires squeal and turned to see what was happening."

"Ever have any surgeries? Any kind of operation?" the nurse once again disrupted the story.

Evan repeated his answer as before "No, ma'am."

"You ain't never been in a hospital?" Ron asked, breaking his silence.

"Nope," Evan stated, rolling his eyes back as far as he could to see his friend sitting in the corner.

"Man … I been in so many emergency…," Ron began to divulge.

"Anyway … on with the story," the doctor raised his voice, obviously irritated with the interruptions.

"Anyhow, I saw the car coming right at us and I really didn't have the time to think about it, but I shoved Ron outta the way and dove as far as I could."

"Any smoking or drug use?" the plump woman inquired.

"Oh, no!" Evan firmly answered.

"Well, Mr. Cierly? While I'm sure you're thankful you weren't hit by a car, I'm thinking you're probably just as thankful this didn't go any deeper into your abdominal cavity."

The doctor extracted a four-inch long section of glass from Evan's right side and held it up for all to see.

"A quarter inch deeper and you and I might have been having this conversation in an operating room."

The nurse, unfazed by the sight of blood, continued with her questionnaire, "Any consumption of alcohol?"

"Oh, yeah!" the two men answered promptly.

"Man, that was big!" Ron added, commenting on the size of the remnant of glass the doctor extracted.

"So, you boys like to drink," the doctor surmised as he turned to throw away the shard of broken beer bottle.

"Yes, sir!" the duo exclaimed.

"Alcohol consumption?" the nurse probed.

"Oh, four or five times a week, maybe?" Evan stated, unsure of his answer as he glanced back at Ron for verification.

"No more than five, I'd say," Ron volunteered.

"Yeah, I believe I drink about five nights a week," Evan confirmed.

"Is that what you guys were doing tonight?" the doctor inquired as he began stitching Evan's wound.

"My man's getting engaged Sunday!" Ron blurted out.

"Really?" asked the nurse, changing to a more chipper tone, "Well, congratulations!"

"My deepest condolences," the doctor muttered as he stitched.

"Liquor, beer, wine?" the nurse resumed, "What do you drink and how much?"

"Everything," Evan declared bluntly.

"All of it," Ron added.

"So…?" the nurse pushed, shrugging her shoulders.

"I might have a couple of beers then move on to bourbon. I'll have several of those," Evan confessed.

"In what kind of time period?" the doctor queried, briefly raising his eyes.

"I don't know. Maybe two hours," Evan admitted.

"I bet your liver loves you," the nurse mumbled.

"The guy is a fish! I ain't never seen anyone hold their liquor like Evan," Ron professed.

"Did you do a complete workup on Mr. Cierly?" the doctor asked his assistant.

"Yessiree," she replied, stood, and handed the lab report to the doctor. He examined the results for a brief moment then silently handed back the report.

"What all did you drink this evening?" the doctor asked nonchalantly, resuming his stitching, "And please, tell me when you started and when you took your last swallow."

"You want the whole rundown?" Evan asked. "Okay, well, Ron and I got to Gardski's about seven-thirty, had some wings and onion rings, and a couple of pitchers of beer."

The nurse stopped writing in her folder and listened to Evan's recount of the night's festivities. The good doctor steadily sewed up the gaping wound under his rib while he, too, listened to the story.

"The guys showed up at about nine and we just sat around talking."

"Do y'all remember what you had to drink tonight?" asked the doctor.

"Kamikazes, Stilettos, DeLoreans," Ron rattled off, as if reciting a list of accomplishments.

"Crown, Jack, Bacardi…," Evan joined in, "then Shiner, Shiner, Shiner…."

"In other words," the doctor interrupted, "you all had more than your fill, right?"

"When you say it like that, you make it sound like it's a bad thing," Ron complained.

"So, all in all, how many shots?" the doctor quizzed.

"Five," Evan answered.

"Highballs?" he continued.

"Five," Ron replied.

"Beer?" the doctor questioned.

"Five," Evan finished, "Not including the pitchers."

The physician tied off the line on Evan's stitches in total silence. He stood up, took off his gloves, then turned and threw them away. It wasn't until he began washing his hands that the doctor addressed his patient.

"Mr. Cierly? To the best of my calculations, you personally consumed over one hundred twenty-four ounces of beer and about seventeen ounces of liquor. Does that sound right to you?"

"I'd say that's in the ballpark," Evan confirmed with a smile.

"Y'all had all that alcohol in seven hours which, in my head, averages out to one drink every twenty minutes, give or take a few minutes," the doctor summarized.

"Now you're making us look bad!" Ron moaned.

"How do you feel?" the doctor asked Ron, crossing his arms.

Ron flashed a devilish grin, shrugged his shoulders, and simply stated, "Heeey."

"I thought so," the doctor commented.

"What's your point?" Evan probed as he sat up on the edge of the gurney.

"My point is this: how is it you've never been sick, never been hospitalized, you have no medical records beyond your childhood immunizations, and after seven hours of steady consumption, your blood alcohol content is point zero, zero, zero, one two?"

All four looked at one another for a moment before the doctor coolly voiced his instructions to his assistant, "I want you to draw enough blood to cover two more complete workups on Mr. Cierly. After you've done that, I want you to run a liver enzyme and full array on one of the pulls. Make sure you get the results to me and send copies to Rankin and Schropture over at Methodist."

"Yes, sir," the nurse acknowledged with a sigh as the doctor turned to leave the ER suite.

"What do you want me to do with the second draw?" she shouted.

As he strode away, the doctor called out over his shoulder, "Send it up to Cryogenics and mark it 'Attention to Doctor Childers for the DNA genome study.'"

CHAPTER 2

EVE

Phoenix. Spring, 1999.

"And we're back!" the disc jockey said enthusiastically, "Ninety-three point three, Tim and Mark with you on a beautiful Friday morning."

"Man, talk about a gorgeous day. It is absolutely perfect outside," Tim's sidekick interjected, "Seventy-two degrees, winds out of the North West at ten miles an hour, and not a cloud in the sky."

"Mark, I don't think my day can get any more perfect than it already is."

"I don't know about that. I can think of several things that can make it even better."

"Better like how?"

"Well, I have a surprise for you."

"For me?"

"Well, not necessarily for you per se, but more for our listeners," Mark clarified.

"I am intrigued. Lay it on me."

"Okay. First, I have a question."

"Fire away."

"When I say *Sports Illustrated*, what do you think of?"

"Let me see. Uh, informative articles, investigative journalism...."

"LIAR! LIAR! Pants on fire!" Mark erupted, pointing and waving his finger.

"What? What?" Tim asked innocently, shrugging his shoulders.

"You think what every other guy thinks."

"And just exactly what, pray tell, do we think of?" Tim inquired, feigning ignorance.

"C'mon, admit it. You think of the bikini issue."

"I do? Oh yeah, I forgot there was a swimsuit issue."

"Yeah, right, you forgot."

"Hey, I can make an honest mistake every now and then."

"Well," Mark began, lowering his voice to almost a whisper, "What if I were to tell you that right now, at this very moment, I have *Sports Illustrated* cover model Chloe Holbrook on the phone, just waiting to talk to you?"

"Me?"

"You!"

"Chloe Holbrook?"

"Chloe Holbrook."

"I'd say you've already been drinking this morning."

"Let's just see about that. Chloe, are you there?"

"Good morning, boys!" the young woman's bright voice called out.

"Good morning, Chloe. I guess Mark hasn't been drinking after all," Tim replied.

"Hey, would I lie to you about something as big as this?" Mark defended himself.

"What's going on, guys?" Chloe asked.

"Wait a minute, where are you?" Mark inquired, "You sound so far away."

"I'm headed north on highway five-fifty, just about fifteen miles south of Durango, Colorado," she informed the duo.

"Ah, I love Colorado. What's going on in Durango?" Tim and Mark commented and asked simultaneously.

"Well, I'm actually on my way to Telluride for the annual Food and Wine Magazine Jazz Festival."

"Do you like jazz music?" Tim quizzed.

"Um, I enjoy all kinds of music, just not rap or hip-hop, but I do like wine and eating," Chloe answered laughingly.

"What's a cover model like you going up into the snow country for?" Mark probed.

As he was speaking, Mark pointed to Tim then tapped himself on the chest. From that moment on it was understood that the two disc jockeys would alternate their questions for Chloe.

"Well, it's really a business trip mixed with pleasure. We're partnering with the American Red Cross on a national blood drive."

"Now, do they draw your blood before or after the wine festival?" Tim followed up.

"I wish after. I hate needles and I can't stand the sight of blood. So if I'm gonna give blood, I gotta be a little schnockered."

"Now, is it just you going on this trip?" Mark probed.

"Oh, no. This is a full-out blitz. It's me, Daniella Pestova, Eva Herzigova, Michelle Behennah, Rebecca Romijn, and Heidi Klum."

"I can honestly say that if I were to see all of you live at one time and in person, I would just let them take all of my blood. Period," Tim confessed.

"Oh, how sweet! But I think you're confused. The festival and the blood drive aren't related, they just happen to be going on at the same time. The jazz festival is every year. The blood drive goes everywhere all the time."

"How did you land this gig with being on the cover?" Mark then asked.

"Yeah, 'cuz aren't you some kind of genius, egghead, bookworm nerd?" Tim added.

"That wasn't nice!" Chloe laughingly exclaimed.

"Tim, how many times do I have to tell you don't insult the bikini girls?"

"Yeah, Tim, don't insult the gorgeous, highly intellectual, internationally famous swimsuit model," Chloe added.

"I apologize, Chloe. As I understand it, you are currently enrolled at MIT. Am I right?" Tim inquired.

"Yes, I'm in my sophomore year."

"Have you declared your major?" Mark queried.

"Biological and mechanical engineering with a minor in nanotechnology. I just don't know what I'm going to do with a degree in nano yet. Maybe computers or robotics. I'm not sure."

"So, how do you go from MIT to SI?" Tim pressed.

"Well, that was really a fluke. My cousin is a cadet at West Point and on the Army wrestling team. And my roommate, Julie, well her boyfriend is at the Naval Academy, and Army was wrestling against Navy last year. We decided to take a road trip to New York and go to their matches and come to find out one of the photographers for *Sports Illustrated* was there and he's the brother of Cheryl Tiegs. After the match, Julie and I went to go congratulate my cousin and the photographer took a couple of pictures of us with the Army team. Cheryl saw the pictures a few days later and liked how I looked and tracked me down. She has contacts with Elite, Ford, Wilhelmina, John Casablancas, IMG … and set me up with a photo shoot. And the rest, as they say, is history."

"So, are you dropping out of school or are you going to try to do both?" asked Mark.

"I am definitely not dropping out! Members on both sides of my family have worked at Los Alamos Labs, JPL, and Johns Hopkins. My great grandfather worked with Oppenheimer on the Manhattan Project and I know my mom and dad would kill me if I threw it all away."

"Okay, speaking of grandfathers, what's the story I heard about your grandpa knowing Daniel Boone?" Tim asked.

"Oh, yeah! Grandpa Isaac. He was my—let me think about this—my great, great … great … great grandfather. He was born a couple of years after the ratification of the US Constitution and died in nineteen-ten, I believe. Maybe nineteen-eleven."

"Shut up!" "You're pulling my leg!" and "Aw, c'mon!" rang out over the airwaves as the radio hosts voiced their skepticism.

"No, I'm serious! He was like a hundred and twenty-two years old when he died. He knew Daniel Boone and Sam Houston, met Davy Crockett, and if I recall correctly, he was in charge of an armory in Texas for the Confederacy during the Civil War. He was called 'The Walking Man' 'cuz he walked everywhere. There's a historical marker about him in China Springs, Texas. That's just northwest of Waco."

"So do you plan on living 'til you're a hundred and twenty?" Mark asked.

"I don't know. I think that would be an incredible experience. My great-grandma Mary Molly lived to be ninety-nine, Grandma Marguerite was ninety-six when she passed away, and my Mimi was ninety when she passed. So I don't know … maybe. We have both Cherokee and Comanche blood in our family and a history of longevity."

"All right, I'm dying to know and tired of waiting … what's your IQ?" Tim boldly inquired.

"Oh, come on, guys, don't make me say that on the air!"

"Tell me! Tell me! Tell me!" the two men squealed.

"Ugh! All right! One thirty-one."

"Wow! Beauty, brains, and blood. Chloe, thank you so very much for speaking with us," Tim stated.

"Oh, you're so welcome! I'll be sure to come by the studios next time I'm in town. Bye y'all."

"Bye, Chloe!" the men said simultaneously.

After the call ended, Tim was first to comment to the radio audience, "Man! If only there was a way to get her brain and bloodline in our bodies. Can you imagine what the world would be like if everyone was as smart and lived as long as Chloe and her family?"

CHAPTER 3

BABEL

In 1955, both the United States and the Soviet Union announced plans for the development and deployment of an artificial satellite. The Russians were first to successfully launch their version, Sputnik, into space in October of 1957. With a low-Earth, elliptical orbital pattern, the shiny sphere transmitted pulses of radio waves for twenty-one days. The metallic ball was visible to the naked eye and amateur HAM radio operators as well as military and intelligence personnel could tune into the satellite's frequency and listen to the 'pings' as it sped across the heavens. Sputnik circled the globe once every hour and a half, racing at an incredible eighteen thousand miles per hour. The tiny hemisphere finally reentered Earth's atmosphere and burned up harmlessly in January of 1958.

The surprising achievement of the Communists ushered in the hysteria and paranoia of the Space Race, precipitating the Cold War between the US and the Reds.

In April of 1958, President Eisenhower secretly met with the leadership of the House, Senate, Department of Defense, the director of Central Intelligence, the secretary of state, attorney general, and Joint Chiefs of Staff. Eisenhower paid careful attention to the public outcry of fear of the Russians spying on the US and possible plans for an invasion. He declared his belief in the strategy of 'maintaining the high ground' and urged his staff, quietly and discreetly, to devise a long-term solution to the new set of problems the Ruskies presented. Ike gave them until the end of the year to come up with, and present, their best and most viable ideas.

During the winter recess of 1958, President Eisenhower met with his team once again in the Oval Office to hear their plans and ideas for combating the progress of the Soviet Union. He sat behind his desk sipping coffee as he listened tentatively to the eager-to-please pitchmen. Some thought the best strategy was to invade Russia and dismantle it from the inside out. A few leaned towards the proposal of bombing Moscow with nuclear missiles. One actually suggested that the US and Soviet Union actually merge the governments to create the first multicontinental superpower. President Eisenhower was not impressed with his limited options. He rose to his feet looking sternly at the carpet and began pacing behind his desk. Eisenhower let out one long breath, parked himself in front of the windows, and began rubbing his chin and scratching his head just above the ear.

"If this is all you've got and this is your absolute best, then gentlemen, we're in for a heap of trouble," he said gruffly.

The president turned to face his think tank and stated, "Unacceptable!"

The faces of the quiet collective sank with embarrassment and disappointment. As if having just received a terse scolding from their fathers, the men lowered their eyes in self-afflicted shame.

"Mr. President?" Samuel Davis spoke up.

Samuel, who served as President Eisenhower's private driver during World War II, was now serving Ike as the White House assistant deputy director.

"Sir: in ancient Greek mythology, Zeus ruled over all of the gods on Mount Olympus. He's referred to as the 'God of the Sky' and the 'God of Thunder.'"

The other men stared at Samuel in disbelief for what he just said. They looked at the president then back at Samuel. The generals and other men of power gazed upon Samuel as if he had Spam on his head.

"Go on," said the president.

"Well, Zeus displayed his judgement for all of Greece to see. He would roll out of the clouds and whoever he felt was in the wrong... zap!"

Seated next to President Eisenhower was Secretary of Defense Neal McElroy.

Without hesitation, the secretary stated "I'm assuming the 'zap,' as you like to call it, is our forward deployment of the SAC Detachment at Incirlik Air Base in Turkey?"

"What does the detachment consist of?" asked Samuel.

"SAC has more than forty B-47s and B-52s, both capable of delivering ten to twenty thousand pounds of conventional and nuclear bombs on seventy predetermined cities, military installations, utilities, and governmental offices, including the Kremlin."

"What else?"

"SAC also has a squadron of U2s that are used in conjunction with the CIA to monitor the movement and telemetry of Soviet missiles and aircraft at Kasputin Yar and Tyuratam. Interceptors, fighters, tankers for midair refueling... we got everything to contain the Soviets."

"What are you driving at?" asked the president.

Samuel quickly rose to his feet and walked a few paces to the corner of the desk. He briefly looked at the ceiling to gather his thoughts, then addressed his commander in chief.

"Mr. President, Mr. Secretary, gentlemen. It's wonderful that we have the means, the tools, the technological know-how to defend ourselves. SAC, the bomb, NORAD... the United States is the supreme world power in all aspects of military capabilities. But in my opinion, Mr. President, we will, as a country, be paranoid and forever looking over our shoulder for fear of not knowing what the enemy is doing and not knowing what they have developed."

"Every country feels that," said the secretary.

"Agreed. But when we dropped the bombs, everybody backed off. We can discuss military strategy against every other country all day long. And for every country, every simulated situation in naval combat, each hypothetical infantry interaction and struggle for establishment of air superiority, the process of engagement and ending the engagement will be different."

"You're telling us what we already know!" Secretary of State John Foster Dulles said curtly.

"No one challenged the US after we showed the world that we had the bomb," Samuel proudly announced, "That was the single most important and constant threat that we had in our arsenal to keep everyone in check. Now the ally we relied on thirteen years ago has got a hold of the magic lamp and is toying with the idea of rereleasing the genie!"

Allen Dulles, the director of Central Intelligence, shifted in his seat as he addressed Samuel, "That's why we have all this. Tools like the U2 help us acquire information and tools of weaponry like the B-52 and the nuclear bomb help us maintain order throughout the world, not just with the Russians."

"What are we going to do when the Soviets sell a shipload of nuclear bombs to Korea?" Samuel inquired.

"Well, I think that we've gotten...," Neal McElroy attempted to redirect the conversation, but Samuel persisted.

"Cuba? What about nukes ninety miles off the coast of Florida? Do we establish a military base in every country? Who's gonna go and stand up to Germany again?"

"Samuel," the president said softly but firmly, "Why don't you just tell us what you've got on your mind."

"Yes, sir. Well, a buddy of mine from VMI is a correspondent in Africa. In '43, he was a tank driver during Operation Husky with the Italian Campaign. He was right behind Patton when he marched on Sicily and rode into Messina with the Seventh Army. He and I were talking about Hiroshima, specifically about when he went there and photographed the damage. Jackson, my buddy, said the buildings simply exploded. Except for those structures made of reinforced concrete and furthest from ground zero, everything else was splintered and vaporized. Jackson is really interested in the pyramids and Middle Eastern culture and said that if Italy or

Germany took control of Egypt and we bombed Cairo, the city would be obliterated but the pyramids wouldn't move."

Ike and his inner circle couldn't quite grasp the idea Samuel was trying to convey.

"You want us to construct a pyramid?" asked Fred Seaton, Secretary of the Interior.

"No, no, no. We don't want a pyramid. We want something higher. We want ... Olympus. Jackson said that had the Egyptians changed the rise and run ratio they used to construct the pyramids, they could have possibly gone as high as half a mile. As it is, the Egyptians didn't even excavate to bedrock. If a bomb were dropped on Cairo, the shock wave would go up and over the pyramids; they wouldn't explode or implode— they're solid."

The room of once quiet and somber men suddenly sprang back to life. As Samuel elaborated on his scheme of a man-made Mt. Olympus, men were pulling out notepads and began creating rough sketches of their own versions of what the mountain might look like.

The president opened a desk drawer and retrieved his own pad of paper.

As he was sketching, he paused and said, "Neal? Allen?"

The director of Central Intelligence and secretary of defense stopped talking to each other.

Everybody stopped talking.

"Yes, Mr. President?" the men replied.

"You're testing the Atlas ICBMs right now. Correct?"

"Yes, Mr. President," Neal McElroy firmly answered. "We anticipate the testing phase will be complete before the end of January with construction and deployment taking place no later than summer. Convair, General Dynamics, and Lockheed Martin have all assured us that deadlines will be met and performance requirements and expectations will be surpassed."

"Thank you, gentlemen," said the president.

He resumed his drawing and casually asked, "Allen, what's the anticipated range of the Atlas?"

"Maybe ninety-five hundred miles, Mr. President. But at least nine thousand for sure."

"Tell me...," the president began, "given what you know about the Atlas, can it be, or for that matter, can any ICBM, be launched horizontally from a fortified structure, say... like a tower?"

***

The Nevada desert, 2019.

In 1964, the United States Department of Defense began storing blood specimens and recording the genetic code for all members of the armed forces, including the Coast Guard and National Guard. The nineteen-eighties and nineties were witness to a breakthrough in genetic cloning. The latter half of the twentieth century and first half of the twenty-first century saw a global, exponential increase in technology, warfare, disease, political unrest, scandal, fraud, terrorism, corporate bankruptcy, ethnic cleansing, fuel consumption, famine, and genocide. The bombing of the World Trade Center and Pentagon in 2001 ushered in a whole new era of heightened anxiety, mistrust, intolerance, media manipulation, finger pointing and bureaucratic, political correctness.

Inside the Engenehem corporate headquarters, Dr. Cain Wyczthack III was presiding over an energetic press conference. He held his hands in front of his chest and with confident, yet elegant authority, spoke to the crowd of journalists, "Please, please, ladies and gentlemen... one at a time, one... at... a... time."

Cain stood behind the podium and slowly cast his ominous glare from one side of the room to the other. When the yelping finally subsided, he inspected the reporters' faces and chose one individual to set the tone of the questions. The man was sheepish, pale, thin, almost gaunt, and unkempt. Cain raised his arm and pointed a bony finger directly at the prepubescent-looking man. With a dry crack in his voice, he said "Yes…you."

"What will the completion of the space elevator do for interplanetary travel?" the reporter asked.

"For over fifty years, we have been working in close conjunction with the likes of NASA, McDonnell Douglas, Boeing, Microsoft, Intel…Texas Instruments, Tesla, SpaceX, Rockwell, Raytheon, Lockheed Martin…numerous corporations and friendly governments to develop deep space exploration and other projects of special interest."

"And by the way," Cain continued after clearing his throat, "we at Engenechem have now renamed the elevator. I would like to introduce to you the new face of lunar and interplanetary space travel…the SUBOS. The world's first Static, Umbilical-Based, Orbital Station."

Dr. Wyczthack stepped back and waved his arm behind him. Two of his assistants pulled back a black silk curtain to reveal a large glossy picture of the tower. A thunderous roar of applause filled the atrium.

Cain silenced the reporters before continuing.

"From here we will launch all future spacecraft, both domestic and foreign. Satellites. Storage vessels for waste material ejection into deep space. Because the SUBOS height reaches into the lower mesosphere, we're at a gravitational pull that's thirty-five percent less than that of the normal pull on the Earth's surface. No longer will we need large external fuel tanks for launching purposes. No longer will we run the risk of exploding gases, burning up on reentry, falling debris and failing O-rings. All craft can now be safely built in the outermost reaches of our atmosphere. Prefabricated pieces of a rocket, or any other craft, can be elevated safely through the bowels of the SUBOS and gently launched into a close proximity orbital pattern to await construction on a docking port."

The brood of hungry information junkies hung on Cain's every word and wrote feverishly in their notebooks, trying desperately to keep up with the outpouring of plans and ideas for the future.

One blogger was typing away on his computer and, without so much as raising his hand, began to speak, "Deep space ejection? What will that entail?"

Just as if he were using a teleprompter, Cain swiftly responded, "Spent nuclear fuel and other waste materials from power plants across the country, and, perhaps, around the world, will be sent to the receiving grounds at the SUBOS, loaded into the elevators, and ejected either into deep space or towards the sun, where they will burn up harmlessly."

"How many staff will it take to run this? Where's the money coming from?" shouted a reporter.

"The SUBOS will have the best and brightest from all over the world working on this project. We foresee the necessity to employ no less than twenty-five thousand military and civilian personnel to see to the security, performance, and progress of this great endeavor. I and the Enenechem Board of Directors will be the principal party responsible for overseeing those day-to-day operations with help, of course, from our nation's military, specifically, the Navy, Air Force, and Marines. We also have the backing of some of the worlds most respected and secure companies, as well as many donations from the private sector. More important, ladies and gentlemen, is that we continue to lead and secure the interests, prosperity, and future of the finest nation on Earth. Thank you!"

Cain stepped away from the podium as camera flashes illuminated the platform. Cheers, applause, and questions from reporters still echoed throughout the massive rotunda as he walked away from the stage with his entourage in tow.

"Are they all here?" Cain asked his secretary as she joined him by his side.

The tall and slender, impeccably dressed woman did not look at Cain when she handed him a black leather portfolio and firmly stated, "Yes, Mr. Wyczthack. All are present and waiting for you."

Cain and his army of secretaries, assistants, publicists, lawyers, and bodyguards, moved through the maze of hallways and meeting rooms like a bulldozer. The slow-moving stampede approached the corridor designated for governmental affairs. At the end of the corridor was Cain's personal conference room. The gargantuan double doors were monitored by two men in black suits, one on either side of the doorway. The muscle bound gorillas stood and reached for the door handles as the entourage approached. Cain simply waved his index and middle finger on his right hand and the polished, mahogany doors parted.

Cain was first to enter the austere and intimate auditorium, followed by Bianca Doyle, his very private and personal assistant. Bianca was tall, blonde, and exotic, a stickler for detail, and hated being late or deviating from one of her carefully crafted itineraries almost as much as Cain did.

An uneasy hush fell upon the room as hundreds of foreign dignitaries, lobbyists, and bureaucratic officials stood and waited for Dr. Wyczthack to make his way to the elevated podium. However, Cain began his oratory as he slowly passed the attendees.

"I've grown too tired of it all I must admit," he groaned. "In two-thousand one, there were three thousand, four hundred and seventy-five homicides in the United States alone. Suicides reached almost two thousand that year. Drug-related deaths passed the thirteen-thousand mark in twenty-twelve. Terrorist-related deaths escalated from four thousand, two hundred twenty-nine to eleven thousand-plus last year alone."

He arrived at the base of the short staircase that led to the stage and podium. Cain took slow, exaggerated steps up the stairs. He rubbed his eyes with his right hand while motioning for everyone to be seated with his left, then tossed his binder on the first long banquet table with an abrupt slam.

"Fuel shortages. Terrorism. Disease. Bankruptcy. Religious intolerance and ethnic cleansing. Genocides. Famine. Politics. It's not working. I have grown weary of my existence on this planet."

He put on quite a show. Pacing back and forth, running his hands through his long grey hair, shaking his head; Dr. Wyczthack was a very good actor. Everyone at that meeting, as far as outward appearances were concerned, bought into the idea that the man truly meant what he was saying. He paused briefly to glance over his right shoulder in Bianca's direction. She rose from her seat, turned to her right, stepped past a stage curtain, and exited the meeting through a side door.

Cain continued with his sermon.

"I've summoned you...specifically...from all over the world...to help me with my plight. Our plight. My grandfather, the first Dr. Cain Wyczthack, was considered a brilliant man, but also a dangerous and delusional man. He had some amazing ideas...some revolutionary for his time. Others crazy for his time. Whether you label him genius or crazy, his plans were....well, genius or crazy."

A moment later, Bianca returned with a man in a blue running suit who appeared to be in his early to mid-thirties. Bianca and the young man stood behind the stage curtain, out of eyesight, waiting for the right moment to step out into the light. She waited for that one perfect moment during Cain's speech to reveal the identity and purpose of the man standing by her side.

"I'd like to show you the two ideas that bring us here together today," Dr. Wyczthack announced.

Bianca and the man stepped out from behind the curtain and a bright spotlight immediately shone on their faces. Not one person spoke or applauded as Cain met them halfway and shook hands with the man. Bianca made an about-face and took her seat at the side of the stage.

The two men held each other in their gaze as they brought themselves before the audience of several hundred people.

Cain leaned towards the microphone and proudly stated "I want to introduce you to my grandfather's first idea...his love...his pride and joy. Ladies and gentlemen, meet Evan Alpha One."

The mass of unimpressed visitors sat quietly and stared at Cain. He was still smiling when he asked "Evan, how old are you?"

"I'm three years, five months, and two days old," Evan replied.

He stood there, innocent and unintimidated, watching the members of the audience gawk at him. They whispered to each other and pointed at Evan.

Cain placed his hand on Evan's shoulder and said, "Evan is but one of almost six hundred male clones generated from a single, cryogenicized blood specimen from nineteen eighty-six."

"Six-hundred?" asked a female geneticist from Singapore, "Like this? Or are they embryos in glass jars?"

"No, no, my dear, not in jars," Cain assured the woman. "There are currently six hundred more just like Evan. All in all, I have three thousand test subjects, in different stages of development of course, that are being grown, trained, conditioned, and educated as we speak."

A very tall and striking gentleman, a biological engineer from South Africa, leaned forward in his seat and commented, "You said male. I'm assuming there are female clones, too."

"Yes, we have females," Cain proudly answered, "Seven hundred strong."

Dt. Wyczthack once again slightly twisted his head and cut his eyes to the right. Bianca took her visual cue and returned to the hallway off the side of the stage. Cain made a few statements about the efforts he and his team have made, stalling until Bianca was back behind the curtain. From the corner of his eye Cain saw Bianca, but this time she had a female companion standing beside her.

He turned to the right, extended his arm, and boldly stated "May I now present to you, Chloe Athena One."

Bianca and Chloe stepped out from behind the curtain and again a bright spotlight illuminated their faces. This time, however, the audience erupted in joyous applause. She wore a blue suit to match Evan and was absolutely glowing. Cain brought Chloe to stand beside Evan near the podium at the front of the stage. Several of those fortunate enough to be in the first row of chairs quickly gathered at the edge of the elevated platform to get a closer look at the couple.

"Chloe and Evan," Cain shouted into the microphone, clapping energetically. He showed off the duo amidst shouting, cheering, whistling, and applause. More of the attendees rushed the stage and raised their hands, desperately wanting to touch them. Cain nodded his head to Bianca, who then briskly gathered Evan and Chloe and escorted them off the stage.

Cain stopped clapping but continued to bask in the limelight, smiling arrogantly as he crossed from one side of the stage to the other. He eventually signaled for everyone to return to their seats.

As the noise subsided, he addressed his audience "As you might have assumed, Chloe is also from a single, cryogenicized specimen, but from nineteen ninety-nine."

A biophysicist from Brazil stood and inquired, "When you say you're 'growing' ... exactly what do you mean?"

"It's taken us decades of man-hours to figure out, but we have at last devised the means to manipulate their genetic coding during mitosis. My colleagues and I have literally dissected the entire sequence of proteinaceous acid formulations in the human genome....and I'm talking about coding in all five stages... prophase, prometaphase, metaphase, anaphase, and telophase...thereby increasing the rate in which their bodies build and develop. Their capacity for understanding, the absorption of knowledge and processing of information, is far beyond that of the average human being. This is due to expanded and accelerated performance in their brains. This exponential rate of increase in intellectual capacity is only surpassed by the amazing physiological development the clones undergo in their first three years. Ladies and gentlemen, we have moved far beyond Dr. Moreau and the Boys from Brazil."

A German neurosurgeon rose from his chair and asked, "Are there any visible or noticeable side effects of these coding changes?" but did not sit down. He placed his hands behind his back, squinted his eyes, and waited for a reply.

"When we were first toying with the idea and began our preliminary experiments, we lost thousands of embryos. I mean tens of thousands, maybe even hundreds of thousands. Male and female. We had to use reverse engineering to understand what was going to happen. Once we had a batch of fertilized eggs survive a new set of coding changes, let's say during telophase, then we had a new and measurable baseline. We lost eggs, embryos, and fetuses at every level of development. Some of the sequence modifications were relatively easy to identify as the source for the loss. The most significant side effect we have seen is the life expectancy. We can harvest an embryo and grow a fully mature clone, male or female, in as little as eighteen months. At that time they will have actually physically aged twenty-five years. Unfortunately, the clones start to deteriorate after four years of maturity and die with a body age of forty-five years."

Cain and the German gave each other a good visual go-over before the man slowly lowered himself into his chair.

The woman seated next to him, a fertility expert from Denmark, stood and stated, "So what you're telling us, if I'm not mistaken, is that these life forms will live for a total of five and a half years, but will experience physical growth and decay comparable to that of a forty-five-year-old. Is that safe to say?"

"You are correct, madam."

People leaned into one another, whispering their doubts and disappointment.

"Why such a short life span?" shouted a woman from the back of the auditorium.

"We believe this is due to the accelerated growth rate and hormone imbalances. To get this, you have to change that. When you do this, it makes that happen. We're dealing with the creation of a new species of humans. I'm talking about breaking down and restructuring the human genome and the bond between atoms. This is all brand new. We are in uncharted territory."

"So you're basically playing God, aren't you?" a man shouted angrily.

"God? Who said anything about God being involved? I am merely replicating human creation through design and engineering. Whether by natural chance or intentional interference, you're going to have losses."

"What will Evan and Chloe be used for?" a woman sheepishly asked.

"They will be very effective in the pursuit of medicines, military applications, physical labor, organ harvesting, blood donations…the list is long with respect to the potential of these wonderful creatures."

"Why these two?" the German quickly inquired, standing once more as he spoke, "Didn't you have genetic samples from all over the world to choose from? What makes Evan and Chloe so special that all other specimens were passed over?"

"You are correct, sir. We had blood, tissue, and other samples collected for testing from all walks of life on every continent. What sets the DNA of Evan and Chloe apart from our vast majority of samples is the fact that both Evan and Chloe, the real Evan and Chloe, are still walking the Earth, have been monitored since the late eighties, and both have exhibited incredible immune systems over the last thirty-plus years. Neither one of them, according to our records, has ever visited a doctor's office, filled a prescription, been hospitalized, or missed a day of work due to illness. Couple that with their family histories of longevity and intellectual capacity, and you have a pretty clear choice as to which DNA samples you would prefer to experiment with."

Satisfied with Dr. Wyczthack's answer, the German slowly crouched into his chair, but never took his eyes off Cain.

A molecular engineer from Spain was next to be recognized for a question. His hips barely rose from the chair when he asked, "Who knows about this program?"

After looking about the room for a brief moment, Cain answered coldly, "No one. And that's the way it will stay. I will make sure of it."

CHAPTER 4

GMO

"I want these capsules registered, sequenced, and staged for final loading into the SUBOS elevator for immediate ejection!" the dock manager barked, pointing at the rows of double-stacked waste vessels.

"Yes, sir!" his pack of roustabouts quickly answered.

The assistant manager reviewed his elevator schedule and noticed a discrepancy in the SUBOS master schedule for the civilian, governmental, and carbon elevators.

"Sir?" the assistant interrupted. "It appears that the CARBEL is already scheduled for ejections throughout the week."

"What?!" the manager snapped.

"Yes, sir. See here, we unloaded and sent up this week's capsules for ejection late last week. Now we have these new manifests from France and Sweden and have nowhere to house them until the Aerie gives us the approval."

"Why didn't you let me know we have a logjam on our hands?"

"I'm sorry, sir, but I thought you knew when...."

"Your job isn't to assume what I do and do not know. Your job is to make sure that all materials received on this dock are distributed to the proper departments on the correct levels. That includes knowing the elevator schedules for said deliveries and distribution!"

"Yes, sir."

"Now, by your estimates, how long will we have to wait before loading the waste capsules to go to the CARBEL?"

"Well, sir, last week we sent up fifty-seven capsules in six load-outs. That's a full eight hours to go from the receiving dock to the...."

"Just tell me the time; don't build me the clock!" the manager bellowed, obviously aggravated with the young man.

"In my estimate, I'd say we won't have an open window for loading until ... next week. Late ... next week."

"Are you out of your mind? What are we gonna do with sixty-four nuclear waste capsules? How are we supposed to unload the trains and trucks with fresh food for more than twenty-five thousand people when my dock is crammed full of radioactive waste?"

The ever shrinking assistant paused before meekly suggesting, "We can load the SUBOS elevator and deliver the capsules to the staging decks on 15A for temporary holding."

The portly and aged supervisor fixed an unsettling squint on the apprentice as he elaborated on his idea.

"The whole mile is Engenechem. We can use the SUBOS to deliver these manifests to 15A until the Aerie is caught up. Once we get the all clear, we can get the capsules up to the Aerie for loading in the CARBEL. We can make the move to the Aerie in a matter of an hour while still receiving new deliveries here."

The manager softened his furrowed brow and turned his eyes to the stacks of spent nuclear waste.

"Get me the deck supervisor for fifteen and the SUBOS Director of Operations."

"Yes, sir."

The puny man scurried away as the manager watched his men drive their tele-handlers back and forth to the primary cargo elevators. He tilted his head to gaze up at the mighty SUBOS and thought back to when he was hired as an assistant to the then-project manager so many years ago. When he was first hired, the tower was a mere two miles in height and projected to be another sixteen years under construction.

"Seventeen miles high," he remembered, scoffing and laughing to himself. Slowly but surely, every few months he would set up deliveries to a new floor and section of the tower.

"All this for space exploration?" he asked himself as wave after wave of trucks came rolling in.

Hundreds and hundreds of miles of new train tracks were laid to allow thousands upon thousands of rail cars to deliver the much needed raw materials to construct the monolithic behemoth. The new airport recorded the monthly landings of hundreds of cargo planes from nearly every country on Earth.

He narrowed his eyes once more as he strained to see the top of the tower.

"Sir?" the assistant dock supervisor called, running straight at him. "I have her, sir."

"Who do you have? Who is her?"

"A representative for Engenechem. Her name is Miss Bianca Doyle. She's on my tablet cam right now."

The eager-to-please young man handed off his tablet to his supervisor.

"This is Chief Dock Supervisor Light Huddleston. To whom am I speaking?"

"My name is Bianca Doyle. I am the senior secretary to Engenechem President and CEO Cain Wyczthack. How may I help you?"

"Ma'am, we have a situation down here with a backup of waste capsules. We do not, and I mean *do not*, have the means to hold toxic materials safely, and the Aerie is scheduled for ejections throughout next week. We just received an additional sixty-four nuclear waste capsules for ejection but can't deliver to the Aerie because they're falling behind on the CARBEL."

"What do you want me to do about it?"

"Well, ma'am, an assistant of mine recommended that we load the vessels and stop at one of your warehouses, specifically 15A, to temporarily house the capsules until the Aerie catches up. Once the Aerie gives us the green light, we can then reload the capsules for delivery to the Aerie for ejection via the CARBEL."

"Give me a moment," Bianca stated lifelessly.

She swiveled in her chair, turning her back to the video camera. Mr. Huddleston glanced over to his sidekick, shrugged his shoulders, and pointed at the tablet. Bianca was mumbling to someone behind her, a man. Light held the tablet closer to his ear. Nothing in the conversation between Bianca and the mystery man was discernable. Whomever she was communicating with didn't sound positive, judging from the tone and volume. Bianca spun around abruptly to face the camera with all of the expression of a chastised child.

"Mr. Huddleston?" she asked politely.

"Yes, ma'am. I'm here," Light answered, startled, and quickly moved the tablet away from his ear.

"Your request has been given approval. You can begin loading your capsules in the commercial cargo elevators."

"Thank you, ma'am. You've saved me a lot of time and headache."

"You're welcome, Mr. Huddleston. But we do have some procedural requirements and restrictions, for security and safety purposes, that you and your employees must adhere to."

Light snapped his fingers to get the attention of his assistant. He motioned for him to come closer and held his finger up to his lips.

"Okay, what do you want us to do?"

"First of all, we're giving you and your staff twenty-four hours to complete this transfer."

"Twenty-four hours? Are you crazy? We've got sixty-four capsules! This will require no less than forty-eight hours. Sixty at the most."

"You have twenty-four hours. Take it or leave it. We will allow you and your staff access to the Engenechem commercial elevators we use. These were designed by our engineers to accommodate our specific requirements. Their speed and capacity surpass the governmental elevators. You will complete your transfer under the deadline."

"Um, okay, if you say so."

"I know so. Secondly, none—may I repeat, none—of your staff is to escort the materials to 15A. You are to load the cab to capacity, notify me when you are ready for delivery, and we will override the access coding from our offices. Upon arrival on our deck, we have the means and manpower to unload the cab and place the capsules in a location that is satisfactory to our needs."

"I don't know about that, ma'am, you gotta be...."

"Mr. Huddleston, we designed and engineered this structure as well as the waste capsules you are so desperately trying to dispose of on a system we created. We also devised the means by which these capsules will be deployed to the CARBEL for ejection. I'm more than confident that my staff is perfectly capable of, and overqualified for, stacking your capsules."

Light paused to take a deep breath.

"Yes, ma'am. I'll have my men begin loading the capsules in your elevator. I'll notify you directly when they're ready for the first delivery."

"Thank you," Bianca stated bluntly and disconnected the video feed.

Light's shoulders sagged as he handed off the tablet to his assistant. "You heard the woman: load 'em up."

***

"Sir? I have an arrival on deck 15A authorized for receipt and unloading. I need supervisor approval to dispatch robotics," said Titan, raising his hand.

A man in a dark grey suit approached Titan, leaned over his shoulder, and asked "What do we have here?"

Evan Titan Forty-Four, one of the cloned Evan offspring, pointed to his screen and video monitor, "The primary SUBOS loading docks have sent up ten nuclear waste capsules for temporary holding. Authority was given by Miss Doyle, directly."

"Is this the only delivery?"

"No, sir. There are a total of sixty-four capsules. We should expect six more deliveries."

"You have my authorization for this load and the remainder of the deliveries," the man said, swiping his hand in front of a camera with an infrared laser and typed a pass code on Titan's computer keyboard.

"Thank you, sir."

"Have the auto-handlers place them next to the blast doors for possible exterior extraction."

"Right away, sir."

"How are you feeling today?" the man then asked, partially sitting on the end of the computer bank.

"I feel fine, thank you. How are you?"

"Fine, fine. Never better. Will you please stand up for me?"

"Yes, sir," Titan answered.

The pod of clones kept their heads facing towards their monitors but strained their eyes to observe the impromptu checkup.

"Any headaches? Nausea? Dizziness?" the man asked Titan as he held up a tiny flashlight to his eyes.

"No, sir. No problems whatsoever."

"Night sweats? Difficulty with sleeping?"

"No, sir."

"How's your appetite? Are you eating well?"

"Fine, sir. I always finish my meals and drink my supplements. I'm nearly always first in my control group to receive injections."

"Any adverse reactions to your supplements or injections?"

"None whatsoever, sir. I eat and drink everything in sight."

"Good, good. How old are you?"

"Next Tuesday I will be two years and seven months."

The man in the dark suit leaned over the console and picked up the notepad and pen lying next to the keyboard.

"Tell me, what is your control identity? And please identify your primary and secondary applications."

Titan hesitated to answer and briefly glanced at his coworkers.

"Don't look at them. You focus on me. What is your control identity and primary and secondary applications?"

"Evan, Titan, 44, communications, sanitation."

The man in the dark suit held Titan in his gaze.

"Subset?"

"Generation B."

The man finished scribbling his notes and ripped the section of paper from the sheet. He slowly and diligently folded the misshapen piece of paper into a square and placed it carefully into the exterior breast pocket of his suit coat.

"Have you received your Arena assignment?"

"No, sir. Our subset is still undergoing training. We should be done with simulations by the end of next week and then deploy to the island for the remainder of our certification testing."

"Are you experiencing any problems with anxiety or feelings of anxiousness?"

Titan once again darted his eyes to the other clones at the communications center.

"Don't look at them. They can't help you. You focus on me."

"No, sir, not really."

"No ... not really. So ... there is something wrong."

The man in the dark suit watched Titan's chest begin to rise and fall as his demeanor changed from confident and stable to nervous and doubtful.

"I ... I just want to do well, sir. But I feel like ... like I'm not keeping...."

"Hey, it's okay," the man said, placing his hand on Titan's left shoulder, "Plenty of people have phobias and fears."

Like a caged cat, Titan began looking about the control center to see if any of his team members were watching.

"Whenever you're finished with your responsibilities here, why don't you come up to the Nursery on seventeen and we can have a more intimate and thorough conversation. Hmm?"

Titan could feel himself shaking and unable to concentrate. He knew the members of his team were watching and listening. He tried to suppress his feelings and control his voice "But sir, I … I don't have any problems that I need to…."

"Just notify the deck officer that I am requesting a session with you and he will approve and assign your elevator codes for access to seventeen. Now, if you will excuse me."

The man in the dark suit turned and removed a vibrating phone from his pocket. He moved about slowly as he mutedly spoke.

Titan returned to his seat at the communications center. He slumped in his chair and wiped his eyes, trying desperately to control his breathing and stifle his emotions. A green flag flashed on his computer screen, notifying him of an incoming message. Titan sat upright, drew in a deep, cleansing breath, and scooted himself to his desk and keyboard. He clicked on the message and a small window opened on his monitor.

The message read: "Don't go."

Titan sat silently, staring at the message. He saw the reflection of his friend on the screen directly to his right.

"I can't not go," Titan wrote out on his notepad and gingerly pushed it to his right.

The clone seated next to him carefully pulled the pad across the console and began to write. In a moment the other man pushed the pad back to Titan. The new message read: "You know what happens when someone complains."

Titan casually glanced around before writing his response and turning the tablet so his friend could read the words, "Nobody dodges Dr. White."

CHAPTER 5

EVALUATION

Engenechem occupied the top three miles of the seventeen-mile-high SUBOS tower. Mile fifteen was used primarily for the creation, development, housing, training, and education of the male clones. Mile sixteen was designated for the very same purpose, with the one exception that it was for the female clone program. Over the years, the clone development initiative came to be known simply as the 'EC Project' to the Engenechem employees. Under their breath, however, the staff referred to the clones, every clone, as 'the twins.'

The US Department of Defense enlarged the Nevada Testing and Missile Range to a massive 22,500 square miles. Even though Area 51, Groom Lake, and Edwards Air Force Base were already within the boundaries of the test range, the Pentagon and Joint Chiefs of Staff all thought it prudent and in the best interest of national security to increase the footprint of the military base. An area measuring roughly 150 miles by 150 miles square was designated as appropriate and defendable by the top brass of the US military.

Representatives of the United Nations overwhelmingly agreed to relocate their operations from the New York facilities to the SUBOS tower. In doing so, not only did the foreign governments of the world expect the American taxpayer to foot the bill for the astronomical expense, but they demanded that each country should have their own military present and that the SUBOS tower and surrounding area should be designated as a neutral international zone to be governed by the UN.

That idea was not met with much enthusiasm.

Engenechem president and CEO Cain Wyczthack made his objection to the proposal abundantly clear when he attended the G20 Summit in Las Vegas the month prior. When the motion was brought before the panel by the Chinese Ambassador to the UN, Cain was asked for his opinion on the matter.

Dr. Wyczthack, in his customary black wool suit, rose from his seat and strode majestically to a podium and microphone facing the representatives. He tilted his head down and calmly but firmly stated "No!" and took one step back away from the microphone. Cain pressed his lips together tightly and slowly cast his notoriously dubious glare across the room. After a brief pause, he bowed, ever so slightly, flashed an insincere grin, and exited the meeting with his lawyers, secretary, and bodyguards following behind him.

***

"Ugh!" the woman groaned. "If I'd have known that all I was gonna do on this project is ask the same questions all day long and take notes, I would never have submitted my application to this stupid company!"

"You and me both!" replied a female coworker standing next to her.

"And this elevator ride … what's it take, forty-five minutes to reach the labs?"

"I don't know, but what I do know is after around sixty seconds I'm ready to bust my way out of this tin can. I'm *extremely* claustrophobic."

"They give me the creeps sometimes with the way they look at me when they're answering the questions. It's almost like they're studying us."

"Doctor White was sitting in on an evaluation right next to me while I was finishing with one of the Centaur class, and I could tell…."

"Oh, don't even get me going on Doctor White!"

"What happened to you?"

"Long story; forget about it."

"Okay, so I'm going through the sleep sequences and out of the corner of my eye I can see Doctor White leaning over towards me. Then I look up into the glass partition behind the Chloe and from the reflection it looked like he was trying to smell me!"

"Ooh! Gross!"

"Tell me about it!"

"Well, all I can tell you is you got out light."

The elevator stopped on Seventeen B and the stainless steel doors quickly parted. The conversation between the two lab assistants came to an abrupt halt as they stepped out. Their faces became void of all expression as they strode to the security gate of the Engenechem laboratory. Dubbed 'The Nursery,' both Seventeen A and B were the locations for the first stage of the clones' evaluation and testing.

"Take it easy," whispered one of the women.

"You know it."

"Ma'am may I see your access badge?" an armed security guard politely asked as the first assistant approached the portal to the Nursery.

"Of course," she replied.

A small army of sentinels, laden with automatic firearms, presided over the only access point to the Engenechem evaluation center, and were under the direct command of Dr. Wyczthack. One of the officers checked her identity badge and verified her accessibility authorization while another authenticated her schedule and zone assignment. Still another guard completed a retinal and thumbprint scan of the woman before she underwent a pat down. The last stage of security inspection required every person entering or leaving the Nursery to undergo a full body scan.

"Have a nice day, ma'am," the last centurion commented.

"Oh, yeah, you do the same!" the woman drolly answered.

Every day, all day long, the clones came to the Nursery to undergo a full evaluation. The Evan clones went from their development zones on Fifteen A to the Nursery on Seventeen A. The Chloes underwent their inspection on Seventeen B, coming from development zone Sixteen A. Every clone, no matter their stage of growth or education, was required to go through mandatory testing once a month.

The first phase of the evaluations was the identity of each clone: name, generation, subset, and primary and secondary applications. Cain, a devout Socialist and atheist, believed that it was the higher power's duty, responsibility, and right to determine the life path of subordinates who lacked the intellectual capacity to think clearly for themselves, and that personal sacrifices from the individual were more than necessary for the advancement of the mass collective.

"Name?" a technician would ask one of the clones as he, or she, would enter an examination room. Even though each clone had an RFID chip embedded in their left shoulder muscle, Cain enforced the idea of psychological submission by making the clones repeat what they were told their plight in life would be.

"Evan, Juno, Twenty-Five, Waste Disposal and Resource Management."

"Evan, Hades, Eleven B, Civil Engineering and Metallurgy."

"Chloe, Atlantis, Four C, Water Purification and Agriculture."

On and on it went, hour after hour, day after day.

"How do you feel?"

"Are you sleeping well?"

"Do you experience any periods of depression or anxiousness?"

Psychological profiles were assembled for each and every clone. Tests written by the likes of Cal-Poly, MIT, NASA, and the CIA were implemented to measure psychological, emotional, and physical progress. Running, weights, swimming, cycling, push-ups, chin-ups, abdominal crunches; the clones were subjected to all manner of physical activities. Survival simulations were conducted, with some going to such a high degree of intensity as to implement food, sleep, and sensory deprivation; there was no end to the barrage of tests and simulations the clones not only had to endure but were required to pass. Or else.

"What do you think of the other members of your control group?"

"If there were a weakest member in your subset, who do you think it would be?"

"Do you think you're special?"

"Are you happy with the way you look?"

"Do you like living here?"

It was all a head game to Cain and Dr. White, albeit a highly lucrative one. To them, the clones were, simply put, disposable and expendable. A new batch of cloned embryos could be generated in roughly one week and artificially inseminated into the birthing mothers well within two hours. One batch, or as Cain referred to it 'a new crop,' contained one hundred embryos at a minimum. Engenechem could, for all practical purposes, produce more than 5,200 clones in one calendar year for both Evan and Chloe. To the investors of Engenechem and the federal government, this number was too conservative. What the US military, pharmaceutical and medical communities needed, and were willing to pay through the nose for, was bodies. Trainable, educated, nontraceable, disposable bodies.

"Chloe, Athena, Nine, Cryogenics and Animal Husbandry"

"Chloe, Hera, Twelve D, Electrical Engineering and Viticulture"

If a clone were, at the time of testing, found to be lacking in physical and intellectual capacity, then both Cain and Dr. White were notified and the clone was subjected to an intense interrogation before being placed in isolation. The clone would then have his or her blood drawn, as well as every other member of their control group. A complete analysis of the entire batch would be conducted with the original clone remaining in quarantine. Once a DNA map was assembled for each specimen, Cain and Dr. White would compare the chromosomes and make the determination if the failure of the clone was due to chemical makeup or a behavioral error. In either case, it ended up not mattering what the explanation was for the failure of the clone to successfully pass his or her testing. Every conclusion resulted in the same correctional action taking place: termination.

CHAPTER 6

The CARBEL

"All right, let's take it down a notch," the man ordered, "My name is Riggs Woodburn and I am the principal instructor for your NBS training and certification. Who can tell me what that acronym means?"

Several of the Evan clones raised their hands.

"Yes, you, what does the acronym NBS mean?"

"Neutral Buoyancy Simulation," the humanoid answered.

"Neutral... Buoyancy... Simulation. Correct. Thank you. Can anybody tell me why you are to undergo NBS training?"

The same Evan quickly raised his hand but did not wait to be called on and promptly stood.

"To prepare us for EVA projects after we have ascended to an island."

"Correct again, thank you. Do you mind telling me your name, class, series, primary and secondary applications? And what is an EVA project?"

"Evan, Armada, Nine, Digital Encryption and Satellite Telemetry. EVA is the acronym for Extra Vehicular Activity... any function an astronaut or cosmonaut performs on the exterior of his or her vehicle is considered an EVA."

The other clones sat silently, staring forward as Riggs and Armada Nine carried on their conversation.

"An Armada class, eh? There's a rumor that several of your kind have blown the ceiling and they're contemplating implementing a third application to your education and training regimen. True?"

"Yes, sir."

"Good, good. We'll double our efforts to keep up with you."

"Thank you."

"Okay, moving on. Behind me are three 80-foot pools. This is where we conduct our training course. You will be divided into three companies consisting of at least thirty members. You will take part in every simulation of EVA. Assembly drills, distribution of materials and parts, inventory control and accountability, suit pressurization, temperature control, and proper safety protocol. The EVA itinerary and project completion schedule as set forth by this company is daunting, challenging, extremely dangerous and, above all, inspiring. You will meet these challenges and surpass all expectations and projections. Now, if you will all please come and get in one of three lines, my staff will fit you for your suits and place you in your respective divisions."

The NBS facilities were massive. The feather in the hat of Riggs Woodburn were the three temperature-controlled 80-foot pools. The enormous tanks were designed and engineered for the sole purpose of conducting large-scale construction project simulations, as well as demolition, salvage, and repair. The clones stood in line, single file, and listened closely to Riggs as he and his team of 'tailors' made measurements and quick alterations to the clones' temporary suits.

"After you have been properly fitted with your suit, helmet, and gloves, please return to the riser and link your identity credentials with that of the helmet. This will enable us to more effectively monitor and track your movements."

When at last the fittings were complete, Riggs again addressed the pod of clones.

"Space is a most inhospitable place to be if you are a human and lack the resources to survive. At any given moment you can be bathed in sunshine and seconds later be in the dark. The dynamics of temperature change can swing from 250 degrees Celsius in direct sunlight to more than -100 degrees in the shade. Our primary construction, preparatory, and assembly zone will take place in the lower levels of the mesosphere. The SUBOS reaches a maximum elevation of 17 miles. Atop of the SUBOS is the Aerie ... a kind of staging and holding area to which the base of the CARBEL is affixed. From there, the carbon elevator rises an additional 8 miles to meet with the temporary landing dock on what we lovingly call 'The Island.' Any questions thus far?"

Riggs noticed that while the group of clones were focused on him and remained silent, Armada Nine surveyed his brethren, looking about as if he anticipated one of them to raise their hand.

"When you are entering the CARBEL, you will be wearing one of two issued suits that are custom fit to each one of you. There are minute differences in your dimensions and weight, but generally speaking you're all the same size. These are not the space suits from yesteryear. We didn't watch *Star Wars* or *2001* to come up with the design. We went beyond. If you will all please stand up, we'll now go through the safety features."

Riggs and his team spent the next hour reviewing the technical aspects of the space suits with the clones. As he and his division leaders took turns explaining the evolution of the garment, Riggs kept his eye on Armada. He noticed that while the class of clones were diligently absorbing the information, they displayed no outward expression of emotion, whereas Armada was obviously invigorated. Armada smiled, looked about the pool room, nodded his head in agreement from time to time, and held direct eye contact with each of the division leaders as they spoke. In the back of his mind, Riggs was thinking that Armada appeared to be genuinely happy.

"Okay, if you'll leave your helmet and gloves and follow me, please," Riggs announced. "We're now going to show you what you will all be working with."

Riggs, the division leaders, and company of clones walked briskly past the bank of recoil spools to the NBS locker room. Gargantuan in size, the facility had an impressive and extensive collection of equipment used in the tanks for making the training exercises as realistic as possible.

"Feel free to take a look around. Here we have examples of the panel sections for the living quarters you're to assemble. The pieces were fabricated to our exact specifications and are made of materials that, when submerged in the tanks, will be remarkably close to the actual handling weight once they are deployed to the Island. We wanted to maximize our lifting capacity while accommodating both size and shape with functionality, so we will be constructing cylindrical dormitories, cylindrical research vessels, and tubular connection tunnels to facilitate the movement and transfer of personnel and so on. These quarter sections will be stacked and tied by size and secured to the landing dock on the Island. The quarters are being fabricated by one of the Engenechem subsidiaries in Ohio. Ten–, twenty–, and forty-foot diameter vessels will be assembled by hand, by you, while orbiting the Earth at over 17,000 miles per hour. Any questions thus far?"

"How many of us do you anticipate deploying at any given moment for EVA projects?" asked one of the clones.

"Well, the answer to that question will be determined at the end of your training. In my mind, and more than likely in the minds and expectations of both Doctor Wyczthack and Doctor White, we would like to deploy your entire class."

"All one hundred of us?"

"Yes, every one of you. In less than ninety-six hours you will all be floating thirty miles above sea level."

"How long will our work details be?" asked another.

"You should complete your EVA assignments well within ten hours. We've also factored in a meal and one lift down and up for urination. Any other questions?"

Armada and his brothers stared back in silence.

"Good. Now if you will follow me, please."

Riggs led his flock back through the locker room to the tank hall.

"Who can tell me about this contraption?" Riggs asked loudly, pointing to his side.

"It's a POG; a pressurized oxygen generator and filtration unit," Armada answered.

"What is the primary function of the POG?"

"It distributes oxygen and extracts carbon dioxide while simultaneously regulating temperature throughout the space suits."

"Why don't we just equip each one of you with your own separate respiration unit? Anybody besides Armada?"

Riggs noticed that with the exception of Armada and one other clone, none of the Evans were engaging socially. Be it participation in conversation with the training leaders, eye contact, answering questions, or even speaking with each other, out of one hundred clones, Armada was the only one willing to exhibit emotion.

"All right, Armada, why a POG?"

"You can control and dispense oxygen much more efficiently. That's relative, however, to the rate of respiration by the individual. Plus, with the spool recoil, you no longer have the need for a separate booster pack for extended EVA."

"Good, good. Armada is correct," Riggs affirmed. "As of right now, every astronaut that has participated in an EVA has been equipped with at least two of three items: a tether strap fastened to their suit, a respiration unit, and or a booster pack."

The clones stepped closer to Riggs and the POG to examine the bank of valves, gauges, hoses, and wires.

"Communications, GPS, vital sign monitors…respiration…the POG is your lifeline. The interior of your helmet will be equipped with a holographic video screen and two way camera so that when we're viewing you and your work, we can send a live feed from any other helmet to assist you and your teams with any assembly problems."

"What are these for?" asked one of the Evans, pointing to a quarter panel by the first tank.

"Push, pull, and propel," Riggs replied, moving away from the gargantuan POG unit.

"Eyes, hooks, handles, and pedals are mounted to each and every quarter panel," he said, directing the clones' attention to the panel. "Eyes and hooks are for attaching draglines to the quarter panel while it's on the inventory dock. Two of you will attach your draglines to a panel, lift the panel off the stack, and grab the handles of the unit you're constructing. You and your partner will pull yourselves across the assembly and the quarter panel will follow right behind you. Your teammates, who are patiently waiting for another piece of the puzzle to connect, will literally catch the panel, connect the corner brackets, and begin inserting the compression bolts into the holes. Once you receive an acknowledgment that your panel is secured and not gonna float away, you will then pull yourselves to the attachment seam, release your draglines, and either push off the panel assembly with your foot on one of the pedals or pull yourselves back to the inventory dock via the handles. In the off chance you lose your grip or you don't have enough momentum, simply pull your breathing line tight, wait three seconds, and the spool will automatically begin to recoil itself. It takes about fifteen seconds to retract the 75-foot hose, so don't freak out. Any questions?"

"Why don't we simply lift the panels one by one and push them to the team?" an Evan inquired.

"A 10-foot quarter panel weighs roughly eleven hundred pounds on the earth's surface," Riggs informed the clone, "But up there, thirty miles above sea level, it'll feel more like twenty. What we don't need is for one of those things, or a pressure hatch, or a gas canister … ANYTHING … to become uncontrollable and drift out of our grasp. If we lose something, even a two-inch compression bolt, it will become a missile when it reenters Earth's atmosphere. An object like a quarter panel will break the sound barrier before striking a jet, landing on a hospital, colliding with a helicopter; any number of things can occur when we try to take shortcuts. Everything, and I repeat explicitly … everything … gets a dragline attached and you are constantly connected to the POG. Clear?"

The school of clones nodded their heads in agreement and lifelessly answered, "Yes, sir."

"All right, collect your helmets and gloves and break into your teams as designated by the colored dot on the back of your helmet. Green, tank one. Red, tank two, and blue, tank three."

The Evans, although doing directly as they were instructed, moved silently with no sense of purpose. All of them, as Riggs noticed, except Armada. To the amazement of Riggs, it appeared as if Armada was skipping to and from the risers near the main entrance.

"C'mon, ladies!" Riggs shouted, "I only have three days to train."

With that comment, the team leaders took the initiative to hurl their own insults at the slow-moving slugs.

"Pick up the pace, granny."

"Hurry it up, ya bunch of worms!"

"What's the problem, chica?"

Riggs and his team leaders spent the next seventy-two hours running drill after drill. Every possible scenario was simulated: tank lights on and off, water heated to just under the boiling point, multiple quarter panels arriving at one time, POG failure, comm-line disruption, and spool recoil failure.

The Evans passed the EVA/NBS training with flying colors. But would their fastidious efforts produce Cain's expected results?

***

"So what, exactly, are we assigned to do?" Titan asked Armada as he secured his dragline to the CARBEL platform.

"If I'm not mistaken, and it's a rare moment that I am, we're assembling an Arena today."

"You are not mistaken Armada," a voice answered. "The task at hand is to construct Arena One."

"Riggs?" Titan called out.

"Hellooo, ladies!" Riggs replied.

One hundred clones let out a pathetic groan of disbelief that their EVA coordinator was none other than their original trainer.

"Yes, it's me, Titan. What? You sound almost as if you aren't happy to have me monitoring your outfit. Like maybe, just maybe, you're a little disappointed to hear the sound of my voice."

"Oh, no sir. No, no, no ... yes," Armada answered for his team.

The school of inexperienced astronauts got a kick out of Armada's quick wit and sarcasm, laughing out loud.

"Very funny, Armada."

"Thank you, sir. I do try my best to please."

"If you and the rest of the sissies will be so kind as to shut up, I can begin my briefing."

"Go right ahead."

"Now, your ride to the hover dock will take approximately one hour. Upon arrival you will notice that there is a considerable gap between the CARBEL Halo and the hover dock. While there is no rigid apparatus connecting the CARBEL platform to the hover dock, we do have our own version of a zip line that loosely joins the two. There is a second line that goes to the waste ejection system, but you don't need to worry about that."

"Sir, what is the Halo?" one of the clones inquired.

"The Halo is a 40-foot square, rigid aluminum alloy frame located at the top of the CARBEL. The primary objective of the last shuttle mission was to deliver and assemble the frame, four carbon fiber braids, eight liquid fueled engines and fuel to the International Space Station. It took several months to coordinate, but with the cooperation of NASA, the DOD, JPL, MIT, numerous corporations and international governments, we changed the orbital path and proximity of the ISS. Not only did we have to calculate and alter the orbital speed of the ISS, but we had to repeat the same process as well for hundreds of satellites."

"I think what my friend is asking," Armada added, "is what specific function does the Halo perform?"

"Well, the crew of the ISS deployed the Halo and attached an engine to each corner of the frame. Once the engines were affixed, the carbon braids were slowly unrolled with a weighted quick release coupler on the end. The ISS had to control the rate of descent of the braid to reenter our atmosphere at a point where we were not only able to retrieve the braid, but to secure the rope to the Aerie at the top of the SUBOS Tower.

"After we had the first braid secured, then the ISS, for all practical purposes, became the Hindenburg. Here was an orbital space station, almost 30 miles above sea level, tethered to a static base. The rest of the construction mirrored the stringing of the support and stabilizing wires and cables of the Golden Gate Bridge. We then used a second coupler and line to send up the first carbon braid and went back and forth, building the carbon braid to the required diameter for supporting the weight and withstanding the stresses. We fabricated the three remaining carbon braids at one of the Engenechem processing plants and hoisted them, one by one, up the first full braid to the ISS, where the men would connect it to the Halo. Once the four carbon braids were attached to the four corners, our satellites triangulated the desired location above the SUBOS and voila ... you now have the world's first Static Umbilical Based Orbital Station ... the SUBOS. We then had to retest and calculate new orbital patterns and recalibrate the telemetry of every satellite after we put the ISS back in its proper place."

"So how often do the positioning thrusters fire off?" asked Titan.

"All four fire off randomly, when needed, to ensure that the CARBEL braids are at a specific point of tension and that the orbital speed of the Halo is at a consistent rate to keep it and the CARBEL perfectly aligned."

"What happens if the engines fail or don't shut off in time?" another clone chimed in.

"Well, several things can occur if we experience any engine failure. One, in the unlikely event that an engine does not automatically shut down, we have the ability to jettison the engine, remotely. We can then send up a team on one of the braids to install a new engine from the emergency inventory on the hover dock. Two, in the unlikely event that more than one, or even all of the engines fail to shut off, we can release the entire halo and use the men stationed on the ISS to install a new halo and engines. The problem with releasing the halo assembly as a whole is the zip line connecting the Halo with the hover dock. If the Halo unit is secured to the hover dock along with the ISS and WES, in theory, the Halo can drag everything with it into deep space."

The clones faced one another; they immediately shared the unsettling idea of being whisked away into the blackest depths of the galaxy.

"Any more scenarios or contingency plans?" Armada inquired.

"Yes, one more. Number three. In the unlikely event that one or more engines fail to fire off to maintain orbital position, there might not be enough time to send the ISS to replace the engines before Earth's gravitational force pulls the CARBEL out of orbit. Not only that, but the hover dock and all of our inventory along with the WES and any ejection containers that might be up there at the time."

"So... in a nutshell, we need to fly on this EVA. Correct?" Armada summarized.

"Right again, Armada. Now, y'all should be about five hundred feet below the Halo. If you look straight up you should be able to see the thrusters firing off."

"Will they burn us?" one of the Evans nervously asked.

"No, you won't get burned. The CARBEL platform will automatically stop one hundred feet short of the Halo. You're in a vacuum. You won't hear it and you won't feel the heat."

The platform rose higher and higher, growing ever closer to the Halo frame and vector positioning engines.

"If you wanna have some fun, slowly let some slack into your tie lines. That is if you aren't a bunch of fraidy cats!" Riggs teased.

From the safety and security of his control center high in the SUBOS, Riggs watched his video screen and the fast-moving images the helmet cameras were capturing. The anxious and nervous pod of identical twins slowly loosened their grips on the tie lines. One by one they began floating, ever so slightly above the platform surface. Riggs and his team watched the video monitors from their assigned posts and listened closely as the clones sprang to life, laughing out loud, and squealing with delight at the new experience.

"Okay, okay, simmer down. Directly above your heads is a wire grid.

Three or four inches below that are your zip lines. Bend down and release your tie lines, then immediately push up with your legs. The grid will stop you and you can secure your tie lines to the zip without having to worry about floating away."

"What about the POG?" Titan called out.

"There's enough oxygen in your suits to sustain you until you reach the hover dock. We already have two POGs ready and waiting. You'll pull yourselves to the hover dock, connect the breathing tube and comm-link BEFORE detaching your dragline and start the POG. Once you're all connected and secure on the hover dock, we'll break into teams and assignments. Does everybody understand?"

The chorus of clones answered with a resounding "Yes, sir!"

The company bent down and released their draglines from the recessed hooks in the platform. In almost perfect unison, they pushed themselves up and gently rose until captured by the grid.

"Excellent!" Riggs complimented as he and his assistants kept a close eye on the clones, "Now, secure your draglines to the zip."

The cameras monitored every movement the Evans made.

"Is everybody connected to the zip?"

"Yes, sir," the twins again answered.

"Now, as soon as you detach your respiration tubes and comm-link, you're on your own until you reach the hover dock and attach yourselves to the POG. We won't be able to hear you, talk to you, or send and receive video feeds. Therefore, until we have the hover dock POG up and running, no one disconnects themselves until ordered to do so. Armada?"

"Sir?"

"You're gonna lead off. Release your tube and link and get to the POG on the hover dock."

"Yes, sir, but don't I need someone to help me start up the POG?"

"No, you don't. This is a one-man operation. Just shimmy on over, attach your tube and comm-link, and initiate the generator. It'll take less than three minutes to complete the startup sequence. C'mon, don't be a weenie!"

Armada turned to look at his brothers and exclaimed "Here I go!"

"Now, until Armada reaches and starts the POG on the hover dock, you remain on the grid and do not, I repeat, DO NOT, under any circumstance, disconnect your breathing tubes and comm-links. Is that clear?"

"Yes, sir" was their only reply.

Armada pulled himself along the zip line cable to the edge of the CARBEL platform. He looked out across the vast expanse of space between the CARBEL and the hover dock.

"Hey, Riggs," he hollered.

"Yeah, Armada."

"How high are we?"

"It's estimated that the thrusters on the Halo are just about 29.5 miles above sea level. Why do you ask?"

"Well, technically speaking of course, I'm more than five miles higher than Felix Baumgartner when he made his famous free fall several years ago. You wanna challenge Red Bull?"

"Just get on with it and we'll worry about world records later."

"See you on the other side, boys!" Armada announced.

One of the helmet cameras captured Armada's face as he disconnected his respiration tube and comm-link.

"Sir, is it just me or is he smiling?" an assistant asked Riggs as he watched the helmet camera monitor.

"It appears as though Wyczthack has a cowboy on his hands," Riggs commented.

Armada took one last quick glance at his brothers and lunged forward with all of his might. He glided effortlessly to the hover dock in a matter of seconds. He grasped the grid wires, pulled himself down to the POG, and took a hold of the first respiration tube and comm-link. After attaching his tube, Armada released his dragline from the zip cable and latched on to a countersunk eyelet on the hover dock.

He unfolded the solar collection arms and uncovered the POG control panel. Once he initiated the startup protocol and entered the authorization code, the batteries slowly kicked in and the oxygen generator began sending fresh air to Armada's suit. A few seconds later, his helmet camera and microphone came on line and immediately transmitted Armada's voice back to the EVA Operation Center at the SUBOS.

"C'mon in! The water's fine!" Armada shouted, "Everyone's doing it!"

"All right, you clowns, you heard the man! Let's get this show on the road," Riggs hollered.

The crew of the EVA center clapped and cheered. The first of many projects was off to a successful start, so far.

***

The transfer of one hundred clones from the CARBEL to the hover dock on the Island took a little more than one hour to complete.

"You boys say bye-bye to your taxi; she's going down," Riggs bellowed.

"When does the CARBEL come back?" a clone asked, nervously, as the platform started its descent.

"It'll be here ready and waiting before you know it. Why don't you focus on the view for a minute? If you boys look straight down, you'll see all the lights on the strip in Las Vegas. The sun is nearly touching the horizon down there."

The brothers let out some slack in their draglines and delicately levitated above the dock. For a moment all communication ceased. The adventurers temporarily forgot about their worries and concerns as they gazed in amazement at the sun, the glow of the lights far below, and the clarity of the oncoming night.

"Hey, Riggs. What's that big glow to the east?" Titan shouted.

"Phoenix, then Albuquerque with Santa Fe just to the north. After that you come to Amarillo and Lubbock to the south. Then Oklahoma City and after that they all kinda blend together. If we left you right where you are, you would watch the sunrise with the inhabitants of Nova Scotia and watch the sunset with native Hawaiians. Eighteen hours of uninterrupted sunlight is what you can look forward to when you're deployed for EVA."

"Hey, Riggs? Not to change the subject, but why is everything in our inventory on the hover dock painted black?" Titan asked.

"Don't any of you ever ask questions besides Titan and Armada?"

Another droll and lackluster "Yes, sir" rang in Riggs' ears.

"The eyes of the world are watching us. They're watching you. They're listening to us. From a satellite a thousand miles above us with infra-red cameras to telescopes with heat sensitivity capabilities we're being watched. The less we're heard and seen the safer we are. Hence the black paint. Now, I want all of you to go to the stacks of 40-foot quarter panels."

The Evans clumsily dragged themselves along the grid wires to the monstrous hovering pile of panel assembly units.

"Now, all of you, take a close look at the exterior surface of the panels and tell me what you see."

"It's not shiny ... like it's a matte finish," one said.

"The surface doesn't feel smooth. It's got a rough and dimpled texture," another volunteered.

"Except for the joining seams, there are no right angles," Titan chimed in.

"What you're touching is, in essence, stealth fabrication. The first of its kind. Resilient to motion–, heat–, and sound-sensitive cameras, scanners and radar, even gamma and X-rays ... these panels, once fully assembled, will enable us to work in complete secrecy," Riggs stated.

"Then that means, if I may summarize, we build what we want, bring up whatever and how much we want with as many people as we see fit and no one will see us, hear us, or scan inside to find out what we got going on," Armada confidently confirmed.

"Yep. The only knowledge any one person, entity, or foreign government can hope to ascertain about our operations will be what they observe from the outside. Now, find your crew leaders and break out into your assigned units. In a few moments, your coordinator here at EVA Control will delegate your group tasks and assembly guidelines. All right, ladies, let's dance."

It was as if an invisible conductor was leading an orchestra. The clones swiftly maneuvered themselves into their work groups. Riggs stood behind his desk, stretched his arms, and began to pace about the operation center. How delighted he was to listen in as the coordinators verbally instructed the clones with no resistance or backtalking, and no break in the chain of command or complaining.

Digital construction schematics were downloaded to every helmet. Team leaders had live video feeds streamed to their holographic visors inside their helmet so they could watch the entire assembly process from different perspectives. Quarter panels, electrical conduit, thermal barriers, wiring for radiant heat, communication kiosks, plumbing; it was a magical moment for Riggs, his trainers, and coordinators.

***

"Sir?" one of the coordinators called, pointing to his video screen, "You should see this."

Riggs stepped closer and leaned over the desk. "Go back and look at the time stamp."

The man reversed the video feed until he came to the point where the first quarter panel was removed from its stack on the hover dock, "Eight twenty, sir."

"Okay, now go to live stream."

"Ten twelve," the man stated.

"In less than two hours they assembled more than half of the entire arena outer shell?"

"I guess so."

"Show me an interior view. Who's got interior video feeds?"

A woman a few feet away raised her hand, "I do, sir."

"Put your monitor up on the big screen," Riggs requested.

The female division coordinator sent the video feeds coming to her desk directly to the large monitor in front of the control center.

The clones worked together just as a colony of ants building a nest. As quarter panels were attached together, electrical conduit and wiring harnesses were applied to the interior. Radiant heat wiring was laid over the remaining surface area, with insulation padding added as the last layer.

"How many sections have they connected thus far?" Riggs inquired.

"They're three shy of completing the cylinder, minus, of course, the caps, pressure hatch, corridor, plumbing, and amenities," the woman replied, smiling broadly.

"We still have another six hours left on this EVA," another coordinator piped up, also smiling.

"Wyczthack has gotta hear this!" Riggs exclaimed, nodding his head. "Don't stop 'em, keep 'em going!"

***

"Would you mind repeating that, Mr. Woodburn?" Cain asked as he motioned for Dr. White to come and listen to the conversation. He put the phone call on speaker while Dr. White pulled up a chair.

"Not at all," Riggs stated. "I wanted you to know that we deployed the first EVA team five hours ago and they've already finished the outer shell construction for Arena One. And to be perfectly honest, sir, I think that I, we, grossly underestimated the capabilities of this batch. I mean, heck, they'll have the end caps mounted and both of the hatches and corridor connected by night's end."

"What was the original projected time for completion of the Arena?" Dr. White inquired.

"One hundred twenty hours, sir. It was our belief that, given that this would be the first EVA assignment, the time frame was fair and realistic, but more important, it was an achievable goal. But after what we've seen here tonight? I can honestly say that, based on what I've witnessed first-hand, we'll complete your remaining projects with an overall reduction in production time of maybe fifty percent or more."

"Excellent!" Cain proudly stated.

"Oh, yeah, I almost forgot to mention ... one of your experiments is acting up."

"Define 'acting up,' please," Dr. White interjected, smugly.

"Now don't misunderstand me. They're smart as all get out, but they don't talk, don't engage, and they absolutely don't show any emotion. However, to their credit, they complete their tasks as ordered with zero problems and no resistance. But one of your boys in particular is ... what I'd label as ... sarcastic."

"Sarcastic?" the surprised doctors repeated, and fumbled to open their notepads.

"Yeah, sarcastic. This one has a real cowboy mentality, like he's not afraid to try anything. He's already a genius and knows it, and shows that he has self-confidence but isn't cocky about it."

Dr. White opened his mouth to speak, but Cain raised his finger to his lips.

"And my team loves the guy! He jokes around with them, looks us in the eye when we talk to him, he asks questions ... we like him. I've seen this guy smile more in the last eight hours than any employee of this company for the past month. And the weird thing about this guy is ... he acts and behaves more like a human than the humans do ... and he's not even real!"

Cain stopped writing, paused, and asked "What is his name?"

CHAPTER 7

BOYS, GIRLS, AND GRAVITY

The red warning lights flashed on and off several times as the speakers emitted a harsh, high-pitched pinging sound.

"Attention, please, attention!" the middle-aged female voice pleasantly announced. "All personnel are required to assemble in the arena at twenty hundred hours."

"What now?" Armada asked out loud to his brothers, flopping his book onto his lap.

"Attention, please, attention," the voice repeated. "All personnel are required to assemble in the arena at twenty hundred hours."

"Probably a debriefing of some sort," Titan answered, releasing the clasps of his mattress restraints.

"Don't you guys get tired of these impromptu briefings and assemblies?" Armada inquired, also releasing his restraints.

"No," his brothers lifelessly answered.

"Well, I don't know about y'all, but I for one wanna finish the EVA objectives and get down to the surface!" Armada declared, putting his book in his foot locker with a slam.

"You said it!" Titan exclaimed, pulling on the zipper of his jumpsuit as he hovered next to his closet.

"They won't ever let us out," one of the twins solemnly stated, floating beside his bed.

"Why do say that?" Armada probed.

"I just know it. They've never let us out of their sight. We've always been on the inside and we always will. I mean, let's face it, we're quarantined; we're lab rats!"

"Oh, don't take it so hard. You never know ... things change," Armada comforted his brother with a pat on his shoulder. He and Titan pulled themselves along the ceiling rungs and floated into the corridor connecting their dormitory to the main transfer tube and Arena One Commons.

"C'mon, boys, last one there is a rotten egg!" Armada challenged his roommates as he and Titan joined the other clones in the transfer tube.

"Do you think he was right?" Titan asked, following close behind Armada.

"About what?"

"Getting out. Going to the surface."

"Nah. He's like everybody else around us. And I mean that; he's just like every one of our brothers. They all have a dismal outlook. It doesn't seem to matter what we're talking about, they all think the same. You and me? We're the ones that are different. You and me, that's it. You and I will get outta here ... just wait and see."

Armada, Titan, and two hundred of their brothers sailed through the passageways until they eventually merged with the main activity area of Arena One. They began living in the adjoining cylindrical dorms after the completion of their 'community center.' As soon as Arena One was assembled and successfully pressurized, Cain and Dr. White instructed Riggs to implement a program for a constant inhabitant presence. Beginning with the first batch deployed to the CARBEL, Arena One became an open living quarter until the Evans completed the construction of the first dormitory. Riggs made sure to include Armada, Titan, and eight of their brothers on the inaugural assignment.

Riggs remained on the SUBOS and thought it best for the clones, socially speaking, to develop their communication skills. The large pod of twins would have a prime opportunity to operate and function as a unit without, of course, the presence of an educational overseer.

Armada and his twins assembled their 20-foot diameter living quarters in a mere four hours. Adding on the end caps, pressure hatch, and corridor was simple enough and took a relatively small amount of time, while marrying the three pieces proved to be the most challenging. Right after the integration and pressurization of the dormitory and corridor, Riggs sent up another team of a hundred clones along with the internal components for the first sleeping quarters and a supervisor to assist Armada, Titan, and the new batch.

Within sixty days, Garret Brock, the new on-site director, had seen to it that all twenty dormitories were constructed and fully operational prior to projected deadlines.

"C'mon, guys, let's shake a leg!" Garret demanded as the clones spilled into the arena.

"Coming, Mother!" Armada announced, passing through the portal separating the corridor from the activity room.

"Very funny, Armada."

"Hey, Garret, what's going on?" Titan asked, not far behind Armada.

"You boys have a surprise tonight."

'Surprise! Yeah, right," Armada commented to Titan. "He thinks showing us *Close Encounters* again is a surprise."

"All right, boys. C'mon in and pull yourselves into four groups, two at each end."

The twins divided themselves into two groups, with the first hundred moving to the far end of the 80-foot long vessel.

"Tonight we're doing something a little out of the ordinary," Garret announced. "Doctors White and Wyczthack think that you clowns need to exert yourselves more than just going out on your nightly EVA adventures. So they, along with Riggs and I, have come up with a game for you to play."

The twins erupted in applause and whistles.

"There are several games we play down on the surface; I bet you've heard about football, right?"

Garret was met with another round of energetic clapping.

"Well, how about basketball and hockey?"

The twins were almost giddy with excitement and began banging their hands on the arena surface.

"Here's what we're gonna do. We're gonna have a demonstration, kind of a mock scrimmage, after I've gone over the rules of the game."

"What's it called?" shouted one of the clones.

"We're thinking about naming it 'ZG Ball.' That's short for zero gravity."

"How many players do you need?" someone hollered.

"If y'all will shut up, I'll explain. Okay, first off, there'll be two teams of ten. The objective of this game is to get this twelve-inch dodge ball through the thirty-inch hoop at the opposite end. You can throw it, kick it, bounce it, or float with it."

The brood of anxious and rambunctious men turned to each other with nods of approval.

"The two teams will scatter themselves on the walls and wait for one of two captains to initiate the play. That occurs when the captain throws, kicks, bounces or floats with the ball. He's gonna wanna pass it off to one of his teammates, who will then pass it off to another and so forth until their player is close enough to throw the ball through the hoop. Are you with me so far?"

"Yes," the twins replied in unison.

"But how does the opposing team stop them from scoring a goal ... point ... basket thing?" Titan asked.

"For starters, you can bat it away or just hold up your hands to block a pass. How do football players stop someone running with the ball?" Garret inquired of his pupils.

"They tackle 'em!" Armada shouted.

"They tackle 'em!" Garret repeated energetically and pointed at Armada.

"You're saying we get to play tackle football?" a clone shouted ecstatically.

"Tackle yes, football no. Look, you can tackle, pull their leg, push 'em outta the way, whatever. But there's no hitting or fighting. The winning team will ultimately be determined by timing and positioning."

"What happens if I'm flying, getting ready to throw the ball, and someone slams into me?" Titan bellowed, "We're gonna be stuck!"

"You bring up a good point and I'm sorry, I forgot one important key element. Each team will also have three players on tethered bungee cords. Every thirty seconds a whistle will blow and each tethered team member gets one pull. That means every thirty seconds a tether can push off and retrieve one of their own, maybe two, I don't know. They get one pull and can bring back a member of their own team, OR... they can pull down an opponent. Either way, as soon as all six tethers retract to their starting position, whoever they retrieved can immediately get back in the game. Y'all get it?"

Two hundred clones let loose with a jubilant burst of applause.

"All right then, since the game this evening is primarily for demonstration purposes, we won't necessarily be focusing on team selections. You guys can decide amongst yourselves as to who will be on what team and who your captains are."

The arena was all a twitter with the Evans literally bouncing off the walls.

"For now I wanna assign tethers. Where's Titan? Titan!"

"Yeah, Coach?" Titan answered to the delight of the twins.

"Funny! That was funny, right? Grab five of your girlfriends and split up... three on each side... and give them each one of these."

Garret threw a bundle of bungee cords and harnesses to Titan. Before he even had the harnesses in his hands, Titan was the recipient of wishful bids for play from the eager volunteers.

"Pick me, Titan!"

"Titan, buddy! Over here!"

"Oh, Titan, please!"

Titan caught the cluster of cords and harnesses and looked about the arena. He pushed off the wall and flew to the side, grabbing a stabilizing rung near Armada's head.

"Wanna play?" he asked with a smile.

"Armada!" Garret shouted.

"Sir!"

"Grab nineteen of your sisters and split up!"

"Sorry," Armada apologized to Titan, shrugging his shoulders, "I'm already playing!"

The company of clones went berserk with excitement. They shouted and whistled, clapped and waved to get the attention of Titan and Armada as they pointed and said "You!" or motioned for a brother while hollering "C'mon!"

In a matter of minutes Armada and his band of twelve, sequestered at one end of 'the can,' devised their strategy. At the opposite end of the makeshift stadium, thirteen identical twins assembled and concocted their own plan of attack.

"Remember what Garret said," Armada barked, "timing and position will determine who wins. I want you all to scatter by pairs on opposite sides from each other. Go up every fifteen feet or so and stagger your launches. I want the first pair to come out when I do. The next pair doesn't push off until the first pass is complete, then the next pair with the following pass. Got it?"

Armada's teammates let loose with a short and boisterous "Yes, sir!" and broke their huddle.

"Where do you want me?" Titan asked quietly.

"I want you in the middle. Let the other two make retrievals. You're gonna be like an eagle getting a fish. Whenever they're getting close and your timer goes off, you go after the leader. Catch 'em and pull 'em back. If you come from the middle, you'll be bringing them backwards."

"Nice! Great plan!" Titan stated, pushing away to join his brothers.

Garret blew his whistle as the two teams settled into their starting positions.

"Now!" Garret shouted, "The rest of you will need to stay behind the goal area while the ball is in play. DO NOT try to catch the ball or push a player back into the playing zone; that's why we have tethers."

"How do we know who's on what team?" a clone asked Garret.

"Good question," he stated, hesitant to answer.

"Armada!" Garret hollered, "You and your boys wrap your identity lanyards around your right arm."

"What's the winning score gonna be?" an Evan hovering nearby asked Garret.

"For tonight let's go to three points. If we start playing this regularly, we might take the game to maybe five points or just see what the score is at the end of one hour. But for now, we're gonna play to three."

Very few, if any, objected to the plan.

"Here we go, boys!" Garret shouted, "Captains, on your mark?"

Armada and his brethren gripped the rungs on the arena walls and squatted low. Garret paused, looked at the two captains, and gave a powerful, shrill blast on his whistle.

Armada prepped himself for a lunge while clutching the ball. He watched the opposing players closest to him and how they were anticipating his initial launch into the game. Armada gave a mighty push with his legs, as did the two opponents. Armada, however, did not release his grasp on the stabilizing rung and did a backward flip. The opposing pair of clones lunged, met in midair, bumped into each other, and levitated helplessly in the middle of the arena.

Armada, free and clear of any opposition, launched his body into the void with a trajectory that placed him within inches of his team's first tether. The clones closest to him jumped and waited for his pass. Armada threw the ball just prior to the thirty-second buzzer going off.

Garret pulled himself to the communication kiosk at the portal entry to the arena. He picked up the phone, dialed Riggs' extension, and turned to watch the game.

"Woodburn," a voice sternly answered.

"It's on! Turn on the live feed from the Arena One commons. You'll wanna see this."

"Hold on," Riggs said, rolling his chair to another desk.

"Have they been playing long?"

"Less than two minutes."

"How do they look?"

"Honestly? I feel like I'm watching my son's first day at peewee league baseball practice. Except, of course, for Armada. He's all over the place. Same for Titan Eleven. He and Armada are inseparable."

"I'm gonna get Wyczthack in on this. Hold on."

Garret turned around just in time to watch Titan get a complete stretch on his line, catch and drag an opponent back, and release him at full velocity. The clone zoomed through the air and slammed against the padded shell cap right above his head.

Garret and two hundred clones burst out with a simultaneous "WHOA!"

"C'mon, Achilles! Get back in there! Don't take that!" Garret shrieked.

"I got Doctor Wyczthack on the line with us," Riggs said.

"Yes, sir. Doctor Wyczthack. Hello, Garret Brock here."

"Mr. Brock, where are you? What's all that noise?" Cain inquired.

"I'm sorry, sir ... THROW THE BALL ... I'm sorry—not you, sir."

"They're playing the game, sir. The 'ZG Ball' we discussed last week," Riggs interjected.

"Yes, yes, I remember, Mr. Woodburn. Tell me, Mr. Brock, how are they responding?"

"Sir, if you'll turn on the live feed from the arena, you'll see for yourself."

"Apparently, sir, Armada and Titan are leading the way, as usual."

"What is their level of functionality, Mr. Brock?"

"Functionality? Have y'all ever put tape around a cat's paw?" Garret asked, laughing out loud as he observed the clones, "Heck, these boys'll get the hang of it soon enough. They're not used to developing strategy, at least not against an opponent while in an environment with zero gravity."

"What's their level of aggression, Mr. Brock?"

"Aggression? Well, this ain't Monday Night Football I'm watching. They're having fun, though, if that's what you're asking."

"Fine; thank you, Mr. Brock. I'll check in again," Cain solemnly stated and abruptly hung up the phone.

"Okay … sir … thank you, sir."

"He's off the line, Garret."

"Oh, okay. Is he always like that?"

"He just wants the facts, not the friendship. Don't take it personally."

"All righty, then."

"Has anybody scored yet?"

"Nah … it'll be a while before anything…," Garret turned away from the kiosk screen to finish his statement, "happens up here."

"Keep me posted on what the score is."

"Yes, sir. Will do."

Garret clumsily hung up the phone as he focused his attention on Armada, who, at that very moment, was attempting to pass the ball.

No sooner had Garret hung up from his conversation with Riggs that almost sixty minutes passed by, and not one point had been scored by either team.

"Titan! Pull me forward! Fast!"

Armada had no sooner shouted to his friend when two tethers from the other team set him, and the ball, in their sights and thrust themselves in his direction.

"Coming!" Titan called out.

Armada floated helplessly, looking for one of his teammates to whom he could pass the ball safely. Titan and the two opposing tethers simultaneously reached out for Armada, grabbing him by his free arm and both legs.

"Don't let go!" Armada grunted to Titan, struggling to keep his grasp on the ball.

"C'mon, Armada! You can't hold on forever!" one of the tethered players griped.

"Help!" Titan shouted to his tethered teammates.

"We can't!" one hollered, "Ten more seconds. The timer is about to blow!"

"Pull! Pull him back!" Garret added.

The thirty-second buzzer blasted and the remaining tethers, along with the rest of the players, hurled themselves at the tug-of-war hovering at midfield.

"Get the ball!" and "Pry his hands loose!" the men laughed and shouted at each other. Garret held on to the rungs at the kiosk as tightly as he could, laughing uncontrollably.

"Get 'em off one at a time!" Armada barked, "One at a time!"

"Start at the legs!" Titan snapped at his brothers.

"C'mon, guys! One point!" Garret yelled, "We want one point!"

"One point! One point!" the onlookers chanted.

"Get 'em off my legs!" Armada again shouted, laughing along.

His teammates managed to wrangle one of the opponents from his left leg and push him to the far end of the arena. They then doubled up on the next man and sent him sailing to join his teammate.

"One point!" Garret and the clones continued to shout.

"That's it, boys! Keep it up!" Titan urged as Armada twisted and flailed to maintain possession of the ball.

Armada's brothers managed to pick off the ten players and send them floating forty feet back, away from their goal.

Now, all that remained of the opposing team were the three tethers.

"Okay, boys, here's what's gonna happen," Armada coached his brothers. "Titan, you three keep your tension constant. When I give you the signal, pull their arms away and let go. They'll shoot backwards and when y'all let go of me, I'll fly forward as your cords recoil."

"C'mon, Armada, that's not fair," the other tethers complained.

"C'mon what?" Titan taunted, "We're here to win!"

"One point!" and "Armada!" Garret and the Evans shouted.

"Help! Help!" the three clinging tethers called out to their stranded teammates.

"Here we go! Time to fly!" Armada warned.

"One … two … three," they counted out loud.

In perfect unison the ten players managed to pry loose the grip of the opposing three tethers. Titan and the two other tethers flew forward, pulling Armada with them. The tethers from the opposite team flew backwards as their cords recoiled. At just the right moment, Titan and his brothers let go of Armada. He soared through the air, virtually unobstructed, directly to the hoop at the end of the arena. Armada lightly pushed the ball away from him and into the net.

From the noise level of the celebration that ensued, one would have thought the last play of the Super Bowl had just occurred.

Armada was met with open arms as he floated past the goal. His brothers plucked him out of the air, patted him on the back, and scruffed his hair.

Garret picked up the kiosk phone and dialed Riggs' extension.

"Riggs," he stated bluntly.

"Game over!" Garret shouted, high-fiving a clone as he floated by.

"Really? Who won?"

"Does it matter? They love it! That's all we were worried about. Right? I mean just listen to 'em! Enable a live feed!"

Riggs turned to his computer and opened the video stream of the arena.

"Wow! How much sugar did you give 'em?"

"You know why they're all wound up?"

"Let me guess—Heckle and Jeckle?"

"Those two are why these guys are so excited. If Titan and Armada weren't leading this thing, it woulda flopped. I guarantee."

"Hold on, I better get Wyczthack in on this."

Riggs keyed in the extension for Dr. Wyczthack.

"Cain," he listlessly stated.

"Dr. Wyczthack, this is Riggs and I have Garret Brock on the line again."

"What's that noise!?" Cain asked, pulling the phone away from his ear.

"Game's over, sir. They loved it!" Garret declared.

"Sir, if you'll activate the live video feed from the arena...," Riggs suggested.

"This is the best test, best experiment you've ever come up with, if you ask me. Better than any other simulation we've implemented, too."

Cain watched the streaming video as he halfheartedly chatted with his subordinates.

"In your own words, Mr. Brock, please give me the reasons as to why you are of the opinion that this experiment is such a roaring success."

"My reasons, sir? Well, if you linked into the video feeds you'll see two hundred reasons. I mean, I've never seen them behave like this."

"Sir, I agree with Garret. In the three years I've been working with the Evans, I, like Garret, have never observed an entire pod interact with one another like we have this evening, let alone two complete classes."

"Was it merely the game, gentlemen? Or is something deeper?"

Dr. Wyczthack leaned closer to his monitor to watch the ongoing celebration.

"Garret thinks it's something more."

"Oh, I know it is! It's not the supplements, it's not the accelerated education ... it's none of that. No disrespect, sir."

"None taken, Garret. Please, continue."

Riggs struggled to stifle his laughter as Garret continued with his lecture. In the meanwhile, Cain quickly accessed the personnel files in the server of the Engenechem Department of Human Resources.

"Hold on," Garret stated and placed his palm over the phone, then picked up the microphone for the speaker system, "All right, guys, that's it for tonight. Lights out in thirty minutes."

The Evans protested just as a toddler whining about an early bedtime.

"Now?"

"It's not even ten!"

"C'mon, Dad, just a little longer."

"Get movin'!" Garret ordered, "Titan, I want all six tethers from you and the other girls."

"Yes, Mother." Titan echoed, sarcastically.

Cain and Riggs waited for Garret to resume the conversation, but did not hesitate to enable the microphones on the video cameras.

The company of clones floated by Garret at the kiosk before splitting off to the transfer tubes leading to the dormitories. As they passed by, Garret was met with a barrage of taunts like "Good night, Pops," "Come tuck me in," and "Will you read me a story."

"Okay, I'm back. Sorry for the delay," Garrett announced.

"Quite all right, Mr. Brock. Tell me, when did they start addressing you as pops?"

"I don't remember them ever being that informal and personal with me. In or out of class," Riggs jealously admitted.

"This is what I'm talking about. Something's happening and it has nothing to do with your experiments or cloning process. It's them."

"Them who, Mr. Brock?"

"Armada and Titan, sir. Something has changed, something internal, intellectually speaking."

"In what way?"

"Garret, if you don't mind me jumping in, I'd like to answer that. Sir, I tend to agree with him. I noticed it as well a few months ago during the EVA simulations. Armada's social interaction was off the chart, comparatively speaking. Not so much for Titan, but it appears that he's slowly catching up to his brother."

"And the two of you believe this is bad?"

"No, sir, not at all," Garret added, "I'm merely saying there's something uniquely and undeniably different about Armada Nine and Titan Eleven. If they hadn't been playing tonight or leading this thing, I honestly think the results would be less than stellar. I'm sure they'd had a good time, but not like this. Those two are affecting the rest of your kids in more ways than you imagined."

"Thank you, Mr. Brock, for your insight and advice," Cain blurted insincerely and abruptly disconnected the call.

"I don't wanna get anyone in trouble, Riggs. I'm just saying that there's something different with Armada and Titan. And whatever it is that's making them appear to be more human won't be found in their blood."

"I know. It's okay; don't worry about it."

Riggs looked at his phone and noticed that Cain was calling him back on another line.

"Hey, Garret, I got another call coming in."

"Oh, okay; say, listen, tomorrow can…."

Riggs hung up from his conversation with Garret without so much as a goodbye.

"Woodburn," Riggs answered.

"I want you to bring down Armada Nine and Titan Eleven tomorrow for an evaluation," Cain commanded.

"Yes, sir. What time?"

"Two o'clock at the Nursery on seventeen."

***

"I don't understand why it's so urgent that we have to undergo another evaluation," Titan complained, "Just you and me? None of the others from either of our control groups is getting this kind of treatment."

"I betcha they just wanna know what we thought of their new game," Armada commented.

The twins removed their helmets as they entered the elevator.

"What time is it?" Titan asked.

"Twelve-thirty. We'll be about half an hour early. Which means you and I have time for a little adventure."

Armada stepped to the control panel and pulled down on a tilt-out keyboard.

"Whoa! What are you doing?"

"Garret said Riggs told him that we were to be at the Nursery on seventeen at two o'clock. Right?"

"Yeah, but…."

"Riggs never mentioned anything about where he wanted us to be before we went to our appointment. Hey, stand behind me to my left and just act normal."

"What are you doing? Where are you taking us?"

With Titan blocking the view of the video camera in the elevator cab, Armada quickly gained access to the records for every elevator in the SUBOS. Armada quietly explained his plans as he altered the time stamps to allow for their unauthorized excursion.

"I don't know. This doesn't feel right."

The elevator came to an abrupt stop, startling Titan. Seconds later the two doors parted.

"What happened? What'd you do?"

Armada pushed the folding keyboard back into the control panel and picked up his helmet.

"That, my partner in crime, is destiny calling. Adventure is ours for half an hour."

The anxious twins nervously poked their heads out to get a quick peek at the new surroundings. With the exception of one security station and two guards, the coast was clear.

"Where are we?" Titan whispered loudly.

"Sixteen A."

"Sixteen A!?" Titan hissed, slapping Armada's shoulder, "Are you freaking kidding me? You know we're not authorized to be up here!"

Titan's comments went unacknowledged.

"We need to get across to the bank of local elevators," Armada muttered.

Titan paced back and forth, mumbling to himself as Armada pondered their predicament.

"Wyczthack is gonna put us in quarantine when he finds out."

"You mean IF he finds out. Here's what we're gonna do: put your helmet on your left side and I'll be on your right. You look the other way so that if the guards see us they won't get anything but a quick glance at my face. We'll simply stroll to the other side of the landing and hop aboard one of the waiting elevators."

Titan stared at Armada with his mouth agape.

"Oh, it's so simple! We'll just stroll out and hop on!"

"You got it! Let's go! We gotta be back in a SUBOS elevator in twenty-five minutes."

The nervous duo placed their helmets under their left arms and briskly strode to the waiting elevators on the opposite side of the hall. Titan looked down and away whereas Armada intentionally turned his head to the right and smiled. Just before reaching out to the elevator buttons, one of the armed security guards glanced at Armada. With a slight nod and halfhearted wave, Armada and Titan entered the waiting elevator, avoiding direct eye contact with the uninterested officers.

"Man, that was close!" Titan declared with a sigh, falling back against the wall.

"I told ya. Just act normal like you're supposed to be doin' what you're doin' and people will leave you alone. Okay, twenty-two minutes left. Where to?"

"I don't care. I don't even know what's here."

"Well, if they're setup is anything like ours on fifteen, then they'll have education, cafeteria, living quarters, R&D...."

Before Armada could finish his statement, the elevator suddenly came to life and quickly ascended.

"What'd you do? Where are we going?"

"I didn't do a thing! How am I supposed to know where we're going when I never touched a button?"

The twin brothers continued their bickering until they felt the elevator slow down then come to a complete stop. Armada and Titan stood frozen, temporarily unable to move or speak as they waited for the doors to part.

A bell lightly chimed and a female voice pleasantly stated, "Sixteen J, Research and Development."

The stainless steel doors parted and the two men were shocked to be standing face to face with their female counterpart. Like scared children on the first day of school, the trio gawked at each other, waiting for

somebody else to take the initiative and begin the communication process. The elevator doors, sensing no movement in the cab, automatically
began to close. Armada and Titan stood in total silence and moved only
their eyes as the stranger disappeared from view. The bell lightly chimed
once more and again the voice pleasantly stated, "Sixteen J, Research and
Development," and the doors parted.

The woman, unmoved, shifted her gaze back and forth, looking over
both of the twins. She slowly stepped in the elevator, just far enough inside
so as to allow the doors to close behind her and turned away. Armada
and Titan remained statuesque, focusing on the physical attributes of the
beautiful passenger. Her face was mere inches away from the elevator
wall when she sheepishly said, "Sixteen X, please." Armada ever so slowly
reached out his right hand and pressed the buttons as she requested.

"You know you're not supposed to be here," the woman delicately
commented.

Titan slapped Armada on his left arm. Armada slapped him back.

After another uncomfortable moment of silence passed, she said,
"My name is Chloe. Chloe Rover Seven."

CHAPTER 8

Big Brother

"What are you doing?" Chloe nervously asked.

"That's exactly what I asked not ten minutes ago," Titan complained. "He started messing with our time stamps, zone authorizations and access codes, and now we're talking to you. C'mon, Armada, quit clownin' around. Someone's gonna catch us."

Armada acted as if he hadn't heard a word as he diligently typed away on the tilt-out keyboard.

"What's on Sixteen X?" Armada casually asked.

"Advanced Genetics. Why?" Chloe replied.

"Who issued your pass and who are you scheduled to meet?"

"Albright issued and White is expecting me."

"How old are you?" Titan shyly inquired.

"I'm one year, two months, and ten days, thank you, and I'm getting the results of my final tests today."

"I'm two years and eleven months," Titan proudly declared.

"What kind of tests?" Armada pressed.

"Tests to determine if I qualify for a third application."

"I already began my third application program," Armada volunteered, pushing the keyboard into the control panel. "What are your primary and secondary applications?"

"What's yours?"

"I asked first."

"Mine are communications and sanitation," Titan awkwardly boasted.

"Satellite telemetry and digital security and encryption," Armada stated, crossing his arms.

"Subterranean excavation and structural engineering," Chloe replied, crossing her arms as well.

"Why don't we drop her off and we can all get to our designated appointments on time. Okay?" Titan jovially suggested.

"Not okay. And the third application?" Armada probed.

"I told you I don't know yet. That's what I'm to be discussing with Dr. White in a manner of minutes."

"My third application program is propulsion systems."

"I want a third," Titan mumbled.

Chloe and Armada quietly held each other in their gaze an extra second or two.

"All right, enough is enough. What are you doing to us?" Titan exclaimed, raising his voice.

"Well, for starters, our schedules got pushed back," Armada flatly stated.

"What?" Titan exclaimed.

"Okay, you two. I want off this elevator now!" Chloe demanded.

"Calm down … just relax and don't get yourselves worked up. I've got it all planned out."

"What'd you do now?" Titan asked.

"We … us three … have an extra hour to explore. The arrival time for our interviews and evaluations has changed to three o'clock instead of two. All three of our zone authorizations and access codes have been expanded. And the video monitor in the elevator is running on a sixty-second loop from over one hour ago when this cab was empty."

Chloe and Titan glared at Armada with incredulity.

"You guys should be thanking me right about now," Armada pointed out.

Titan and Chloe remained transfixed on Armada, unable to overcome the shock and amazement at his actions.

"Okay, where to now?" Armada asked nonchalantly, running his fingers over the buttons on the control panel.

"I don't care. What does it matter? I've been kidnapped," Chloe complained.

"Not to change the subject and detract from our little jaunt, but what's that?" Titan quizzed Chloe, pointing to a device hanging from her right hip in what looked like a large, modified holster.

"What? This thing?"

"Yeah, that thing. Looks like a tablet."

"All right, we're going to … Fifteen G. I've yet to see the medical facilities," Armada blurted, pressing the buttons.

"Oh, goody. Well, since you asked—this, boys, is the L-Gen," Chloe confidently stated as she removed the device from its cradle and handed it to Armada. The heavy tablet-shaped device was just over twelve inches in length, around six inches wide, and no more than two inches thick.

"L-Gen, meaning…," Titan prodded.

"Laser Resonance Frequency Generator."

"Like Tesla?" Armada asked.

"Better than Tesla. He designed and built a steam-powered oscillating generator. This uses waves focused in a laser beam, pulsing at a rate of 32,000 cycles per second with a penetration depth of 40 feet."

"Fascinating!" Armada commented.

Titan had the look of a fazed deer staring at a pair of headlights.

"Will you please explain to my friend, in English, what this device does?" Armada requested and backhanded Titan's chest.

Chloe chuckled softly as she reached out to take the L-Gen from Armada. As she did, her fingers lightly brushed the back of his hand.

"If I were at a location, say a quarry or a mine, I could walk all over the place, aim this lens on the end and push … this button here on the corner, and wherever I am, whatever direction the L-Gen is pointing, the laser shoots out and penetrates what I'm aiming at ... up to forty feet deep."

Chloe directed her attention to Armada as she spoke and watched him as he looked her up and down. Titan, oblivious of the immediate connection between Chloe and Armada, was lost in the details and design of the fabulous toy he held in his hands.

"And in about thirty seconds, the laser will detect the minerals that are in that location. Tesla theorized that everything vibrated when a certain sound wave was produced and amplified. So gold ore vibrates at a specific frequency, coal, copper—you name it—everything has a resonate frequency. This goes through a very broad and expansive range of frequencies and wave forms and can successfully identify no less than seventy compounds.

"So just push this button right here?" Titan asked Chloe while pressing down.

"Yes, but don't...."

A bright green beam of light flashed out of the L-Gen lens and struck Armada on his left shoulder.

"What're you doing? Ya idiot!" Armada snarled.

"What? I'm sorry! That was an accident!"

"Hey! Hey! It's all right. It's completely harmless, just so long as you don't aim it at anyone's eyes."

Chloe took possession of the L-Gen while the brothers perpetuated their argument.

"Way to go! You could have blinded me!"

"Well, I didn't so don't be such a big...."

The confrontation was ended by a sudden ping of Chloe's device.

"Ah-ha!" she exclaimed. "Let's see what Armada's made of!"

"Oh, now you're the funny one?"

"I like her," Titan sneered as the men stood on either side of Chloe, trying to interpret the information on the display screen of the L-Gen.

"Well?" Armada asked.

"Uh ... this is ... strange."

"What does it say? What's in Armada?"

"This says you have platinum, silver, silicon, copper...."

"That doesn't sound right," Armada commented.

"Ha! You're a cell phone," Titan guffawed.

"Shut up!"

The trio were so consumed with the results of the impromptu scan of Armada that they failed to realize their destination was fast approaching. When the elevator stopped, a friendly female voice interrupted the threesome, saying, "Fifteen G, Emergency Medical Services."

The doors parted quietly and smoothly. Chloe and the twins dared not move a muscle for several seconds. When he realized no one was waiting to board the elevator, Armada ducked back against the wall with the control panel. Chloe and Titan leapt backwards to join him.

"Are you having fun yet?" Armada whispered with a smirk.

"See?! I told you not to mess around! Now Wyczthack will quarantine all three of us!"

"I'm never gonna get my third application now! All because of you two morons!" Chloe hissed.

"Me? What'd I do?"

"How about you two shut up so I can think!" Armada demanded.

Armada squatted low then gingerly crept to the threshold and poked his head around the open elevator door. He turned to his left and saw only a long corridor of office doors. To his right was a department directory with arrows pointing in different directions.

"Follow me and keep low."

"Where are we going?" Titan whispered.

"Just trust me and don't say a word."

"If I don't get my...," Chloe threatened.

"I know! Your application! I know, I know! I get it! Follow me."

Armada led the way with Chloe sandwiched in between the brothers. They stayed close to the wall and scurried down the right side of the corridor to a set of electric double doors marking the entrance to the radiology department. Armada swiped the identity card on his lanyard and was given immediate access.

"Why did you take us to radiology?" Chloe hissed.

"I don't care where we go, but we can't very well sit in an elevator and wait to be discovered."

Armada reached for the doorknob of the first office he came to and gave it a jiggle.

Locked.

Before Armada had the chance to release the knob, it suddenly twisted in his hand and the door to the office quickly swung open. Two Engenechem employees exited the room and marched purposefully down the hall, away from the cowering trio. Armada extended his arm to stop the door from closing. He turned to Chloe and Titan, jerked his head to the left, and cautiously entered the room.

Once inside, Armada slowly rose from his crouched position and surveyed the area.

"Keep quiet," he said, motioning for them to follow.

Armada determined they were in a waiting room for one of several radiologists. However, thankfully, at that particular moment there was no sign of a receptionist. They waddled to the doorway leading to the radiology lab and delicately pushed it open. Once it was established that they were truly alone, Chloe broke the silence.

"I can't believe this is happening to me!"

"All right, scan me again," Armada ordered as they erected themselves.

"What? You've kidnapped me and derailed my confirmation and you want me to scan you?"

"C'mon, Armada! Let's make a plan, get her off our back, and...."

"Whoa! Hold on! Get me off of YOUR back? What? Now I'm slowing you down?"

"Look! Just scan me again and we'll put you right back where we found you. Okay?" Armada sweetly suggested.

Chloe looked over the inept twin assailants.

"Just a scan?" she confirmed.

"That's it. All you have to do is aim and shoot."

"C'mon! Just scan him before we get caught. He'll take you right back to ... to...," Titan impatiently begged.

"Sixteen J."

"Sixteen J. We'll put you right back where we found you on Sixteen J. Tell her, Armada, and let's get outta here."

"Sixteen J, just like the man said," Armada softly assured.

Once again Chloe looked over the brothers, drew in a deep, cleansing breath, and released it with a sad shake of her head.

"Okay," she said, removing the L-Gen from its holster, "one scan coming right up."

Chloe moved a few feet away, took careful aim at Armada's left shoulder, and gently pressed the button on the corner. The bright, fluorescent green laser beam flashed out onto Armada's jumpsuit. In a matter of seconds, the L-Gen beeped and the LED screen lit up. The three runaways stared at the illuminated display as Chloe read the results.

"It's the same as before. Platinum, silver, silicon, copper...."

"Your gizmo is out of whack!"

"It is not! This has been field tested by Phelps-Dodge at the copper mines in Morenci. They tried it out in Kentucky and Virginia at the coal mines. They...."

"I don't care who tested when with what in the big whatever where," Armada snapped.

"Okay, she scanned you and it's jacked up. Big deal! C'mon, let's go!" Titan anxiously urged.

"The L-Gen isn't wrong. I helped with its original design. Maybe you had some kind of surgery or broke a bone ... I don't know."

Armada, having passed beyond the point of frustration, unzipped his jumpsuit and began pulling his sleeves off his arms.

"Geez, you two! Drop it already."

Chloe's eyes grew as large as saucers watching Armada remove the torso of his jumpsuit and undershirt.

"Do you two see any scars?" Armada gruffly asked. "Deformities? Abnormalities?"

He stepped toward Chloe, grasped her left hand, and placed it on his shoulder as he turned away from her.

"Now! Does anything feel strange to you?"

Delicately running her index and middle finger across his left shoulder, Chloe softly rubbed from side to side. After a couple of swipes she stopped and repeated the process on his right shoulder.

"What? What's wrong? Why'd you stop?" Armada nervously asked, looking over his shoulder.

"Titan, come here please. Do something for me."

"What do you want me to do?"

"Hey! What're you doing?"

"Shut up, you big baby," Chloe said with a slight slap to the back of Armada's head.

"Rub your fingers right here and the same on the right," Chloe directed.

Titan did as he was instructed, going back and forth between the two shoulders.

"You feel it?"

"What? C'mon, feel what?" Armada asked.

"Yeah. Yeah, I can feel the difference. She's right, Armada. You got something in you."

"That's impossible! I've never broken a bone, never had surgery... never been sick, for that matter!"

"I'm telling you, we can feel it. There's something in you."

Chloe resumed rubbing her fingers on his left shoulder.

"I can't tell if it's in your trapezius or levator scapulae. It's right in between. Maybe something happened when you were younger and just don't remember it?"

"I'd remember it if I had surgery," Armada angrily stated, pulling his shirt over his head.

Titan looked at the clock on the office wall.

"Let's worry about this later. Okay? We gotta be on Seventeen G and she's gotta be on Sixteen J in forty minutes."

Armada briefly leaned against the counter.

"Can I see that thing for a moment?" he pleasantly requested.

Silently, Chloe again removed the L-Gen and handed it to Armada. He indiscriminately looked over the toy, then quickly aimed it at Chloe and fired the laser.

"Hey! What'd you do that for?"

"What's wrong with you? It's not her fault you have whatever in your shoulder!"

The L-Gen pinged and the display screen began listing the results of the scan.

"Read it and tell me what it says," Armada demanded, handing the device back to Chloe.

"Platinum, silver, silicon, copper...."

Before she could finish her statement, Armada yanked the scanner from her hands, directed the lens at Titan, and fired the laser. Chloe stood in awkward silence as Armada slapped the resonance generator in her hands. Once again the scanner beeped and the machine displayed its results.

"Read it!" Armada ordered.

Chloe's voice cracked as she started speaking "Platinum...."

"Platinum, silver, silicon, copper, aluminum," Armada loudly finished for Chloe. "All right, unzip your jumpsuits."

With expressions resembling those of chastised children, Chloe and Titan slowly peeled off their jumpsuit sleeves.

"Show me where," Armada demanded, grabbed Chloe's hand, and placed it on Titan's left shoulder.

She slowly slid her fingers across the trapezius and levator scapulae muscles until she identified the exact location of the foreign object.

"Do I have it, too?" Titan meekly asked.

"Yep," she replied.

Chloe then coyly turned her back to the twins. Titan stood by

Armada's side as he timidly extended his hand and lay his fingers, ever so tenderly, on her soft and exposed skin. He pushed his hand under the strap of her tank top and gently rubbed back and forth until he, too, discovered the tiny bump in the muscle. Without a word, Chloe turned slightly to her left and made direct eye contact with Armada. He nodded his confirmation and pulled up Chloe's sagging uniform.

"So, what are we gonna do? She's gotta be there in twenty minutes. We need to be on one of those elevators like right now."

"Platinum, silver, silicon, copper and aluminum," Armada quietly stated.

"You two can discuss this all you want. I'm leaving. There's no way I'm missing my interview on account of you!"

"They're tracking us," Armada growled. "We have RFID chips inside our bodies! They know where we are every second, every last one of us."

Titan and Chloe traded short glances with each other.

"Can we remove them? Surgically?" Chloe innocently asked.

"We don't have the time."

"C'mon, Armada! Let's go! We'll think of something later!"

"I got it!" Chloe excitedly stated. "We're in radiology, right? So let's fry 'em with X-rays."

"It'll be too suspicious. Three clones have their transponders fail simultaneously due to overexposure to radiation? That'll send up a red flag for sure."

"Okay, talk and walk. Let's go; work with me, talk and walk!" Titan nervously spouted.

Titan assumed control of the situation as Armada and Chloe churned out different plans and schemes to either remove the chips or render them useless. While Titan was on the constant lookout for any and all forms of danger, Armada and Chloe strolled lackadaisically behind him, fully erect and speaking freely without a care in the world. When they arrived at the bank of elevators, Titan pushed the button and slumped against the wall.

"Hey there, buddy, you don't look so good," Armada casually commented.

"I'm fine. I just haven't had any of my supplements since early this morning."

The green 'up' arrow illuminated and a muted bell chimed, alerting the clones the elevator had arrived. The stainless steel doors split and the trio briskly boarded.

"I agree with Armada. All of a sudden you don't look all that great. And you're sweating! Are you sure you feel okay?"

"Sure I'm sure. I get this way whenever I'm on an unplanned adventure. Just do your magic and take us where we need to go."

Armada pulled down the keyboard and typed away. Chloe kept a careful watch on Titan as Armada rearranged the time stamps and authorization codes for their final destinations.

"How will I get in contact with you? Will I ever see you again?" Chloe asked.

"Did you enjoy yourself today?" Armada inquired with a smile.

"Well, I don't know how much I enjoyed the past hour, but I will say it was definitely an adventure."

Armada stopped typing, folded the keyboard into place, and turned to face Chloe.

"Do you trust me?"

"Her trust you? I've known you all my life and I don't trust you! She's known you for all of one hour. Trust you? Ha!"

"Well, maybe the answer to that question should be that I'm open to the idea of growing to trust you over a period of time."

"Then I can definitely promise you that yes, you'll see me again and we'll figure something out."

"I hope to see you again sometime soon, Titan."

"Thank, Chloe. It's been a real thrill."

Titan slid down the wall, closed his eyes, and leaned his head back. Chloe adjusted her stance to face Armada. The couple didn't speak as the car sped upwards. In a matter of moments, a woman's voice said, 'Sixteen X, Advanced Genetics,' and the elevator stopped. Chloe slowly stepped past Armada, out the elevator, and into the hallway. Knowing that she would be under immediate surveillance, she didn't show any kind of reaction when Armada whispered, "Go on and find out if you'll ever get the chance to be as smart as me."

Chloe shook her head, then smiled to herself when she heard Armada call out, "I'll find you."

CHAPTER 9

THE NEW BABYLON

"I want to show you the next phase of our plans," Cain gloatingly stated as the digital schematics shone on the screen. "We call them 'Clouds.' Complete self-sustaining environments."

The modest assembly of engineers, scientists, and designers gazed upon the illuminated blueprints in both awe and doubt.

Amanda Castro, a trainer with EVA aquatic simulators, asked, "Doctor, do you have projected dates for construction of this...Cloud, as you call it?"

"Nine to ten months. Eleven as the worst-case scenario."

"Can you project the arena and dormitories on screen along with the Cloud?" another man inquired.

"Bianca? Will you be so kind as to display both sets of schematics?" Cain requested.

In a matter of seconds, Bianca Doyle, Cain's personal assistant, had the original design blueprints of the arena and dormitories alongside those of Dr. Wyczthack's newest project. An immediate hush fell upon the intimate audience. As if viewing a picture of David and Goliath, the perplexed collective began voicing their opinions out loud to themselves.

"Correct me if I misunderstood you, but you expect assembly of this unit to take no more than nine to ten months?" Riggs Woodburn inquired.

"Eleven months as...."

"Okay, eleven months; you honestly expect to complete this project just shy of a year?"

"Do you have an objection you wish to express?" Cain inquired with an obvious inflection of his voice.

"Well, sir, just look at it. That's gotta be at least ten times larger than the Arena. And I'm not even considering all of the internal components. With all due respect, Dr. Wyczthack, this obviously is a very ambitious undertaking and I'm not so sure we can meet the anticipated construction deadline."

Cain leaned his weight on the podium and, with his infamous scowl, simply stated "Ten."

His intimate audience silently sat, waiting for him to finish his statement.

"Ten?" one of the engineers spoke up, slightly rising out of his seat, "What do you mean by 'ten,' sir?"

"Ten Clouds," Cain smugly replied.

Riggs, Garret, Amanda, and the EVA departmental heads turned to face each other, as if what they just heard was spoken in a foreign language. Cain briefly glanced at Bianca who, in turn, cracked the smallest of smiles and shrugged her shoulders. The think tank was so focused on the discussion with themselves that for the moment they forgot where they were and who was watching and listening.

"We can't...," and "We don't have...," was the start of almost every statement and comment.

Amanda stood and raised her voice, drawing the attention of her associates, "With your proposed schedule, judging from what I see here right now, in my best estimation, we should complete all ten Clouds in nine-and-a-half years."

Cain and Bianca quickly darted their eyes at one another. As he chuckled softly, Cain glowered at Amanda and said, "Ten Clouds, ten months. Not one Cloud in ten months."

Cain shouted into the microphone, "Ten! I want ten…in… ten…months!"

"How?" Light Huddleston asked.

"Thank you!" Cain hollered, clapping his hands. "Finally, one of you geniuses asked a question instead of caving in with a blanket 'We can't!' Now, if you're finished with your whining and complaining, I'd really like to proceed. Is that okay with you all?"

Not one person moved or cleared their throat.

"Thank you!" Cain snarled. "Moving on now. Bianca, play the video and loop it."

There was an uncomfortable hush that hung over the room as they waited for the short animated video to begin.

"Turn off the volume; I'll narrate and explain as we go along."

The projection screen came to life as the Engenechem logo and name faded in.

"Remind me to call about the music for the new commercial; I hate it."

The computer-generated animated short began with a distant aerial view of the CARBEL from space.

"Okay, Bianca, pause it right there," Cain requested, moving away from the podium. He stepped down off the miniature stage and moved directly behind the table of doubtful scientists.

"Here," he barked, circling the Aerie and the CARBEL with a laser pointer, "we currently have how many CARBELs in use?"

The moping brood was slow to answer.

"One. That's one! We currently have one CARBEL in use," Dr. Wyczthack growled. "That will change with the addition of four new elevators and the enlargement of the Aerie. How many square feet of pay-load space do we have available at this moment?"

"Sixteen hundred, sir," Light meekly answered.

"Sixteen hundred. You are correct, thank you. How long does it take to deliver a full payload, unload the platform, and descend back to the SUBOS?"

"Roughly speaking, sir, on average we're experiencing a six-hour turnaround," Riggs replied.

"Marvelous," Cain commented. "Moving right along. We assembled the CARBEL in less than twenty-four hours. As we speak, there are sixteen nine-mile-long carbon braids in transit from one of our subsidiaries in Ohio. Pratt and Whitney and Rolls Royce are wrapping up their tests and performance trials on thirty new maxi-mount, solid fuel, vector thrust engines. The Aerie can be enlarged without suffering any downtime. When the braids and engines arrive, we can, and will, deploy the framework for the Halo modification and have all four new CARBELs in operational status before Monday of next week."

All of a sudden, the facial expressions and mood of the team began to change for the better.

"And how many square feet of cargo space will you have access to once the new elevators are operational?" Cain asked.

"Eight thousand," Garret excitedly called out.

"Eight thousand square feet of cargo space every six hours. Technically speaking, ladies and gentlemen, that comes out to thirty-two thousand square feet of available cargo space every twenty-four hours."

The once disgruntled group of scientists started smiling, nodding their heads, whispering and scribbling notes.

"Moving on. At this point you're probably asking yourself: who? Who will be responsible for the construction of the Clouds? Well, to put it bluntly, I—we—have at our disposal an unending supply of metal workers, welders, fabricators … virtually every skilled position required to see this project to fruition."

Bianca merged the schematics of the proposed Cloud project and a picture of the Arena and dormitories back on the screen.

"This…," Cain said, directing the attention of his team to the dormitories with his laser, "we managed to deliver the raw materials, assemble, pressurize, test and certify as safe and operational in under sixty days.

That was accomplished by no more than two hundred personnel working five days a week, in one ten-hour shift per day. Dorms, Arena, transfer tubes, all of it … in less than two months and we came in WAY under budget."

"So, how many Evans are up there now?" Amanda inquired, twisting back to look at Cain.

"The original two hundred," Garret answered.

"We're going to use that facility and those workers to begin piecing together prefab units. Things that can be deployed and put together now but aren't necessarily vital at this point," Cain added.

"So, the dorms and Arena house two hundred personnel, right?" she asked.

"Yes."

"Well, just who are you planning on taking up there? I mean, honestly, sir, these things are gigantic. How many inhabitants do you intend to house?" Amanda pressed.

Dr. Wyczthack held up his hand to hush the room, dug into his back pocket, pulled out his cell phone, and began pressing buttons.

"White," a deep and coarse voice answered.

"Alan? Cain. I'm in the conference room on seventeen with the EVA team and I have you on speaker phone."

"Okay."

"The question was just asked as to how many inhabitants we intend to place in each Cloud."

One could plainly assume, judging from the silence, that Dr. White was searching for his notes.

"Three thousand with a maximum of forty-five hundred," he stated.

"I thought that was the number we agreed upon."

"That's it?"

"That's it. Thanks."

"Sure."

Cain disconnected the conversation and placed the phone back in his pocket.

"Well? Does that satisfy your curiousity?" he asked Amanda, nonchalantly.

The small ensemble of brilliant scientists sat slack-jawed, shocked by the information Dr. White just shared.

"Does he mean three thousand total? Or is that per Cloud?" Garret queried, breaking the barrier of silence.

"Per Cloud."

Riggs and a few of his subordinates pushed themselves away from the conference table and began pacing. Whether seated or standing, the band of twelve geniuses mumbled in disbelief and vigorously shook their heads in disagreement.

"Thirty thousand? You're seriously contemplating sending up thirty thousand people?" Light asked with incredulity.

"That's more like forty-five thousand." Riggs piped up, "Potentially, forty-five thousand."

"Forty-five thousand?" Garret repeated, anxiously running his fingers through his hair.

"Two hundred Evans can't possibly assemble a structure of this magnitude, let alone ten, in less than a year!" Riggs defiantly claimed.

"You're absolutely right," Cain admitted. "Two hundred cannot realistically accomplish that size and scope of a project. That's why we're quadrupling the number of personnel for the Arena and dormitory."

"Quadruple?" Garret asked. "We're already crammed in up there! There's absolutely no room for an additional six hundred!"

"I know, Garret, I know," Cain replied. "We took that into consideration when Dr. White and I were devising our production schedules."

"Sir?" Amanda called out. "Will you please go back to the original schematics? I have a question that may or may not relate to our current conversation."

"Bianca? Original schematics, please? And lose the overlay."

In a few seconds the full-size, computer-generated blueprints shone on the screen.

"Will you explain exactly what those three oblong structures are next to the Clouds?" Amanda asked.

"These?" Cain confirmed, circling the shapes with his laser pointer.

"Yes, sir. Are those Clouds but in different size and shape?"

"Well…," he began, rubbing his chin, "Clouds yes, function no. Those we dubbed as 'Arks.' We…."

"Sir?" Light interrupted, "It's obvious that you, Dr. White, Engenechem, NASA, and others have a grand vision for this … these … structures. Will you please just tell us what you're gonna do?"

"Everything?" Cain asked. "You want to know where we're going with this?"

The answer was a resounding "Yes!" from each of the attendees.

"All right," Cain agreed. "Here it is: the facts and the black and white of it. In three weeks, we will add another two hundred Evans to the EVA agenda. Another four hundred will have completed their training and education one month after that. Are you with me so far? That's six hundred Evans in seven weeks' time. Okay?"

Cain looked about the conference table and paused to focus on each pair of eyes.

"Dr. White and I are on schedule to authorize the simultaneous release of six hundred Perseus-class Evans and one thousand Aphrodite-class Chloes, with a duplication of the Armada-class to be released within an additional thirty months."

Amanda, Riggs, and their teammates struggled to jot down the flood of information, along with the corporate and governmental objectives.

"Each Cloud will be constructed with the intention of housing no more than 4,500 civilian personnel. Every Cloud will be equipped with Halo docking capabilities and multimount vector thrust engines. The original two hundred Evans will begin assembling three replicas of their dormitory and Arena. In the meanwhile, the Perseus class will undergo EVA training with Riggs and Amanda. Garret will still oversee all EVA objectives, project construction, and safety. Once Garret's team has completed the first dormitory, we'll begin sending up the next batch of two hundred and someone to assist Garret."

"What about the Chloes you mentioned? Where do they fit in?" Amanda asked.

"I'll get to that in a moment," Cain politely replied. "There's more to this that we need to cover. Now, where was I...? Oh, dormitories, that's right. We'll build a dorm and Arena, then house it. Four hundred will build the next dorm, then so on and so forth until we have all eight hundred up there and living in their own separate facilities."

Cain stopped and reached for a bottle of water. As he rested his voice for a moment, he guzzled his water.

"After the dorms and three Arenas have been completed, the receiving department will begin sending up the materials to hold in the staging areas. Clouds, Arks, the Garden—it doesn't matter what—every project will have a staging area for inventory control and assembly. Light, Bianca, Riggs, and Garret: you four will need to be in constant contact with one another as to what's down below being unloaded from the trucks and trains, what elevators are operational, what's going to which staging area. You're going to have your hands full."

"When do you foresee us piecing the next dorm together?" Garret asked.

"First, you'll complete the Halo expansion. Second, the multimount engines will need to be attached. Third, CARBEL platform assembly on the SUBOS Aerie. Fourth, connecting the carbon braids from the Halo to the Aerie and then, finally, the fifth task, attaching the braids to the CARBEL platforms. When we've completed that task, we'll fire up the vector thrust engines and GPS. Today is Tuesday... braids and engines arrive late tomorrow. We should receive everything... Halo frames, braids, engines, solid fuel capsules... everything, by midmorning Thursday. That gives you eighty-four hours to accomplish this assignment. Are you and Armada and Titan up to the challenge?"

Garret felt the attention of the room suddenly turn to him. He could tell by the wide-eyed expressions of his peers that the task and the short window of time to wrap up the CARBEL, Halo, and Aerie expansion was no easy undertaking.

"Sure!" Garret blurted with a slight crack in his voice. "I mean yes, sir. I'll see to it that Armada, Titan and the boys get the job done."

Everyone let their silent focus on Garret linger a few uncomfortable seconds.

"What? I said we'll get it done, so ... we'll get it done."

Garret's comrades slowly shifted their attention back to Dr. Wyczthack.

"What's your ideal duration of deployment for the inhabitants of the Clouds?" Amanda asked.

Cain hesitated to directly answer her question, "Let me come back to that in a while. There are more pressing details to cover first. Okay?"

Amanda and the others at the table nodded in agreement.

"Okay. So, all eight hundred Evan clones are in the four Arenas and dormitories. Right? Now, we assign the Evans to assemble each Cloud. One Cloud, one month. We split them into two companies of four hundred working in twelve-hour shifts. Every day we have eight hundred highly intelligent and reliable workers connecting pieces of a giant jigsaw puzzle. Minus the Garden and the Arks, all ten Clouds will be pressurized, tested, and certified and ready for placement in a close proximity, low altitude orbital position."

"You mean the Clouds won't be in an affixed location adjacent to the Arenas or ISS?" Riggs questioned.

"No, all ten Clouds will be placed in very strategic locations, as determined by myself and Dr. White, NASA and JPL, the Department of Defense, Solar Dynamics, and others. One over each pole, and the others will be moved on a rotating schedule. The Arks and Garden, however, will be in a somewhat fixed location, either with the Halo or ISS, or maybe one of the Clouds. We'll see what the future holds in store."

"What's the purpose of these Clouds?" one of Amanda's assistants inquired.

"Well, that's a good way to put it. The 'purpose' of all this ... the clones, the SUBOS ... the 'purpose' for this elaborate agenda is ... life.

Designing, creating, supporting, and extending…life. Life for you and me and those that come after us. We're testing new ways to live, new life forms, medicine, agriculture, reproduction, cryogenics, hydroponics, energy creation, storage and usage. We are, boys and girls, on the cusp of redesigning, reengineering, and restructuring creation. Everything is on the table. Options are open. Nothing is forbidden or taboo from exploring or experimenting with."

Cain's face lit up like that of a child on Christmas morning, dashing to the tree to see what Santa had left them.

"That brings us back to Amanda's question: 'how long' will they, the civilians, be in their Clouds. We are aiming for a self-sustainable, multigenerational environment to be inhabited for no less than twenty years with a maximum of thirty years."

One could have disrupted the stillness and quiet of the room with the blinking of an eye. Riggs, Garret, and Light exchanged looks of panic. Amanda was unable to take her eyes off the Cloud schematics on the brightly lit screen.

"Judging from your facial expressions, I guess you're all experiencing a sense of 'sticker shock,'" Cain stated, amused with the obvious display of panic. "Let me recap what we've discussed thus far. We're expanding the Halo with a new frame that will allow us to add four more CARBELs. We're going to assemble the Arena and dormitory facilities necessary to adequately house an additional six hundred Evan clones. We will then construct ten Clouds in ten months to house up to 45,000 civilian inhabitants for testing programs that have a duration period of twenty to thirty years. Do you understand everything thus far?"

Cain momentarily studied each face as he slowly paced the length of the table.

"Sir?" Light said, "Uh … can you … um, go back and … um…."

"I'm moving forward, so if you have any questions or comments, write them down and we'll address everything after I've presented the whole plan. Now, in response to Amanda's inquiry regarding these three oval-shaped structures—and may I include another unit I will debut in a moment—we've dubbed them as the Arks... Arks One, Two, and Three. The 1,000 Chloe subjects I and Dr. White are scheduled to release will spearhead the greatest, most expansive safari and scavenger hunt in human history. We'll make Noah's Ark look like a puppy sale out of a car trunk at a flea market. Our collection will be different in that not only will we capture a male and female of every specie, we're going to do it in triplicate. One pair for each Ark."

Every statement made by Cain was met with gasps of astonishment and disbelief. Riggs and his cohorts were drowning in a sea of information, details, and objective deadlines. Answers to questions only raised more questions and inquiries. Each time Cain explained the 'how and why' of a certain project, he revealed another set of goals that were more magnificent than the one prior.

He wanted samples of every living thing: mammals, primates, reptiles, plants, trees, insects, bugs... everything.

"The Chloes will be divided evenly between the three Arks and the Garden," Cain stated. "Two hundred fifty for each craft."

"For the sake of our sanity, would you let me summarize what you've revealed thus far?" Riggs jokingly requested.

"Certainly. By all means, feel free."

Riggs rose from his seat as Dr. White entered the conference room.

"Ah, Alan," Cain greeted his partner. "Right on time."

"I hope I'm not interrupting," he coolly stated.

"No, no, not at all. Mr. Woodburn was just about to regurgitate our little endeavor to his teammates. Weren't you, Riggs?"

Riggs looked down at his notepad, rubbed his hands together, and drew in a deep breath.

"I'm going to review this in bullet point form and not elaborate on each topic."

Doctors Wyczthack and White sat at the adjoining table as Riggs made his way to the stage and podium.

"Okay; first, braids and engines arrive this week. In the meanwhile, the Evans will enlarge the frame of the Halo. Engines and braids get sent up, we mount engines and attach braids, lower the braids to the SUBOS, and construct the four new platforms. Right?"

"So far so good," Cain smugly replied.

Dr. White answered with a lifeless "Yes."

"Next, we assemble another Arena and dormitory facility to house two hundred new clones that you will deploy for NBS and EVA training while the dorm is under construction. Right?"

"Yes," Dr. White answered, already showing signs of irritation.

"We build, then inhabit, two more times for a grand total of four Arenas and dorm systems and eight hundred clones. That should take us, in theory, six months to accomplish, if everything goes according to plan."

"It will, trust me," Cain confirmed.

"Once the dorm systems are completed, we'll begin construction on the Clouds. We'll work twenty-four hours a day in two twelve-hour shifts with four hundred clones on each shift. At that rate, you have an anticipated deadline of one month for each Cloud. At the end of the ten months, you will begin sending up thirty to forty-five thousand civilian personnel to inhabit the Clouds for a duration period of twenty to thirty years."

The doctors, unwilling to show any emotion, silently stared at Riggs as he expounded on Cain's presentation.

"Okay; next item. As the three Arks are being pieced together, you're going to conduct a global safari and excursion to gather three sets of two for every living creature and multiple samples of every tree, plant, insect, bug, seed, and so forth. The Chloe series, all one thousand of them, will be divided evenly and placed in charge of the three Arks and Garden."

Light, Garret, and Amanda turned to face Cain and Dr. White and waited for their reaction to Riggs' summary.

Dr. White sat with his arms folded and legs crossed and said not one word. Cain, on the other hand, leaned forward, placed his palms on his legs, and tapped his kneecaps with his fingers.

"Did I get it right?" Riggs impatiently asked. "Did I leave out anything?"

"Oh, no, you did fine," Cain snarkily answered, "but there's more."

"More what?" Riggs asked, "Did I skip something?"

Dr. Wyczthack turned to Dr. White and nodded.

Dr. White stood, looked at Riggs and his team, and stated, "There's more."

CHAPTER 10

AWARE

"I found it!" Armada quietly exclaimed as he floated next to Titan.
"Found what? Why are you whispering?" Titan responded.

"Sshh!" Armada hissed.

"What? Okay, I'm whispering. Geez! What'd you find?"

Armada looked up and down at his brothers as they hovered in line, waiting for one of their three daily doses of liquid supplements. He grabbed a rung on the wall of the transfer tube and said, "Follow me."

Titan and Armada pulled themselves to the end of the cylindrical corridor. They passed by their last brother and maneuvered into the entrance of their dormitory.

"C'mon, Arm. What's so important? Garret's gonna wonder where we are."

"I found the program!" Armada triumphantly declared.

"How?"

"I hacked White's credentials and scoured the entire Engenechem database."

"Are you crazy? You know every access point to administrative programs and files are tracked and recorded!"

"Who's gonna check up on Dr. White? C'mon, think about it. Do you honestly believe that with all of Wyczthack's responsibilities he's gonna not only suspect Doc White of something nefarious but that he'd actually take the time to look at what all program files White has gotten into?"

"No, Cain wouldn't do that. But still, even though you logged on using his credentials, the access stamp will show your terminal number."

The ecstatic look on Armada's face suddenly went to one of regret and concern.

"Not to mention the video footage that's recorded. I think you ought to drop this espionage gig and forget we even found out about it."

"That's the whole reason why I hacked White's credentials! I found the tracking program, the kind of chip they're using, what data they're storing in us...everything."

Titan poked his head around the corner to check if anybody was approaching as Armada continued.

"I also located the RFID implant history for not only us but the Chloes as well."

Titan was anxiously hanging on to every detail and bit of information. Armada noticed Titan's interest but suddenly stopped speaking.

"And? What about it?" Titan impatiently asked.

"Nah, you don't wanna know. You were right; I should just forget the whole thing."

Armada started to exit the dormitory but Titan punched him on his arm and pulled him back.

"C'mon, you idiot! You started this whole thing! Tell me!"

Armada laughed out loud as his friend pummeled him.

"All right, all right! I'll talk! A while ago I looked at the bandwidth of all the currently running programs and applications. One of 'em takes up nearly twenty-five percent of total bandwidth usage. That program is called 'WATCHER,' and it's the one tracking our movement and whereabouts. But...come to find out, the chips we have in our shoulder, and in Chloe, are not transmitting chips. They're not powerful and big enough. What's embedded in all of us is merely for basic identity purposes and 'snapshot' tracking...a kind of 'where are they now' monitor that's activated every fifteen minutes."

"What are they looking for?"

"It appears that the program is set up to automatically scan for activated chips, then download the information to all of our individual records."

Titan peeked into the transfer tube and noticed the corridor of his waiting brothers was now empty.

"What do you think they're doing with all of that data?" Titan curiously inquired as he stretched out of the dormitory doorway to get a better look down the connecting tunnel.

"That I don't know. But two things I do know are: one, they're crunching a lot of data, and two, I discovered the correlating chip numbers for each one of us."

"How many chip numbers are in the registry?"

Armada pushed himself into the corridor to join Titan.

"That's the bizarre thing. It showed that almost seven thousand chips have been implanted, but less than three thousand are activated."

The brothers quietly stared at each other.

"We had almost one hundred in our class, right?"

"More like ninety. Remember? In the nursery? There were several that didn't...."

Titan's words trailed off as he turned away from Armada.

"Yeah. I remember," Armada sorrowfully admitted. "So ninety of us, in one batch. Then the Cronus class after us, that's another hundred-plus. The Perseus class will have three batches in eight weeks. That's five hundred. I have no idea about Chloe."

"So? What's your point?" Titan asked, lowering his volume and moving closer to Armada.

"My point? We know here in two months' time that there'll be eight hundred of us and I don't know how many there are of Chloe and her kind, or about to be released. But let's just say, for the sake of argument, that there'll be a total of eight hundred just like us. Okay?"

"Okay ... and?"

"And what? C'mon, Titan, think! That's only sixteen hundred current activated and trackable chips. The registry showed over seven thousand have been implanted and activated."

"That's a discrepancy of more than five thousand!" Titan stated as he felt a knot in his stomach begin to tighten and beads of sweat suddenly appeared on his forehead.

Armada slowly nodded his head in agreement and asked, "So where are they?"

CHAPTER 11

A PLACE FOR EVERYTHING

"I'm telling you Amanda, we don't ... have ... the room!" Light clearly stated.

"What about the switchbacks? Can you store anything there?" she growled into her headset microphone.

"No, ma'am. Like I said earlier, I got eighteen hundred rail cars waiting to be unloaded right now. All ten switchbacks are packed as it is without trying to designate a temporary holding zone. And we haven't even addressed the capsules for the WES."

"Now for that I can guarantee that the additional ejection tubes will be up and running by tomorrow night," Riggs confidently declared from the comfort of his office.

"That's fine and dandy for the day after tomorrow, but for right now I can't unload any more," Light complained into his phone, "I'm lookin' right at it! I got a conveyor that I can't start up because the SUBOS is stuffed. Because I don't have any extra available rail space, this train will remain right where it is, backing up the one that's already sit'n and wait'n behind it. And, to make matters worse, San Diego departed two hours early and El Paso is less than three hundred miles away!"

"What about delaying receipt of delivery from Houston and Galveston and the others?" Riggs asked. "I mean most of this stuff, or at least a great portion, will be reloaded for relocation in Kansas and Colorado anyway. Will the ports be willing to off-load and hold our orders? Say, maybe thirty days? Forty-five at the most?"

"I don't know if they'll buy in to that," Light replied. "That's an awful big chunk of change. I don't rightly think I'd like to be the guy responsible for making sure that somebody else's inventory is safe and up to snuff."

"The only thing we need for NBT are all the prototypes," Amanda stated. "Once I get my hands on those, I can let Wyczthack and White know that they can release the next batch for training."

"Let me get the Evans focused on the WES. Maybe Garret and the boys can chop off twelve hours and then we'll start shooting 'em out five at a time," said Riggs.

"If y'all will push Garret on the WES, I can cut down my time on the capsules and focus on staging for the new Arenas," Light added.

"Find out which cars the carbon braids are in, move everything else, and get 'em up here. The Evans finished the Halo expansion a few hours ago, so all we need to do now is connect the new platforms," Riggs instructed.

"Have the multimount engines arrived yet?" Amanda inquired.

"No, ma'am," Light quickly answered. "Lockheed is flyin' 'em in ... should be touching down in an hour or so."

"Okay, so, let's wrap up. These logistics are making my rear ache!" Riggs hurriedly suggested, "Light, locate the braids and Arena prefab prototypes. Move everything else back when you find them and send 'em up pronto! Amanda, as soon as Light notifies you regarding the prototypes, alert White and Wycz. They'll release the batch for NBT and your team, Amanda, can be fitting them for suits. Light, as soon as the flight from Lockheed arrives, send up the engines. With any luck we'll beat the Monday deadline. We all clear?"

"Yes, sir," Light and Amanda confidently answered.

"All right then," Riggs replied and disconnected from the conference call.

***

"Attention, please. Attention, please," said the sensuous female voice. "All personnel are required to assemble in the arena at zero seven hundred."

The dormitory was suddenly illuminated as the lights automatically came on. Armada, Titan, and their brethren were slowly, and reluctantly, showing signs of life when the female repeated her orders, "Attention, please. Attention, please. All personnel are required to assemble in the arena at zero seven hundred."

"We heard you!" Titan bitterly shouted as he unfastened his mattress restraints.

"Loud and clear, Sasha, loud and clear," Armada happily chimed in, unlocking his bedding clasps.

"Sasha?" asked one of Armada's dorm mates. "Who's Sasha?"

"Sounds like a Sasha to me," Armada replied, "Just listen to that voice. A Western European Sasha. Long hair, long legs, exotic, intelligent, and sophisticated."

"You wouldn't know what to do if she walked right up and bit you," Titan snapped, then broke into a coughing fit.

Armada and the eight roommates turned in unison and looked at Titan as he wearily slipped his legs into his jumpsuit.

"Hey, buddy," Armada gently called out, hovering in front of his locker. "You're, uh ... kinda moving in slow-mo. You feeling okay?"

"I'm fine!" Titan growled, struggling to dress himself. "I just need to get to the commons and take my supplements."

Armada zipped his jumpsuit and motioned for the others to leave. As his brothers finished dressing and floated out of their barracks, Armada pulled himself next to Titan. His skin was pale and discolored with patches of light yellow and hints of green and grey. Tiny beads of perspiration glistened on his neck.

"Hey, c'mon pal," Armada said. "Let's take a look at you."

Armada tenderly spun his friend around to face him. Titan's cheeks were sunken in and he had deep, purplish brown bags under his eyes. There was a thick, golden crust near his tear ducts and dried clumps of blood just inside the nostrils.

"Okay, cowboy. Let's you and me go to the Nursery and get you checked out."

"No! No!" Titan emphatically stated, "I'm fine. Just gimme my supplements and I'll be all right. Don't take me down there, Arm. Please! You know what happens when one of us complains, don't you? They get held back and quarantined!"

"Nobody's gonna quarantine anyone," Armada chuckled and hugged his brother.

Titan grasped at Armada's jumpsuit, buried his face in his friend's chest, and wept uncontrollably.

"Hey, it's okay; you're just run down. I'm sure you probably caught a bug from something down on the SUBOS. We'll go to the Nursery; they'll know what to do and have you fixed up in no time at all."

"I don't want you and the others to think that I can't handle everything," Titan confessed.

"No way, man! You? They won't give it a second thought."

"I'm not a failure. Am I?"

"C'mon, stop it now. No one, and I repeat no one, will ever think you're a failure."

"You sure?"

"Sure I'm sure. They might think you're a dork, but a failure? Never!"

Armada's chummy insult caught Titan off guard and instantly made him laugh. Titan launched a large volume of mucus from deep inside his sinuses. The blood-tinged glob splattered on Armada's chest and both men stared at it in quiet shock. After a moment of silence, their eyes met and the best friends laughed out loud.

"Thanks, oh, so much, idiot!" Armada snarkily commented, then pulled himself to the sink and mirror.

"Oh, man! I am so sorry! I couldn't help it," Titan lightheartedly apologized, following Armada.

Titan floated next to Armada and saw his reflection in the mirror. His smile abruptly disappeared and a sense of panic washed over him.

"All right, snot slinger. Let's make you presentable."

Armada turned Titan away from the vanity and grabbed a hot wash-cloth from the steam box. Titan bowed his head and tried to suppress his tears. As he wept, blood began to drip out and away from his nose. Armada quickly yanked several tissues from the dispenser and pressed them against Titan's nostrils.

"Slow down, slow down. You don't want them to know you're crying, do you?"

Titan shook his head.

"I didn't think so. C'mon, straighten up your big, fat, ugly face, blow all that crap outta your nose and let's change into our EVA suits."

Titan blew his nose repeatedly while Armada changed suits. Armada helped Titan out of his jumpsuit and, noticing that it was saturated with sweat, grabbed a stack of steamed washcloths.

"Mm, mm. Nothing screams brotherly love quite so loud as giving your roommate a sponge bath!" Armada drolly exclaimed as he wiped Titan's skin clean.

"A little more on the rear end, please, Helga," Titan laughingly demanded.

"Oh, may I?" Armada replied and popped Titan on his bottom with the washcloth.

"Ow!" Titan squealed and rubbed his stinging derriere.

"Say just one word. Please!" Armada threatened, twirling the cloth in preparation for another strike.

"Okay, I give!"

"That's what I thought you'd say. See? You're gonna be okay."

Titan reached for his friend and embraced him once more.

***

"I want you to stay with him and the both of you come back on the same CARBEL," Garret ordered, connecting Armada and Titan to the POG. "The last thing I need is to have Wycz or White on my butt because you two are wandering around unsupervised. Got it? You stay with Titan and come back together."

The brothers nodded their heads in agreement.

"You're gonna be just fine," Garret said with a smile and a tap on Titan's helmet.

Garret's face, however, told a different story as soon as Titan turned away.

The twins secured and tightened their tie-down straps, sat on the platform, and leaned back against the POG. The descent to the SUBOS would give the duo more than an hour to close their eyes, gaze out at the stars, or watch the land below greet the sun.

***

Armada and Titan stood in front of the desk in the reception area of the Nursery hospital on floor fifteen. The man behind the desk was dressed in blue scrubs, had a breathing mask hanging around his neck, and wore a face shield. Feeling weak and light-headed, Titan leaned against Armada for support. The brothers waited quietly for several minutes, unacknowledged.

"Control identity, subset, primary and secondary application?" the man finally said without so much as a polite glance in Titan's direction.

"Evan, Titan, forty-four, communications and sanitation."

"And you?"

"Me? Oh, I'm not here to...."

"Control identity, subset, primary and secondary application?" the man rudely repeated, unwilling to look at either of them.

"I'm only accompanying my...," Armada tried to explain.

"Control identity!" the man snarled, slamming his fist on the desk. "Subset! Primary and secondary applications!"

"Evan, Armada, nine, satellite telemetry, digital encryption and security."

"Thank you!" the man sarcastically snapped as he entered the clone's data. "Was that such a difficult question to answer?"

"Look, they sent me down to help. He's been feeling...."

"What I don't need is to hear you tell me what is or isn't wrong with your ... friend," the man again rudely interrupted Armada.

The man rose from his seat, snatched a pair of gloves from the wall dispenser, and stepped around the end of the desk. He then pressed a button on the underside of the countertop and briskly approached Armada.

"We'll take care of him now," he gruffly informed Armada and took Titan by the arm. Just then, three more men quickly entered the waiting room. They, too, wore scrubs, masks, and face shields.

"Help me with this one," the man ordered his assistants. "And watch the other; he's got a bad attitude."

"Arm?" Titan said groggily.

"We'll take over from here," one of the three assistants stated as he wedged himself between Titan and Armada. He hefted Titan under his left shoulder and aggressively pulled him away.

"Hey!" Armada snapped. "Be careful with him!"

"Arm! Arm!" Titan shouted as he was carried to the double door entry of the hospital.

"Don't worry about your friend," one of the two goons insincerely growled, grabbing Armada by his wrist.

"He's in good hands now," said the second man, yanking Armada's left arm behind him. "We'll know exactly what to do with him."

"I'll be right here!" Armada hollered.

"Armada! Don't let them take me!" Titan pleaded.

Armada heard the horrific panic and fear in his brother's cries. Armada struggled to break free to help Titan, but was overpowered by his captors.

"Wait! Where are you taking him?" Armada yelled.

"That's none of your concern," one of the men hissed.

Armada helplessly watched as the double doors swung open and Titan was whisked away into the corridor.

"Armada!" Titan frantically wailed, "Armada! Don't leave me!"

Armada's heart was torn to shreds watching the doors close behind Titan as he screamed.

The two men holding Armada dragged him backwards across the waiting room, out the door, and into the main hallway.

"You better leave, right now!" one of the men said, pushing Armada away.

"I can't. I have my orders. I'm supposed to stay with him and wait until he's been checked out."

"Well, the orders have changed," the second man sarcastically added.

The men crossed their arms and glowered at Amanda. They were both at least a foot taller and probably outweighed him easily by a hundred pounds.

"When can I see him? Where do I wait?"

"Where?" one of the men repeated. "That's up to you and your supervisor, but it won't be in here. Dr. White doesn't want any disturbances while he's … investigating."

The second man sneered at Armada and added, "That's right. And you're being a disturbance."

***

Armada meandered aimlessly down the long hallways. He couldn't stop replaying Titan's cries for help as he listlessly strode along. The image and sounds of his brother being hauled away were seared into Armada's brain and heart.

After a good half hour of roaming the exterior corridors of the Nursery, Armada approached a darkened section of the floor that, for all intents and purposes, appeared unused. Cubicles, desks, offices, phones, chairs, computers; everything was set and ready to go, but where were the people? Armada made sure the coast was clear and quietly opened one of the office doors. He tiptoed to a desk, rolled the chair back, and took a seat. Armada bent down, reached under the desk, and pressed the power button for the computer, then scooted the chair forward and waited for the monitor to come to life. After a few seconds, he heard the whirring of the hard drive and the screen flashed a window asking for log on credentials. Armada had no problem bypassing the security systems he helped to create and, in a matter of moments, gained access to the Engenechem Master Server, ran a search for 'Chloe Rover Seven,' and opened the files.

Armada studied the results of the 'WATCHER' program and found the exact department terminal numbers where Chloe was stationed throughout the day and the times she was actually logged on. With very few exceptions, Chloe was in the Research and Development Lab on Sixteen M every day, between 9:00 and 4:00. From there, she went to the Testing and Evaluation Center from four-thirty until almost seven. Armada noticed a definite alteration in Chloe's schedule over the past two weeks. For the previous six months, the WATCHER scan placed her in the Child Development Center from 7:00 p.m. until 10:00. Now, she went directly from R and D to Advanced Application Studies for six hours of training on her third application.

Armada smiled to himself.

The clock on both the phone screen and computer monitor read 11:45. Armada opened an interoffice e-mail with a false heading, addressed it to Chloe, and typed out his message: 'Do you honestly believe that you'll ever be as smart as me?' Satisfied with his flirtatious taunt, he clicked 'send.'

While waiting for a reply from Chloe, he ran a search for 'Evan Titan Forty-Four.' He opened the digital file and, curiously, the most recent WATCHER scan report placed Titan in an area two floors above the Nursery medical services.

Armada's monitor flashed a green flag, notifying him of an incoming message. He opened the note which read: 'I know I am! Where are you? You're going to get us in trouble.' Before he had a chance to respond, another green flag appeared. This message read: 'So, when do I get to see you?' Armada was about to write a sarcastic reply when his gut told him to check in on Titan. This time, Armada ran an unscheduled WATCHER scan for an up-to-the-minute report on the status of all activated RFID chips. He speedily typed a response to Chloe: 'On Fifteen J, medical services. Titan is ill. I'll log on from the Arena tonight and contact you.'

A window in the bottom left corner of the monitor read 'Scan Complete' and had an attachment. Armada opened the document and found Titan's chip number and current position. The report showed that Titan was now at the Aerie loading docks high atop the SUBOS.

"Crap!" Armada whispered to himself in disbelief. "Why are they sending him up by himself? Idiots!"

Armada hastily typed his farewell to Chloe: 'Can't talk now; got to go, will explain later. Check your inbox first thing tomorrow. Armada.' He sent the letter, logged off the terminal, and shut down the computer.

Armada gingerly cracked open the office door and popped his head out to make sure he was still alone. He noiselessly scurried past the cubicles to the main artery of the Nursery. As he neared the entry to the Medical Services lobby, Armada felt his heart beating faster. He grasped the door handle and gave it a strong twist while pushing with his right shoulder. It was locked. Armada kicked and pounded the door and twisted the knob with all of his might. He stepped back away from the door and looked to his right and left. *How odd*, he thought. *Here it is almost noon and the Nursery looked like a ghost town. The halls and offices should be buzzing with activity.* A sudden and uncomfortable chill swept over him.

Armada ran the length of the corridor to the elevators. He repeatedly pushed the button, growing evermore impatient as he waited. The doors to one of the elevators finally parted. The lonely clone entered the cab, pressed the button marked 'CARBEL,' and sat on the floor for the long ride up.

The elevator cab came to a stop on the top floor of the SUBOS. Armada exited the cab, dashed to the locker room, snatched his helmet, and swiped his identity card on the security panel next to the door that led to the Aerie CARBEL loading stations. He walked onto the deck and visually scanned the area. Armada looked up and saw CARBEL One was ascending to the Halo. He turned around to check the timers and noted that the other four CARBELs were in different stages of construction.

Armada turned to his right, grabbed the stabilizing bar, and made his way to the CARBEL Registry Office. Once inside, he removed his helmet and approached one of the many clerks manning the service counter.

"Excuse me," he said politely, "I was supposed to be on the last personnel transfer to Arena One. When will the next CARBEL be departing?"

The young man looked at Armada as if he were speaking Greek.

"What transfer?" he asked.

"The personnel transfer that just left. I was supposed to be on it with my buddy, but I got detained unexpectedly and couldn't make it in time."

"Uh, I don't know exactly what you're referring to, but CARBEL One began its ascent almost half an hour ago with a shipment designated for WES purposes only."

"WES? Are you positive?"

"Yes, sir. They loaded twenty-four capsules for ejection. Gonna be another thirty arriving in two hours to send up."

"May I speak with the deck officer?"

"I'll see if he has a moment."

The attendant turned, walked to the back of the office, and leaned his head into a glass walled cubicle. Armada watched the young man speak to his supervisor, point in his direction, and the supervisor turn to look at Armada.

The attendant left the office and stepped toward Armada, saying, "He'll be with you in a moment."

Armada gazed about the large office and the hustle and bustle of the staff. Something that caught his eye were two men filling in time blocks on a large dry erase board that spanned the entire width of the office. There were dedicated columns for each individual CARBEL with clocks above the column. Every SUBOS elevator was numbered, had a digital display showing its position, and a dispatch number telling the men marking the board what was in each car. There was also a column showing the estimated arrival times for each SUBOS elevator to the Aerie. Armada took a close look at the information in the box for CARBEL One. There was no mention of any personnel accompanying the WES capsules.

"Can I help you?" the supervisor asked, startling Armada.

"Yes, sir. I was supposed to be on CARBEL One for the personnel transfer, but was unable to make it in time. So what I need to know is when will the next CARBEL be departing for the Arena?"

"What's you're control identity?"

"Evan, Armada, Nine."

The deck supervisor looked up the shipment number on his tablet and shook his head, "I'm not showing any record of a transfer in personnel today. The most recent activity was four days ago, minus, of course, your arrival at 9:31 this morning."

"Any chance that one of your boys messed up and didn't make a notation of who was on the platform?"

"Mess up? My boys? Not a chance!"

"Do you have a copy of the manifests for today?"

"Sure do."

The man pressed a few buttons on his tablet and pulled up a digital copy of the manifest for the load in route on CARBEL One. He then placed the tablet on the counter for Armada to inspect. There it was in black and white, twenty-four capsules marked for delivery to the WES.

As he looked over the digital document, Armada thought to himself, *Something weird is going on.*

"I know the manifest doesn't mention anything about a transfer, but is there a possibility that someone just didn't think about it or notice someone on the platform?" Armada politely inquired, pushing the tablet away from him.

"After everything has been loaded, either myself or one of two other supervisors examines the cargo, compares it with the accompanying manifest, and if the content of the cargo on the platform matches what's listed in the manifest, then we'll authorize the release and up it goes. The manifest is signed by hand, scanned, and downloaded to the daily records.

After we release the platform, we take four pictures of the load and combine them with the manifest. The cameras are in a fixed position at the top of all four master couplers connecting the SUBOS to the carbon braids."

The man spun his tablet around, pressed several buttons, and brought up all four images.

"Here you go," he said, spinning the screen toward Armada. "WES capsules, just as the manifest, my boys, and I have said."

Armada carefully examined the pictures.

This is wrong, he thought.

"Could it be, perhaps, that it is you that is mistaken?" the man asked, retrieving the tablet.

"Yes, sir," Armada confusedly answered. "If you'll please include my control identity on the manifest for the next transfer, I'd appreciate it."

"Will do," the man said, turning to face the dry board. "Load up will commence at two-thirty. You can wait in the locker room if you like."

"Thank you, sir. I was wondering if you have a terminal I can use to send a message to my supervisor?"

"Who? Garret?"

"Yes, sir."

"You can log on from the desk in the corner."

"Thank you, sir," Armada humbly replied.

Armada went to the desk, sat down, and immediately logged on to the terminal with administrative credentials. He quickly pulled up the WATCHER program and activated a scan. While waiting for the results, he sent a message to Chloe that read: 'Titan missing. Will give you details soon. Armada.' He then sent a message to Garret that read: 'On SUBOS waiting for loadout.'

There was a sudden ping of the computer and a window that appeared on the monitor, reading 'Scan Complete.' Armada opened the report and found Titan's chip number and current location. The scan now showed Titan, and five others, to be on CARBEL One and in transit to the Halo.

"This can't possibly be right," he told himself. "Six people are supposed to be on the CARBEL and not one sign of them anywhere."

To check for accuracy, Armada looked up both his and Chloe's identity numbers. The WATCHER scan correctly identified both of their locations.

Armada reluctantly logged off the terminal. He leaned back, rubbed his eyes, and drew in several deep breaths. Utterly confused, Armada retraced his steps, pondering all that he did and said, what he saw and heard and read. He couldn't figure it out; there was something missing, something wrong. Could it be the scan? The manifest? Then, like a bolt of lightning, it hit him. The pictures.

Armada sprang from the desk and made a dash to the supervisor's office.

He felt a horrible pain in his heart when he asked, "Can I see those pictures again?"

Growing weary of Armada's persistence, the supervisor begrudgingly reached for his tablet, pressed some buttons, and handed it to Armada.

"Didn't we just go through this not ten minutes ago?"

"Yes, sir, but I need to verify something."

Armada looked closely at the four pictures and counted the number of capsules in each shot. Twenty-four capsules appeared in all four images. In the last picture, however, something captured his attention. On the top row, in the very last stack, that capsule was only half as long as the others and had no markings of hazardous materials.

"Can you show me where these WES capsules came from?" Armada anxiously asked.

"I hope you're going somewhere with this; my patience is wearing thin," the man said, aggressively pushing the tablet buttons.

He forcibly pushed it at Armada, "Here."

Armada scrolled through the digital manifest and felt the blood drain from his head. The records showed that the original load of hazardous capsules from the SUBOS was only twenty-three in count. That was it! Wyczthack and White, he theorized, would have to have placed Titan in an extra capsule, along with the other five clones in poor health, and dispatch the capsule to the Halo. The container of dead and dying clones would then be ejected, along with the WES capsules, into deep space. That's why the WATCHER records didn't show the location of nearly five thousand RFID chips. They're systematically being disposed of, secretly.

Armada handed back the tablet.

"Is that it?" the man asked sarcastically.

Armada turned away from the man without answering him. He tried to maintain his composure as he approached the door to leave. Visions of Titan lying in a pile of bodies, dead or alive, bombarded his mind.

"Hey, I'm talking to you!" the man shouted, exiting his cubicle. "Did you find what you were looking for?"

The men in the office stopped what they were doing to witness the verbal altercation.

"Yes, sir," Armada sorrowfully replied, grabbing his helmet. "Unfortunately, I found exactly what I needed."

CHAPTER 12

VOICES

"**A**rmada?" Garret called out. "Has your team finished installing the cleft seals on the joints and seams?"

Several seconds passed with no reply from Armada; Garret tapped into the live video feed from his helmet camera.

"Armada!"

"Sir?" Armada sluggishly replied.

"Didn't you hear me calling you?"

"I don't know."

"You don't know? Well, who knows if you don't?"

"I'm sorry, Garret, I wasn't...."

"Pay attention!" Garret barked, "You're my eyes and ears out there! You got almost two hundred men depending on you! You might be floating, but don't let your brain float away!"

"Yes, sir," Armada meekly replied.

"Now, I'll ask once more: has your team finished installing the cleft seals on the joint and seams in the dormitory?"

"Give me a moment to get to the interior."

Armada left his place on the Arena Two docking port by pulling himself on the rungs mounted on the exterior of the shell. He looked down and to his right at the multitude of his clone brothers as they floated around their areas of work. He pushed off the not yet completed Arena and flew to the end of the adjoining dormitory. As he neared the end of the massive cylinder, from the corner of his eye he observed something strange. From high above the Earth, Armada saw the lights going out. He took hold of the bottommost rung on the dorm shell and focused on the bizarre sight.

"Garret? Are you seeing this?"

"Seeing what?"

"The lights in Las Vegas!"

"What about Las…?" Garret asked.

The speaker in Armada's helmet began to crackle with static.

"The lights. It looks like…."

The communication link with the SUBOS suddenly erupted with feedback and distortion.

"Ugh!" Armada grunted from the loud and annoying sound.

He watched as darkness slowly consumed the land below. Like a wave on the ocean reaching the shore, blackness swept over the city.

"Garret?" Armada shouted. The volume of the static grew louder and louder, almost to the point of being unbearable. The buzzing abruptly subsided and the holographic visor in his helmet stopped glowing.

"Garret? Can you hear me?"

Garret didn't answer.

"Hey, guys, do y'all…," Armada began and rotated to face his brothers.

His mind raced and his heart filled with horror at the sight that greeted him. There they were, nearly two hundred of his brothers, floating lifelessly around the Arena. The soft purple and green glow of the interior helmet visors were dark. No one moved, no one responded.

Armada grasped his airline, pulled the slack tight, and waited for the automatic recoil to engage. After three seconds, the POG reel started drawing Armada in.

"Guys!" he shouted, panic-stricken. "Riggs! Garret!"

He reached out in front of him, grabbed the tube, and began to pull himself toward the generator.

X^N

"Riggs!" Armada screamed, gasping for air. "Garret? Anybody!"

As he neared the POG, Armada peered down and watched the black-out creep to the base of the SUBOS.

"Garret!" he again screamed. "It's coming! It's moving up the SUBOS!"

Helplessly he watched as the darkness slowly crept up the tower, squelching out the brilliantly illuminated exterior floor by floor. The POG spool stopped and Armada attached his tether line. He gazed upon his immobile brethren, then the SUBOS, and saw that the shadow was now rapidly ascending the tower. Armada briefly glanced at the CARBEL and noticed that not only had the elevators stopped, but the multimount engines on the Halo were inactive and the carbon braids were beginning to buckle.

"Hey! Riggs! Garret! Anybody!"

Desperation took hold of Armada. He watched the power outage conquer Arena One and the dormitories, along with the unexplainable shutdown of the ISS.

Armada was trapped.

He sat on the POG and stared out at the void of space. The sun wouldn't rise for another five hours and the moon was on the far side of the planet. The whole state of Nevada was experiencing a blackout, at least it appeared that way from thirty miles away. The darkness closed in on Armada.

Wait a minute, he thought to himself. *The SUBOS generates its own power. There are thousands of wind turbines and solar collection panels on the exterior. How could a local, isolated power outage affect the tower, Arena, and the ISS?*

As he rationally collected his thoughts, the sense of desperation disappeared. The analytical side of Armada took over and, for some strange reason, he felt confident about his somewhat dismal and bleak situation.

"Okay," he said, "the POG batteries will generate oxygen for ten hours. If I'm the only one using it, then I should be okay for about sixteen hours. That'll be enough time for them to figure out the power failure and ... wait a minute. We have triple redundancy on every power source. If the outage affected the whole state, even the ISS...then why is my POG functioning? Everything else is down but the oxygen generator still operational?"

Armada sensed a strange warmth in his suit, but not created by the suit. His eyes felt heavy, but he wasn't at all sleepy. Although completely relaxed, he was fully aware of his surroundings.

"Evan," a man softly called out. "Evan."

Armada didn't move. He sat on the mounting frame of the POG and stared out at the twinkling stars. He didn't recognize the voice but knew it wasn't that of Garret, Riggs, or any of his brothers.

"Evan," the man said with more authority. "Evan."

The man's voice was all around him; it wasn't coming through the speakers of his helmet, but from inside his suit. Although he was in a precarious situation, Armada found the tone of the man's voice to be calming and soothing.

"Why is he calling me Evan?" Armada said out loud, still gazing at the stars. "My name is Armada."

"Evan," the man called once more. "Evan."

The voice was as comforting as a soft, fluffy blanket.

Before peacefully closing his eyes, Armada faintly replied, "Here I am," then leaned into the POG coil and fell fast asleep.

***

"C'mon, Armada, wake up," Garret said, gently rubbing Armada's left arm. He knew it was Garret he heard, but Armada hesitated to open his eyes.

"I know you can hear me. I'm about to run out of sympathy, so wake up."

Armada's eyes fluttered open; he stared up at the bed above him. Garret floated beside the section of bunk beds, waiting for him to speak. He unlatched Armada's mattress restraints and maneuvered himself to the end of the bed.

"You wanna tell me what's going on?"

"Me?"

"Yeah, you. Ever since Titan got himself reassigned, you've been acting weird. Tonight is a prime example."

"I'm acting weird?" Armada huffed, rolling off the bed. "What've I done that's so weird?"

"When you tell me 'Wait a minute' and don't respond to me or your subordinates for more than ten minutes and...."

"Whoa, whoa, whoa. I didn't respond? I screamed for you, Riggs, and the others! You don't answer my request for help and you complain that I'm weird?"

"Request for help? Help with what? You didn't say a word about needing help."

"I was trying to warn you about the blackout."

"The blackout? What blackout?"

"The one on the SUBOS! It wiped out Las Vegas and even took out the ISS."

Garret furrowed his eyebrows.

"What ... are you talking about?"

Armada paused, scratched his head, and tried to gather his thoughts.

"I moved to the end of the dorm, looked down, and watched the blackout happen. It took out Vegas, came up...."

Garret focused on Armada's story with a look of confusion on his face.

"What's that expression supposed to mean?" Armada asked snarkily, mocking Garret.

"What? You mean my 'This guy is off his nut' look? That's exactly what it means. What am I gonna tell Riggs, and how am I supposed to tell Wycz and White when the EC Program poster boy is experiencing a total meltdown?"

"I'm not experiencing a meltdown, Garret! I know what I saw! I'm not crazy!"

"Well, something's not right. You're telling me you observed a blackout occur, so powerful that it not only wiped out the SUBOS, it knocked out the ISS as well. Somehow two hundred workers didn't witness a blackout and lo and behold, miraculously, thousands of governmental employees didn't observe any sort of power outage in the SUBOS. This is the kind of thing I'm supposed to be watching for and report to Dr. White."

"I'm not seeing Dr. White!" Armada defiantly declared, "He'll find some reason to have me...."

Armada had to stop himself from completing his statement.

"He'd have me reassigned in a heartbeat!"

Not knowing what to do, Garret closed his eyes and repeatedly ran his fingers through his hair.

Does he know about the WES capsules? Armada asked himself. *Maybe I said too much.*

"So, do I simply just forget this incident ever happened and hide it from Dr. White?"

"I don't know. But I'm telling you, Garret ... I will not see Dr. White."

"Well, then, what do you propose we do?"

"Look," Armada quietly stated, moving closer to Garret, "for all anyone is concerned, the valve on my comm line seized up and I couldn't get any oxygen."

"I don't know, Arm...."

"No one has any idea what I've told you. Right? So if anybody asks you, just tell 'em my oxygen got cut off and I blacked out. It makes sense."

The two men backed away from each other when suddenly, one of Armada's dorm mates entered the room. The trio exchanged quick glances as the intruder glided past them. While the clone was digging through his locker, Garret elected to break the silence.

"So," he began, "I'll, uh, have that coil checked out and, maybe, um, go ahead and replace the tubing and pressure valve."

"Thanks," Armada stated, winking at Garret. "I really think it was the valve that locked up."

"You all right, Armada?" the clone asked, closing his locker door.

"Yeah, I'm fine. I was out for only, like, ten minutes or so."

"I guess you're pretty lucky Euclid was so close."

"Is that who brought me in?"

"Yeah. You came to the rim of the new dorm and then we couldn't hear you anymore. That must have been the moment your comm line malfunctioned."

"Did you see what happened?" Garret asked.

"Nah, I was at the opposite end attaching the cap. But Euclid was right there, you can ask him. He told me you started moving in, but then your visor shut down and you stopped moving."

"I think that's when he called me," Garret added.

"So how long was it from the time Euclid called for you and I was connected to a new breathing coil on the POG?"

"I don't know. You'll need to talk to Garret and Euclid about that. I gotta go."

The man swiftly flew to the dorm entry and exited into the transfer tube.

"How long was I unconscious?"

"I'd say from the moment Euclid made me aware of your situation, to the moment you got hooked up to the POG . . . two minutes . . . two and half . . . three minutes at the most."

Armada listened to Garret's recounting of the emergency, biting his lower lip in the process.

"And how long did it take y'all to get me to my bed from the POG?"

"Oh," Garret thought out loud, "Another four or five minutes."

"Okay, that's eight minutes max so far that I was unconscious. How long was it before I woke up once they got me on my bed?"

"Let's see . . . Achilles checked your vitals, then he left and . . . I'd say ten minutes."

"That's eighteen minutes ballpark, give or take. Right?"

"I think that's about it. This'll have to go in my report, you know? I can't hide or cover up something like this, Arm."

"Hey, it's all right. Just so long as White doesn't get wind of this, I don't care what you come up with."

"But that still won't get you out of your monthly eval with him."

"That I can handle."

"Why are you so afraid of Doc White? What'd he do that's got you all worked up?"

Armada turned away from Garret and dragged himself to the tiny window at the end of the dorm.

"It's just that…." Armada's words froze in his mouth.

I wonder if he knows what's going on at the WES? he asked himself, and *What if he knows that I've discovered their secret?*

"It's just what?" Garret pushed.

"Nothing," Armada answered nonchalantly, spinning around. "Really, it's nothing to worry about."

"You sure?"

"Yeah, I'm fine."

"'Cause if you wanna talk, I can call him and schedule a…."

"No!" Armada firmly interjected. "No. Thanks, I'll be all right."

Garret looked Armada up and down, contemplating how he should end the conversation.

"Okay," he said, patting Armada on his shoulder. "Why don't you take it easy for the night. We can handle the dorm."

Armada nodded his head and watched as Garret pulled himself to the entryway and float out into the transfer tube.

Eighteen minutes, he thought. *But I wasn't unconscious. I couldn't have been. That was no hallucination.*

He reached out for the rung at the head of his bed, pulled himself under the top bunk, and secured his mattress restraints.

No way I imagined that! Armada told himself. *The helmet camera would have….*

"My helmet camera!" he shouted from the confines of his bed.

He lifted his head from his pillow to see if anyone was coming or maybe overheard his exclamation.

If I can get to the Arena kiosk later, he silently rationalized, *I can access the Master Server and examine my files. I bet they keep everything. Tracking movement, audio and video recordings … I can prove there was a blackout!*

$$X^N$$

***

Three a.m.

"Evan," the voice summoned; not too loud, but enough to roust Armada from his deep slumber. "Evan."

Armada felt for the mattress restraints and, one by one, delicately unlatched the clasps. He stealthily swung his legs out and pulled himself from under the top bunk. He floated beside the stack of beds, listening carefully. Once he determined no one else was awake, Armada ever so slowly extended his arm to grab one of the rungs mounted on the ceiling. He focused on controlling his movement so as not to activate the motion sensors. If he moved too quickly, or made too broad a stroke of his arms or legs, the sensors would automatically turn on the lights and the video cameras would engage. Armada folded his arms towards his chest and locked his legs straight. He gripped and released the rungs directly in front of his chest, as if he were dog paddling in a pool, floating as lifelessly as possible.

Suddenly, the lights in the transfer tube came on. However, Armada neither saw nor heard anyone in the tube. He waited for a few moments and the light in the tube shut off. He gingerly eased himself into the corridor and waited. Armada peered into the darkness and could see only the tiny green glow of the video cameras on the ceiling. He crept through the connecting tunnel until, at long last, he reached the entry to the Arena.

Armada extended his left arm and grasped the underside of the lip where the Arena joined the connecting tunnel to the dormitories. He steadied his torso, released the ceiling rung from his right hand, and drew himself into the Arena. Even though the communication kiosk was just inside the entry, there were still two motion-sensitive cameras he had to contend with. Armada moved in as close and slow as possible to the kiosk screen and keyboard. Once he powered up the terminal, Armada ran a risk of the light from the monitor activating the cameras. He pressed his chest against the screen and pushed the power button. The screen briefly flickered, then went black. He backed away from the terminal and, after a moment, the monitor flashed the Engenechem logo and a window appeared, prompting the user to enter their log on credentials. Armada entered the administrative name and password, then proceeded to hack his way into the Master Server. Once the security systems were bypassed, he logged in as Dr. White, but rerouted the log on to reflect the address of a terminal from a different department on the SUBOS.

Armada ran searches for 'Evan Armada Nine' and 'POG AV.' While waiting for the search results, he ran another search for 'WATCHER' and 'Chloe Rover Seven.' In no time at all, a green flag appeared in the bottom left corner of the screen, and then, almost immediately after receiving the first notification, a second green flag appeared. Before he opened the reports, Armada created an internal e-mail to Chloe's terminal number.

'Haven't communicated with you recently,' he typed, 'but have much to tell you. I know it's late, but hopefully you will find this early. Armada.'

He clicked 'Send,' retrieved the search reports, and was just about to open one of the attachments when an e-mail alert blinked off and on several times.

'So you're actually saying something instead of just repeating my name over and over?' the message read.

Armada read the note several times before responding.

'What are you talking about? I haven't sent you anything in weeks. By the way, why are you awake at this hour and at your terminal?'

Confused by the meaning of Chloe's message, Armada opted to wait for a reply instead of opening one of the reports. The computer 'dinged' with another incoming letter from Chloe.

'Uh-huh, likely story. We're modifying the L-GEN; addition of Geiger meter.'

'How many times did I contact you?' Armada quickly typed in response. 'When did I attempt to contact you? If you still have messages, give me the terminal number and address they came from.'

He felt a yawn coming on and was preparing to straighten out his arms for a good stretch when he remembered where he was. Armada tried his best to stifle the yawn by gritting his teeth together.

He opened the reply from Chloe as soon as the bell chimed.

'Week before last, two times back to back; this Monday, two times back to back, and eight hours ago, again, two times back to back. No terminal number or IP address. Just a time stamp. What's going on? I'm confused.'

'Me too,' he wrote, followed by, 'I heard someone call me 'Evan,' almost eight hours ago. The voice came from inside my helmet.' He placed his hand on the button to send the message, but hesitated to do so.

Something weird is going on, he thought, *and now it's happening to Chloe.*

Armada sent the note to Chloe and instantly regretted telling her anything at all.

Why weren't there any identification properties in the e-mails? he asked himself.

He opened the notes from his conversation with Chloe and all three letters had properly populated fields with information identifying where and when the communiques were generated; terminal number, address, time, file size…everything was there.

The bell chimed once again and Armada pulled up the newest letter from Chloe.

'You know what's really strange?' she wrote, 'As I was leaving my class Monday night, I entered the hallway and the lights went dim; I could have sworn I heard someone call me. It was a man's voice.'

'Let me do some investigating,' he suggested. 'If you can, be at your terminal at 3:00 a.m. I'll contact you then. By the way, the lights and cameras are all motion and sound-sensitive. Be quiet, move slow, and take small strides. Talk to you in twenty-four. Armada.'

Chloe sent an immediate and short, 'Til then.'

This made Armada smile.

After clearing out the mailbox, Armada retrieved the four attachments and opened all of them at one time. He focused his attention, however, on the 'POG AV' report. The list contained data like who was on which comm-link, what time they connected to the POG, how much time was recorded in both video with voice from the individual helmets, and another amount of time recorded in just that person's communications. Tonight, there were nearly two hundred clones attached to the POG. Armada scoured the report for 'Evan Euclid Four' and 'Evan Achilles Two.' Once he located their individual POG data lines, he copied both lines and pasted them into a new document. He compared the two, but nothing obvious jumped out at him. The second line entry of the 'AV' report was his, so he copied and pasted the information about him in the other document. Armada studied the grid entries and thought back to the events from several hours before.

When he looked closely at the 'video' columns for the grid, Armada said to himself, *If there was no blackout or power outage and I was supposedly unconscious for almost twenty minutes... then why do I show to have an additional ten minutes of recorded video footage?*

CHAPTER 13

THE ARKS

"Mr. Wyczthack!" the reporter shouted. "When do you anticipate these artificial habitats to go active?"

"Well, as I stated earlier," Dr. Wyczthack began, "that date will be totally dependent on construction first. After that, we'll make decisions on when to move forward."

"Sir! Sir!" one of the journalists hollered, jumping up from her seat. "A moment ago you referred to these... environments, as you describe them... in the plural tense. How many will be produced and exactly which species will you be housing?"

"Three... and every specie."

"Every specie of what specifically?" a tech-blogger called out.

"Every specie, every animal, every breed. When I say every specie, I mean... every... specie."

"So, the three habitats will be designated for different animals?" a news anchor loudly asked.

"No, no, no," Cain said, shaking his head. "Look, people, let me say it again. We are in the process of constructing three artificial habitats to house every breed, every specie of every living creature. There won't be a 'bird' habitat, and then a carnivore habitat and so on. Three separate environments and a male and female of every living creature will go in each environment."

The horde of journalists, reporters, and bloggers had looks of befuddlement on their faces.

"Let me give you an example," Cain stated, obviously frustrated by the lack of understanding, "There are eight species of bears. We have the black bear, both North American and Asiatic, that's two. The panda, three; the brown bear, four; the sloth bear, five; then the polar bear, that's six; the spectacled bear, seven, and coming in at number eight is the sun bear. Now, we plan on capturing a male and female for each of those eight species of bears, and placing all sixteen bears in each of the three environments. For those of you who happen to be mathematically deficient, that comes out to forty-eight bears."

"And you're gonna do this ... why?" a woman asked, sarcastically.

"For the future of our planet, young lady. As we have all known for nearly five decades now, our world is slowly dying ... and we're the ones killing it!"

"Since when did Engenechem become such a benevolent corporation with a conscience, especially about conservation?" the same woman followed up.

"We have always had a soft heart for the survival of Earth's creatures. That's why we're partnering with more than one hundred forty zoos, universities, conservation groups, corporations, individuals from the private sector, and friendly governments from around the globe to assist us in this undertaking. It will take the people of this world working in unity for the one common purpose of saving it for future generations."

"Can you be more specific about how these affiliates will be assisting you?" a television reporter shouted.

"Sure I can. I don't want to name names just yet, but one in particular will be gathering specimens from the Pacific Northwest, British Columbia, Alaska, and the Arctic Circle. Muskox, bison, bighorn sheep, caribou, and so on, until such a time as we are properly and adequately prepared for the Arks to go live. Once we know the Arks are stable, then we'll relocate all specimens to the SUBOS for transfer."

"Transfer to where, sir?" a woman seated in the front row asked.

"To the Arks, my dear."

"Well, when you say 'transfer,' it makes it sound as if they, the animals, will be going somewhere else, after arriving at the SUBOS," she replied.

"The animals will be received at the SUBOS be it by air, rail, or truck. They are then to be quarantined for seventy-two hours to recover from their journey before boarding the SUBOS to be transferred to the Arks."

"Wait a minute!" a man shouted, leaping from his chair. "You're not building these Arks on the base... you're assembling them at the Aerie. You're building them as orbital stations. Aren't you?"

All eyes and ears were fixed on Cain in anticipation of his answer. He surveyed the faces of the anxious newshounds knowing that whatever his reply may be, the coverage of the press conference would focus on his next spoken word.

"Yes," he softly stated with a slight smirk in the corner of his mouth.

The throng of reporters, bloggers, cameramen, and photojournalists leapt from their seats. They clambered about the stage and podium to get their microphones and cameras as close to Dr. Wyczthack as possible. Cain held his hands in the air in an attempt to regain control of his press conference. Those in the back of the room stood in the chairs vacated by the hungry information seekers.

"Ladies and gentlemen: please, return to your seats," Cain firmly instructed. "I will not proceed with you behaving in this manner!"

"How will these animals be fed?" and "Isn't this unfair to the animals?" the reporters shouted angrily.

"What gives you the right...?" followed by, "Do Greenpeace and PETA know of your agenda?" the journalists shrieked.

After a few shoving matches and Cain's silent resolve, the crowd in front of the podium slowly dissipated and everyone eventually returned to their seats.

"Yes, we are constructing three artificial environments with varying habitats to house, preserve, study, and reproduce the beasts of the Earth. And yes, PETA, Greenpeace, the ASPCA, Ducks Unlimited, the Sierra Club and World Wildlife Federation … they're all fully aware of our intentions and plans. In fact, many of the world's leading animal rights and advocacy groups have played an integral part in the development and design of this program."

"But why place them in a space station?" a woman shouted.

"Well, let's think about this for a moment. When Al Gore released his documentary, he stated that due to all of the man-made global warming, the polar ice caps will melt, thereby causing our oceans to rise by more than twenty feet. Billions of people would either be killed or displaced, and hundreds, if not thousands, of different animal species would be wiped out, followed by a global economic collapse. Do you all remember that? Then, there was the summit in France, where all of the rich, developed countries agreed to a worldwide carbon tax to redistribute the wealth to the poorer, underutilized and underdeveloped regions of our fare planet. What, I ask you, has changed since then?"

Cain looked about the room and snarkily stated, "That wasn't a rhetorical question, boys and girls. I'm waiting for one of you to answer my question."

It was as if the reporters were suddenly transported back to their days of elementary school. Not one of them was willing, or brave enough, to engage Cain one on one in a room full of phones, cameras, and microphones.

"Nothing has changed!" Cain blasted. "So we at Engenechem have spearheaded the programs and initiatives to bring about the desired changes and results of the global populace that the governments were unable to provide. Now, if Earth does not survive the meddlesome and destructive actions of mankind, where can humans go to reestablish the species? How do we get there? Who gets to go? How long will it take to get to wherever we're going?"

The brood of reporters sat quietly in their seats, mesmerized with Cain and his speech.

"The closest Earthlike, rocky planet, Kepler 452B, is fourteen hundred light years away. It's five times the mass of our own planet and has a sun that's estimated to be 1.5 billion years old, in a stable burning phase and has 20 percent greater luminosity. But that information does nothing for us right here and right now."

"What does it matter if a planet is rocky or not?" a man in the back of the room asked.

"It's a sign that means there are heavy elements present and available, and that the sphere isn't primarily comprised of gases. But the surface gravity on Kepler 452B is double that of Earth. If we were to look closer to our neighborhood for a habitable planet, our only choice is Mars. On average, the red planet is roughly one hundred forty million miles away. IF we were to journey to Mars, and depending on when we launched, the distance might be as little as thirty-three million miles or as great as two hundred fifty million miles away. Once we get there, we'll have to contend with surface gravity that's forty percent less than that of Earth's gravity. The list goes on and on and on as we expand on this plan. Gravity, atmosphere, soil, temperature, water, natural resources, energy … it's staggering when you compile all of the 'what ifs' and…."

"What you're telling us," a woman in the first row rudely interrupted, "is Engenechem is collecting animals on a grand scale to conduct tests that will determine if life can be relocated and sustained on another planet. Is that correct?"

Cain leaned from left to right a couple of times, took a sip of water from a bottle under his podium, and cleared his throat.

"That's an oversimplistic way of putting it, but in the nutshell of it, yes, we will be conducting animal experiments that will…."

Once again the crowd of activists jumped to their feet, all in a hot and lathered dither over the mere mention of animal experimentation.

Cain reached for his water bottle and took a step back, away from the microphone and podium. He calmly twisted the cap and took another sip. Dr. Wyczthack placed the cap on the bottle and held his hands behind him. He glowered at the faces of the rabid pack of reporters until, finally, they got the hint and took their seats.

"Are you done?" he sarcastically inquired, leaning into the microphone. "If not, I'll end this conference now and ban you AND your networks, your magazines, your newspapers, and your websites from ever entering this facility again!"

No one dared make a move or a sound.

"Now, as I was saying before I was so rudely interrupted … yes, we will be conducting animal experiments in the Arks. But these tests are not what you're thinking. We need to determine if the Sumatran and Javran species of rhinoceros can adequately adapt to a zero-gravity atmosphere temporarily and in the long term adapt to and reproduce in an artificial environment minus sixty percent the gravity of Earth. Muskox, javelina, elephant, Saint Bernard, a parakeet, the hummingbird, sea otters—everything needs to undergo proper testing for determining if the species is salvageable and transferable."

"Can you give us some examples of the kinds of tests you'll be implementing?" a man called out.

"Certainly. The three Arks will be positioned in specific locations and elevations above the Earth for varying periods of time. A problem we currently have is the loss in both muscle and bone density our astronauts experience after prolonged exposure to a zero-gravity environment. Upon their return, the impact of adjusting to Earth's gravitational force is noticeable. It can take anywhere from fourteen days to several weeks of adjustment to gain a sense of normalcy. What will the rate of decline be for an ostrich or hippopotamus? Will certain species retain their muscle density while others deteriorate more rapidly? No one knows. This is one example of what we mean by 'testing.' No toxic chemicals, no unnecessary experimental operations on the brain or spinal cord. This massive undertaking is intended and designed to extend the life cycles of our planet's wildlife, wherever they may live … be it here or in a new home."

"How are you gonna feed them all? What will they drink?" a woman standing off to the side asked. "The Nevada desert isn't exactly an oasis, and the last time I checked, the lake levels are down about thirty feet."

"I'm glad you brought that up." Cain smiled and pointed at the woman, "I concur with your statement; the water level of Lake Mead is lower than it's ever been. We anticipated the use and consumption to be right around two hundred fifty thousand gallons of water a day for the SUBOS. That was our initial estimation from many years ago. However, upon the activation of this facility, that number ballooned to over four hundred thousand gallons of water every day. That's been placing a heavy strain on the state's freshwater supply. Particularly, Lake Mead and the Colorado River. Early last year, in 2021, we devised a strategy to not only meet the requirements and needs of the residents of Nevada, but one that will fulfill our needs as well. Engenechem, in conjunction with the Department of Defense, the Army Corps of Engineers, Department of the Navy, the Department of the Interior and several corporations, is proud to announce that we are building a pipeline."

As Cain spoke, a large projection screen was lowered behind him and off to his right. A digital projector illuminated a map and zoomed in on the lower half of Nevada, northern Mexico, and the Gulf of California.

"Here," Cain said, using his red laser pointer, "Isla Montague, the northernmost point of the Gulf of California. With the approval and cooperation of the Mexican government, we are in the final stages of constructing the facility that will soon house the equipment necessary for the desalination of seawater."

"By what means will that happen?" a reporter close to the podium asked.

"Nuclear reactors will power the building and grounds, and desalination, but nothing else. The reactors will not be considered a substation for providing power to the local residents."

"What kind of capacity are we talking about?" another woman inquired.

"The aircraft carrier U.S.S. Carl Vinson has four saltwater distilleries that can produce one hundred thousand gallons of fresh water … each.

That's four hundred thousand gallons of desalinated water every twenty-four hours. By way of comparison, the Isla Montague location will incorporate fifteen of these distilleries, producing a total of 1.5 million gallons of fresh water every day. Our scientists worked with the Army Corps of Engineers, Shell, and Xylem Pumps on a delivery system that would accommodate that kind of volume. Right now, we're assembling sections of pipe that are six feet in diameter and twenty feet long. The pipeline will be above ground and stretch across nearly three hundred fifty miles of rugged landscape, from the Gulf of California to its final destination here at the SUBOS."

As Cain was giving the basic information on the pipeline, a slide show began with pictures of the sections of pipe being mounted in their concrete cradles and welded together.

"What do you intend to do to purify the water after it's been pumped hundreds of miles?" a woman shouted from the rear of the conference room.

"The Engenechem team of engineers created a unique filtration system that, once implemented, is sure to revolutionize the desalination process around the world. The distilled water will flow through a series of ten filters every ten miles. The first set of five filters are electrically charged membranes of differing porosity. The second set of filters are thicker, fibrous filters that are also electrically charged. As the water travels along its three hundred fifty mile journey, it will undergo reverse osmosis while simultaneously passing through nearly four hundred filters. When it finally reaches the SUBOS, the level of impurities, salt and dissolved solids will be less than three parts per billion. That's billions with a capital B, folks."

"Do you intend to use all one and a half million gallons of water every day?" someone shouted.

"No, not all of it. We anticipate our consumption to be somewhere in the neighborhood of one million gallons. Some days more, some days less … it'll vary. All excess water can then be pumped either directly to the City of Las Vegas or back to Lake Mead."

"If you don't mind humoring me for a moment, sir," a woman said as she stood, "I'd like to get your take on my summary of this conference thus far."

"Fire away!"

"Engenechem and more than one hundred entities are planning to capture six of every known creature and temporarily house them in three artificial environments that will be placed in orbit. You devised this plan in the off chance our planet doesn't recover from the effects of man-made global warming and extreme changes in climate. You also anticipate possible colonization of Mars. To ensure that the SUBOS tower and the collection of animals have plenty of water to drink, you're currently constructing a three hundred fifty-mile long pipeline from the Gulf of California to the SUBOS. The desalinated water will be produced by fifteen distilleries, powered by aircraft carrier-style nuclear reactors. Does it sound to you like I got the guts of it correct?"

Cain and the audience applauded the woman who, in turn, jokingly curtsied and bowed before taking her seat.

"Wonderful!" Cain warmly stated. "It's a rough sketch but yes, you captured the guts of it!"

"One follow-up question, please," she said and again stood up. "With all of these plans, projects, agendas … schedules and goals you have going on, I mean … you do have a lot going on. Do you ever find yourself feeling like Noah before the great flood?"

Cain tilted his head back and drew in several deep breaths.

"If I recall correctly," he began, still looking up at the lights, "Noah … was a devout Jew, and did what he was told to do, and said to the people what he was told to say. That, to me, says that Noah was merely a servant and messenger."

Cain turned his attention to the woman and arrogantly declared, "I am not a messenger and am a servant to no one. Honestly, I find myself becoming more like God!"

CHAPTER 14

SHOPPING LIST

Arena One, 3:00 a.m.

'So, after Riggs sent up the new batch,' Armada typed, 'Garret had us play a game of ZG Ball with a few of them before we went back to Arena One.' He pressed 'send' on the communication kiosk fold-out keyboard and waited for a response from Chloe.

Several minutes went by, then his mailbox flashed a green flag. Armada opened and read Chloe's reply.

'Who won?' she inquired. 'How many points did you score? Did it feel at all strange with Titan not being there?'

'We did, four points, and yes, it's just not the same without him here. I know we're all supposed to be the same, but I have come to realize that he and I are vastly different from the others.'

'Different how? In what way? I can't agree or disagree with you; you and Titan are the only ones of your kind that I've been exposed to.'

'I think in our personality. I can't put my finger on one specific thing, but it's something inside my head that I'm unable to fully express. Do you ever get that feeling whenever you're with your sisters?'

'Sometimes. I have these urges to tell Cain and Dr. White that I'm not the property of their corporation. I find myself growing more and more angry with each passing day, especially when we have our monthly evaluations and the nurses speak to all of us in such a condescending and patronizing manner. I swear, there are those times when I want to tell some of them 'Shut up! Who do you think you are? I've accomplished three times what you can even dream of in less than four years.' These idiots are ten times our age and think themselves superior to you and I."

'Whoa! Simmer down! Sorry for asking,' Armada typed.

'I apologize. I don't really have a close relationship with anyone down here. At least not like what you had with Titan. I spend so much of my time in class or at the lab, there isn't anybody available to just sit down and talk with.'

'It's okay. Except for Euclid, I don't have that glamorous a social life either.'

'Have you been monitoring the RFIDs? Do you still suspect that they're ejecting bodies via the WES?'

'Yes, and YES. Typically, after you and I have said our goodbyes, that's when I do a WATCHER scan and review the packing slips and manifests for loads going to the WES. They don't have a set schedule for deploying the capsules coming from the Nursery. But nine times out of ten, there's nothing to worry about with loads making the full ride from the SUBOS dock. It's the loads that take a Nursery pit stop prior to reaching the Aerie that are suspicious.'

'How many chips do you estimate have been rendered inactive?'

'Last month, when we were constructing Arena Three, I saw two platforms being off-loaded for the WES. That night I ran a scan and compared it with WATCHER reports I ran two weeks prior. The new report showed that in the first week they deactivated seventeen chips, and in the second report that number almost doubled. The discrepancy in RFIDs, in a fourteen-day period, was nearly fifty. Fifty of my brothers and your sisters.'

'Oh, my gosh!' Chloe replied. 'That's almost half a batch for us. How do we stop this? I'm scared stiff to even suggest I might have a hang nail or something simple like that. I'm afraid Dr. White will send me to the Nursery and no one will ever hear from me again.'

'I know what you mean,' Armada typed. 'They think we don't know when someone's been replaced, but I immediately notice the change.'

'Have you completed construction on all of the Arenas?' her next message asked.

'Yes, three new facilities and dormitories for six hundred brothers. The other night, Riggs sent up a new batch, the Hyperion class, to stay on Arena Four. We now have eight hundred of us to begin the next stage of assembly.'

'What are they building now?'

'Garret says we're basically building a zoo. He's freaking out with all of the inventory we have floating around and so many staging areas to keep straight. Plus, Riggs has been sending up some larger, preassembled pieces that look really bizarre. Some of this stuff I don't even know what it is, and neither Riggs nor Garret will tell us."

'Like what? Describe some of it to me; I might can tell you.'

'One piece is about thirty feet square, with rows of half-inch-thick steel … I think it's a magnesium and tungsten composite. It folds down on itself and the strips of steel have notches cut out every six inches or so. A second piece, the same size, looks like it would attach to the first, perpendicularly, and the notches on those strips of steel would fit in the strips of the first piece. Garret won't let us unfold it and is all hushed up about the whole thing. Honestly, it looks like a giant vegetable processor.'

'You're right, that does sound bizarre. Did Garret say anything about when you'll be putting it together?'

'No. He won't even tell us what it's called or who authorized the off load. Another weird thing is the underside is covered with a fabric I've never seen before. It's thick, and looks as if there might be copper wires woven through it.'

'It could be a cloak or deflecting tool. If it had mirrors attached to the bottom, I can see it being used for blocking out thermal radiation waves for infrared resonance imaging,' Chloe suggested, adding 'In other words, whoever delivered this thing doesn't want anybody knowing what it is, what it does, or where it is. Right?'

'Precisely,' Armada confirmed. 'I almost forgot; this came with a halo frame and four multimount, vector thrust engines.'

'Whenever it's fully assembled, you just watch; they're going to operate it remotely and make it portable,' Chloe predicted.

'I agree. But I can't figure out what it's supposed to do.'

'Time will tell, Mr. Spy.'

'I want your help and input on an investigation. Are you game?'

"I don't know,' Chloe pecked, then followed with, 'We're probably being monitored as we speak. I already don't feel safe.'

'All I need you to do is just review some documents, packing slips, and invoices. I'll send them to a public folder on the Master Server and you only need to open the folder and look at the individual images.'

'Won't I get caught or flagged?'

'No. I'll set up your accessibility permissions and credentials. No one will even know the folder exists.'

'What's this about? Can you give me a hint?'

'Last Friday, after our conversation, I ran a WATCHER scan and waited a couple of minutes. The report didn't come up. I looked at programs running in the background on the Master Server that might be slowing it down. It showed hundreds of running applications being active, but one in particular, called 'Groceries,' was taking up an enormous amount of bandwidth. This program has so many access permissions, data is being sent in from all over the world.'

'Groceries? What's it for?' she inquired.

'To me, it looks like someone created a massive shopping list and sent orders out all over the planet.'

'Shopping for what? Where?'

'One invoice I saw was for something called a Komatsu PC650. I have no idea what that is.'

'That's an excavator made by a Japanese company. It's huge.'

'Well, Engenechem bought ten of them for nearly half a million dollars each. Then they purchased twenty Wirtgen asphalt reclaimers. Those are coming from Germany.'

'I don't get it. What's the problem? What are you looking for?'

'They purchased one hundred telehandlers. Two hundred light plants. Two hundred fifty 60-kilowatt generators. Twenty-two hundred miles of copper wire in fifteen different gauges. Ten thousand solar generators with one hundred thousand collection panels. Twenty-five thousand, fifteen-gallon liquid propane tanks. Fifty thousand assorted styles of shovels. I found forty subfolders for all kinds of equipment and machines.'

'Sounds to me like Engenechem is preparing to break ground on something big,' Chloe commented.

'Maybe so. The majority of these purchase orders were generated with shipping instructions to send everything to Hutchinson, Kansas, to a place called Strataca.'

'That's a salt mine!' she quickly informed him. 'That's one of the locations where Engenechem took my L-Gen for testing. I wonder why they're delivering that type of equipment to a mine? The only thing an excavator of that size and capacity can do is drive in and sit. There's not enough room for the boom to be raised or the arm extended. What else?'

'Drywall, tile, tools, copper and PVC tubing and pipe,' Armada began, 'Toilets, sinks, faucets, water hoses, barbed wire, hundreds of thousands of LED lightbulbs, paper goods, and lumber. LOTS of lumber. I'm talking millions of linear feet! Two trains worth.'

'The more items you name, the more it gives an impression that Engenechem isn't about to build, they're stockpiling for something.'

'Exactly,' he typed.

'What would spook a corporation as big and powerful as Engenechem into stockpiling?'

'Good question. Is it something they think might happen or will definitely take place? Another question to ask is could this be something Engenechem is preparing to do themselves?'

'You mean Engenechem create and initiate a crisis or event themselves?'

'Bingo! Why not? They've become the largest self-sustaining, off-the-grid corporation in the world. They have the biggest, most technologically advanced private military in the history of mankind. It wouldn't surprise me one bit if Engenechem instigated a catastrophic global event. They could literally take over everyone and everything.'

'Okay, now you've really got me worried!' Chloe confessed.

'I'm sorry, but I can't stop this feeling like something big is about to happen, and you and your sisters, and me and my brothers are directly involved. I'd even go so far as to say we're partially responsible for what lies ahead in the not too distant future.'

'Us? You and I are to blame for what's coming?' she hastily asked.

'Well, in a way, yes. But not in a conscious, deliberate way. We're the ones doing all the heavy lifting when it comes to research and design to create and build their machines, systems, and structures. We need to dig deeper and find out what Cain and Doc White have up their sleeves with all of this. Why would this massive company feel the need to buy millions of bandages and doses of antibiotics, thousands upon thousands of pairs of pants, socks, shoes and boots, millions of freeze-dried meals, and then send it all to a salt mine nearly eight hundred miles away? There are scanned copies of packing slips for one million seven-hour votive candles, flares, axes, chain-link fencing, matches, water storage containers, filters and purifiers, and iodine tablets. There's some in the folder for thousands of one-gallon jugs of hydrogen peroxide, portable surgical kits, and tools for field dressing wild game ... this whole thing is screwy. Engenechem is directly involved with something nefarious. I know it.'

'I'd suspect that they're planning on deep storing all of that stuff. There are miles and miles of tunnels at Hutchinson. It's a perfect location; temperature-controlled environment, no humidity, no light, it's out of public sight, one way in and one way out. Plus, depending on what they put where, ground-penetrating radar and thermal imaging won't be reliable after a certain depth. I think that's where the FDA and Department of Agriculture are storing all of the seeds. There's also an undisclosed location in the Arctic Circle. I believe that facility is submerged as well.'

'You're the mining expert; do you think that Engenechem is using

Strataca as a depository to avoid radioactive fallout from an atomic bomb? Could the mine survive a direct hit from a nuclear warhead?'

'I don't know. I guess that all depends on several factors: Where exactly does the warhead strike? What is the megaton force of the bomb? Is it an aerial detonation? If so, at what altitude? All in all I'd say Strataca is a safe bet, more than any other location, as far as nonhuman collateral is concerned. Subterranean advancement of radiation would be minimal. Is this what you really believe? Engenechem is stockpiling food and supplies in a Kansas salt mine in order to survive a nuclear war they plan to initiate?'

Armada pondered Chloe's question and the implications of his answer. He typed the word 'Yes' and clicked 'Send.'

CHAPTER 15

EDEN

"That's all changed as of right now," Riggs said, pushing away from the conference table.

"Changed as in permanently? Or temporarily?" Armada inquired as he watched Riggs stroll to the digital projector.

"I probably should have said 'altered' instead of changed. This is what I would call a 'minor adjustment' on paper. But in reality, with regards to the allotment of time, this really does change our plans for the immediate future."

Riggs connected the projector cables to his tablet and powered it up.

"So, are we gonna be freed up for a while?" Euclid asked. "Do we get a break or something?"

"Yes, Wycz and White and I are all in agreement; you boys deserve a vacation."

The two brothers turned to face each other, smiled, and nodded their heads.

"Your class, more than any other, deserves some downtime," Riggs praised as he finagled with the tablet. "Not so much the Hyperion class on Arena Four, but definitely you boys and your sisters on Arena Two. Who deserves what more than the others doesn't really matter at this point.

What does matter is all eight hundred of you sissies are coming down to spend a week getting reacquainted … with me."

The two clones leaned back in their chairs and moaned loudly.

"That's no vacation!" Euclid complained.

"No doubt!" Armada chimed in. "That's more like a sentencing!"

"If you girls cry real loud, I'll make it two weeks of reconditioning instead of one."

"One week is enough for me," Euclid stated.

"We're good with the one week," Armada added. "But I don't know if you can handle all eight hundred of us at one time."

"Well, Armada, I guess you and your sorority sisters will have to find out just how prepared we are."

"Ooohh!" the twins replied, wiggling their fingers at Riggs.

"What are you trying to…." Armada began.

Right at that moment, the projector shone a brilliant blue screen with the letters CEA, capitalized in bold white print, centered in the field of blue.

"There we go," Riggs commented. "Finally!"

"You do know that I'm a computer super genius," Armada bragged. "And if you…."

"Shut up!" Riggs snapped, not even looking at Armada.

"What's 'CEA'?" Euclid drolly asked.

At that very instant the door to the conference room swung open, and in came Garret, followed closely by a woman.

"Sorry we're late," Garret apologized, walking to the chairs nearest Riggs and the digital projector.

"Oh, good," the woman stated, placing her belongings on the table. "You haven't started the presentation yet."

"Armada, Euclid?" Riggs called out, "I'd like to turn things over to Dr. Ashlynn Phu."

"Good morning," the beautiful stranger politely said. "Boy! This tower is something else! It took me over three hours just to get in the gates, parked, and authorized for elevator access."

"Armada Nine," Armada pleasantly announced, rising from his chair to shake Ashlynn's hand.

"Armada, so good to meet you," she replied.

"Euclid Eleven," Euclid said as he, too, stood to greet the newcomer.

"Euclid, Euclid," Ashlynn repeated, firmly shaking his hand. "Thank you all for taking the time from your busy schedules to meet with me."

"Our pleasure," Riggs replied, pulling out a chair to sit. "The floor is yours."

"Thank you, Riggs. Well, before we get started, I'd like to tell you about myself. I received my PhD in agriculture management from Texas A & M and my master's in horticulture from the University of Michigan. For several years I was doing private consulting in the bioscience community, as well as conducting my own research and development projects. I was principal investigator for a few studies conducted by the National Science Foundation, and that led to my eventual involvement with Richard Stoner and Colorado State University. Mr. Stoner pioneered the idea, the study, everything … of aeroponics."

"Is that what 'CEA' is about?" Garret asked.

"Yes, and no," Ashlynn answered. "The acronym stands for controlled environment agriculture. Indoors, outdoors, hydroponics, aeroponics … any type of agriculture production needs to have a system of controls put in place to effectively monitor growth, ensure quality, detect pests and disease, regulate water usage and consumption, and record yields and waste. These are all primary factors for agriculture production."

"We're gonna be gardeners?" Euclid asked.

"You guys? You and Armada? Oh, no. No, no, but what Mr. Wyczthack and Dr. White plan to do is apply the skills and talents you, Armada, and the others possess, to assist in the creation of a carefully designed and engineered environment. We have devised a system for the perpetual production of organic food. The system will employ techniques of aeroponics, primarily, with nuances of hydroponics."

"Can you explain this, please, in a stripped-down version?" Garret pleaded.

"Okay. Bare-boned ... we're growing plants in vertical sections without soil for a nonstop, year-round source of food. CEA."

"How ... how does that work?" Armada probed.

Ashlynn strode to the tablet and projector, accessed the presentation folder, and brought up an animated model of the process.

"First, we have seedlings that we do grow in soil. Seedlings will be transplanted from the soil to aeroponic generators. It's here the aeroponic aspect kicks in. The root system is isolated from the body, or trunk, of the plant in an enclosed box. Underneath a rigid sheet of food-grade PVC, the roots are exposed to a burst of vaporized water. Purified water, infused with liquid nutrients and ODC, is pressurized then forced through tiny, tiny holes in a valve made from special polymers. The water used, anywhere from five to fifty micrometers, is pumped in via automatic timers. We'll be spraying, on average, once every two minutes for approximately one-and-a-half seconds."

"You can grow crops with no soil and that little water?" Garret sneered. "C'mon. You gotta be doing something else."

"Yes, really, we can," Ashlynn proudly answered, walking briskly to the head of the table. "Here," she said, opening a satchel. "This is an average-sized, every day Honeoye strawberry."

Ashlynn pulled out a plastic container, opened the lid, and held up a sample of the berries. She handed it to Garret and explained, "It's a little bit larger than a silver half-dollar, has a pleasant aroma, and is typically an early season producer of bright-red fruit, as you can see."

Garret examined the berry, smelled it, and handed it to Riggs.

"Now," Ashlynn added, "compare that Honeoye, grown in a greenhouse, in raised beds with compost and drip irrigation, with this."

Smiling broadly, she opened a larger plastic container that housed one strawberry bigger than an apple.

"That's a strawberry?" Euclid asked amazedly. "No way!"

"What's the difference?" asked Armada.

"Plenty," said Ashlynn, handing it to Armada. "That second one? It weighs about nine ounces and was grown without the use of soil. We controlled the water dispensed to isolated, exposed and oxygenated roots, with little to no change in temperature. The cultivars were on a rigid PAR schedule, which stands for photosynthetic active radiation. It's a range of solar radiation that goes from about four hundred to seven hundred nanometers that plants use for photosynthesis. We use LEDs on timers for that. Then there's the daily carbon clouding … the list goes on and on. But keep this in mind these are both examples of the same strawberry varietal. There are currently more than one hundred strawberry varieties being grown and cultivated all over the planet."

"We're going to be strawberry farmers?" Euclid asked, unassured.

"No, you're not going to be farmers," Ashlynn answered with a giggle. "But you will build us a farm."

"Ashlynn," Riggs chimed in, "what kind of space and volume of produce are we looking at? I mean, how much space for how much food?"

"Typically," Ashlynn began, "we'd plant the strawberry cultivars in a row, about eight inches apart, or in a raised bed, on one-foot centers. Now, because of aeroponics, what once took an acre of land to grow we can now produce in vertical sections. With the timers, pumps, liquid nutrients, and temperature and UV controlled, we can harvest year-round in a fifty-foot tall column of shallow, five-foot-by-five-foot boxes."

"Do you have any of the blueprints for the 'farm'?" Armada inquired.

"Sure, sure," Ashlynn replied, walking back to the tablet and projector.

"Now," she said, "please realize that Dr. Wyczthack and Dr. White have been working with the staff at NASA, Hanoi, General Dynamics, Ames, me, the NSF, DOA, and others on this project for quite some time."

The CEA image was quickly replaced with that of what appeared to be an aircraft carrier.

"We're building that?" Euclid asked, already intimidated by the size of the ship.

"Whoa!" Garret grunted.

"What are the overall exterior dimensions?" Armada asked, intrigued with the craft.

"Let me double-check," Ashlynn answered, glancing at her notes and specifications. "Twelve hundred feet long, sixty feet wide, and nearly seventy feet deep."

"What?" Euclid exclaimed.

"Has everybody gone just plain, flat-out crazy?" Garret asked, rising from his seat.

"I know, I know," Ashlynn confessed, shaking her head. "Just the sight of it is daunting."

"Everyone calm down," Riggs gently ordered, walking towards the screen. "Give the woman a chance to explain."

"Thank you, Riggs," Ashlynn gracefully stated.

"Twelve hundred feet long?" Euclid repeated, as he, too, rose from his chair and stepped closer to the screen.

"What kind of timetable are you shooting for?" Armada inquired, standing up.

"With the assistance we received from NASA, the folks in Newport, MIT, UC Davis, Monsanto, JPL, and SpaceEx, we concurred that, with proper and exacting prefabrication, Dr. Wyczthack can have his Eden in roughly ... one year."

The small gaggle of men stood outside the image on the screen and stared in awe and amazement, but felt somewhat overwhelmed by the sheer size of the orbital greenhouse.

"By my estimations," Armada began, "that thing would give you more than five million cubic feet of vertical gardening space."

"You're absolutely right," Ashlynn commented. "We plan to use the additional 40,000 cubic feet for storage, water, and air filtration systems, and...."

"What about pollination, photosynthesis, and all that?" Euclid asked.

"Well, not every plant responds to sunlight in the same manner," Ashlynn stated. "Some need very little, some require direct sunlight all day ... that goes back to what I was saying about PAR and the range of...."

"How do you intend to fertilize?" Riggs interrupted. "Five million cubic feet of differing plant species will take a fair amount of time to pollenate by hand."

"We'll be incorporating both hands on and the use of bees for purposes of pollination," Ashlynn politely answered.

"Bees?" Garret repeated. "How can bees fly in zero gravity?"

"Actually," she began, "honeybees have shown to be quite adaptive to an environment free of gravity. If given a surface to cling to and oxygen and carbon dioxide, they can be very productive. We've created artificial wind conditions in which the bees can be fully functional. There will be massive fans on all four sides of Eden. The air intake will be located all along the floor base, like baseboard molding in an office. The air will be dispensed in varying velocities, elevations and directions, thereby simulating their natural habitat."

"Where will the bees be housed and how many do you plan to introduce to the garden?" Armada inquired.

"For the bees," Ashlynn responded, pointing to the diagram, "we'll bring in at least a hundred thousand and divide them into two colonies, one at either end of the garden. The hives will be encased in a Plexiglas shell that has a continuous source of filtered air. The shell looks kind of like an upside down bell with a long, four-inch diameter tube sticking out of the bottom for the bees to enter and exit the hives. This is ideal for their protection when we gas the garden."

"Gas?" Euclid asked, "What gas?"

"Every twenty-four hours we'll implement what we call 'Carbon Clouding.' I mentioned it earlier," Ashlynn answered, stepping to the table for her strawberry samples. "After all personnel have been cleared from the area, we inject carbon dioxide gas into the garden for an exposure period of no more than twenty minutes. After the gas has been circulated, it'll be pumped out. The air then passes through the filtration system, we test the oxygen levels and, if all goes accordingly, the staff can resume their duties."

Ashlynn held up the small strawberry and said, "Remember, guys, dirt and no gas," then held up the large, nine-ounce version. "And this is with gas, but no dirt. You oughta see our peaches!"

"You're gonna grow peaches?" Garret shockingly asked.

"Oh, yeah!" Ashlynn excitedly answered, placing the berries on the table. "Our record for peaches is one pound, five ounces."

"How are you gonna grow mature, fruit-bearing trees?" Riggs asked. "Correct me if I'm wrong, but don't fruit trees occupy a large footprint and consume a lot of water?"

Ashlynn started walking towards the projector as she responded, "Normally, my answer would be yes and yes. However, in this case, I'd be wrong."

After several taps of her fingers on the tablet, the screen switched pictures. What was a monstrous, metal monolith seconds before now looked like closely hung, horizontal rows of vines.

"What's that?" Garret laughingly asked.

"That, gentlemen, is a peach tree," Ashlynn proudly replied.

"Shut up!" Euclid snapped. "That's a peach tree?"

"Yes, Euclid, that is a peach tree."

"What happened to it?"

"Yeah!" Garret jumped in. "Where are all the branches? Why isn't it shaped like a tree?"

"It's undergone espalier modification," Ashlynn answered.

"A Spaniel?" Euclid tried to repeat.

"Espalier. Espalier," Ashlynn restated. "It's a French term, and a form of trunk and branch pruning and training. With this system of growing, we can take a tree that is typically fifteen to thirty feet tall with a twenty-five-foot diameter, and yield the same amount of fruit, sometimes more, while reducing the overall height and footprint by as much as eighty to eighty-five percent."

"What kind of trees will you be growing and how many of each?" Armada asked.

"If I remember correctly, we'll have an orchard consisting of over one thousand trees," Ashlynn stated, tapping on the tablet screen, then began naming off the different varietals from her list, "We'll be growing several varieties of peach, apple, and cherry, along with plum, nectarine, apricot, orange, persimmon, lime, lemon, grapefruit, pear, tangerine, olive, pomegranate, plumcot, mango, quince, and passion fruit."

"How are you gonna fit all that in Eden?" Garret asked.

"Gentlemen," Ashlynn addressed the group, "what Doctors Wyczthack and White want, and what I absolutely and desperately need, is for you and the rest of your company to bring this project to completion by, or before, the deadline date. We're on a tight schedule with very little wiggle room, and I can't even begin to explain to you how vital this...."

"Pardon me for interrupting," Riggs said, "but other than reasons for experimentation and testing, why are we constructing this ... greenhouse, on such a grand scale?"

"I agree," Armada joined in. "Who are we building all of this for?"

Ashlynn bit her lower lip, concentrating on her words, then said, "It's not so much a question of 'who' is going to benefit from Eden. It's more of a question as to 'who and when.'"

CHAPTER 16

SPUD

"Dis apsur!" Ri Su-yong blasted in his best broken English. "We contin to be deny assess to SUBOS! The Democatic People's Republic of Kowea ha given genously to US. Fo decade we offu suppot and money to build towa. Kowea wi not...."

"Will the minister please refrain from making comments until he is recognized?" said Chairman Patterson with a pound of his gavel.

"We wi not be sirent whi Engenechem secetry build...."

Chairman Patterson banged the wooden mallet, "Minister Su-yong, you have not been recognized!"

The quarterly summit for the Independent Council of International Affairs had, once again, suffered derailment at the hand of Ri Su-yong, the venomous and outspoken minister of intelligence for North Korea.

The council, comprised of representatives from nearly every country on the planet, was a creation of Dr. White and designed to be a proactive alternative to the corrupt and impotent UN. To add insult to injury, the ICIA intentionally scheduled their assemblies to coincide with those of the UN, on the same floor of the SUBOS.

"As I was saying," said the minister of defense for Canada, "we are in total agreement and alignment with Engenechem and the NSA. Canada will be a great benefactor of the proposal, along with the nations gathered here today."

"Mista Chaiman!" Ri Su-yong yelled, leaping from his seat, "Mista...."

"The Chair recognizes the minister to North Korea," Chairman Patterson announced with a crack of his gavel.

"Noth Kowea wi not stand fo lyi and spyi!" Ri shouted, pointing at Cain Wyczthack, who sat quietly behind and to the right of Chairman Patterson.

"We ha bee lie to by Cain! Dis Impealis company lie!" Ri Su-yong declared, turning to the council delegates.

The auditorium exploded with angry displays of objection from council members. Ri Su-yong stepped from behind his desk and quickly approached the minister to South Korea, two desks away. Had it not been for the Norwegian representative blocking the path of the irate North Korean and the swiftness of the ICIA security detail, there surely would have been a brawl.

ICIA Secretary General Adolphus Bleakly abruptly rose from his chair and headed straight for Chairman Patterson.

"Order!" Chairman Patterson shouted into his microphone, "Order!"

"Cain lie!" Minister Su-yong continued to scream, even as body-guards dragged him back to his seat.

"Mr. Chairman!" and "Mr. Secretary!" the delegates shouted, tossing their headphones aside.

Cain slowly withdrew his cell phone from the interior left breast pocket of his suit coat. As he visually monitored the situation that lay before him, Dr. Wyczthack nonchalantly dialed the number for Jay Hickman, the director of the NASA STEREO Telescope Program. Cain waited impatiently as the phone rang over and over.

"Hickman," the man said flatly, finally answering the call.

"Jay? Cain."

"Good afternoon, sir. I'm sorry I didn't answer my...."

"No time for apologies," Cain quickly interrupted. "I need you to update me on the exact position of the Kwangmyongsong Three satellite. Now."

"Now? As in right now?"

"Yesterday!"

"Sir, we're recording the largest CMEs we've ever seen! These coronal ejections are capable of hitting Earth in less than…."

"Now, Jay. You have two minutes."

Cain coolly disconnected his phone call and immediately dialed Riggs.

"This assembly will come to order immediately!" Adolphus blasted, leaning in to the chairman's microphone. "And remove that man! At once!"

"That won't be necessary," Cain calmly and softly stated, rising from his seat, still on his phone. He slowly sauntered to the elevated stage and podium.

"Woodburn," Riggs dully answered.

"Riggs? Cain. Call Jay at STEREO in sixty seconds. Be prepared to deploy the SPUD as soon as he gives you the trajectory and telemetry for the Kwangmyongsong."

"Are you kidding? North Korea, sir? Are you sure you want to…."

"Just do it. I'm tired of dealing with this fat punk. Call me when it's a go."

Cain deftly slid the phone in his coat as he approached Chairman Patterson and Secretary General Bleakly.

Ri Su-yong was still shouting at his fellow ministers as Secretary Bleakly moved the podium microphone to the side.

"Don't have the minister escorted out," Cain softly requested. "By all means, please, let the man stay. This should be interesting."

"Dr. Wyczthack," Secretary Bleakly whispered, "the minister's behavior is unacceptable in this…."

"Adolphus, please, return the man to his seat. Everything will be just fine."

Secretary Bleakly shook his head and reluctantly stated to the armed security guards, "If you gentlemen will please escort Minister Su-yong back to his chair, I'm confident we can bypass any further unpleasantries."

As he watched Minister Su-yong and the armed security guards, Cain reached for his phone once more and called his friend, Luther Parks, at Jet Propulsion Labs. Without so much as a pleasant hello or polite greeting, Cain immediately, and quickly, gave Luther his orders as soon as he answered the call.

"Call Riggs at the SUBOS and Jay Hickman at NASA STEREO. After the three of you track and calculate the orbital pattern for Kwangmyongsong, launch the SPUD for immediate interception."

Cain didn't wait for Luther's delayed response of "Uhhh…." and hung up.

The auditorium was still at a dull murmur when Dr. Wyczthack motioned for Patterson and Bleakly to take their seats. He momentarily studied the delegates' facial expressions and body language. Ri Su-yong appeared unmoved at the calamity and chaos he caused. The North Korean wore his arrogant pride as a badge of honor, with a smug and despicable grin to go along.

"Ladies and gentlemen," Cain pleasantly stated, "I humbly apologize for the disruption. I think that we should take this moment to indulge our friend and give him the opportunity to air his grievances with this council."

A look of bewilderment washed over the faces of not only Chairman Patterson and Secretary Bleakly, but even Minister Su-yong was surprised by the kind gesture of Dr. Wyczthack. Cain backed away from the podium and, with an insincere smile, began clapping. The delegation was slow to join in on the applause and void of enthusiasm.

***

"Riggs? Are you there?" Jay frantically called out.
"Yeah, I'm here. Where's Luther?"
"Hold on, guys," Luther shouted.

"Riggs, is SPUD ready to deploy?" Jay asked.

"Yes, sir," he proudly replied. "Garret initiated remote assembly and both blades are fully erect, locked, and functional.

"Okay, okay," Luther cried out into his headset. "Are you boys ready to party?"

"Bring it on!" Riggs hollered back.

"Here it is! Get it right 'cause this thing is flying! All right, semimajor axis is 6,921 kilometers; eccentricity 0.0065; perigee 492.5 kilometers; apogee 584.9 kilometers; inclination 97.4 degrees, and a period of … 95.42 minutes."

"An hour and a half?" Riggs asked, astonished.

"I told you! This thing has a motor on it."

"What's the mass? What are the dimensions?" Jay inquired as he began configuring the speed and inclination for the SPUD.

"Five hundred twenty-five pounds and four-foot square," Luther quickly answered.

"Four by four?" Riggs exclaimed, "We might as well be trying to catch a butterfly."

"Hey, man! This is what it's supposed to do!" Luther barked.

"I thought when Sohae launched this that Korea said it was for communications and monitoring weather patterns?" Riggs commented.

"That's what they told the UN, ICIA, and IAEA. That's what they wanted the world to believe," Luther stated.

"So when did that all change?" Jay asked as he speedily worked through his calculations.

"Earlier this year, Cain had some of his secret supermen hack into the Kwangmyongsong. They discovered imbedded coding in Korea's digital transmissions that proved our military installations were being secretly monitored and attacked by their cyberpunks."

"What's my inclination and speed, Jay?" Riggs impatiently inquired.

"All right, y'all ready? SPUD inclination needs to be 74.8 degrees with a burnout of eighty-seven seconds to rendezvous with target at perigee of 526.8 kilometers."

"Cain usin Koea! Dey bill towa to spy on us! Dey ty to...."

"Thank you, Minister Su-yong," Dr. Wyczthack interrupted, stepping up to the podium. He slightly bumped the much shorter man with his hip and again applauded the minister.

"Thank you. Thank you," Cain repeated.

Just as Minister Su-yong marched off the stage, Cain felt a vibration in his coat pocket. He retrieved his phone and opened a text message from Luther at JPL. The note simply read: '17 minutes.'

Cain placed his phone on the podium and opened a timer application, entered a countdown of seventeen minutes, and pressed 'start.'

"I remember when my grandfather, Cain Wyczthack, took me on a road trip," he said. "He took me to New Mexico, Arizona, Utah, Nevada, and California. That was, gosh ... over fifty years ago."

Cain took off his suit coat and draped it over the back of the vacant chair immediately to his right.

"Anybody here enjoy just ... getting outta town and driving? Anywhere?"

The ICIA audience of two hundred sat quietly but scanned the room, looking for someone to raise their hand in response.

"Come on! There's gotta be at least one other person that loves getting in the car and heading out on an adventure!"

A female aid, seated at a table that housed the ministers of foreign affairs for both Australia and Denmark slowly and cautiously raised her hand.

"See? I knew it! I knew it! Thank you, miss. Where do you enjoy traveling to?"

Like a bunch of kids on the first day of school, the delegates leaned and strained to see who was brave enough to answer one of Cain's rhetorical questions.

"Ah lak trekin' in thu bak cuntry ... otsada Sidney."

***

"Where's the point of intersection?" Riggs asked excitedly.

"From their inclinations and velocities, it looks like northeast Canada," Jay volunteered.

"Jay!" Luther jumped in, "Get ESA on the horn and see if Newton can track Kwangmyongsong. I'm gonna check in with Chandra Observatory and find out if they'll track and record."

"What about the SOFIA?" Riggs inquired.

"Get on it, man!" Luther snapped. "Don't wait for both of us to tell you what to do. Wyczthack's gonna want to know where and when SPUD completes the objective. If SOFIA is in the air, have them track and record as well."

***

"So my grandfather would go to all of these out-of-the-way, one-of-a-kind, local mom and pop dives whenever we traveled together. No chain restaurants, he wanted the good stuff. You know what menu item we fancied ourselves to be aficionados?"

Two hundred sets of eyes were glued to Cain's every word, waiting for him to supply an answer.

"French fries," Cain said. "We developed such an appetite… for French fries. Can you believe that?"

The mood in the room lifted and suddenly, the stiff ICIA representatives began to smile, nod their heads, and quietly converse with their neighbors.

"Who here likes French fries?"

The delegates now felt comfortable enough to raise their hands.

"What about you, Minister Su-yong? Do you enjoy eating French fries?"

The staunch North Korean turned his head to see who was watching.

"What is flench fly?"

Several of the members chuckled out loud, but even more turned away in embarrassment for the minister. He covered his microphone as an aide leaned over and explained what the food item was.

"Oh!" Ri Su-yong exclaimed once he understood. "Tatu tot! Yes! Yes!" The entire assembly roared with laughter, smiles, and applause.

Cain's phone vibrated and a text message appeared, reading: 'Eight minutes. Point of contact Nova Scotia. Newton and Chandra tracking.'

Cain smiled and said, "Me? I'm partial to the fries at Blake's Lotaburger in New Mexico. Some prefer McDonald's or Burger King's, while there are those who lean towards Jack in the Box and their curly fries, or maybe Sonic and their tater tots."

The Nigerian representative boldly stood at his desk and proclaimed, "Or de krees kut potato at Chick-fil-A."

"Yes, yes," Cain jovially agreed, clapping his hands. "Waffle fries. Good … but not Blake's good. Don't you ever wonder how all these French fries are made? It's fascinating!"

The phone vibrated again with a new text message that read: 'Five minutes. Debris field seven miles SE of Hofn, Iceland. SOFIA over White Sea, tracking in infrared.'

"I was watching a program on the History Channel one evening and the show focused on potato production and the different ways we use them. In vodka, restaurant menu items, potato chips, mashed potato flakes in the grocery stores…everything. So, globally, roughly four hundred million tons of potatoes are grown and harvested. The US is responsible for about twenty million tons, and China is in the ballpark of eighty-seven, eighty-eight million tons. Did you know that there's as many as five thousand different potato cultivars?"

***

"We have less than two minutes, boys! Is everything in order?" Luther asked his partners.

"SPUD blades are fixed and locked," Riggs stated confidently, leaning into his phone base. "SOFIA is monitoring both the Kwangmyongsong and SPUD in infrared."

"Newton, Chandra, and STEREO are all fixed on point of intersection and recording," Jay added.

"JPL is monitoring, as well as Hawaii and ASU," Luther stated. "Ninety seconds! Keep your fingers crossed!"

***

"Ore-Ida processes hundreds of thousands of tons of potatoes every year. The delivery trucks pull in, tilt back, and dump their loads into several huge loading bins that feed the potatoes onto conveyor belts. They pass through these massive sorting machines that separate the various sizes, then they're washed and partially peeled. This is the interesting part."

The smart phone on the podium vibrated, and a new text message flashed across the screen: 'Sixty seconds.'

Cain turned slightly to his right and leaned on the podium with his left elbow. As he began speaking, he focused his attention on Minister Su-yong.

"The potatoes, now clean and peeled, are dumped, along with the water, into a twelve-inch diameter tube. The water is pumped through the tube at a velocity of nearly thirty miles an hour. Unbeknownst to the potatoes, waiting for them is a grid of razor-sharp blades that are spaced one quarter inch apart. The potatoes cannot avoid the grid. Anything that goes through the tube will be cut to a quarter-inch square. Voila! French fries!"

Cain gloatingly stared at the pompous and pudgy North Korean. Minister Su-yong had no idea of the drama unfolding four hundred miles above his head.

Most of the global elite sat politely through Cain's spew of specificity, careful not to distract him. There were those, however, who slyly darted their eyes to see how others around them were responding.

The Kwangmyongsong collided with the SPUD at nearly 18,000 miles per hour. At that speed, the spy satellite stood little chance of surviving the impact. The grid of tungsten and magnesium composite blades on the SPUD shredded the satellite into thousands of tiny fragments. Gravity would quickly draw the debris into Earth's atmosphere, where the pieces would either burn up on reentry or fall harmlessly into the sea off the coast of Iceland.

Cain's dubious glare was broken by a blinking mobile phone screen that simply read: 'Sliced and diced!'

"Sshh!" Cain hissed, holding his finger up to his lips. "Can you hear that?"

The international bureaucrats froze, struggling to hear any obscure sound. Cain slowly crept down off the platform and extended his arms. He bent his knees and spread his fingers while stepping heel to toe, ever so slowly.

"Dr. Wyczthack!" Secretary Bleakly snapped, "I find this whole...."

"Sshh!" Cain again ordered, motioning for him to sit.

The delegates cocked their heads and rolled their eyes from side to side, listening, as if trying to decipher Morse code.

"Do you know what that sound was?" Cain pleasantly asked, straightening himself. He placed his hands behind him and approached the table where Minister Su-yong was seated.

Once he was directly in front of the minister, Cain stated, "That, my dear friends, was the sound of a potato being diced."

With that, Cain smiled, bowed slightly to his audience, turned around, and strode to the podium. He leaned over the table and grabbed his coat, then reached to the top of the podium and snatched up his phone.

"Dr. Wyczthack?" Chairman Patterson asked, rising from his seat.

"I don't imagine you'll be experiencing any more problems with Minister Su-yong," Cain stated, glancing over his shoulder. "Call me if you need me."

Cain snapped his fingers and his three-man security detail sprang to their feet. Two men hurried ahead of Dr. Wyczthack as he crossed the floor of the ICIA Conference Hall, opened the doors, and checked the hallway. The third personal security guard followed closely behind Cain.

As he and his bodyguards briskly walked to the elevators, Cain pulled out his phone. He dialed Riggs' phone number and waited.

"Yes, sir," Riggs confidently answered.

Cain quickly stated, "I want three more SPUDs!" and hung up.

CHAPTER 17

AGENDA

"With Eden now online and fully operational, we can focus our attention and energy on the Arks and Clouds," Dr. Phu stated confidently before sitting down.

The crowded conference room broke out into a tepid round of applause.

With almost fifty engineers, scientists, physicists, and designers packing the hall, there wasn't much space to maneuver about.

"Thank you, Ashlynn," Dr. Wyczthack politely remarked from his office via the monstrously large flat screen monitor on the wall. Cain had so many cameras and microphones hidden in the conference room that he could listen to every little whisper and watch each individual keystroke on a computer or phone. He also tracked and recorded all phone conversations in the SUBOS. There were very few occasions where Cain and Dr. White didn't know exactly what was being said to whom and when.

"When do you anticipate achievement of full production?" Cain asked.

"Fruit trees should begin producing in as little as eighteen months," Ashlynn began, rising to face the monitor. "With nut-bearing trees coming in around thirty-six months. Hydroponics will begin producing in a few weeks, four or five at most. We can safely predict that pretty much the entire organic root and herb program will be fully operational in one month, as my team and the Chloes are transferring seedlings around the clock."

""Excellent!" Cain said, semijovially. "That will be all for now."

Dr. Phu nervously looked about the room for a moment, lowered her head, shut her laptop, and quickly gathered her belongings. No one uttered a word as Ashlynn left the meeting under the intimidating glare of Cain.

The door to the conference room hadn't been closed for more than a second when Dr. Wyczthack suddenly changed his demeanor, smiled, and visually scanned the faces of the remaining collective.

"Where is Mr. Huddleston?" he gleefully asked. "Is he in attendance?"

"Yes, sir!" Light answered energetically with a loud chuckle and wave of his arm. "I'm here! Present! Don't mark me absent!"

Light Huddleston had been leaning in the corner, obscured by the other attendees.

"Ah, yes, Mr. Huddleston. Just the man I want to see."

"Yes, sir! Anything you need … just … count me in! I'm here to help!"

Light's overexuberance didn't go unnoticed, as the pear-shaped man clasped his hands together and wrung them.

"Tell me, Light, how many switchbacks do you currently oversee at the SUBOS shipping and receiving docks?"

"Uh, that'd be ten switchbacks, a roundhouse, and nearly five linear miles of track."

"Good, good," Cain replied, nodding his head.

"Now, Dr. White and I have been in close and constant contact with both Burlington Northern and Union Pacific, as well as the Department of the Interior, Department of Transportation, Department of Parks and Recreation, and the BLM. To ensure that Engenechem and its partners are on target with our schedules, projects, and agendas, we have come to the decision that we must expand our resources on the ground and increase our capabilities with the staging, efficacy, and efficiency of the SUBOS and CARBEL elevator systems."

"Yes, sir!" Light answered, slightly rocking his hips from side to side, still wringing his hands together.

"We're laying two additional track lines from two different hubs, El Paso and San Diego. I've been told that Engenechem can expect complete cooperation and that both double lines will be ready in eighteen months."

The team of scientists looked about the room in amazement at the projected time of construction.

"Sir," said one man, "that's almost twenty-one hundred miles of new track."

"Yes, we're all well aware of the distance," Cain smugly admitted.

"What about the EPA? The conservationists? Permits and Bureau of Indian Affairs? I think this ...."

"Yes, yes, I know. We've secured the assistance of the Railroad Commissions for Texas, New Mexico, Arizona, Nevada, and California. Everything has been agreed to regarding private land, eminent domain, wildlife, natural habitat restoration ... there is absolutely nothing we haven't thought of or developed a contingency plan for. We'll have our rails down and running in eighteen months."

Cain singled out and stared at the man, concentrating his glare on the one who dared to question his idea.

"Sir?" Light peeped, "What do you need from me? How can I help?"

"That's what I want to hear!" Dr. Wyczthack bellowed. "Optimism!"

"You will soon be in contact with the engineers for Burlington-Northern Suffolk, and will coordinate a time when they'll come out to the SUBOS and plot the locations for the additional switchbacks and load-outs for the Ark and Cloud prestaging zones. Those locations are of high importance. The more that we can assemble prior to deployment on the CARBEL, the faster we'll complete the projects."

Light stared at the mammoth monitor as if waiting for additional instructions.

"That will be all, Mr. Huddleston," Cain politely remarked, smiling at the eager man.

Like Dorothy and her friends in the presence of the great and powerful Oz, Light stared in curious awe and fascination at Cain's image.

"You can return to your duties now," Cain suggested.

"Yes, sir. Yes, sir," Light stated, bowing slightly. "Thank you, sir."

As Light scurried to the conference room doors, the remaining staff cleared their throats, shifted in their chairs, and stretched their arms.

"All right," Cain began, "moving on. Arks and collection. Where do we stand? Where's Larry and Gary?"

The Tartt Brothers and their assistant, Floyd Arp, were handpicked by Dr. White to oversee the safe capture and relocation of the world's animals. All three men were experienced outdoorsmen, survivalists, hunters, and conservationists. With degrees from Texas A & M, TCU, and Cal-Poly, the trio had more than forty years of education and combined had almost eighty years of animal study in their natural habitats. From the Amazon basin to the deserts of New Mexico, the frozen tundra of the Arctic Circle and Siberia to the jungles of Africa, these men of men had seen and done all.

"I'm here," Gary hollered in his Texas drawl, waving his arm from the back of the room.

"And where is the rest of your team? Where's your brother?" Cain inquired, looking about.

"Sir, my brother Larry just ain't feeling well; he couldn't make it. And Floyd is in South Africa on safari, tagging and tracking elephant, black rhinoceros, and impala."

"And what is our current status with Project Noah?" Cain probed.

"Well, sir, that's all kinda dependent on the situation with the progress here in Nevada. We been collecting blood samples and tagging everything we come up on, but hadn't really seen a need for extraction and relocation ... thus far."

"What does your team require to know to begin the process of transferring your acquisitions?" Dr. Wyczthack asked, visually aggravated by the news of the slow progression.

"Well, for one, the water. How're we looking at getting the pipeline finished?"

"Xylem has around ninety percent of the pipeline completed," Cain announced. "The long-term underground storage vessels have been put in place, and the DOD and Navy have assembled all fifteen distilleries. We need only to complete the last thirty-five miles of pipeline installation and will be ready to begin pumping soon thereafter."

"Well, to be perfectly honest, as soon as I get wind of the pipeline performing to its full capacity, we can have at least thirty to forty percent of our captured specimens on your front doorstep in just about a week."

The staff was all abuzz when Gary revealed the speed at which the animals of the world would arrive.

"Excuse me, Gary," a woman seated at the table spoke up, "but when you say forty percent of your 'specimens' will be on our doorstep, what exactly does that entail?"

"That means you're gonna get six elk, twelve anacondas, eighteen North American bison, twelve silverback gorillas ... we're ploppin' everything we can lay our hands on right in your lap. That's the whole point of this endeavor. Right? These artificial environments y'all been constructing, cisterns, and the subterranean enclosures ... we're ready to...."

"Yes, Gary, I know the objective! There's no reason to be condescending about it!"

"Who's being condescending? I'm just answerin' your question. Look, I got nearly three thousand people scattered all over the world that do nothing but follow, track, capture, tag, and take blood samples of every living creature they encounter. That doesn't include the schools and universities, private institutions, conservation societies, zoos, reserves and sanctuaries and so forth we're partnering with. There's about twenty thousand individuals out there finding beetles, centipedes, scorpions, rattlesnakes, ostriches, loons, cranes, orangutans, giraffes, and wild boars. So when you ask me what's coming? That's what's coming! And like I said, when the water starts flowin,' gimme a shout and you'll have what we have in a week."

"I hate snakes," whispered the man sitting next to Gary.

"Thank you, Gary," Cain said. "I would advise you and your teams to begin centralizing your specimens in preparation for delivery in roughly three weeks."

"Yes, sir. I'll pass that along to Larry and Floyd."

Gary tipped his hat to Cain, pushed himself back away from the table, and made his way to the door. He hadn't yet reached out for the door handle before everyone began discussing what particular species of animals they would be most interested in seeing up close. The reality of the Ark program struck a nerve with the brood of intellectuals. Before, it was just one of hundreds of intangible aspects of the Engenechem project calendar. But now, particularly after listening to Gary, the prospect of placing a hand on a hippopotamus, peacock, lemur, or Arctic fox sent a surge of emotional energy throughout the collective minds and hearts of Cain's think tank.

"All right, children, settle down," Dr. Wyczthack instructed. "Each of you will have more than enough time and opportunity to visit the petting zoo. For now, I need you to…."

"Sir?" Amanda Castro called. "Three years ago Riggs, Light, and I had a lengthy discussion regarding incoming freight, supplies, and materials. At that time, Mr. Huddleston made it abundantly clear that he hadn't any room for more incoming cargo. And that was with all ten switchbacks filled to capacity. If I may be so bold as to inquire, how many switchbacks do you intend to install and where?"

"Yes, Miss Castro," Cain responded flatly, removing his glasses. "Tell me, how does this affect you and your job?"

"Well, sir, it affects my job tremendously!" she stated, slightly raising her voice as she clicked open a file on her laptop. "When you instruct Mr. Arp and the Tartt Brothers to ramp up for delivery in three weeks, that greatly impacts my ability to prioritize and shift cars coming out of Houston and Galveston. This increase in rail traffic doesn't even address our backup for Kansas. I got…."

"Okay, okay, Miss Castro," Cain quickly interrupted. "I'll visit with you in private and address your questions and concerns."

"But sir...."

"Miss Castro!" Dr. Wyczthack growled. "I trust that I made myself clear when I said I will speak with you in private!"

"Yes, sir," Amanda meekly replied, bowing her head in embarrassment as she closed her computer.

No one moved while Cain surveyed the fear-stricken faces of his employees.

"I will now run through, and briefly touch on, what we've discussed here today. Before I begin, are there any more questions, concerns, or comments?"

Cain again slowly scanned the room, just itching for anyone to question his authority.

"Good. Now, in three weeks' time, Xylem will have completed the pipeline installation and the DOD and Navy will initiate the distilleries. Mr. Arp and the Tartt Brothers will immediately consolidate their specimens in preparation for delivery to the SUBOS. Eden is now operational and they're currently transferring seedlings and roots to the hydroponic containers. The BNSF engineers will meet with us to determine where to place the new switchbacks and load out zones for Ark and Cloud staging. Twenty-one hundred miles of new track lines from El Paso and San Diego will be laid in, or under, eighteen months."

Cain finished his summary with all the fanfare of a wet paper towel. No one smiled, no one spoke, and nobody dared look up at his face on the monitor.

"Thank you all for your time. That's it for today. Miss Castro, please come to my office at once."

The image of Dr. Wyczthack suddenly disappeared and the monitor went black. A couple of seconds later, the Engenechem name and corporate logo popped up on the behemoth screen. It was at that moment that the staff in the conference room felt free to relax, slouch in their chairs, and speak to one another.

"Man! What's his problem today?" asked a man seated next to Amanda. "He's got a God complex…."

Amanda immediately turned to face him, placed her finger over her lips to shush him, and discreetly pointed up at the ceiling. The man stopped at midsentence and glanced upward. On the ceiling were dozens of small, dark-colored glass domes, spaced across the ceiling tiles in a grid.

Amanda reached into her bag and pulled out a miniature yellow legal tablet. She quickly scribbled a note and showed the man what she wrote. 'Cain is watching and listening. EVERYTHING!' the message read. Amanda ripped off the sheet of paper, wadded it in a ball, then placed the notepad and ball of paper in her bag.

"Have a great week," Amanda said with additional volume, trying to end the conversation. "I need to go up and visit with Dr. Wyczthack."

"Wait a minute," the man hissed, reaching out for Amanda's arm. "Why did Cain interrupt you? What's so important about Kansas?"

Amanda twisted back to face the man, turned her eyes upward, and whispered, "There's a lot of amazing history about the Kansas salt mines on the Internet. You oughta take a close look and *see* for yourself."

CHAPTER 18

HARVEST

'I wouldn't have believed it if I hadn't seen it with my own eyes,' Chloe's message read.

'Why not? This was the whole point of Eden, right?' Armada speedily typed and clicked 'send.'

He turned back, slowly, away from the computer. The glowing green light of the overhead camera didn't flicker as he gingerly inched his way to the observation window. He remembered how vast, expansive, and beautiful Earth's upper atmosphere looked from this vantage point. Arena One and its connected dormitories, once the largest man-made objects in space, were now dwarfed in comparison to the three Arks and the even larger Eden.

The communication kiosk binged, alerting Armada that he had received a response from Chloe.

'It's a far cry from reading and imagining to actually holding a strawberry that weighs almost half a pound. I understand the chemistry of it, but it's the rate of growth that's fascinating. Have you ever watched anything grow? And I don't mean by time-lapse photography. But actually sit and do nothing but watch one plant grow?'

'No, I can't rightly say I have,' he admitted. 'Not a whole lot of

agricultural and horticulture observation opportunities in computer programming and encryption.'

'Very funny. There are strains of corn down here that are accumulat-
ing ten to twelve inches of growth in under twenty-four hours.'

'Pop any yet?'

'Funny. You're a real funny guy tonight. But seriously, this is the most
exciting thing I've ever been part of. Dr. Phu is now scheduling harvests
every forty-eight hours.'

'Forty-eight hours? That's impossible!'

'That's exactly what I would have said twelve months ago. I am constantly recording yields; almost half of my shift is spent doing nothing but
weighing, tracking production, taking pictures, and data entry. Dr. Phu
said we broke projected yields for the month ... in seventeen days.'

'You're joking!' Armada declared.

'No! Really! In twelve hours we harvested three-and-a-half tons.'

'That would be an awesome sight to see.'

'Speaking of sight, when do I get to see you again? I've almost forgotten what you look like. Terminal screens and keyboards aren't an
acceptable replacement for a real person.'

'I wish I could arrange another visit,' Armada typed and paused
before sending the instant message.

He waited and waited for Chloe's reply.

'Do you really want to see me again?' her incoming message read.
'Because it would mean the world to me to spend a little time with you.
Messaging a few nights a week for a few years just isn't satisfying.'

Armada smiled to himself and struggled to stifle his giggle. Before he
could answer Chloe's intimate inquiry, another green flag appeared on the
monitor with an accompanying ding.

'This might sound strange, but I have to ask you something,' she
wrote.

Armada waited, but a follow-up message didn't appear.

'Hello?' he typed, along with, 'Are you there?'

As he was finishing his note, Chloe sent her message.

'Have you been feeling well lately? Specifically, has anything happened to you, or has there been any strange or odd occurrences?'

Armada read through the note several times and selected his words carefully before answering.

'Strange, like how? I feel fine, but have noticed that I feel differently. I'm not sick and I don't feel bad in any one particular way; I just feel different. Somehow I know my end of life cycle isn't kicking in, at least not like Titan. Why do you ask? Are you all right? Did something happen?'

Armada hovered next to the kiosk, impatiently waiting for Chloe to respond to his questions.

'I'm like you,' her letter began., 'I don't necessarily feel bad, but just since the day before yesterday I've felt more, if that makes any sense. And yes, there was a specific and significant occurrence. I've tried not to make a big deal of it and have spoken to only a few of my station mates about this, nonchalantly of course. As we were dressing to go to the commissary, I swear that I heard a man say 'Stay' right after morning announcements. I asked a couple of my sisters if they heard what the man said, but they all stared at me as if I were crazy. After the other girls left, I finished dressing and stood up from tying my boots. I didn't even get one foot off the ground and that same voice said, 'Stay here.' It was louder, firm, and direct, but it didn't sound mean. I heard it in me, inside me, but I wasn't afraid. If anything, somehow I felt comfortable, maybe even good. I haven't had any supplements for nearly three days. Is this weird? Do you think they'll find out I'm not going to the commissary?'

Armada read and reread Chloe's intimate admission.

'I'm so relieved to know you're not hurt or feeling ill,' he declared. 'And no, it's not weird at all. To be perfectly honest with you, I, too, had a very similar incident happen to me, and if I'm not mistaken, probably right about the same time as you. Euclid and I were preparing to enter the transfer tube to go to the Arena, get our supplements and assignments, and suit up for EVA. I heard a man say 'Stay here,' just like you, but I thought it was Euclid messing around with me. I asked him, 'What do you mean stay here?' and he told me he didn't say a word. He went into the tube and I was right behind him when I heard that voice again. I didn't follow Euclid and never went to the Arena for my supplements. No, I don't think we'll get into trouble for not taking our supplements. That is, unless we both simultaneously happen to get sick or our life cycles begin to deteriorate."

'Have you noticed any changes in the way you feel without having taken the supplement drink?' she inquired.

'No, nothing significant or of major importance. However, I have been perspiring more than usual. But now that I think about it, Euclid and I got into an argument last night. That's never happened before, as far as I can recall. He said that I've been acting irritable the past two days.'

'I've felt the same way!' Chloe confessed. 'I'm feeling impatient and anxious, but it's over simple things, things that normally I wouldn't give a second thought to. Yesterday, after we tallied the second harvest yields, I actually started crying.'

'Crying as in a few tears?'

'No!' she admitted. 'I started weeping. I couldn't control or suppress it. I had to leave the clean room and hide in one of the decontamination chambers for almost twenty minutes. It was so bizarre. Do you think that not taking the supplements could have something to do with this?'

'Maybe. You never know what Wyczthack and White will do. I do know that none of the Engenechem or SUBOS officers take supplementation like we do. It could be that they're introducing something in liquefied form they can hide in the supplements. We drink it three times a day, so it can obviously be flavored to taste just like the primary base. Do you think you could keep a sample and take it to your lab on Eden?'

'I'm not so sure about that. These suits don't exactly leave room for imagination, let alone a container big enough to store a pint of liquefied supplements.'

'You shouldn't need an entire pint. All it would require is a half-ounce or less. What about using your L-GEN? Wouldn't that give you a molecular breakdown of the supplements?'

'It doesn't work that way. The generator emits a laser and can tell what kind of mineral it's pointing at by how quickly vibration waves are reflected back and their strength. Liquid samples aren't applicable.'

'I'm stumped. We don't have access to a lab up here. I know that I could smuggle mine out of the Arena to my dorm, but after that it'll get tricky.'

'If you can manage somehow to get me a sample on Eden, we can test it here,' Chloe suggested.

'That's the problem. How do we reach Eden from Arena One? Anywhere I go, WATCHER scans will pick up my movement.'

'Can you delay the program?' she asked.

'No. It was designed to monitor automatically and record movement of RFIDs. If I go in and alter the coding, then tracking reports won't get compiled. That'll send up red flags and then we'll really be in trouble.'

'Do you trust Euclid enough to ask him to remove the RFID?'

'I trust him plenty, but I'm not about to let him start cutting on me. Besides, where am I supposed to lay my hands on a scalpel and all that? Remember, we still come all the way down to the SUBOS Nursery for our evaluations once a month. No lab, doctors, or medical facilities up here.'

"What about bringing the sample with you when you have your next evaluation?'

'That won't work either. My next evaluation is two weeks out. We need to know now if there's something in the supplements that's keeping us alive or under Wyczthack's control.'

Armada stretched his arms and momentarily peered out the Arena observation panel. From where he stood, he could plainly see Eden, the three Arks, the WES platform, and launching tubes. He could also see Arena Two and Three, the Cloud staging zones, all five CARBELs, and the four SPUDs. Like a bolt of lightning, it hit him.

'I figured it out!' he typed. 'I'll go to one of the SPUDs and cut out a tiny piece of the fabric from the underbelly. It's perfect! I can cut out enough for both me and you.'

'What's the SPUD got to do with testing the supplements?'

'Don't you get it? The fabric on the bottom of the SPUDs is

impermeable. Heat, infrared, sound waves, laser, nothing can penetrate it; the fabric can either deflect or absorb anything you throw at it. It's space stealth. This means that you and I can place this on our shoulders, under our suits, and WATCHER won't be able to track us. Except for the cameras, we'll be free to go where and when we want.'

'Are you positive? What do we do about the cameras? They're every-where, even in the restrooms and shower stalls.'

'If we move slowly and keep our voices low, the sensors won't pick us up and the cameras won't be activated.'

'What do we do when I'm in Eden or you're working on Cloud assem-bly? They'll know something's up when all of a sudden a male and female have their RFID chips disappear at the same time and then reappear in unison at another location. I don't like it.'

Armada received Chloe's reply and quickly read through it. His enthusiasm began to diminish as he reread the text and considered the negative consequences. Chloe was correct. If she and Armada were not being monitored with their whereabouts, how would he explain an abrupt presence in another location not related to either one of them? How could they account for the tracking of the WATCHER program without inter-fering with, and altering, its coding structure? If Armada were to rewrite the coding, could he disable the entire scanning process and substitute data to the individual records? No, that would take an incredible amount of time, not to mention the enormous volume of information needed to fill each file.

Armada pondered the situation for both him and Chloe and weighed out his options before responding to her last comment.

'As I see it now, you and I, all of us, are in a very precarious situation. We don't know if our food and liquid supplements are being tampered with. We do know that Wyczthack and White are tracking each of us, and that Engenechem is preparing for a disaster of immense propor-tion. Furthermore, sub-outs and replacements have been increasing and our life cycle has already reached five years. I can't say I know how you feel, but if you're anything like me, then you're well aware that things are going to be headed downhill for us and soon. I would suggest, if we can't safely disappear for even a little while, then perhaps we should disappear permanently.'

Armada sent his message, and had no sooner than taken his hands off the kiosk keyboard that he received Chloe's rebuttal.

'WHAT?' she asked, followed by, 'Are you out of your mind? How? When? Where would you suggest we go? How do you propose we get off the SUBOS and air base?'

'First, I'll get the SPUD shielding fabric,' Armada typed. 'Then I'll generate passes for the CARBEL, go down to the Aerie, then up to Eden for you. You'll join me for the SUBOS descent, and as soon as we get to the Nursery we'll have our chips removed.'

'But that still doesn't address the problems with the cameras, recognition scans, and getting off the SUBOS.'

Armada could sense that Chloe was stressed with the seemingly impossible idea of escape.

'I can generate passes, establish new parameters for motion sensitivity on cameras, and completely erase all records of our existence. Dr. White scheduled evaluations for the entire Cronos class for tomorrow. I'll create a false ID to board the CARBEL, remove the transponder from my helmet, and disable my microphone. There'll be at least sixty of us hooked up to the POG, so I'll blend in with everyone on the CARBEL. Plus, there aren't any recognition scanners on the platforms. So when you stop and think about it, getting off the Arena and down to you isn't that big of a problem.'

'Pardon me for pointing it out,' Chloe blasted back, 'but we go straight from the SUBOS to Eden and back. Forget WATCHER, there's cameras and recognition scanners everywhere. From the moment you step foot on the Aerie you're on camera. You have to enter a preset authorization code to board the platform to get up to Eden. Once you're there, you have another security gate to pass through and that authorization code is separate from the CARBEL code. Just to throw salt in your eye, we're timed from the instant we dock to entering Eden, then the dressing room, decontamination and sterilization, and finally, the clean room and actual Garden. I'm sorry, but this won't work, Armada. There's no way to bypass all of Cain's cameras and scanners. We'll always be trapped.'

Armada ran his fingers through his hair and scratched gruffly in frustration. Once again, Chloe was correct. While deleting one's digital existence was a relatively simple task, it would be something entirely different to evade, hide, and escape.

'I'm curious to know something: when do you dispatch your harvests to the SUBOS?' Armada asked, not at all addressing Chloe's comments.

'Every six hours,' she quickly typed.

'How do you pack the produce? What type of container do you use?'

'The harvested produce is weighed and recorded before being loaded in temperature-controlled, insulated cubes. Containers are kept at a constant sixty-two degrees for the hour-long descent. Why?'

'When do you receive empty containers? When? Where?'

'The harvests are taken directly to the lab on fifteen, and if everything tests okay, the produce is sorted for distribution. I believe I overheard Dr. Phu saying that the SUBOS has eighty-five kitchens. Back to the Eden containers. Once everything has been off-loaded, each container undergoes sterilization with hot, pressurized, chlorinated water. After that, they're sent to a kind of oven where any stagnate water is blown off and the interior is dried. The lid is then shut, locked, and the remaining air inside is pumped out. On top of that, the sterilized containers are shrink-wrapped prior to deployment to the Aerie. Depending on yields for the day and CARBEL availability, we can receive as few as thirty containers every six or eight hours. But I have noted that on more than one occasion they've delivered almost sixty.'

'Darn!' Armada commented, 'I was thinking that perhaps I could stow away in one of the incoming units.'

'That wouldn't help us with the objective of escaping.'

'What about gas? When do they refill canisters and tanks?'

'That's all done externally. CO_2, nitrogen, ammonia, everything comes to us in massive tanks that are swapped out on Eden's exterior.'

Armada glanced at the clock in the lower right corner of his monitor. It was half past 2:00 a.m., and in a little more than an hour, the sun would be rising. He knew that Garret began his day at 4:00 a.m., but also remembered that Garret experienced bouts of insomnia. The last thing Armada needed was someone wandering the dormitories and activating the video cameras.

'I hate to do this, but I have to go,' he stated. 'Garret will be up and around soon and I don't want to be caught out of my room.'

'Do you absolutely have to leave?' Chloe asked. 'This whole thing scares me and we haven't solved any of our problems. If anything, I have more questions than before!'

'Yes, I must. I'm sorry and I wish that we had more time, but it's necessary. Before I sign out, can you tell me anything about the solar arrays? Who services and replaces the panels?'

'I have no idea. On occasion I've seen several technicians exchanging panels, but have never really paid attention to the uniforms. I would assume that Engenechem is sending up their own people for maintenance of the energy systems.'

Armada took his hands off the keyboard and turned back slowly to the Arena window. He peered down at the CARBEL and its platforms and how Eden was tethered to the five interconnected Halos. By his estimates, the bottommost row of collection panels on the lower section of Eden's solar arrays was thirty to forty yards away from Halo Five. He also noted that the platform for CARBEL Five was equipped with a POG. The platforms for CARBEL One and Two were also equipped with POGs. Platforms three and four didn't have a POG, as those were used primarily for shipping and receiving material without human accompaniment.

Armada visually leapfrogged a path from Arena One to the CARBEL Halos. If the timing were right, he could exit the Arena, cross over to the staging zones for the Clouds, and hook up to the POG next to the SPUD dock. He could then remove a miniscule amount of the shielding fabric and return to the Arena. After that, Armada reasoned, it should be fairly simple to get from the Halo on CARBEL One to Halo Five and up to

Eden. It wouldn't be difficult at all to locate the maintenance and service records for the solar arrays. He could then generate access codes to gain entrance on Eden, go in, get Chloe, cross back over to either CARBEL One, Two, or Five, connect themselves to the POG, and enjoy the hour descent to the SUBOS Aerie. Once safe on the SUBOS, Armada could generate zone authorization passes and sneak into one of the Nurseries. After they've removed the RFID chips, he could back out all records and medical files, and delete the entire history for both of them.

Armada felt reenergized with his newest epiphany and typed out the brilliant scheme as fast as he could. Just as he sent the detailed plan to Chloe, he looked at the clock on his monitor. The time was 3:15.

The chime for a new message faintly rung and Armada hastily read Chloe's reply.

'There's plenty of ifs in this idea of yours. There's also plenty of opportunities for being caught, stranded, and suffocating. I don't even want to entertain the thought of becoming detached and floating away, or worse yet, being drawn into Earth's atmosphere and vaporizing on reentry.'

'I know there's several areas where things can go wrong, but I genuinely feel positive about this. I sincerely believe we can do this. Furthermore, we both know what the future holds in store for us if we were to stay put.'

As he was composing his message, Armada suddenly became aware of his heart beating faster. He also realized he was perspiring, the palms of his hands were moist, and his cheeks were flush.

'I just know that something inside....' Armada stopped typing. This time, however, he had to wipe his eyes.

Why is this happening? he asked himself.

The more he thought about Chloe, the more his heart pounded. Armada shook his hands out and took several deep breaths. He felt a buzzing in his lips and his chin quivered, 'is compelling me to come to you,' he admitted, finishing his statement, 'I'll figure this out and will find a way for us to escape. Trust me.'

'I trust you,' Chloe's next message stated. 'I'll be waiting for your letter.'

'Goodnight,' Armada typed and clicked 'send.'

Armada copied the content of their conversation to a file he created on the Master Server, then deleted the entire strain. He backed out the imposter terminal number from the Arena server and erased all incoming and outgoing communications from Chloe's terminal.

After he shut down the kiosk computer, the room went dark. With the exception of the green light of the overhead cameras, there was very little natural light.

Armada turned towards the connecting tube entrance and prepared to launch himself to his dormitory. He noticed he was casting a shadow on the wall, but not from the green of the cameras. Armada rotated and gazed in wonderment at an orb hovering in the transport tube. He was drawn in by the comforting glow and warmth of the almost transparent and growing sphere.

Armada felt his eyelids growing heavier and heavier, until he could no longer keep them open.

As he peacefully closed his eyes, he heard a man softly call out, "Evan."

CHAPTER 19

INVITATION

B ianca's perfectionism, impeccable taste and sense of style, coupled
with Cain Wyczthack's wealth, was in top form. She wore a simple,
black silk Armani evening gown and draped her soft and flowing golden
locks over the front of her left shoulder. Cain's attire consisted of a char-
coal-gray suit and pocket square kerchief, but in place of his traditional
white shirt and tie, he opted for a powder-blue, V-neck cashmere pullover
with a white undershirt. Whenever he wanted, or found himself in need
of new clothing, Cain wasn't the kind to shop. Even with easy access to a
handful of fine and reputable clothiers in Las Vegas, he didn't much care
for the 'off the rack' format of purchasing his wardrobe. Instead, Cain
stayed at the SUBOS while the likes of Alexander Amosu and William
Westmancott came to him to handcraft his suits.

Cain's private and personal entertainment and lodging facilities were
palatial, to say the least. They took up the entirety of the first two floors
at the one-mile mark of the SUBOS. The first floor consisted of several
banquet halls, a main dining and conference room, a couple of bars and
lounges, a coffee house, swimming pool, day spa with massage parlor,
gymnasium, and a minor medical treatment center. The second floor
served as temporary living quarters for invited guests and could easily
house a thousand individuals in spacious, lavish luxury.

The second floor also contained a heliport. Engenechem constructed a monstrously large hangar at Nellis Air Base just to keep up with the demands of those who required absolute secrecy and privacy when travelling abroad. Guests would land at Nellis, taxi to the hangar, and transfer from their private plane to a helicopter that would whisk them to the SUBOS. It wasn't that uncommon to find forty or fifty jets parked next to the massive hangar at any given moment. Gulfstream, Bombardier, Embraer, Dassault, Airbus; the runway was littered with the best in personal air travel.

After a cocktail reception, dinner was to be served in the main dining room, a cavernous dining hall Cain had come to fondly refer to as Bacchus, in honor of the Roman god of wine and festivity. The Bacchus Hall kitchen was equipped to rival those of the world's most renowned restaurants, and was the envy of many Michelin three-star chefs. It wasn't so radical of an idea to bring in a chocolatier from Switzerland, a pastry chef from France, or saucier from Sweden, for an evening of exquisite gastronomy. Cain spared no expense when it came to fine food and wine.

Those fortunate enough to be invited to dine with Dr. Wyczthack were treated to a visually stunning feast for the eyes prior to the meal being served. Intricate crown molding, fifteen-foot walls, and ornate sixteenth-century tapestries hung from the cathedral-style ceiling. Colorful Chihully glass sculptures, fireplaces, fountains, rare flowering plants, and a mammoth wet bar kept Cain's attendees delightfully distracted until time for dinner.

Cain and Bianca commissioned the production of twenty-five tables and three hundred chairs specifically for Bacchus Hall. The round, one-piece tables, large enough to seat ten people comfortably, twelve at most, were lovingly sculpted and carved from exotic hardwoods from around the world. The master craftsmen incorporated combinations of Afromosia, Cocobolo, Ebony, Mahogany, Tiger and Zebra woods, burled Walnut, Bubinga, and Carpathian Elm. Because of the beautiful and brilliant artistry of the tables, a conscious decision was made to not cover them even during meal service. The only linens provided to the guests during their dining experience would be that of their napkins.

For the evening's entrees, Bianca and the chef decided on Russian caviar to be paired with Alaskan Salmon and Maine lobster, and a choice of hand-carved Japanese Kobe or Nebraska grass-fed bison steaks. With fresh floral centerpieces, Swarovski crystal candle bases, Christofle silverware, and Raynaud fine bone China, it was more than appropriate that the Chateau Latour be poured in Riedel glasses.

***

The steak was flavorful and juicy, the salmon tender and flaky, and the Bordeaux luscious, deep, and robust. The meal had been executed without so much as one hiccup.

Once the attentive staff had cleared the plates, the diners were left to enjoy their coffee and Bollinger champagne.

Cain's speech and spiel had progressed nicely, right up to the point when he casually said, "Fifty million dollars. Each."

"Fifty million dollars?!" the audience repeated with incredulity.

Of the one hundred invited guests, a dozen silently rose from their seats and promptly exited the lavish dinner. The remainder of attendees, while voicing their strong objections to such an astronomical cost, did not leave the opulent feast.

"How many inhabitants did you say will be in each Cloud?" a man seated in front of Cain rudely called out.

"We will deploy three thousand individuals to each of the Clouds," Cain replied.

"That's more than three trillion dollars!" another man shouted.

"Yes, it is," Cain stated.

Several more dinner guests stood and departed in quiet protest.

"Do you plan to introduce any of the selected inhabitants to your EC's?" asked Muhammad bin Ibrahim, the governor for the Central Bank of Malaysia.

"No," Dr. Wyczthack flatly answered. "There will be no direct contact with any Cloud inhabitants. We do not intend to introduce human interaction of any kind."

"Well, if you don't mind my asking, then what motivation is there for me to surrender my wealth for an experiment?"

The gaggle of elite financiers, corporate presidents, intellectuals, and filthy rich began to mumble and whisper. Although deep down inside Cain despised the brood of real estate moguls, railroad magnates, and financial wizards, he was forced to admit to himself that Engenechem, while more powerful than Amazon, Apple, Google, and Wal-Mart, lacked the cash reserves necessary for self-funding the Cloud Program. Engenechem had more than enough means to see the Cloud Program to fruition, but it meant lengthy delays in construction, fabrication, and assembly of the Clouds. Waiting for cash reserves to build themselves up again would take years, maybe a decade. If Cain wanted his Cloud Program to stay on course, he'd be forced to ask for outside assistance.

"Mr. Ibrahim, ladies and gentlemen, this is more than a grand experiment. We're not conducting a summer internship at some community college or running a contest for nominees to live in a bio dome for a week. This isn't space camp for teenagers. The Cloud Program will be ... is ... the pinnacle of scientific research, the standard by which all future endeavors will be judged ... the crowning achievement in mankind's quest to establish human life beyond Earth. As we are all well aware, our planet is dying. We're killing it! Every day, little by little, ever so slowly, we are destroying this precious world. Drilling, mining, excavating, deforestation, air pollution, water pollution, soil contamination ... doomsday is fast approaching, whether we want to admit it or not. We are now, and have been, preparing for Earth's inevitable demise, be it next week or next century."

The subdued and emotionally deficient snobs were unappreciative of Cain's semimotivational speech.

"But a thirty-year experiment?" Mr. Ibrahim again spoke up. "And you expect us to foot the bill?"

"This might seem a bit awkward," Cain stated, "but it's an absolute necessity. The fifty million-dollar price tag for this privilege is, at least to you in this room, all but a trifle. Think of this in the context of corporate sponsorship, in place of a fee or expense. Imagine that you're Phil Knight in the late nineteen-eighties, and your company, Nike, is on the hunt for the next Michael Jordan."

The intimate crowd still wasn't biting.

"Meesta Cahn," said Akio Mimura, the director and president of Nippon Steel, "You wi find that insuting our interregence make us weary of doing business wit Engenchem. Why do you make such pwopostwous wequest?"

"Mr. Mimura, please believe me when I tell you that no insult was intended. While Engenechem has always positioned itself with generating, and sustaining, a vast source of income, the costs for the Cloud Program have, shall we say, expanded beyond our immediate means. Total costs for Cloud construction is $125 billion dollars . . . each. Bathrooms, dormitories, propulsion systems, air and water filtration and purification systems, lighting, waste management and collection, communication systems, clothing, medical facilities . . . food . . . it's mind-boggling when you consider everything it takes to sustain life in an environment where it's impossible for life to exist."

"I can appreciate your position," Anette Olsen, the CEO for Ganger Rolf stated, "but just now you said that 'we' . . . would be on the lookout for the next Michael Jordan. To me that says not only are we being solicited to finance your project, but we're expected to locate and identify your staff?"

Anette sipped the last drops of her Bollinger, turned to her side, and loudly snapped her fingers.

"Miss Olsen . . . ," Cain began as he stepped away from his chair. He intercepted the briskly moving waiter and relieved him of his fresh bottle of champagne. Approaching Anette on her right, she slowly raised her glass to receive a refill.

"I'm in no way suggesting that any of you be responsible for selecting candidates for Cloud deployment," he stated as he poured the golden bubbly.

Cain twisted back to Bianca and nodded. Bianca rose gracefully from her seat and walked a few paces to something covered with a shiny black fabric. She faced the guests and stood silently.

"A simple misinterpretation, Miss Olsen," Cain charmingly stated with a slight chuckle.

Dr. Wyczthack again glanced at Bianca and nodded. She pulled back on the black coverlet and revealed a handsomely ornate wooden service cart with a large pyramid-shaped stack of black boxes. Bianca gently pushed the cart to Cain as he spoke.

"I'd be more inclined to label this arrangement as a 'joint venture' of sorts. It would serve both of our interests well to have each of you not only financially involved, but your intellect and ingenuity as well."

Cain handed off the bottle of champagne to the waiter, turned, and was given the box from the very top of the pyramid. Bianca smiled as she released the perfectly square, velour-covered case into Cain's hands. Dr. Wyczthack faced Anette, placed the box on the table in front of her, and then stepped away. He winked at Bianca, giving her the go ahead to dispense the boxes to the dinner guests.

Anette Olsen, daughter of famed Norwegian shipping and offshore drilling magnate Friederick Olsen, grasped the small box. She firmly held the base in her right hand and delicately pulled back the lid. Bianca continued to pass out the tiny black cases as Cain addressed his guests.

"This," he said, "is the extent of your requested involvement."

Cain reached out to the opened box in front of Anette and removed a piece from the scarlet silk-lined interior. He motioned for the others around him to open their boxes.

"What are these for?" Mr. Ibrahim asked. "What am I supposed to do with them?"

Inside each small, tissue box-sized case, in neat little rows, there lay one hundred micro USB thumb drives with shiny, black teardrop-shaped bumps on the outer edge.

"All I ask," Cain began as he held up the microdrive, "is that each of you use extreme prejudice and bias when informing your potential candidates of the Cloud Program."

"How…," Mr. Imura started asking.

"When you find yourselves in a position to approach your candidate," Cain interrupted, "you will inform him, or her, that you are in possession of information that they might be interested in. Information regarding a highly secretive project that you believe he or she could easily qualify for and become directly involved in, and they possess certain talents, etc., etc. Then you hand them this … and you're done."

The intimate crowd sat in their chairs, perplexed. They picked up and examined the chips, then looked about at each other, and placed the chips back in their boxes. This process was repeated several times.

"We're…," Miss Olsen started, then paused. "You're placing the burden on us … to handpick thirty thousand individuals … to send up to your orbital habitats … for thirty years?"

Cain laughed out loud.

"You?" he asked, patting Anette's shoulder as he tried to suppress his giggling. "All eighty of you? Eighty people to select thirty thousand? No … no, no, no. My dear lady, I have thousands of employees dedicated to this one endeavor alone. Throughout the month I will be conducting this same presentation. I'll travel to New York, Los Angeles, Rio de Janeiro, Sidney, London … Madrid, Frankfurt, Moscow … Beijing, New Delhi, Jerusalem, Budapest … Copenhagen, Milan, and Abu Dhabi. While I've made preparations to accommodate one hundred guests at a few of those meetings, other locations will see three and four hundred guests, and even more still at the remainder of my presentations. Like you, each of them will be given one hundred microdrives, identical in every way, to dispense how they so choose, and to whom. So by month's end, I will have a potential one hundred thousand additional sets of eyes scattered throughout the world … leaving me with as many ten million candidate options for deployment to the Clouds."

"Why dis cheep?" Mr. Imura inquired, raising his hand and microdrive.

"When activated," Cain stated, walking to his seat, "the applicant will be immediately connected to my staff here at the SUBOS."

He held up his empty champagne glass and motioned for the waiter to bring the bottle as he explained, "Whatever device the individuals choose to use, these microdrives will ensure that all information is encrypted, the GPS chips rendered useless, and all communications will be untraceable by the NSA, CIA, DHS, or Google."

The waiter promptly returned and filled Cain's glass from a fresh bottle of Bollinger. Before he placed the glass to his lips, Dr. Wyczthack glanced at his guests and pointed to his glass, then pointed to them and raised his eyebrows, as if to ask "Would anybody else care for a refill?"

Everyone quickly held up their glass. Cain snapped his fingers, bringing the waiter back to his table. He draped his arm across the young man's shoulder and whispered in his ear while motioning to his guests.

"Yes, sir, Mr. Wyczthack," the man quietly replied and dashed away.

"Now, where was I?" Cain asked, sipping his champagne.

"You were explaining the importance and significance of the microdrives," Bianca answered, gently placing her left hand on Cain's right arm.

"Oh, yes, Mr. Imura. How silly of me. I apologize," he said, bowing slightly.

Just as Cain opened his mouth to speak, the waiter returned with two bottles of chilled champagne in each hand.

"Ah!" he said and began clapping.

Behind that waiter was another, and another, and another, all laden with multiple bottles of the fine, crisp, and expensive French champagne. Cain turned to Bianca and smiled as she, too, applauded the arrival of the delightfully delicious intoxicant. Bacchus Hall exploded with raucous applause as more and more staff streamed out from the bar and delivered to each of Cain's guests their own bottle of champagne.

Applause turned to laughter as another wave of dining staff entered the room. This time they bore handcrafted wooden boxes filled with fine cigars and sterling silver trays of assorted Swiss chocolates and cheeses, blueberries, and strawberries. The giddy patrons stood and clapped. Robust aromas from nicely aged Bolivar, Montecristo, and Partagas cigars filled the air. Fragments of broken chocolate bricks from Frey, Cailler, and Teuscher chocolatiers were scooped onto chilled plates. The pairings of soft Brie, luscious chocolates, bright fruit and crisp champagne was the topper to a dynamic meal.

"Getting back to our topic of conversation," Cain announced as he stood, "My staff will conduct a thorough interview with each of the candidates you select. At that time, he or she will be given full disclosure regarding the Cloud Program and what our long-term expectations and goals are. They will then go to their physician of choice for a series of draws for blood work that will be conducted here at the SUBOS. The vials will be special air-freighted from wherever they are in the world. Once we receive the samples, the blood will go through hundreds of tests. In the meanwhile, my staff will conduct a genealogical history search for the candidates, going back as far as five generations."

"Why the genealogy?" Mr. Ibrahim asked, puffing his cigar.

"We're looking for irregularities in their family history," Cain replied, exhaling a plume of smoke from his Partagas. "We need to know if the people we're sending up there have a history of emphysema. Did their mother have cystic fibrosis? Does their paternal grandfather suffer from Alzheimer's? Maybe a maternal great-grandmother had Lou Gehrig's disease. This will greatly affect and influence medical treatment facilities and protocols, not to mention reproduction results."

"Wait a minute!" Anette Olsen hollered, slapping the table. "You plan on bringing babies into the picture? How will that work? I mean, why? You're already sending up families, why have more babies?"

A few of those seated around Anette agreed and applauded her question.

"Miss Olsen," Cain began. "No one mentioned families. Ever. One candidate will go, whether married with children or single."

This revelation startled Anette and many of the others as well.

"So, just like that, you're going to separate a father or mother from their family?" Anette inquired, obviously disturbed by the idea.

"I'm not separating or dividing anyone. That's up to the individual candidates to decide. Furthermore, testing will determine who goes and who stays. Just because a person might be married and qualify for the program doesn't necessarily mean his or her spouse qualifies."

The slightly intoxicated diners spoke candidly with their seated neighbors, some with more volume and slurred speech than others.

"Ehrwier you stated tuty tousen go to Crowds," said a very inebriated Mr. Imura, trying desperately to speak clearly. "But aso say foty-fy tousen can go to Crowd. Which numba twu?"

"You're correct, Mr. Imura, I did say both of things. And both of those statements are true. We fully intend to send, and are preparing for, an initial deployment of thirty thousand individuals for a test span of thirty years. Ideally, we'd prefer to house each Cloud with two thousand females and one thousand males. Through genetic testing, chromosome research, and genealogical research, we'll identify the prime female candidates for impregnating via artificial insemination. We expect to achieve a ninety-five percent success rate and produce five hundred offspring every year."

"Whaz dis tessing aboutt?" Mr. Ibrahim attempted to ask. "Why s'much tessing?"

"We require the absolute best of what this world can offer. The individuals we select must be of the highest caliber intellectually, physically, genetically...every last one. Chemical engineers, architects, physicists, mathematicians...our future rests on their shoulders. So when you're contemplating who to approach with the microdrive, remember that while good looks are temporary, knowledge is life lasting. People who we don't need to waste our time on is someone like...like, uh...oh, who was that singing punk all the girls were so crazy for about fifteen years ago?"

The befuddled group tried and tried to think of the popular singer Cain was referring to, but no one could recollect his name.

"Oh, come on, please, somebody help me out," Cain pleaded.

"Jusin Beeba!" Mr. Imura gleefully shouted, jumping to his feet.

"Justin Bieber!" the semisloshed crowd repeated, clapping for the smiling Japanese man.

"Justin Bieber!" Cain and Bianca echoed, as they applauded Mr. Imura who bowed over and over.

"I can stan Jusin Beeba!" Mr. Imura proudly declared. "My gandata jove mi cazy wit him muzic!"

Everybody stood, laughed, and clapped along.

"Can any of you imagine what our world would look like if we left it up to Justin Bieber to repopulate the planet?" Cain shouted, raising his glass, "No Justin Bieber!"

"No Justin Bieber!" his guests shouted, then gulped down their bubbly.

"Oh, my," Cain said, fanning himself. "Seriously though, the birthing calendar is of the most importance. Just imagine it: at the end of the thirty years, we will have created the very first wave of stable, clean, and genetically pure humans!"

"Yeah?" Anette piped up. "For whom? For what?"

Bianca stood next to Cain as he coolly responded, "For the New World!"

CHAPTER 20

THE LOTTERY

'I don't get it,' Chloe's message read.

'Well,' Armada began typing, 'we can pretty much count on Wyczthack and White having something up their sleeves.'

Armada sent his simple statement to Chloe, and immediately reopened the file folder named 'Contestants.' Awaiting a response from Chloe, he resumed his investigation by randomly clicking open the numbered subfolders.

'Why number the folders?' the next message asked.

'I don't know. But for whatever reason they're collecting this volume of personal information, you can rest assured that it's of major significance. You're the engineer, you tell me what you think.'

He sent the message and opened the program monitor for the Master Server to see what programs were running in the background.

'Oh, I agree with you … it's something big,' her message began. 'Maybe numbering the folders instead of inserting an individual's name is a secret method of identification. It's like a placebo; they'll make their decision based strictly off of data, not gender or race. Eight-digit numbers might mean one thing and six-digit numbers something else. Or maybe the first digit in the sequence is the identifying variable. Do you see what I mean?'

Armada quickly skimmed through Chloe's message. He then opened the 'Contestant' tab, selected one of the numbered subfolders, and copied it.

'Check this out,' he typed, attached the copy, and sent the message.

While waiting for Chloe to examine the content of the folder, Armada reviewed the properties of the 'Contestant' file. It was massive, to say the least. More than seven million subfolders had been created in the last three months. On the day the file was created, its first subfolder was generated and given the peculiar title 'Basket of Eggs.' Armada was intrigued. However, upon reviewing the 'Eggs' file, he found a paltry eighteen thousand subfolders with the similar eight-digit numbered titles.

'Did you look at each page?' Chloe's newest message asked. 'I mean, are the pages in this file similar to the other files you've examined?'

'Yes and no,' Armada pecked. 'Some have way more content than others, whereas a few I picked out have very little. And by little, I mean thirty to fifty pages. I did open one that was, at a minimum, a hundred and fifty pages.'

'Judging from the information in this one file, it would appear that White and Wyczthack are conducting the same battery of tests and exams they subject us to. This woman, whoever she is, has normal levels of HDL, LDL, CRP, THS, U/E, and so on. But why subject millions of randomly selected people to this deep of an investigation? I see that she's employed by Qualcomm and is one of their top microprocessor engineers. She's divorced, twice, is forty-three years old, and smokes. So why pick her out of six billion people?'

'Your guess is as good as mine,' Armada stated and sent his answer.

'Anything else of interest this evening?' Chloe's next letter inquired.

'Yes,' Armada swiftly responded. 'In the parent file is a folder called 'Basket of Eggs.' But the files in that folder appear to have the same kind of content.'

'Pick out five from Eggs and send them to me. You choose five from Contestant and we'll compare them.'

'Deal,' Armada typed and sent his note.

He clicked the 'Eggs' tab, highlighted five separate folders, and copied them as an attachment to his message, 'Don't say I never gave you anything.'

Three years had quickly come and gone since he and Chloe began their secret late-night correspondence. Although he deleted all traces of their communications, Armada kept digital copies of every conversation. On the rare occasion he was unable to connect with Chloe, he would reread the transcripts until the early morning hours. He came to realize that she'd become a permanent and vital presence in his life. However long that life might last, he felt himself growing more and more dependent on Chloe for support, both mentally and emotionally.

After a good thirty minutes had ticked by, a message alert appeared on Armada's screen.

'What's the answer to question twenty-five?' Chloe jokingly asked.

'Stalactite,' he replied in jest.

'Oh, I put Sasquatch.'

'Okay, professor, very funny.'

'Are you ready?' she asked. 'What'd you find?'

'For one,' Armada started, 'none of this is going through Engenechem HR. Whoever these individuals are, they're submitting everything directly to Wyczthack and White. Moving on, I pulled files for both male and female applicants between thirty-two and sixty-one years of age from all over the world. All five are in positions of power and prestige within their organizations. I found a forty-three-year-old single father of three that's the senior project manager at Imabari Ship in Japan. Next, a thirty-eight-year-old single mother of one who's a senior site development manager with Glencore Xstrata, living in Australia. Third, and the oldest of the bunch, a sixty-one-year-old professor who's the chair of Systems and Software Engineering at Cornell in Ithaca. He smokes a pipe, drinks, and underwent double bypass heart surgery two years ago. Number four, a widower from London who works in the Department of Alternative Propulsion for BAE Systems in England. He's in his fifties, smokes, and never had any children. And finally, in fifth place, a married woman in her late forties, five kids, doesn't smoke, drinks a couple glasses of wine a week, and works for Parsons Brinkerhoff Engineers as their Western Hemisphere senior site manager. She lives in Poulsbo, just out of Seattle, but travels all over. From northern Saskatchewan down to Chile, she goes everywhere. All of these individuals are supersmart and excel at what they do. Salaries range from a hundred twenty thousand dollars to more than half a million. Wyczthack and White went way beyond the conventional psychological profiling and physiological makeup of these people; they did a complete genome panel and ancestry search as well.'

'All five of my picks had something in either their direct past or a close family member's, like polio, influenza, diabetes, cancer, macular degeneration, ALS, Alzheimer's; something hereditary and passed down through the bloodline. Going by what I've read in these random selections, Cain went back at least five generations in each of their family trees. A few had members who suffered from an autoimmune disease, whereas some were diagnosed as schizophrenic, clinically depressed, or had bipolar and multiple personality disorders. That about sums it up for me. What did you find?'

Armada dispatched his lengthy and in-depth assessment, and resumed his investigation into the background programs currently running on the Master Server.

As he suspected, Watcher was taking up a considerable chunk of bandwidth, followed by Grocery List. But the Contestant program occupied the lion's share of available bandwidth space. Contestant had no less than two thousand users logged on at any given moment, day or night. The file history showed that, on average, Contestant was receiving, compiling, and storing a terabyte of data for fifty thousand individuals a day.

'Are you ready?' Chloe's newest message asked.

'Fire away!' Armada answered smartly.

He waited and waited for a letter, but it never arrived. Just as he began typing 'Hello,' he received Chloe's message.

'I found many similarities between Contestant files and those in the Eggs folder. Like the individuals in Contestant, those in Eggs are at the top of the food chain. Plenty of engineers, managers, and designers. My five candidates, however, are no older than thirty-five and no younger than twenty-seven. Out of the five, only one had children, and three of them, two male and one female, are still single. None of them smoke, but they all drink alcohol, mostly wine, and all five have a clean history for substance abuse.'

'Their blood and genome panels are exceptional, and the ancestral ties are, for the most part, nil of anything significant. One individual, the principal engineer for Robotics and Nanotechnologies with Hitachi, had a maternal grandfather who died of leukemia. Other than that, nothing here to report. One thing I will comment on is that from all outward appearances, this information is identical to the oceans of data Wyczthack and White have been collecting on us for years. Not to toot my own horn, but I'm more qualified and have a current, hands-on education that far surpasses the vast majority of these people in three separate fields of study. Our IQ scores probably put all of theirs to shame. Plus, our DNA is pure. I don't know what's going on, but why go through the hassle and expense of selecting and testing candidates, knowing all the while that the person, and end results, will be inferior?'

Armada carefully pondered her questions. Chloe made a good point. Why indeed would Cain and Dr. White be gathering so much information on that many people? Why select thousands of individuals who, intellectually, were well below the par of those in the EC Program, and genetically flawed?

'What would you say is the overall mortality rate of your kind?' Armada asked, 'Factoring in substitutions and end of cycle swaps, I'd estimate we're at fifty percent.'

'That sounds about right,' Chloe replied, 'Dr. White is releasing a new batch every month. But out of two hundred sisters, almost half die off within sixty days or so. How often does he release a batch for your kind?'

'We received a new batch, the Hercules class, two months ago,' he answered, 'but ours are roughly three hundred in number, and die off is also in the fifty percent range.'

'How many Clouds have you constructed? How many in total are scheduled for production? How many inhabitants can one Cloud house?'

'Eight so far, ten, and forty-five hundred each,' he swiftly responded.

Armada hovered in front of the Arena One communication kiosk, slightly illuminated by the underglow of the terminal keyboard. He spun around and gazed through the wide, panoramic window at the collection of Clouds, Arenas, Arks, and Eden. The mammoth structures loomed over the dinky, cylindrical dormitories connected to the Arenas. He focused on the three dormitories, then the Clouds, and then back to the dorms.

"The dormitories hold two hundred," he whispered to himself. "Four dorm systems means eight hundred inhabitants. But two hundred experience end of cycle every two months. Two hundred die off, but two hundred are brought up. It's a wash. They cancel each other out."

"It's a wash! It's a wash!" he repeated, almost shouting. Armada glanced up at the video camera, and was relieved to find the green light still glowing.

'Contestant, Eggs, and Grocery List are all connected!' he speedily typed and sent to Chloe.

He started to expand on his epiphany when Chloe's reply of 'WHAT!?' appeared on his screen.

'Cain and Dr. White are using us to construct and assemble the Clouds, so that when the time is right, everything will be up and running for the people in the Eggs file. Do you get it? Wyczthack and White are putting all of their best 'Eggs in a Basket.' That's why they're purchasing a million toothbrushes, two million pairs of shoes, five hundred thousand packs of underwear. Engenechem is planning on some global catastrophe to justify taking the selected applicants up to the Clouds. It's perfect!'

Chloe read through Armada's letter three times. At first, she thought it too extravagant and elaborate of a plan to be pulled off. The second time, she started putting the pieces together and found herself growing angry as her pulse rate increased. When she read it the third time, a chill ran down her spine and a wave of fear, panic, and dread washed over her.

Chloe began crying as she typed, 'Oh, my gosh, Armada! What are we going to do? I don't want to be killed off.'

'You're not going to be killed,' he tried to console her. 'You're not going to die, not if I have a say in it. Let's think this out. Okay?'

'Okay,' she replied.

'Do you trust me?' Armada inquired.

'Yes.'

'All right, we'll be just fine. First, let's assume that I'm correct and Wyczthack and White, and you and I, are the only ones who know about the end game. If too many are in on the plan, it'll create a panic and chaos. Cain doesn't want that; he's a spoiled brat and a control freak. Agreed?'

'Agreed,' Chloe typed, wiping her nose and eyes.

'Good. Who's your buddy? Who makes you laugh?' he pecked, smiling to himself, knowing it would cause her to smile and lighten up.

'You.'

'Okay then, moving on. Cain needs everything to run smoothly to pull this off. Whoever he's working with, they're either not fully aware of his ultimate goal, they're just plain stupid, or they're in on it. Next, Wyczthack and White can't initiate their plans until the Clouds are finished. We're currently working on Cloud Eight, and modules for Cloud Nine have begun arriving at the Aerie. I can slow things down for a little while with staging, but as a long-term stall tactic, that won't work.'

'Who can we tell? Isn't there someone we can talk to and explain what's really going on?'

'I wish there was,' Armada answered.

As he was about to elaborate on his hypothesis, the monitor suddenly went dark as well as the keyboard. Armada looked for the illuminated power button, but that, too, was dark. He turned his attention to the video camera and the miniature green light refused to shine. Once more, he pulled himself to the large panoramic window and peered out at the hovering community of metal structures. He was shocked to find that the power failure had not affected Eden, the Arks, Clouds, or Arenas and dormitories. In fact, looking down he noticed that the exterior lighting for the staging zones, the Aerie, the four SPUDs, and all five CARBEL Halos was fully functional. Even the SUBOS appeared to have avoided a power outage.

Chloe, in the meanwhile, was awaiting a reply from Armada. Suddenly her computer screen flickered, and the window with Armada's last message disappeared. She fell back in her chair and held her hands up in confusion. Her mouth was agape in shock as an automatic notification flashed in the bottom right corner of her monitor: 'Terminal Error: Source Signal Lost.'

"Oh, no," she mumbled. "No, no, no, no! Armada! Don't leave me hanging!"

She restarted her terminal server and immediately looked for any incoming messages. There were none. Again, Chloe felt the nervous panic building inside her. Her heart pounded fiercely, and she could feel the heat in her face and cheeks radiating to her throat and upper chest.

"C'mon, Armada," she whimpered softly, scooting closer to the monitor. "C'mon, c'mon, c'mon. Please, answer me!"

Chloe refreshed the mailbox, but no new messages were received. She pushed away from her desk, buried her face in her hands, and silently wept.

Please! she thought to herself, *This can't be how it ends! It just can't. Armada, I need you! Please!*

$$***$$

Armada was stumped as to why the Arena would experience a loss of power. He again glanced up at the video camera and still no lights, red or green, showed from the base. He pushed away from the wall in the direction of the kiosk, and before reaching out to grasp a hand bar, something caught his attention. The tunnel connecting the dormitories was not fully lit. Normally, a quartet of powerful LEDs, placed every ten feet, illuminated the tunnel in brilliant, white light. Now the tube was very dim, and the source of light was moving.

After timidly sticking his head into the tunnel, he looked to his left and to his right but observed no one. What he did observe was the movement of a faint glow at the end of the tunnel, and the video cameras weren't functioning.

"What?" he asked out loud, as he withdrew from the tunnel back into the Arena.

Armada turned around to make sure the camera on the ceiling hadn't been activated. It sat motionless.

He pulled himself completely into the connecting tunnel and noticed that the light hadn't changed its position. But as he began to propel himself along the hand rungs, the glow continued to advance ahead of him. If Armada stopped, the light stopped. He tried playing a trick by stopping and backing up to see how the opaque and transparent orb would react. Surprisingly, the glowing apparition reversed itself and waited.

Whatever path the light traveled, Armada noticed that all lights and video monitors ceased to function. He followed the sphere all the way back to his dormitory entrance portal. Once directly in front of the portal, he felt compelled to pursue the light rather than enter the dorm and go to bed. He made the conscious decision to evaluate his situation, how he felt, and make a mental note of his thought process.

Armada turned to face the hovering beacon and pushed away from the dorm portal. He trailed the cloudy mass past the remaining dormitories, Garret's private offices, the communications center and kitchen, until it finally stopped at the EVA prep area, Arena One docking station, and air locks. Just as he noticed the absence of electrical power in the connecting tunnel, so, too, was the obvious lack of energy in the receiving bay.

He had a firm grasp on one of the hand rungs and maintained his position at the entrance to the bay. The translucent orb floated further away from him to the very end of the docking station. It stopped moving once it reached the last staging zone and pressurized air lock. Armada fixed his gaze on the ethereal cloud. The hues in the vaporous mass alternated continuously from warm yellows and orange, to cool shades of blue, green, and purple.

'Okay, what now?' he half-jokingly and silently asked himself.

He stared and waited, not fully knowing what he should do next.

"Go to her," a voice called out. "Go to her now, and fear not."

CHAPTER 21

AN INTRODUCTION

Chloe shut down her terminal and wiped her eyes and nose as she briskly exited the research center. Instead of taking the elevator to the dormitories on Sixteen M, she opted for the stairs, even though it meant climbing almost twenty flights.

She entered the cold concrete and steel stairwell. The door slammed behind her with a loud thud that echoed throughout the cavernous chamber. She never felt so alone. Fear and confusion consumed her as she climbed, weighing her down more and more with each step. It took Chloe more than an hour to ascend the stairs to the dormitories connected to the Nursery.

As she approached the landing for floor Sixteen M, she brushed away the tears running down her cheeks. She tried to calm down by taking a few refreshing breaths before opening the door, so as to not draw attention to herself should she encounter anyone prior to reaching her dorm room.

After passing the retinal scanner, Chloe bowed her head and quickly made a beeline for her dorm. She entered the corridor that led to her room, walked past the shower stalls and restrooms, and typed her pass code on the exterior keypad. The door's magnetic lock disengaged, granting access to her room. She tiptoed past the rows of bunk beds to the last stack and gingerly squatted on the mattress. Her eyelids felt heavy and swollen.

He can't be right! Chloe thought, lying down on the bottom bunk, *Engenechem is plotting, and preparing, to exterminate six billion people? And not save us? Armada's not thinking clearly. He's overlooking something or hasn't factored everything.*

She shut her droopy eyelids, drew up her knees, and tried not to think.

As she was drifting to sleep, Chloe suddenly felt the uneasy sensation of someone watching her. She opened her eyes, but instead of feeling dreary and listless, her body and brain were invigorated and alert. She lay on her left side and tried looking to her right as far as she could. There was no sound. In fact, she didn't even hear her nine roommates breathing as they slept. She slowly pulled her left arm up to look at her watch. The digital screen was dark.

She abruptly sat up, turning to her right to face whomever was watching her. Chloe blinked and rubbed her eyes and shook her head. There, in front of the door and first stack of bunk beds, was a glowing, pulsing, mass of haze, floating in midair. The feelings of despair and fear that earlier had inundated her psyche were instantly replaced with those of tranquility and peace. She smiled as she witnessed the vaporous cloud slowly roll past the beds, row by row. Chloe's rapidly beating heart began to wind down. She couldn't not stare at the light as it drew closer to her. How warm and relaxed she now felt, but not at all sleepy or tired. When the orb was perpendicular to the end of her bed, she peered straight through it at the wall-mounted clock. The second hand, she observed, had stopped moving.

Chloe slowly shifted her weight, turning back to lean on her left arm. The cloud of dazzling colors crept towards her, but quit advancing when it was nearly parallel with her hips. Curious to know what it was, she delicately raised her right hand and gradually extended her arm. The smoothly swirling ball of light backed away, just beyond the tips of her fingers. She again smiled, lowered her arm, and the glowing haze moved closer.

She moved her left arm from behind her and gracefully lay herself down, keeping her focus on the apparition.

"My precious child," she heard a man softly say, "Fear not, and know that I am with you."

***

Armada removed the transponder chip and pulled out the microphone before clamping down the locking mechanism on his helmet. He then started pulling himself towards the last air lock and glowing orb.

"How am I supposed to enter the air lock when all of the power is out?" he asked.

He gazed in astonishment as the orb passed through the air lock door into the vacuum chamber. Once he was in front of the door, he peered through the tiny, round window. Without warning, the vacuum chamber was immediately pressurized and the interior door to the air lock began to swing in. The orb, however, was no longer on the inside of the chamber. Armada secured the interior door of the vacuum chamber and thrust himself to the exterior door. He grabbed two rungs to steady himself, leaned into the portal door window, and watched the orb begin to back away from the docking port.

"How do you expect me...?" Armada started to ask.

Before he could finish his question, the chamber instantly depressurized and the outer door to the docking portal slowly swung open. He had to laugh to himself. Even if he decided to tell Euclid about his encounter and experience this evening, he doubted Euclid would believe one word of it.

"Come," the voice instructed, and smoothly bobbed over the Arena until out of sight.

The outer door to the last vacuum chamber had no sooner shut when the power supply to the Arena was instantly restored.

Armada pulled himself along the hull exterior and came upon the orb, hovering just above the pin that connected Arena One to the five

CARBEL Halos. The pin held a tether cable, roughly four inches in diameter, securely in place, ensuring that if something happened to the vector engines on one of the Arenas, the cable would keep a constant tension and not allow the station to fall out of orbit.

Just as Armada took hold of the pin and cable, the orb moved out and away from him.

"Fear not, and know that I am with you," the voice firmly commanded.

Armada watched the orb as it sped across the cable to the Halos and on to the four SPUDs. From there, his eyes tracked the swift and shiny mass as it travelled back to the Halos and down CARBEL One. Like a streaking comet, it zipped down the elevator, and, when it reached the SUBOS, flickered brilliantly.

Armada gathered his thoughts and reviewed the trail the shiny sphere just travelled.

"Okay," he muttered. "Arena to Halos, Halos to SPUDs, SPUDs back to Halos, CARBEL One to the SUBOS. And … no oxygen canister."

He gazed down below at the sparkling beacon on the SUBOS Aerie.

"Ten miles down, and no oxygen," he told himself, reluctant to advance any further.

"Come, now," the voice urged. "Trust in me, and know that I am thy God."

At that moment Armada looked down, and far below him he could faintly see the flashing lights of a CARBEL platform. As he focused on the platform, he traced the cables up to its Halo. The platform for CARBEL One was rising, but more important was the fact that CARBEL One had a POG mounted to its surface.

Oxygen.

Armada estimated he had around twenty-five minutes to get over to CARBEL One before it began its descent. Twenty-five minutes to the SPUDs and back before he suffocated on his own CO2.

He released his grip on the rungs and grasped the cable. Due to the large circumference of the tether wire and smoothness of the palms of his gloves, Armada found it difficult to get a good grip. It was nearly impossible to drag himself along the wire hand over hand. He decided to clamp both hands at the same time and propel across the cable with one mighty tug.

He darted his eyes to the top left corner of the holographic screen on the interior of his helmet.

"Eighty-five percent," he grumbled as he reviewed his oxygen levels.

Armada temporarily lowered his head to get a fix on the swiftly ascending platform. He then set his sights on the interconnected Halos and yanked harder on the thick tether cable. After accidentally losing his grasp on the wire, he thought it best to lightly pinch the metal tie line between his feet.

Once he came in contact with the outermost arm of the frame for Halo Five, Armada found it relatively easy to traverse the two hundred feet to Halo One. Using the grid wires on each Halo frame, he was more than happy to advance hand over hand. Like Tarzan swinging on a vine, Armada tightened his fingers on one wire, pulled, and simultaneously reached out with the opposite hand to grab the next. He successfully navigated the five grid sections in just over two minutes.

Armada again focused on the CARBEL One platform, gauged its speed, and checked the gas levels in his suit.

'Sixty percent oxygen,' the screen read in blinking yellow lights.

He turned away from the Halos to determine the fastest and shortest route to the four SPUDs. Should he go by way of the tethered staging zones for the Clouds and on to the interceptors? Or would his remaining time be put to more effective use by making one mighty lunge, allowing his inertia to deliver him to the corralled quartet of stealth satellite hunters?

Armada looked back at the rising elevator, and once more at his oxygen supply.

"I'm trusting you!" he shouted.

He faced the SPUDs, curled his legs underneath him, and placed his boots on the corner of the Halo frame where it joined the tether cable.

"This is crazy! This is crazy! This is crazy!" he repeated, mustering the courage to let go.

"Two hundred … maybe two hundred fifty yards," he guestimated, and glanced at his O2 levels.

The holographic screen flashed 'Forty-five percent' in bright red digits.

After drawing in one deep breath, he pushed against the Halo frame and, with every ounce of strength, launched himself into the cold, black vacuum of space. Armada tried to regulate his intake of air by breathing in as much he could, holding it in as long as possible, and exhaling long and slow. He stared at the not too distant objective and concentrated on his respirations, forcing his brain and body to ignore the fact that he was free floating, nobody knew where he was or what he was doing, and running desperately low on oxygen.

Thankfully, Armada covered a great deal of distance in a short span of time. He was fast approaching the SPUDs and had only a few seconds to determine where best to grab on. If he missed, or lost contact with the SPUD, there was a strong chance he could bounce past the remaining three vessels.

Armada stuck his arms straight out in front of him in preparation for the impact. He spread his fingers open and visually scanned the surface for the best location to place his hands.

Unable to identify an ideal spot to grab, he hit the SPUD squarely in the upper chest, knocking the wind out of him. He struggled to regain his breath while straining to hold on to the SPUD. Armada felt dizzy and lightheaded from lack of fresh oxygen. The digital hologram in his helmet now blinked 'Twenty percent.' Having the air pushed out of his lungs, he was forced to take a greater number of breaths, thereby removing more and more oxygen from his suit.

He twisted his torso to find the CARBEL One platform nearing the Halo.

"No, no, no, no!" he complained loudly between gasps. "You gotta be kidding me!"

He turned to face the SPUD, worked his way to the corner, and wrapped his right leg around the tether cable. Just as he removed his multitool from the exterior pocket of his suit, the hologram in his helmet flickered 'Fifteen percent,' and a piercing, high-pitched buzz began ringing.

"This isn't helping!" Armada shouted, desperate to identify and unfold the blade on his tool. He pried the knife open and thrust it through the radar-deflecting fabric on the underbelly of the SPUD. Withdrawing the knife, he again glanced at the platform.

"C'mon, c'mon, c'mon," he blasted, retracting the folding pliers.

Armada started coughing and was experiencing blurred and double vision. He jabbed one jaw of his pliers into the slit in the fabric, squeezed tightly, and began tugging. Little by little, the dense material gave way until an inch or so protruded to the side.

'Ten percent,' the hologram flashed.

"Aauugghh!" he screamed, approaching a state of unconsciousness.

From the corner of his eye, he saw the safety lights of Halo One flicker to life. The lights automatically came on when a sensor in the carbon braids was activated. The sensors were placed one hundred feet and two hundred feet below the Halo. When the rollers on the four corners of the platform struck the lower sensor, the floodlights were activated, as well as four red, flashing beacons mounted to the underside of the Halo frame. When the CARBEL platforms came in contact with the second sensor, the four electric crawlers would disengage, stopping its rise.

Armada began to panic, as he knew he was almost out of time and O2. 'Nine percent.'

With one final surge of energy, Armada squeezed the pliers and leaned back as quickly as he could, pulling with his arms, back, and abdominal muscles.

Had he not wrapped his leg around the tether cable, Armada would have launched his body to the farthest reaches of the Milky Way. He held his pliers close to his helmet and examined the tip. The stealth material was torn in a tiny strip, measuring no more than one inch by a half inch.

Armada didn't waste any time by collapsing the pliers. Instead, he tucked the tool and swatch in the upper arm pocket of his suit and zipped it up.

'Eight percent.'

Armada's vision was growing cloudier and his coughing intensified. He turned towards the Halos and watched as the elevator platform arrived at Halo One, two hundred yards away. How could he reach the POG on the platform prior to its descent? If he was late, there wouldn't be enough oxygen to sustain him for a return to the Arena. As things stood, even if the platform were to wait for him, he'd be out of oxygen before connecting with the POG.

Armada clung to the tether, weighing out his options. With no one single solution to his problems, Armada stretched his left arm back behind him until he felt the tether cable. He did his best to predict the location of the platform for an interception as he turned his attention to the forest of distant carbon braids.

"Okay!" he belligerently shouted. "Here I go! I'm trusting you again."

'Seven percent.'

He strained to focus on the Halo and platform while he played out his options. It didn't appear to matter whether he attempted to reach the CARBEL, try and intercept the elevator during it's descent, or make the long trek back to the Arena; the end results were the same: out of time and out of O2.

'Six percent.'

"I know! I know! I know!" he screamed. "I see it, I get it! I'm low on oxygen!"

The decision was made for him when CARBEL One released its brakes and activated the four crawlers to begin the hour-long journey to the SUBOS. Armada placed his boots on the outer frame of the SPUD and drew his knees close to his chest. Delirious and exhausted, he adjusted his stance and calculated the anticipated point of contact with the platform. Armada went all out in his last-ditch effort to survive, exploding from his crouched position into the void.

'Five percent.'

"C'mon! Be there, please!" he softly pleaded between coughs.

He wanted to shut his eyes and be done with it all, but the thought of Chloe gave him some hope, albeit very little. Condensation began collecting on the interior of his helmet, making it difficult to determine his proximity to the CARBEL carbon braids and the platform. By his best estimates, the point of intercept with either a carbon braid or the platform was around three hundred yards away. Earlier, on his first free-flight from the Halos to the SPUDs, Armada approximated the gap at two hundred yards. That leap sucked out twenty percent of his suit's remaining oxygen supply and cost him ninety precious seconds. Now, he didn't know if he would last another minute.

'Four percent.'

After floating for nearly two minutes, he turned back and up to his eight o'clock position. Armada was panic-stricken to see the blinking white beacon lights of the platform almost directly above him. His trajectory and speed had him passing far below the CARBEL platform, and way too early. He felt his heart race as he twisted to see in front of him. With his arms open wide, he squinted into the darkness, struggling to see through his helmet visor.

Armada suddenly struck one of the carbon braids with his left arm. The semiflexible cord gave way, slightly, and absorbed much of his energy, so the force of impact was not so severe. However, the collision deflected him into a flat spin, away from the elevator cables.

'Three percent.'

Armada couldn't suppress his anxiety any longer. He started laughing at his dire situation: no oxygen, no reserve tank, free falling thirty miles above the Earth's surface, and not one person knew of his plight. His body shivered uncontrollably as the suit's internal temperature continued to plummet. Not only was he experiencing dizziness from the intake of carbon dioxide, but coupling that with the flat spin was more than his brain could bear. Armada succumbed to the idea of dying, prepared to draw his last breaths, and turned his thoughts to Chloe, Euclid, and Titan.

As he closed his eyes for the last time, his flat spin came to an abrupt stop. Armada struck one of the carbon braids for CARBEL One, and hovered motionless next to the gigantic cable. He had no sooner raised his eyelids when he felt a mighty thump from above. The CARBEL was on top of him, pushing him down.

'Two percent.'

Unable to see where he was, and almost out of air, Armada rotated to face the underside of the platform. He blindly reached for the outer edge of the elevator, curled his fingers on the corner, and, in one swift motion, pulled himself topside. He couldn't inhale anymore carbon dioxide and waited until the last possible moment to exhale. His lungs ached to release the pressure building inside him. Armada dragged himself across the platform's surface, not knowing if the POG lay ahead. His heart pounded, his temples throbbed, and the dropping temperature wreaked havoc with his coordination. Then he felt the base of the mounting brackets securing the pressurized air bank to the CARBEL. Overcome with joy, he released the poisonous gas from his lungs. He clenched his jaws and pressed his lips together in an attempt to stifle the urge to cough.

'One percent.'

Armada's stiff fingers clumsily fumbled on the POG power control panel, refusing to bend to his will and grasp the tiny protruding tab. Starving for fresh oxygen, his body began to thrash about, buckling at the waist. For the briefest of moments, he managed to join his two index fingers and tug the panel cover open. He depressed the power button for five seconds to initiate the oxygen generator, then flailed violently against the bottom row of spooled comm-links.

In his haste to reach for one of the comm-links, he inadvertently released his grip on the POG and began floating away from the descending platform.

'Air!' his brain screamed. 'I need air! I'm so close!'

With his eyes nearly frozen shut, he felt himself drifting to unconsciousness. Without his tether strap securely fastened to the CARBEL, surely Armada would have floated away had his arm not become wedged between two comm-link spools. With his free hand, he groped for the coiled umbilical that housed the oxygen, communications, and power for his suit's built-in radiant heat. He yanked the tubing from its spool and awkwardly joined the quick coupler of the comm-link with that of his suit.

'Zero percent.'

Armada broke free of the rack housing the retracting spools, allowing the CARBEL platform to continue its downward journey without him. He opened his mouth to breathe and felt his diaphragm trying to expand, but nothing happened.

The piercing bing of his emergency alert suddenly stopped, delivering some much needed silence. However, even with his eyes closed, the blinking red light of his holographic screen shone through his eyelids. Every time it flashed, Armada was reminded of his impending doom.

'C'mon, just die!' he told himself. 'It's over now, let go.'

His arms and legs, he noticed, were no longer twitching, and he could feel the radiant heat of his suit. The light penetrating his eyelids transitioned from blinking red ... to stable green. He smelled the odor of fresh oxygen pouring into his helmet and expanded his lungs. Like a newborn baby, he moaned and gasped loudly as more and more clean, filtered air filled his aching chest. His eyes fluttered open, revealing a frost-free helmet visor and hologram screen that showed an internal oxygen level in green double digits, and climbing.

"Woo-hoo!" he shouted. "Chloe! Chloe!"

As her name was leaving his lips, Armada was suddenly bathed in a blazingly hot and blinding white light. He raised his hand to the edge of his helmet and drew down a reflective filter. There, on the eastern horizon, the sun rose above the blue, translucent edge of Earth's atmosphere. He gazed at the burning star, reveling in its glorious warmth.

"Fear not, and know that I am with you," he heard the man whisper.

Confident and assured, Armada closed his eyes.

CHAPTER 22

AWOL

"Great!" Armada grumbled. "Now what do I do?"

The deck of CARBEL One was nearing the Aerie at the top of the SUBOS, and, as he peered down, the reality of potential danger struck him. In the excitement of the moment of following the orb, Armada failed to consider his options upon arriving at the SUBOS. Without his identification lanyard, he had no means of accessing the inner tower. He didn't have any zone authorization codes or passes, and was incapable of generating artificial permissions to the SUBOS elevator systems. Once he reached the Aerie and was found to have left the Arena without an authorized release from Garret, dire consequences were sure to follow.

Armada scooted away from the platform's edge and rolled over on to his back. Gazing up at the carbon braids and multitude of stars, he proceeded to talk his way through the anticipated scenario of being caught.

"Okay, any minute now we'll trip the first descent sensor, triggering the load lights. Right after that comes the second sensor, which will cause the dock beacons to begin flashing. Then the locks will engage, and the deck officer on duty will come and ask me why I'm on the CARBEL without an authorization code. He'll ask the staging and dispatch clerks to check their incoming and outbound manifests for any individual…."

He stopped talking to himself when something caught his attention.

Staring up at the four vertical deck support posts, it suddenly occurred to him that the load lights didn't engage. Not only that, but the four mounted video monitors weren't recording as they normally should. He knew this to be true due to the absence of illumination by either a red or green miniature LED status light on the camera's exterior.

"Why are there no load lights?" he wondered aloud. "And the cameras should have started recording the moment the platform pulled away from the Halo."

Curious as to the extent of malfunctioning gadgetry, he rolled to his chest and crawled to the edge of the CARBEL deck. Just as he thought, the platform had indeed passed the descent sensors and should have, technically, engaged the lights and beacons. But as he pulled himself over the elevator's edge, he saw the beacons on the deck's underside, like the monitors and floodlights, were void of life.

Even though the CARBEL was nearing its final destination, from his temporary vantage point, Armada could easily view the entire Aerie and staging zones. The Aerie's footprint was nearly equivalent to that of a soccer field. All five CARBEL prestaging areas were filled to capacity. Each CARBEL had three prestaging zones, and were aptly named PSZs. So CARBEL One, more commonly known as CE1, had PSZs One, Two, and Three. CARBEL Two, CE2; CARBEL Three, CE3; and so on, followed by a PSZ number. CARBEL One, Prestaging Zone One would read CE1 PSZ1, and on down the line.

The platform touched down with a deep and mighty thud. Armada remained motionless as he lay on his chest. After looking about the Aerie, he slowly and cautiously erected himself.

He first observed a digital clock on the wall above the bank of opened SUBOS elevator doors. 05:10 it read. The more he observed of the Aerie deck, the more the irregularities he noticed. Without so much as stepping one foot off the platform, it became apparent that his strange experiences were not isolated to just the Arena and the CARBEL.

This place should be swarming with people, he thought. *And the elevator doors to the SUBOS should be closed at all times, except for load outs.*

One of the strangest sights was that of the CARBEL and SUBOS Elevator Status screens. The large monitors, mounted next to the clock and load out schedule, showed all ten SUBOS elevators to be in standby mode...at the loading docks on Earth's surface. Furthermore, every CARBEL platform had a status of 'HALO Off-Load Pending' in flashing red letters, when in reality, all five were in 'dock lock.'

After making sure his suit registered a full supply of oxygen, Armada released the quick coupler of his comm-link and powered down the POG. The self-coiling spool slowly drew in the deflated oxygen and communication line.

He gingerly crept off the deck to the rows of gargantuan CCs. CC was the anagram given to the 40-foot-by-40-foot 'CARBEL Cubes' that the Aerie personnel constructed from the cargo that arrived in the SUBOS elevators. A full load out on a CARBEL platform occupied a 40-foot cube. And, to avoid confusion as to when a load out was to be placed on the schedule, a deck officer assigned CC numbers to the cargo in a PSZ. CE1 would have CC1 in PSZ1, and CC2 would occupy PSZ2. Once a CC was given the okay to be placed on a CARBEL deck, a 40-foot long strip of metal emerged from underneath a hinged, folding plate of steel in the floor. Hidden hydraulic cylinders would then press the raised metal lip against the bottom of the CC, pushing the enormous, one-piece parcel out of its assigned PSZ, by way of rows of closely spaced rollers, and onto its designated CARBEL platform. That was another glaring oddity: the status screens showed all PSZ s to be vacant. Plus, not a single CC existed, according to the monitors.

Armada popped his head from behind CC3, in line for CARBEL Five. He chuckled to himself when he spied the Aerie cameras were incapacitated.

"All right, I see it!" he hollered, "Whoever...or whatever you are...thanks."

Feeling a bit brave, he casually strolled out into the open and walked the length of the Aerie towards the offices for the CARBEL supervisor and deck officer.

He sauntered past the open elevator doors and nonchalantly paraded by the dispatch clerk's kiosk. Unhindered, Armada maneuvered through the stacked pods of nuclear waste awaiting ejection via the WES System.

As he neared the Aerie offices, Armada pressed his back to the wall and sidestepped the remaining distance. Gradually leaning over to peer through the door's window, he was pleased to find the entire staff gathered around the glass-enclosed, private office of the deck captain. Every one of them faced away from the door. Relieved to have not been spotted, he briskly walked to the security portal. The only thing standing in the way between him and Chloe was the door's magnetic lock. He cautiously approached the frame and security panel and remembered to look up for the video cameras.

"I don't know what your point is in all of this," Armada stated, focusing on the blackened power light, "but I'm glad that so far as I can tell, you're on my side."

As soon as he wrapped his fingers around the door's handle, the magnetic lock disengaged and the authorization screen switched from red to green. The automated retinal scanners and motion sensors within the security portal failed to acknowledge his presence.

"This … is … so bizarre!" he declared as he removed his helmet and pressed the button for the elevator.

Armada had barely removed the multitool from his left upper arm pocket when the doors parted to an empty cab. With helmet in hand, he entered the compartment and looked at the video monitor and scanner above the elevator door. He didn't give it a second thought after noticing the loss of power to both.

"Okay," he mumbled, staring at the control panel to the right of the sliding door, "how do I enter my zone access authorization code and floor selection … when I don't have a zone access authorization code and don't know what floor she's on?"

As the words were leaving his lips, the digital keypad suddenly sprang to life. The display showed asterisks stretching the width of the screen, triggering the elevator doors to close. Above the control panel another digital screen lit up with 'Sixteen M,' and the cab immediately began its descent.

"Thanks!" he shouted, removing the piece of SPUD radar-deflecting fabric from the teeth of his multitool. Armada tucked the invaluable swatch in his front pocket, collapsed the multitool, and tucked it into his lower leg zipper pouch.

"The Aerie is more than half a mile above Sixteen M," Armada stated, looking up at the clock above the elevator doors. "That should take no less than twenty minutes. It's almost five-thirty; Chloe said she and her dorm mates wake up at six. That gives me ten minutes to find her, explain what's going on, and find a safe and secure location to hide before the Nursery staff arrive."

Without warning, the screen above the elevator door flashed Sixteen M.

"What?" Armada asked, confused. "That can't possibly be right!"

The cab doors separated, revealing a wall with 'Sixteen M' painted in a large, bright-red font.

"I didn't even feel it stop," he continued lecturing himself as he exited the elevator. "I'd have to be in total free fall to descend a half mile that fast."

Not knowing Chloe's room or dormitory sector numbers, Armada couldn't decide which direction he should take to find her.

"And those drive motors weren't designed for speed," he reasoned looking to his left, then looking right. "The retarders would have engaged if we were descending too quickly."

Finally, he committed to turning to his right in search of Chloe. He hadn't yet raised a foot to move when the overhead lights went out. To his right all was dark, while the lighting in the corridor to his left suddenly returned to normal. Walking slowly down the darkened hallway, he observed that ahead of him there lie an intersection.

"Perfect!" he grumbled. "Another choice ... left, right, or straight."

As he drew closer to the intersecting hallway, the lights in the corridor breaking off to the right abruptly went dark.

"No ... way!" Armada exclaimed.

Before turning to his right, he glanced left at the ceiling-mounted cameras and spied the green LED status lights on all of them; every recessed lightbulb shone brightly. To his right, however, he saw nothing but blackness.

"Okay!" he hollered, picking up his pace. "I understand!"

He then broke into a brisk jog as he steered through the darkened maze. Whenever he came to an area where he wasn't sure which direction he should go, the telltale sign was the absence of light. At all times his movement was concealed in darkness. Be it by human eyes or video camera, his presence was known to no one.

Armada entered one particular corridor and noticed that all the doors had keypads and retinal scanners to the right of the handles. At first glance, he estimated there to be twenty doors, at least, all of which required a zone access authorization code to enter.

"Now, which room is she in?" he asked, panting heavily.

About halfway down the hall, to his left, one of the digital keypad screens began blinking off and on, over and over. He briskly stepped to the door, laid his fingers on the handle, and pushed down. The keypad flashed green and the magnetic lock disengaged. Once in the room, he passed through a lounge area with a couple of cushioned armchairs and sofa, then down a short hallway. Armada crept towards the sleeping quarters, trying desperately not to make a sound.

Emerging from the hall, he was astonished to find the same glowing, vaporous mass hovering near the lower mattress on the last stack of bunk beds. Not knowing what to say to Chloe, or how he should wake her, he stepped forward ever so slowly, keeping his gaze upon the shining cloud. He hadn't yet reached her bunk when the orb rose straight up and levitated against the ceiling.

Armada passed under the illuminated sphere and crouched down beside her. He remembered her being pretty, but now, seeing her again by only the light of the ethereal cloud, she was the most beautiful thing he ever laid eyes on. Delicately resting his elbow on her mattress, he extended his other arm and gently brushed the hair away from her face.

It was at that moment he knew, deep in his heart, he truly loved Chloe. Overjoyed to be reunited, he would have been content to simply sit and watch her sleep.

The shining orb suddenly pulsed with a brilliant flash.

Armada stood, turned away from Chloe, and raised his head. He smiled as the light intensified and penetrated him; through his eyelids, through his suit, it consumed him. How warm and relaxed he felt. As if being hugged internally, the radiance of the dazzling colors soothed away his fear and doubts. The light emitted by the cloud gradually faded, prompting him to open his eyes.

He turned, bent over, and eased himself on to Chloe's bed. Reaching out with his left hand, he tenderly grasped her right shoulder, and, with a gentle shake, softly whispered, "Chloe," but received no response.

He glanced back and up to his right at the clock on the wall.

"Chloe," he repeated, with more volume and a firm nudge. "Hey, c'mon … it's ten 'til six. We gotta move."

Chloe began to stir and yawned deeply. She extended her arms straight out, clenched her fists, and arched her back. After completely stretching, she lay flat on the mattress and rubbed her eyes.

"I don't wanna get up," she groggily complained. "I'll write to you tonight."

"Hey, we can't stay; it's time to go," he said, trying not to laugh.

Then reality hit her.

"Armada!" she ecstatically shouted, springing up with her eyes wide open. "You're here!"

Chloe wrapped her arms around his neck and squeezed tightly as she continued calling his name.

"Armada, Armada! Oh, my gosh! I was so scared! All of a sudden, my terminal lost connection with…."

"Okay, sshh, be quiet. I'm glad to see you, too, but right now…."

Without warning she drew back, placed her hands on his cheeks, pulled him to her, and kissed him.

Surprised by her own impulsive, aggressive actions, she abruptly pushed him away. With a gasp of shock she covered her mouth. Armada sat on her bed with his mouth agape and a quickening pulse. Having formally broken the ice, the long distance romantics lunged at each other. Their mouths met for a more intimate and lengthy replay.

After reveling in the impromptu moment, the couple separated their lips but remained embraced.

"Wow!" Armada blurted, chortling slightly. "Didn't see that coming."

Sensing something wrong, he leaned back and saw tears running down Chloe's cheeks. She quickly covered her face and fell forward against his chest. Her torso shook as she silently sobbed.

"Hey now," he said tenderly, rubbing her back. "Take a breath, let's calm down. Everything's gonna be okay, you'll see."

"How can you say that?" she loudly whispered, sitting upright. "How do you know we'll be safe? Remember what they did to Titan? There's no telling what Wyczthack and White will do when they catch us! And I haven't even told you about what happened a couple of hours ago after I lost connection with you. You won't believe me when I...."

"Sshh," Armada lowly hissed, pressing his finger against her lips. "I have something to tell you as well, but first, you need to see this."

He lowered his hand, took Chloe by her right wrist, and began pulling her arm as he stood up.

"You're absolutely gonna flip when I...," she started to say.

Her words fell short when she clambered out of bed and observed the hovering, shimmering cloud of many colors. She and Armada tightened their grips on each other's hand. They stood next to the bunk bed and gazed in awe at the floating orb. Shutting their eyes, they remained motionless as the ethereal sphere's light suddenly intensified. The illumination was so brilliant that for all but a few fleeting seconds, darkness and shadows ceased to exist.

After a moment, the brilliant light grew dim and the duo opened their eyes.

While staring at the glowing mass, a man's voice reassuringly stated, "Fear not, my children, and know that I am with you."

The cloud suddenly and swiftly crossed the sleeping chambers and passed through the wall, leaving the room pitch-black.

With the dormitory void of all light and power, the twosome reached for one another, entwined their arms, and gently swayed from side to side.

"We gotta go now," Armada whispered. "Take only what you truly need ... you're not ever coming back. Also, do you or one of the other girls have a knife, or pair of scissors? And we'll need something sticky, like tape or Band-Aids."

"Go look in the drawers in our vanity," she whispered back. "One of them is bound to have a couple of bandages. I have a utility blade in my supply trunk. Go to the washroom and I'll get my things together."

"Okay, but hurry; we don't have much time."

"All right."

"Be sure to bring your L-Gen scanner. I have a feeling it's gonna come in handy."

"I will."

Cloaked in darkness, they kissed once more and separated.

Armada clumsily felt his way through the sleeping chambers, past the bank of lockers, and arrived at the doorway to the restrooms and vanity. Not knowing where they kept their personal hygiene supplies, he blindly fished about the countertop. After knocking over something obviously made of glass, he decided to just stay put until Chloe was ready to go.

"Armada," she soon hissed, feeling for his body, "where are you?"

"I'm over here, next to the sinks."

She found his outstretched hand and clutched his fingers tightly as he reeled her into him.

"Did you find anything we can use?"

"I can't see a thing and I don't know what I'm touching. I think I broke something."

"Here," she said, releasing her grasp on his hand. "Let me check the L-Gen. Maybe when I power it up there'll be enough light to help us find what we're looking for."

Chloe removed the laser pulse generator from her small duffle bag and depressed the power button. Sure enough, the rechargeable, battery-powered generator lit up the entire vanity area of the restroom. The pale green underglow of the miniscule keyboard and digital display screen emitted just enough light, allowing her and Armada to inspect her roommates' drawers and personal belongings.

"Ah-ha!" she lowly exclaimed, reaching to the back of a drawer, "I knew it!"

She withdrew her arm and in her hand she held a roll of medical tape.

"Aphrodite Five doesn't like wearing gloves during harvesting, so she's always getting cuts and blisters."

"Excellent! Let's go."

Chloe gently squeezed his bicep and drew him closer.

"Where can we go?" she asked, powering down the L-Gen.

"Don't freak out when I tell you, but I have no clue as to where we're supposed to go. But," he paused and delicately pressed his cheek to hers, "what you're about to witness ... just ... trust me ... you'll have absolutely no worries. Okay?"

She quietly nodded her head in agreement.

"All right, you lead the way."

Chloe grasped his wrist and instinctively led him out of the bathroom, down the short hallway, through the den area, and out the door to the dormitory corridor. Once in the hallway, Armada paused then reached for his upper left arm pocket.

"What're you doing?" she excitedly asked. "Why are we stopping? They're gonna catch us!"

"I don't have time to explain right now, just gimme your utility blade."

Armada removed the tiny swatch of radar-deflecting fabric from his pocket. Chloe reached into her bag and pulled out the small, retractable utility knife.

"Now," he said, taking the knife, "get out the medical tape, and tear it into six four-inch long strips."

He firmly pressed the fabric against the wall and began slicing it down the middle. The dense metal and carbon fiber material was extremely difficult to cut, especially with such a short, thin, and flimsy blade. But just as Chloe finished ripping the last strip of tape, he managed to cut through the few remaining strands of woven wires.

"Here we go," he stated, handing her the tiny patch. "Locate the RFID in my shoulder, lay this directly on top, then tape it in place. This will be our only protection against the WATCHER scans."

"What?" she exclaimed, as Armada unzipped and peeled back his suit. "You didn't disable the program?!"

"No … I didn't. At the moment I was more focused on breathing and staying alive, rather than…."

"Great!" she sarcastically declared. "Now they'll know exactly where we are."

"Just … will you please keep your voice down … and tape the swatch," he snipped.

Chloe gruffly felt his shoulder, located the imbedded microchip, and firmly patted the fabric and tape in place.

"Thanks," he sternly said, pulling up and zipping his suit. "My turn."

Chloe turned away from him, pulled her hair to the side, and tilted her head. Armada poked her exposed flesh, not at all trying to find the transponder buried inside her.

"Ouch!" she complained. "Is it necessary to jab me that hard?"

"All right, found it," he said.

He lay the fabric on her shoulder and swiftly secured it.

"Now, prepare to be amazed," he stated.

With an encouraging smile, he held out his hand and the couple laced their fingers together.

Looking up, he confidently declared, "Okay, we're ready now."

Not knowing what to expect, Chloe's eyes darted about the dimly-lit dormitory corridor. She twisted her neck to see behind them, but nothing out of the ordinary appeared. Feeling fearful, she leaned against Armada's right arm and squeezed tightly.

"I said we're ready!" he repeated with much zeal. "Show us where you want us to go. We'll follow you. Please!"

The brightly illuminated keypads of the secured dormitory doorways suddenly ceased to shine, leaving Chloe and Armada once again stranded in total darkness.

"Uh...is this where I'm supposed to be amazed?" she smartly mumbled.

"Hold on," he snapped. "Just...hold on a second."

From out of nowhere the shimmering orb appeared, passing between them, and zoomed down the corridor.

"C'mon!" he said, with a yank on her arm.

"You can talk to it?" she asked as they broke into a run.

"It hears me, I know that much!"

Chloe chased after Armada as he followed and tried to keep in pace with the glowing cloud of swirling colors.

She watched in amazement and curiousity how the orb controlled and manipulated the power. At first she didn't catch it, but after completing their third turn, it suddenly dawned on her: wherever the orb goes, the lights, video cameras, motion sensors, and embedded microphones shut down. Furthermore, power doesn't return until after they pass through the darkened areas.

It's protecting us, she thought as she ran. *It's shielding us from being seen.*

She surmised that this thing, whatever it was or wherever it came from, had chosen to reveal itself to them, specifically, and was purposely guiding and leading them to safety.

Armada rounded the next corner and froze in his tracks.

The shining mass was hovering in front of a junction of three hallways and an elevator. Suddenly, the orb increased in size, as if to block the duo from advancing any further. Chloe joined him a moment later and stood silent and still by his side.

"I think we're supposed to stop here," he suggested. "What is this place?"

"This is one of the unutilized wings of our dormitories," Chloe replied. "I heard they're different from our normal rooms. I think that these come with larger beds, private restrooms, and showers. But I've never known of these suites being used … ever. It's like a hotel just waiting for customers."

Armada pondered the information, then humbly asked the sphere, "Are we supposed to stop here? Is this where you want us to go?"

He waited for a sign of some sort, but the sphere showed no response.

"Or, maybe we're not supposed to go down this corridor or use that particular elevator?"

The sphere emitted a brilliant flash of purple light.

"That's it? Don't use this elevator and corridor? Is that what you're trying to tell us?"

The orb confirmed his guess by once again emitting a pulse of purple light.

It quickly shrank to its original size, meandered down the hallway to Armada's right, and came to an abrupt halt at the next-to-last doorway on the left. Armada witnessed the door swing open and watched the orb enter the room.

They approached the half-opened door, entered the suite, and swiftly inspected their surroundings. Chloe then lowered her bag to the floor and followed Armada out of the room to the end of the wide, lightless hallway. He reached out and began feeling the wall for a motion sensor or manual light switch. The couple was caught off guard when the glowing orb passed through the wall, rose above them, and shone brightly. Both were amazed with what lay before them.

"It's an atrium," Chloe remarked, lowly. "It brought us to an atrium."

Armada briskly moved ahead of her to a series of several wide doors, hinged on both sides, and two stainless steel, roll-down shutters. Chloe followed a curved walkway to a vast open area with stacks of boxes containing unassembled tables and chairs. Only a few had been removed from their cardboard shells and put together.

"Chloe!" Armada loudly whispered. "Come check this out!"

She hurriedly doubled back to the pathway entrance and saw the orb on the far side of the atrium, hovering next to one of the multihinged partitions.

"Chloe! C'mon!" he beckoned.

"Okay, I'm here," she announced. "What is it?"

"Do you know where we are?" Armada laughingly asked.

"No, not really. But from the looks of it out there, I'd say we're in a general social area, like a commons."

The sphere of swirling colors unexpectedly zipped to the middle of the atrium, swelled up like a hot air balloon, and blazed magnificently.

"It brought us to a cafeteria!" he ecstatically hollered. "It led us directly to a source of food and water. Isn't this amazing?"

Now bathed in radiant white light, the food service area sprang to life. Stacks and trays of fine China, silverware, boxes containing crystal glasses, pots, pans, and utensils; everything essential to the preparation of food. Steam tables, flat grills, convection ovens, deep fryers, gas grills; the discoveries seemed endless.

They excitedly wandered through the gargantuan kitchen, calling out to each other what they spied.

As they approached the spacious dry goods area, the two split up and repeated the process from both sides of the enormous shelving units. Similar to a home improvement store, the distance between aisles was wide enough to accommodate a forklift or electric pallet jack.

"Crackers, potato chips, pasta, mixed nuts, peanut butter…," Armada rattled off.

Chloe answered with "Sugar, brown sugar, flour, corn grits, steel cut oats, honey, syrup…."

After a sightseeing tour of the palletized bulk food, they then came upon three humongous refrigerated units resting side by side. Each was equipped with a tall, roll-down overhead door on one end and several extremely wide steel doors that were disbursed evenly down the length of one side.

"Shall we?" Armada asked cordially, bowing slightly.

"Yes, let's shall," she replied with a curtsey.

He gave a slight tug of the handle and pulled the heavy metal door open. After passing through a hanging plastic curtain, the duo were amazed with what they saw.

"See?" Armada asked. "This proves my point! Wyczthack and White are up to something big and they're prepping for a limited number of survivors. Let me rephrase that: a well-planned, limited number of pre-selected survivors."

Chloe didn't respond.

Stacked high on industrial shelving units, the couple found pallets and crates of frozen food. The reality of Armada's hypothesis became clear as they slowly strode the gargantuan deep freeze.

"Sirloin, ground beef, chicken breast, ribeye steak … this is incredible."

Chloe walked ahead of Armada to the opposite end of the chilly storage container.

She began calling out the content of the shrink-wrapped boxes as she slowly stepped in Armada's direction, "Frozen catfish, salmon, shrimp, squid, trout, albacore tuna, thresher shark, mako, tilapia, mahi-mahi…."

"Meatloaf, pork chops, pork tenderloin, filet, baby back ribs, roast, brisket…."

The pair hollered their findings to one another as they gradually approached the center of the frigid storeroom.

"How high would you estimate these racks are, including inventory?" he asked.

"No less than twenty feet. Twenty-one to twenty-two feet maximum," she replied.

They stood in the middle of the freezer, gawking in disbelief at the volume and variety of frozen food. After a few moments of silent incredulity, the twosome turned and exited through the door at the end of the unit.

They faced the overhead door and looked above the top of the frame. There, below an amber-domed flashing light, was a sign reading 'FZ1.' As they strolled over to the next unit, its sign read 'FZ2.' Continuing on, the third unit was labeled 'RF1.'

"What're we doing?"

"I want to confirm something," he said.

Armada tugged on the handle and the couple entered the refrigerated unit. The door closed behind them with a dense thud that echoed throughout the cavernous room.

"Ah-ha!" Armada stated, pointing, "See? Empty! I knew it!"

"So? What does that matter?"

"This unit is for fresh, perishable foods. Milk, fruits, vegetables, stuff that's gonna be used and consumed now, or very soon."

"I still don't understand where you're going with this."

"It's empty. There's nothing here. They haven't started sending up perishables from the docks, or down from Eden. We've still got time to figure this all out."

Chloe's face lit up when she understood Armada's observation, "Oh! No fresh food means Wyczthack isn't ready!"

"Exactly!"

"So when we find them sending up perishables, that'll be the signal that Cain and Dr. White are getting ready to pull the plug!"

"You got it!"

Chloe sprang at Armada in joyous excitement, wrapping her arms around his neck. He clutched her firmly against him, swinging her from side to side.

"Oh, my gosh!" she exclaimed, releasing her grasp.

"What's wrong?" he asked, lowering her to the floor.

"C'mon!" she demanded, yanking his hand. "I just thought of something."

"I don't know why I didn't notice this earlier," she confessed as she briskly led him out of the cooler. "Look at the floor markings."

Chloe pointed down at the black and yellow 'Caution' stripes running throughout the maze of shelving.

"It's painted for forklift traffic. They go into the deep freeze and refrigerated units through the overhead doors on the ends and people use the side entries. Which tells me they can deliver anything at any time, from the docks or Eden. There's another elevator chamber we haven't seen yet."

The two followed the markings past the dry goods and bulk storage shelves to a battery charging station. There they found three six-thousand-pound-capacity electric forklifts. Beside those were four electric pallet jacks and extra batteries for all seven machines.

Armada climbed up into the driver's seat on one of the forklifts and turned the key.

"It's got a full charge," he said, looking at the gauge.

Chloe walked ahead of Armada, out of the charging station, and stopped in front of the hidden SUBOS cargo elevator. Armada joined her, staring at the shiny metal overhead door.

He noticed that the door opened and closed by way of digital keypad and retinal scanner.

"Well, I'm assuming that when someone is notified of an arrival, then that someone is responsible for confirming that what's on the manifest matches up with what's actually on hand."

They both stepped toward a freestanding kiosk to the side of the rolling door. Armada powered up the tablet and logged on using his forged Dr. White credentials. The screen had only a few preset commands and functions and three input tabs named 'MANIFEST #,' 'MANIFEST SEARCH,' and 'S/R AUTHORIZATION.' He tapped the 'MANIFEST SEARCH' tab and selected the 'History' command. In a flash, a list of materials and goods received filled the screen. Dates, manifest numbers, time, and release and receive authorization codes, every item sent to Sixteen M was listed in chronological order.

"When was the last harvest from Eden shipped out?" he asked Chloe as he perused the data.

"Um, I'd say at eight or nine last night. Why?"

"And who generates manifest requests from Eden?"

"Who specifically, we don't know … we never deal with names, just ID numbers. Orders for distribution are inserted in descending sequence. Everything is harvested, sent to seventeen for cleaning and portioning, and crated up. That's where they physically set the manifests in order. All we do is tend the garden, harvest the produce, and record yields. Why?"

"Well, if I can create fake login credentials, I should be able to generate an artificial distribution request. That's if we can find a terminal. The trick will be making an order big enough to accommodate us for a short while without much waste, but not so small that it sends up a red flag."

"How then do we receive the order when it arrives?" she inquired. "We'll be found for sure when we use the retinal scanner to open the elevator door."

She was right. Even though they covered their RFID chips with the radar-deflecting fabric from the SPUD, the retinal scanner would show exactly where they were and at what time the scanner was accessed.

"I'll just have to figure it out later, not right now," he said as he powered down the kiosk tablet.

With one final glance at the roll-down door, the pair made their way to the main kitchen entrance.

When they reached the dry goods storage area, Armada plucked a shrink-wrapped case of bottled water and hefted it atop his shoulder. Chloe opened a carton of organic crackers, removed one box, and peeled back the top. Armada glanced up at the tops of the industrial-grade shelving units, stopped dead in his tracks, and lowered the case of bottled water from his shoulder.

"Why'd you stop?" she asked.

"Look!" he said, flabbergasted. "Look at the lights!"

Chloe cast her gaze upwards as well, slowly turning in a circle. "What? Am I missing something? What am I supposed to be looking at?"

"I'll be right back," he excitedly stated. "I wanna check something."

Chloe stood in the middle of the aisle and watched as Armada began running to the rear of the kitchen.

"It's in the prep area!" he shouted.

A few seconds later, she heard him yell out, "It's in the freezers and refrigerator, too!"

"WHAT'S IN THERE?" she hollered as he ran out of sight towards the charging station and elevator.

"Woo-hoo!" he screamed, "It's everywhere!"

He suddenly came racing out of the charging station, shouting as he ran, "Chloe! Chloe!"

"Armada, Armada!" she mockingly replied, waving her hands.

He ran directly at her, swooped her up in his arms, and spun them around and around, laughing out loud as they twirled. She squealed in girlish delight at his display of genuine, heartfelt joy.

"What? Tell me, you idiot! Why are you so excited?"

"Look up and tell me what you see," he instructed, panting heavily as he released her.

"I have been. I still don't understand what it is you want me to notice."

Armada laughed as he spoke, "Look at the lights and tell me what you see. C'mon, look hard, think."

"Ugh! You're beginning to annoy me!" she complained, half smiling. "Okay, looking hard, thinking about the lights. I'm looking, I'm looking, at the lights. Well, that one isn't on, and ... those two aren't turned on, and...."

Chloe immediately twisted around to face Armada and covered her mouth. Tears welled up in her eyes.

"Oh, my gosh, Armada. They're all off!"

"I know, I know!"

"But how? That's impossible!"

"I don't know! But whatever that thing is out there, it's powerful enough to send light through walls and around corners. Look at the leg of the shelving unit."

It was at that moment they both realized the shelves, support brackets, and frames didn't cast a shadow on the tile floor. Not only that, but the more they concentrated on what they were looking at, it was quickly discovered that there were no shadows anywhere, including themselves.

"Oh, Armada! Look at us!" she laughed.

He picked up the case of bottled water, took Chloe by the hand, and led her to the atrium.

Armada let go of her hand, crossed the atrium, and delivered the water to their room.

Chloe stood almost directly under the orb, basking quietly in its brilliance. As he was returning, it began to shrink and diminish in luminosity. In just a few moments, the massive sphere resumed its original size. It came down from its position near the ceiling and hovered in front of them before leading them back to their room. The couple entered the suite, followed by the orb.

The door closed behind it without a sound.

Armada and Chloe sat on the end of one of the queen-sized beds as the glowing mass levitated in front of them.

"Fear not my children, and know that I am with you, always," the man's voice reassuringly stated.

"How long are we supposed to stay here?" Armada humbly asked. "How will we know when it's safe to leave the atrium and kitchen area? I mean, how do you want us to communicate with you?"

"I will show you miracles, signs, and wonders. Trust in Me, I will not forsake you."

"Do you...," Chloe started to speak, but the glowing mass of light abruptly evaporated, leaving the couple alone and in the dark.

They sat quiet and still.

Armada rose from the bed and pulled Chloe to her feet. They held each other and gently rocked back and forth. He withdrew himself from her arms, then guided her to the second bed. He gently pushed her back on the mattress, knelt down, and removed her shoes and socks. Remembering he saw where the closet was located, he awkwardly fished his way through their new dwelling. When he touched and recognized the closet doorknob, he swung it open and groped for a blanket and pillow.

"What are you doing?" she asked, giggling.

"I'm looking for the bedsheets."

His hand landed on a shelf with four pillows and, above that, another shelf holding two thick, fluffy blankets. He grabbed two of the pillows and both blankets, tossed one of each on his barren mattress, and walked back to Chloe's bed. He playfully flung the pillow, smacking her square in the face.

"Uh ... thanks!" she sarcastically grunted.

"My pleasure!"

She tucked the new, billowy pillow under her head and rolled on to her right side. Standing over her, he clutched the edge of the blanket, shook it open, and spread it out evenly across the bed, covering Chloe in the process. He sat down next to her, extended his left arm, and, without a word, delicately ran his fingers through her soft hair while listening to her breathing. She scooted closer to him until her head was nearly touching his hip.

"I can't hardly believe what all has happened today," she mumbled.

"You and me both," he whispered back.

"Wanna know what else I can't believe?"

"Sure."

"That you actually came for me."

"I told you one day I would."

Chloe grinned and reached for his left hand. She pulled it down out of her hair and pressed his palm against her cheek while lightly clinging to his fingers. Although she had always been surrounded with a multitude of sisters, for the first time in her life, Chloe didn't feel utterly and completely alone.

The room was dark and the pillow, blanket, and bed were soft and warm. She yawned deeply, closed her weary eyes, and fell fast asleep.

CHAPTER 23

MIA

"What?" said Garret, "Would you please repeat that?"

"I said I'm unable to establish contact with Armada Nine," Euclid stated. "In addition, I've yet to determine a physical location for him."

"What you're sayin' is you haven't seen him and you haven't spoken to him. Correct?"

"Yes, sir."

"Hold on, Euclid."

"Zeus," Garret said, muting his headset microphone. "Do a quick scan of all comm-links and transponders. Make sure they're all paired up."

"Yes, sir," Zeus replied.

"Euclid?" Garret called out. "What's your current position? And at what time did you couple up with your POG?"

"I'm on the underside of Cloud Eight. Armada Nine and I usually transfer to the POG together at around 6:40. I arrived at our normal time, powered up the POG at ten 'til, and have been waiting on Armada to coordinate the CC disbursements. What do you want me to do? Everybody's just ... waiting. Should I begin...."

"Have you observed any emergency strobes?" Garret asked, interrupting Euclid.

"Sir, all transponders are showing to be matched," Zeus whispered. "I'm showing no irregularities."

"Hold on, Euclid," Garret snapped. "Zeus, shut up when I'm talking!"

"Yes, sir."

"Armada Nine, this is Nest Command, do you copy?" Garret asked, waited, and repeated his call, "Armada Nine, this is Nest Command, do you copy?"

Armada failed to reply.

"Now, Zeus, repeat that, and then shut up."

"Yes, sir. I was saying that my scan shows no signal irregularities between helmet transponders and comm-links. Every one of them is matched."

"So you found Armada's comm-link signal?"

"His specifically, no. But every comm-link signal has been identified and Armada Nine isn't being recognized. So, from the looks of it … he's not out there."

"Well, then … let's…," Garret stammered, and again muted his microphone. He bit the inside of his lip while contemplating his next move.

"Okay," he began. "Zeus? You, Perseus, and Mercury, go search his dorm, his locker, the bathing stations, everywhere, and find what you can."

The three amateur sleuths removed their headsets, unfastened their seat restraints, and swiftly exited the Nest.

"Attention! Your attention, please," Garret commanded, opening all communication channels. "This is Garret Brock, Arena One supervisor. I'm issuing a Code Red Emergency Directive. All personnel, I repeat, all personnel are to return to their assigned POG immediately. Please retract your spools and remain at your POG until further notice. If you're currently in transition, or have already received your CC allocations, please secure your loads and recoil to your designated air bank as soon as possible. All communication transmissions will be temporarily suspended until further notice. Garret out."

Garret turned his gaze to the wall of video monitors and watched as Zeus, Mercury, and Perseus wandered through the cylindrical corridors.

One by one the brothers reached their destinations. He watched them inspect Armada's dorm room, the cafeteria, Arena, bathing stations, cargo bays, air locks, and EVA Deployment Center.

"Sir, there's nothing here," "I'm not finding any trace of him," and "We can't seem to locate Armada anywhere" were the only responses to Garret's request in tracking down the missing clone.

"All right," Garret grunted in frustration, "get back here, pronto!"

He reopened all communication channels and barked, "Once all spools have recoiled, power down the POG units for thirty seconds. After completing the shutdown cycle, you will then disconnect your comm-link quick couplers. Only after confirming that ALL comm-links have been disconnected are you to restart the POG units. DO NOT, I repeat, DO NOT connect yourself to the oxygen generator until the transmission signal has full strength. Once the Nest has synched up with the generators, you can then reattach yourself to your spools. That should reset everybody's EVA suits to the POGs and the Nest, and allow us to identify and locate Armada Nine. Garret out."

Perseus, Zeus, and Mercury, emerged from the cylindrical corridor, floated by Garret, and briskly fastened themselves into their seats at the Nest control panel.

"Okay, let's see what happens now," Garret stated optimistically.

The four men watched the monitors displaying the signals being received from the quartet of POGs. In near unison, the screens went black.

"All four oxygen generators are now off-line," Perseus commented.

Garret gazed out the Nest windows at the four hundred men hovering about the dormant air banks and spool carriages. Even though they weren't receiving fresh oxygen, the EVA suits retained a fifteen-minute supply of air that was continuously filtered via a battery-powered purifier that recharged itself whenever the suits were connected to the POG.

"Thirty seconds," Zeus stated.

"All right, all right, all right," Garret interjected, clapping his hands. "Now we'll find him!"

The video monitors remained dark and lifeless.

Garret glanced again at the throng of inanimate clones.

Suddenly, one of the monitors flashed with activity, then another, then the last two. All four screens displayed the message 'Acquiring Signal,' with a stopwatch symbol underneath. In no time at all, the screen headers appeared identifying each of the four oxygen generators: POG 1, POG 2, POG 3, and POG 4.

"I'm showing all four generators are now online with full signal strength, and no disruptions or irregularities," Mercury informed Garret.

"Now … if I'm correct in my thought process … we should, in theory, be able to watch everyone hook up and identify which line Armada Nine is using."

"And then what?" asked Zeus.

"First things first," Garret replied. "We need to find him. Keep your eyes open for his transponder to register."

The anxious quartet stared at the brightly colored computer screens.

Like the fireworks at an Independence Day celebration, the four monitors busily displayed the comm-link and transponder signals as each of the clones connected themselves to their POG generators.

"Anybody see him yet?" Garret loudly asked.

"No," and "Not yet," the trio answered.

"Ugh!"

It wasn't long before the Nest stopped acknowledging new signals from the four POG units.

"Sir?" Mercury spoke up, "I'm showing that all comm-link and transponder signals are correctly paired up, and there are no isolated or unmatched spools."

The three brothers turned to face Garret. He sat at his chair, stewing in anger, frustration, and confusion.

"I don't get it!" he blasted. "Will one of you please help me to understand this? Armada isn't anywhere to be found on this vessel. We can't connect to the transponder in his helmet. He hasn't activated his emergency strobe. Euclid hasn't had contact with him, visually or verbally. None of the four POGs are acknowledging his EVA suit, and he isn't responding to repeated requests from me or Euclid to identify his location."

The triplets sat in silence, absorbing Garret's flustered recitation.

"Am I forgetting something?" he bellowed.

"Sir?" Perseus spoke up. "His suit was missing from his locker."

"Which one? From where?"

"From the EVA deployment center. Everything is missing."

Garret rapped his fingers on the arm of his chair, fuming over the inexplicable disappearance of one of the clones. But not just any clone was missing; it was Armada Nine he couldn't locate, the best and brightest, and potentially the most dangerous.

"Okay, listen up," Garret snapped. "Here's what we're gonna do. Zeus, review the video feeds from his dorm starting at 10:00 p.m. I wanna know when he left his bed. Mercury, open Armada's data file and see where he went last night, beginning at 10:00 p.m., up 'til 8:00 a.m. Perseus, open all audio records for the entire Arena... he's bound to have spoken to somebody. Somehow, someway, our boy has devised a method of making himself disappear. What we need to do is find the secret to make him reappear."

The three stooges blankly stared at Garret.

"Well?" he growled. "Get to it!"

Garret's crew hurriedly set themselves to task while he reached out for assistance and placed a call.

"Aerie Dispatch Office," a man said. "How may I direct your call?"

"This is Arena One Supervisor Garret Brock. Tell me, who's the deck officer on duty?"

"Lucas Shipman, sir. If you'll please hold while I transfer your call."

Garret sat and observed his trio of sleuths as they investigated Armada's vanishing act.

"Shipman," a voice suddenly stated.

"Lucas? Garret, up on Arena One. Say, have any of your people come across an individual transfer in the last eight hours?"

"From or to?"

"From."

"I believe that would be a no, sir."

"Well, would you mind double-checking for me?"

"No, I don't mind at all. But it's not a case of whether I mind or not. We just conducted our shift change, oh, not more than fifteen minutes ago, and all manifests were signed off. From 9:00 p.m. last night to 7:00 a.m. this morning, every CARBEL load out has been accounted for … and not one blemish. Captain Anderson and I spend near half an hour every morning going through discrepancies and miss-ships. And I can assure you, no one has been accidentally overlooked for an individual personnel transfer."

"What about your cameras and monitors … are you experiencing any problems?" Garret pushed.

"What do you mean by 'problems'? Problems like what?"

"Sir?" Mercury loudly whispered.

"You know…," Garret stammered, waving his hand at Mercury, "glitches, hiccups, gaps…."

"Sir?" Mercury again interrupted.

"Shut up!" Garret hissed.

"Excuse me?!" Lucas quipped.

"Not you, Lucas. I'm in the middle of … of … oh, let me call you back."

Garret disconnected his headset and pulled the earpiece away.

"What, Mercury? What? What is it you don't understand about 'Shut up!' whenever I'm conversing with another person?"

"I'm sorry, sir, I just thought…."

"Just tell me what's so important and then shut up."

"Yes, sir. If you'll watch the monitor…."

Mercury extracted a video record of Armada and his dorm mates from the previous night.

"What am I supposed to be looking at?" Garret asked, scratching his head.

"Notice the time stamp … this is the audio and video feeds from Armada's room, beginning at 11:18 last night."

"Okay, I'm noticing."

"Well," Mercury began, moving his mouse cursor in a circular motion on the monitor, "Odysseus Two rolled on to his side and cleared his throat, activating the cameras and microphone. The condenser mic is calibrated to engage when a sound of thirty decibels or more is detected. So a cough, sneeze, yawn … anything literally above that of a whisper, and both camera and microphone will automatically begin recording."

"Yes, Mercury, I'm fully aware of the calibrations."

"Okay, so there's a timer programmed into the cameras. They'll record as long as there's detected movement or a sound of thirty decibels or more. As soon as the sensors stop registering motion or noise, fifteen seconds later the cameras automatically stop recording."

"All right already! I know! I know! What?"

"Sir, here's Odysseus turning over and rustling around. And on this bunk … is Armada Nine. Now watch. Eleven eighteen, then eleven nineteen, and … eight, nine, ten, eleven, twelve, thirteen … and … camera off."

Garret slumped to his side and rested his chin in the palm of his hand while Mercury made the transition to a different video file.

"Okay, so just now we saw Armada in his bunk as of eleven-nineteen. Right?"

"Right," Garret mumbled.

"And now, at … two minutes past twelve, we find … this."

Mercury played the 27-second clip, but Garret remained unimpressed. "And?"

"And what, sir? Didn't you catch it?"

"Catch what? I didn't notice anything."

"Sir," Mercury began and restarted the video, moving his cursor in a circle on the monitor, "keep your eyes on the last stack to the right. So Hades Thirteen turns to his side … cameras come on, and … stop."

Mercury paused the digital video and pointed at the screen.

"See? He's gone. At some point, between 11:19 and 12:02, Armada disappeared."

"What…?" Garret grumbled. "Show me both clips, back to back."

Zeus and Perseus put their investigations on hold as they focused on Mercury's discovery. Mercury brought the two video segments to the main monitor screen and placed them side by side. He played them several times for Garret and his brothers.

"All right, I've seen enough."

Garret silently peered out at the stars for a moment, then addressed his assistants.

"Thanks to Mercury, we now know that Armada managed to leave his dormitory, undetected, between 11:19 and just after midnight. So ... what we now need to figure out is ... where did he run off to? I wanna see all recordings, for every camera, from eleven o'clock to twelve fifteen, PRONTO."

Garret reached out for his headset floating next to him and reconnected it to the transmitter that hung from his belt. As he watched the video monitors, one question kept running through his mind: *How? How could Armada elude the retinal scanners when entering or exiting a room? How was he able to avoid detection by the video camera motion sensors? How did he manage to gain entrance to the EVA deck and activate the air locks without an authorization code?*

Reluctantly, the burly supervisor surrendered himself to the Engenechem safety protocols and entered the extension number for Riggs Woodburn on his cordless transmitter.

"Woodburn," Riggs said, drolly.

"Riggs? This is Garret. Have you got a minute?"

"A minute? Sure. What's up?"

"I ... I got a situation ... we ... we got a situation on our hands that's giving me...."

"What's the problem, Garret?"

"Somebody's missing ... and we can't seem to locate them."

"Missing?" Riggs repeated, sitting back in his chair. "Who's missing?"

"Armada Nine," Garret sheepishly replied.

"Armada?! Armada Nine? How did you...? Armada Nine? Really?"

"Yes, sir."

"Have you conducted a full sweep?"

"Yes, sir."

"Did you attempt to contact him? What about the EVA transponder?"

"Yes, sir, we attempted both verbal communication and location positioning via the transponder, but failed to make contact."

"Did anyone observe an emergency strobe?"

"No, sir."

"What about POG verification? Did you ensure all comm-links are correctly paired? Maybe there's a digital anomaly."

"Yes, sir, we did a hard shutdown cycle on all four generators, but he didn't register during the reboot. And we didn't show any anomalies."

"What about 'WATCHER'? Did you track his chip?"

"Uh...."

"Have you not been given access to the chip tracking program?"

"No, sir. I knew they had them, but I was never...."

"All right, all right," Riggs repeated, spinning around in his chair to face his computer. "I'll see to it you get clearance, but for now I'll take a look."

Garret waited for Riggs to open the RFID chip tracking program and report his findings. The trio in front of him had already identified and isolated several video and audio files for the time period he'd requested.

"Okay...," Riggs suddenly stated, "Evan...Armada...Nine. Let's just take a peek at where Mr. Sneaky Pants has gotten off to. Here we go. Ready?"

"Yes, sir."

"Armada went to his dormitory sleeping quarters at, oh, somewhere between 9:30 and 9:45. It looks like he was in his room at 9:45, 10:00, 10:15...up to 11:15. At 11:30 a.m. he was in Corridor One, between the cafeteria and Dormitory D. At 11:45 he...."

"Hold on, Riggs," Garret interrupted. "Y'all listen up...stop what you're doing and pull the video records for these zones as I call them out. Okay, Riggs, tell me again where he was at 11:30?"

"Corridor One, between Dormitory D and the cafeteria."

"Eleven thirty, Corridor One, from Dormitory D to the cafeteria," Garret repeated loudly.

"At 11:45 Armada was in the Arena and remained there up 'til 3:45."

"Arena One, 11:45 to 3:45."

"At 4:00 he was back in Corridor One, between Dormitory A and the shower station."

"Four a.m., Corridor One from Dormitory A to the showers. Perseus, go to the Arena kiosk and review the user history. I wanna know what all he was doing for four hours."

Perseus quickly unbuckled his seat harness, disconnected his headset, and jettisoned himself from the Nest into Corridor One.

"All right, moving on," Riggs announced. "Four fifteen, Armada was…."

"Was where?" Garret anxiously inquired. "Where does it show he went?"

"I don't know if this is accurate, but it shows him out with the SPUDs."

"I want all HALO camera records," Garret snapped.

Zeus and Mercury turned to briefly face each other before taking a quick glance back at Garret.

"Don't be looking at me; do your job!"

"Garret, HALO cameras and all video feeds can only be accessed by me, the Aerie deck officers, and CARBEL deployment supervisors. I'll review them myself and let you … wait a minute … something's not…," Riggs voice tapered off, as if he were suddenly distracted.

"What? Something's not what?"

"WATCHER shows Armada in Corridor One at 4:00 a.m., he was with the SPUDs at 4:15, and at 5:15 he was on the Aerie. Geez! This can't possibly be right! At 5:30 he entered the SUBOS, and at 5:45 he was on Sixteen M."

"What?" Garret hollered, staring wide-eyed at Mercury and Zeus. "Repeat that last statement."

"The WATCHER scan shows Armada entered the SUBOS at 5:30, and on Sixteen M … at 5:45."

"That's impossible!" Garret again shouted. "Those personnel elevators cannot descend almost a mile in less than fifteen minutes. The retarders would have engaged and slowed 'em down."

"Hey, I'm just telling you what the program reported. I know the elevators weren't meant to descend at that speed."

"Okay, so where is he now?" Garret asked. "It's almost 9:00. Where's he been for the past three hours?"

Garret waited for Riggs to answer his question but received no answer. Mercury and Zeus again twisted around towards Garret.

"Riggs? Are you there?"

"Yeah, I'm still here. But…according to the scan, as of 6:00 a.m. … Armada doesn't appear to be … anywhere."

"What do you mean by 'anywhere'?"

"By anywhere, I mean his RFID chip isn't registering a physical location … it's like he just disappeared."

As Riggs was finishing his explanation, Perseus called out to Mercury over the kiosk microphone. "Merc, open a live feed to Arena camera 0509."

"Hold on, Riggs, I'm putting you on broadcast," Garret stated. "Riggs, are you there?"

"Yes."

Zeus tapped into camera 0509 and brought the live stream onto the large monitor screen. Perseus had his face directly in front of the camera lens.

"Perseus, can you hear me?" Garret hollered.

"Yes, sir. I have you patched through the kiosk terminal speaker."

"Good. I have both you and Riggs Woodburn on broadcast here in the Nest. Now, what all did you find?"

Perseus pushed himself back and away from the camera and grasped the edge of the kiosk top.

"Okay, I logged onto the terminal and went through the user history."

As he spoke, Perseus would occasionally glance up at the video camera.

"There hasn't really been much activity. Until, that is, I discovered that almost every night, right around midnight or so … someone has been logging on and staying on 'til 3:00 or 4:00 a.m."

"What are they doing? Who's logging on? Is it Armada?" Garret inquired.

"Well, it's weird … and I don't know if this is right, but … this terminal shows that Dr. White has been using it."

"What?" Garret shouted.

"That's what the history says … it's Dr. White's credentials."

"Perseus?" Riggs hollered out.

"Yes, sir?"

"I want you to go back one day at a time and tell me the times when Doc White was logged on. I'll compare those days and times with the scan and Armada's movements. Zeus? You and Mercury pull up camera video records for Armada's dorm at the same time. We'll go back one day at a time, every day, whether or not the Arena kiosk terminal shows anyone has logged on."

The five men spent several hours reviewing taped footage of Armada's dorm and the Arena, cross comparing those video clips with the dates that Dr. White was supposedly logged onto the kiosk terminal to see if those dates matched up with the records of Armada's movement in the WATCHER scan.

At around two o'clock, Riggs gave his summary on their findings.

"I've come to the conclusion that Dr. White wasn't really remotely logging on to the Arena server. That was all Armada. Second, the scan on his chip, coupled with the video records for his dorm, line up perfectly with dates and times he was in the arena, AND they match on the nights he didn't leave the room."

"I agree with you on those aspects," Garret commented, "but, that doesn't answer the questions: Where is he now? Why isn't WATCHER picking him up anymore? How did he gain access to the Aerie, the SUBOS, and the Nursery on Sixteen M without any zone authorization codes, AND bypass every retinal scanner? Why do the motion sensors not appear to function properly whenever he's in the Arena?"

X^N

"Garret, I don't know!" Riggs barked. "I don't know. We'll … we'll just have to figure it out. But for now … we gotta call Wyczthack and White."

"I'm outta here," Perseus commented, and powered down the kiosk terminal.

"Crap!" Garret hissed, vigorously scratching his head with both hands. "Crap! Crap! Crap!"

Zeus and Mercury stared straight ahead at their monitors, pretending to be working and oblivious of Garret's comments.

"Sorry, chief," Riggs offered, "but we gotta follow protocols."

"I know. Wyczthack's gonna flip, and then they're gonna kill me."

Riggs called Dr. White's extension.

Garret put his headset on and disconnected the broadcast conversation. Perseus entered the Nest and made a beeline for his seat without so much as one word, or look, in Garret's direction.

Just as Perseus was situated at his chair, Garret felt a vibration coming from his transmitter. Pressing the blinking light, he was instantly connected to Riggs and Dr. White.

"Garret Brock," he said, as jovial as could be.

"Garret, I got Dr. White on the line."

"Yes, sir."

"Mr. Brock, Riggs tells me that the two of you have a peculiar…."

Dr. White stopped in midsentence at the sound of a knock on his door.

"Excuse me, gentlemen…. Yes? … Oh, do come in. You're right on time. I have both Mr. Woodburn and Mr. Brock on the line. Something about a peculiar situation."

"This is Dr. Wyczthack speaking. Why, pray tell, do you consider your situation to be peculiar?"

Garret and Riggs winced in mental preparation for the verbal assault they were about to receive.

"Hello? Is anyone there? Or is this simply a waste of my precious time?"

"No, no!" Riggs exclaimed. "No, sir, this will, uh … definitely not be a waste of your time."

Garret started with the encounter he and Euclid had earlier that morning, and Riggs jumped in with his involvement that began at 9:00 a.m. At first, doctors Wyczthack and White didn't sound concerned at all that Armada was missing. However, as the conversation progressed, both men stood, removed their coats and ties, and paced about as they shouted out their questions.

During the conference call, Riggs and Garret heard another knock at the door to Dr. White's office.

"Not now!" Dr. White gruffly roared. "Riggs, I don't care if you...."

The person on the other side of the door dared to defy Dr. White and not only knocked again, loudly, but opened the door.

"What do you not understand about 'Not now'?" Cain shrieked.

"Sir?" Cassandra Hall called, poking her head around the door. "I'm so terribly sorry for intruding, but we have an emergency that's really quite extraordinary."

"We're in the process of diffusing our own emergency!" Cain shouted as Cassandra entered the office.

The handsomely dressed woman, who happened to oversee Curriculum Development for the female clones in the Nursery, was more than persistent and shut the door behind her. "Yes, sir, but, you see ... one of our clones...."

"Thank you, Cassandra, but we've already been made aware of the predicament and are attempting to resolve the problem as we speak. So, if you'll please...," Dr. White added.

"How did you know she's missing?" the woman confusedly asked. "We just figured out ourselves she's gone!"

Cain and Dr. White blankly and silently stared at the woman for a moment.

Dr. Wyczthack closed his eyes and barked "She!?"

CHAPTER 24

DRINKING BUDDIES

"I'm hungry," Chloe stated. "Are you?"

"I'm getting there," Armada replied.

"Do you think they've discovered we're missing yet?"

"Oh, yeah. Definitely! For me, I'd say Garret knew something was up at around 7:30 or so. He probably freaked out and asked Riggs for help in locating me. What about you? When do you think they realized you were MIA?"

"Well," Chloe began, leaning back in her chair. "If it was Ashlynn, she would have noticed me not being at my station by at least 8:00, if not soon thereafter. We have very small windows of time to ascend to Eden from the CARBEL. Once we reach the Halo, every transition is monitored until each of us has registered our boarding authorization codes and logged into our designated stations. Since I wasn't on the Aerie for loading on the CARBEL, I wouldn't show up then as a worker that wasn't accounted for. But if it was Cassie, she wouldn't know until late this morning, like at 10:00 or 10:30."

She sat at the table for four, in the far corner of the suite, next to a low standing chest of drawers. Armada lay on his left side on the bed, leaning on his elbow.

Although they had been communicating with each other for well over five years, their sudden change in physical proximity was not at all an easy and smooth transition.

"So...," Chloe said, allowing the word to linger, "what now?"

She wobbled back and forth, tipping her chair. Armada rolled onto his back and gazed up at the ceiling.

"Well?" he stated, "I suppose we could go to the kitchen area and see what we can rustle up for dinner? Maybe take another look around the atrium ... we didn't check it out entirely. Besides, you're out of crackers and I'm in the mood for something more substantial than water."

Armada rolled to the foot of the bed and sprang to his feet.

"C'mon!" he enthusiastically demanded, reaching out to Chloe, "let's have an adventure! Whadyasay?"

Chloe smirked at the boyish, comical comment, and begrudgingly took his hand.

"When are we gonna be there? When are we gonna be there?" she jokingly pestered, tapping him repeatedly.

Even as he stepped toward the door, Chloe continued to pepper her beaux, "Are we there yet? Are we there yet? Are we there yet?"

Armada flung open the door and darted down the hallway, laughing out loud as he ran. Chloe tore after him, hollering her agitating questions, "But when are we gonna be there? How much longer? I'm hungry! I'm hungry!"

Once they entered the spacious atrium, Armada quickly reversed his tactics and began chasing Chloe. She squealed in delightful joy upon realizing that he was now after her. She led him through the front of the kitchen, out into the area with stacked boxes of chairs and tables, and finally came to rest in what appeared to be a cocktail lounge.

The breathless couple strode by a grand piano, elegant coffee tables, ornate candelabras, handsome leather couches, armchairs and love seats, and a beautiful selection of chaise lounges. Armada broke away from Chloe as she sat on and appreciated the different choices of luxurious furniture.

"Hey, Chloe!" he shouted, leaning over a long black-and-silver granite countertop. "Have I got something to show you!"

Chloe took her time and made sure to look over each piece of furniture before responding to Armada.

"Hold on, I'm coming," she repeatedly answered with each call of her name.

"Finally!" he declared as she entered a room that was cordoned off by a wrought iron gate, "Where've you been?"

"I was just looking at some chairs," Chloe nonchalantly replied, spinning in a slow circle. "What is this place?"

"It appears to me that we've stumbled upon ... a bar."

They passed cases of bourbon, vodka, Scotch, gin, tequila, rum, and exotic distilled spirits from around the world. Hundreds upon hundreds of boxes were palletized, shrink-wrapped, and loaded onto heavy-duty, industrial-grade shelving units, similar to those they found earlier in the kitchen. Row after row, the selection and volume of alcohol on hand boggled their minds.

"What's Frangelico?" Chloe asked as she pulled away the plastic wrap from one of the pallets, "And Midori? And Tuaca? And ... Rumplemintz?"

"Rumple what?" Armada inquired, laughingly, investigating the outer label of the box, "Peppermint schnapps."

"What's schnapps?"

"You're asking me? I've never laid eyes on any of this stuff, let alone tasted it. Your guess is as good as mine what it is ... the one thing I do know is this is all alcohol. And we've never consumed beer, wine, or liquor. So I'd say it's best to not get in trouble with this stuff."

"Oh! What are ya? Scared?" she playfully teased as they moved onto the next row of shelving.

"Me? Scared? Nah. Just playing it smart."

Chloe turned her head and resumed reading the label names aloud as they strolled by.

"Jim Beam, Johnny Walker, Maker's Mark, Weller's, Baker's, Booker's. Why don't we pick one out and try it?"

"Ha!" he laughed. "You're a nut!"

"I'd rather be a nut than a coward!" she declared and turned away from him with her nose in the air.

"Coward? You callin' me a coward?"

"You? Oh, no. Never."

"'Cause I'm not afraid, and I'm no coward."

"No? Then prove it."

The challenge was made.

"All right," Armada stated with a gleam in his eyes. "We'll both do it at the same time. But! I get to choose what we drink."

Chloe placed her hands on her hips and bit the inside of her lower lip as she looked Armada up and down.

"Deal!" she snarkily agreed.

"All right then, you go on and take a look around and I'll pick one out."

"Fine. Take your time."

"Oh, I will. Remember now … you said anything."

"I know. A deal is a deal."

Chloe snootily turned around and resumed her visual investigation of the gargantuan supply of liquor. Armada went in the opposite direction to search out the winning selection.

"Sambuca, Amaretto, Kahlua…," he heard Chloe faintly calling out, "Bailey's, Grand Marn … Marn … Ouzo … Absinthe…."

Armada hurriedly scanned the labels on the outside of the cellophane encased boxes. While not knowing exactly what he was in search of, or what the contents would taste like, he knew that his choice had to be something powerful enough to take Chloe's pride down a notch or two. After another ten minutes of browsing, he came upon two pallets resting side by side with a large, black-and-gold bat on one side of the pallet. Seeing the winged creature was enough justification for Armada.

"Found it!" he triumphantly shouted, "C'mon!"

He peeled the shrink wrapping off the top level of boxes, pulled back on the cardboard, and extracted a bottle. Chloe rounded the corner of the aisle he was on and observed him tucking the red-and-white bottle into his suit.

"Whatcha got there?"

"Oh, nothing much," he playfully replied, keeping his back to her.

"If it's nothing, then let me take a look," she sarcastically grunted, jumping on him.

Armada reached behind him, grabbed both of Chloe's legs, and began spinning and hopping about. He'd jog a few paces, then jump and turn, and acted as if he intended to throw her off backwards. Chloe wrapped her arms around his neck, laughing as Armada ran up and down the aisles.

The bronco ride came to an abrupt halt as soon as the couple approached the gate to the liquor vault. However, instead of releasing her legs, Armada kept his firm grip and strutted to the bar and cocktail lounge. Chloe lowered her chin to rest on his shoulder and tilted her head to the side 'til their skulls came in contact. Closing her eyes, she enjoyed the slight bump of his stride.

"Okay," he announced, coming to a standstill, "off you go . . . let's get down to business."

He loosened his grasp and Chloe was slow to lower her legs and slide off his back. Armada turned to face her, gave her an impromptu peck on her lips, and brashly stated, "Glasses!" and entered the bar.

"We need something to drink out of. So find us some kind of glass," he said with Chloe close behind.

The duo looked in the cabinets above and below the bar top but found none. Chloe looked out into the lounge and spied stacks of cardboard boxes containing a multitude of glassware styles. Pilsners, champagne flutes, wine, martini, daiquiri, squall, snifters, cordials, and highball glasses were in vast supply.

She climbed over the bar while declaring, "Found 'em," to her beaux.

"What kind of glass do we need?" she asked as she crossed the lounge.

"Well, whatever you choose; it doesn't necessarily have to be big. We're not exactly drinking a whole bottle's worth."

Chloe checked the names of the different glasses, as well as the size.

"How about an eight-ounce highball glass?" she hollered, looking over her shoulder.

"That's plenty big. Just grab a box, it doesn't matter which one."

Chloe picked up a case of twelve highball glasses and skipped back to the bar.

"Thank you," Armada said as he tore back the top of the box. He pulled out two of the short paneled glasses, turned on the hot water, and waited for the cold water to run out.

"Hey, bartender, whatcha got to drink?" she playfully inquired.

"Oh! You'll love it. It's something new, and unlike anything you've ever tasted!"

The running water began to change temperature.

"Oooh, I'm intrigued!" she stated, pulling her knees up onto the bar stool. "What's it called? What is it?"

"Lady, it's so new I've actually forgotten the name," Armada admitted as he ran the dirty glasses under the hot water.

"But I'll let you be the first to see it," he said, turning off the water.

After letting the excess water drip off, Armada turned the highball glasses right side up and set them in front of his single bar patron.

He partially unzipped his suit, spun away from Chloe, and withdrew the secret bottle.

"Oh, yes. I remember now!" he exclaimed as he turned to face her. "It's called 151."

He placed the shiny bottle directly in front of Chloe, as if to gain her approval.

"Well, what is 151 precisely, and what's with the bat? Who's Bacardi?" she inquired, inspecting the label closely.

"Don't know, don't know, don't know. And … don't care. I only picked it out because of the bat. Looked promising to me."

Chloe held the bottle up to the light and gazed into the caramel-colored spirit.

"Shall we?" he asked, removing the bottle from her grasp.

He twisted off the metal cap and discovered a metal strainer affixed to the rim. Armada raised the bottle to his nose, inhaled, and was overcome by the aroma of the high-octane spirit.

"And?" Chloe stated as his eyes began to water.

He extended his arm and tilted the bottle toward her. She timidly leaned over and sniffed, ever so slightly.

"Spicy," she coolly commented.

Armada slowly poured the potent distillate until the glasses were more than half full. He watched Chloe's facial expression change from one of cocky confidence to nervous concern.

"You sure about this?" she inquired.

"Sure I'm sure. What? Are you scared? No longer intrigued?"

"No, I'm not scared!" she snapped. "It's just that you poured so much, and ... and we've never tasted alcohol. So...."

"Okay, okay," he interrupted, pulling her glass away, "we don't have to...."

"Hey! Put that back! I'm not wimping out ... I'm simply being cautious."

"Oh, thank you for looking out for my well-being and safety."

Armada again placed the half-full, eight-ounce highball in front of Chloe.

"All right. Here's how we'll do this. I'll count to three and we'll drink the whole thing together, at the same time."

"All of it?" she asked in bewilderment.

"What? Don't tell me you sip your delightful daily supplements."

"Oooh! No! That stuff is disgusting!"

"Then when I say three, just tilt your head back and take it all in one mouthful. We'll have it done in a flash."

Chloe gave a worrisome look at the small glass of liquefied fire, then at Armada.

"Okay ... let's get it done and over with."

They smiled at one another and raised their glasses while Armada announced the count.

"One ... two ... three."

The two inexperienced amateurs closed their eyes, raised their glasses, and quickly tossed back the powerful elixir.

Chloe immediately lunged forward, placed her hands on the bar, and moaned loudly from the painful sensations her tongue and throat were experiencing. She then quickly erected herself onto her knees, wrinkled her face and puckered her lips, and flapped her hands in anguish. Armada pulled his hand up and pressed his lips together in order to avoid spitting out the rum. They stared at each other with panic in their eyes, while infernos raged in their mouths. As tears welled up, they both wanted to end their pain and suffering but weren't willing enough to be the first to admit it.

With liquid lava in their mouths and painful waves of air entering their lungs each time they inhaled, the couple reached a stalemate of pride. In an attempt to play down the severity of the bonfire in her mouth, Chloe gently lowered herself onto her bar stool and calmly folded her arms. She unclenched her jaws, but kept her lips pressed tightly. Armada tilted his head back, opened his mouth, and breathed in and out several times. Each had successfully lowered the rum from the roof of their mouths momentarily. They were both too proud to lose, yet too chicken to swallow.

Armada lowered his eyes and stared at Chloe.

With a mouth full of rum, he tried to make Chloe laugh by saying, "Harrow."

Chloe chuckled at the sight of Armada and the sound of his voice. Her small laugh was enough to disturb her concentration and had to lean over the bar once again to gain her composure. Chloe's chuckle in turn made Armada laugh, causing him to partially choke and dribble some rum from his lips.

Chloe witnessed the minimal spill from his mouth. She slammed one hand on the bar, pointed at Armada, and loudly hummed "Ah-ha!"

Armada tried to object by shaking his head and humming, "Uh-uh!"

Chloe laughed harder and couldn't keep her lips from parting. Several spurts of rum freely dribbled down her chin.

Armada now had the upper hand, and pointed at Chloe and sarcastically hummed, "Ah-ha! Ah- ha!"

He thrust his fists in the air and started dancing in a circle. His less than graceful routine was unbearable to watch, causing Chloe to laugh uncontrollably. She climbed on top of the bar, leaned over the sink, and spat out the distilled spirit. The fumes from the rum filled her lungs and what remained in her mouth scorched her throat. She jumped down behind the bar, turned on the water, lowered her mouth to the faucet, and drank heartily to wash away the taste; her tongue felt like it had been incinerated.

Armada stood and waited for his 'drinking buddy' to quench her thirst.

As soon as the fiery flavor was neutralized, Chloe turned off the water and erected herself.

"I bet you're feeling mighty proud of yourself. Aren't you?" she commented, wiping her mouth on her sleeve.

Armada had yet to ingest his shot of rum. He held his hand up to stop Chloe from speaking, then pointed to his mouth and hummed, shaking his head in the process.

"Oh, you're kidding me. Right? It's bad enough that I spit mine out, but you're still gonna drink it? Just to show me up?"

"Mm mm," he replied, nodding his head vigorously.

"You creep!" she exclaimed and proceeded to slap his biceps and pinch his waist.

"Well, c'mon then. Hurry up and drink it! Hurry! C'mon, finish it!"

"Mmmm! Mmmm!" he loudly hummed, turning away from his attacker.

"What's wrong, tough guy?" she asked, switching her tactics from pinching to tickling.

Armada concentrated and forced the rum down his throat.

"Augh! Okay! I give up! Yuch!" he announced as she jumped on his back.

With Chloe clinging to his neck and hips, Armada suddenly straightened himself and stood very still.

"Oh, whatsa matter now? Are you...."

"Wait a minute! Stop! Hold on," he snapped, lowering his voice.

Chloe eased herself off his back and slowly relaxed her arm from around his neck.

"What is it? What's wrong?"

"Don't you smell that?" he whispered.

CHAPTER 25

SIGNS

Chloe sniffed the air and wrinkled up her nose in response.
"Oooh! What is that?" she asked, lowering her volume. "Smells like something's burning."

"That's what I'm thinking. But what?"

Armada gazed across the lounge as Chloe reached out for the two empty highball glasses. Just as Armada turned to exit the bar, there was a sudden crash of breaking glass. He spun around to find that Chloe had accidentally dropped one of the glasses into the bar sink, shattering it to bits and pieces.

"Man, that scared me! Are you okay?"

"Armada ... the bottle! Look at the bottle!" she nervously stated.

He stepped to the bar, picked up the bottle of rum, and turned it to examine the label.

"What?" he asked, confused, then glanced again at Chloe.

The once bright-red, white, and gold label now looked as if it had been set on fire. While the rum itself wasn't discolored or cloudy, the colorful labels on both the neck and body were black and charred. With the face of a frightened animal, Chloe pushed herself back against the liquor cabinets.

Armada pulled the bottle to his nose and inhaled deeply.

"Hmm," he mumbled and once again visually scanned the cocktail lounge.

"Hmm what?" Chloe inquired. "Armada!? How did that just happen? I mean, we were both standing right here."

"I don't have a clue. The past eighteen hours have been just as bewildering as this. Smokeless, flameless paper. Huh."

Chloe relaxed and drew in close to him. She removed the bottle from his hand, inspected the labels, and took a whiff. Armada peered up to the ceiling lights and repeated his statement "Nope. No smoke."

"This isn't the same odor," she said, smelling the label, then held it up for Armada.

"You're right, that's not the same odor. To me, it had kind of a bitter scent."

"Really? I thought it smelled more like burnt or smoldering rubber … maybe plastic."

"Yeah," Armada agreed, then turned in the opposite direction and held his nose high in the air.

"There it is again," he quickly stated, inhaling through his nostrils.

The couple sniffed and smelled their way to the bar entrance.

"Smells stronger over here," Chloe commented, pointing to the gate that led to the liquor storeroom.

Armada was reaching for the gate handle when the fumes overwhelmed their senses.

"Ugh!" Chloe gasped, covering her mouth and nose. "That stench!"

They opened the ornate metal gate and cautiously proceeded back into the massive warehouse.

"Still no sign of smoke," said Armada as he looked up at the lights.

They had barely cleared the entryway wall when Chloe grabbed his hand and exclaimed "Oh, Armada!"

They stood partially paralyzed at the sight that lay before them. Tears of fear and confusion welled up in Chloe's eyes as she firmly clutched Armada's hand. His heart raced and his breathing became shallow and short. They couldn't wrap their brains around what they saw.

A mere ten minutes earlier, the two of them wandered the aisles of the storehouse admiring the amazing selection of exotic liquors. What was once a collection of every conceivable form and flavor of alcohol complete with beautiful, intricate, and detailed artwork on the boxes and outer labels now looked as if a bomb had been detonated.

"How?" she asked, appearing to be genuinely frightened. "We were just in here."

"I ... I can't explain it," Armada replied, dumbfounded.

They soon relaxed and gingerly approached the first stack of utility shelving units. When the duo came to the pallet lying on the ground underneath the lowest shelf, they knelt down to inspect it.

Armada leaned over and sniffed at the neatly stacked boxes. Chloe did the same and gently plucked at the plastic shrink-wrapping material.

"I think this is our culprit," he declared, tapping his finger on the uppermost box.

"I agree," Chloe added, pulling at the now brittle and blackened plastic. "But, how? What melted the plastic, and how could the labels on the boxes be scorched ... without creating a flame? And no smoke?"

"And raise the temperature to combustion level but not incinerate the cardboard," he added.

Armada ripped away the bubbly and scorched plastic, pulled back one of the top flaps, and reached into the box.

"What're you doing?"

"I'm curious."

"So am I! I got a couple hundred questions I want answers to!" she confidently stated.

Armada extracted a bottle, examined the front label, and laughed.

"What's so funny?" she inquired as he inspected the interior of the case.

"You want answers? Well, can you answer me as to how this happened?"

With a mischievous twinkle in his eyes, he handed the bottle to Chloe.

"Explain that!" he proudly challenged.

Chloe took the bottle and turned it label side up.

"No!" she declared, chuckling, as she examined the glass bottle. "Shut up! Armada! This is amazing!"

"How did the label get scorched, inside the cardboard box ... and the interior remain unscathed?"

Fear and confusion quickly subsided as wonder and intrigue filled their hearts and minds. Chloe set the bottle on the ground before both she and Armada tore into the cardboard case. One by one they retrieved all twelve bottles and set them down, side by side, all in a row.

"This is undoubtedly the most amazing thing I've ever seen," he announced, waving down at the line of liquor.

"You and me both," Chloe agreed, nodding her head.

"Okay, let's review what we know."

"All right."

"No flames present."

"No smoke either."

"Correct. No visible damage to the interior or exterior of the case. Except the label, of course."

"No smoke damage to the immediate surroundings," Chloe added, inspecting the underside of the shelf.

"No visible damage or change to the rum, even though it's highly flammable."

"I'm at a total loss of words," she laughingly admitted.

"I know what you mean. Physics just flew out the window."

"I wonder if...," Chloe began as she stepped out from between the rows of shelving.

"You wonder what?" Armada inquired, trailing behind her.

"Well," she thought, peering at row after row of shelving, "if we're to go by outward appearances only, we can then safely assume that the phenomenon affected all of the cases on this first aisle in the exact same manner. Agreed?"

"Agreed."

"So the question now becomes," Chloe stated, walking to the next aisle, "did the phenomenon affect all of the cases in the warehouse? Or … is this restricted and confined to a specific form of alcohol or section of the warehouse?"

"Hmm," Armada hummed, glancing down the aisle. "How about we go through each aisle, making sure that every box has been scorched, and we'll randomly select a carton and inspect its interior and bottle conditions."

"Oooh, I like that idea," she cooed.

"All right then, after you."

They joined hands and slowly strolled up and down every aisle in the expansive storehouse. The sleuths carefully eyed every shelf and the exterior condition of the boxes. Chloe chose one case from both sides of each aisle to undergo examination. One by one the cardboard boxes chosen for inspection yielded the same results as the first. Finally, after more than a couple of hours of investigation, they reached the last shelving unit.

"Well, that wasn't very productive," Armada sorrowfully stated.

They turned toward the warehouse entrance and walked silently, still hand in hand.

"Man! I'm burning up!" Armada admitted while unzipping his body suit.

He casually peeled it off his shoulders and pulled out his arms, exposing his tight fitting, ribbed undershirt. The upper half of the one-piece suit hung down from his waist, inside out, with the sleeves dragging the floor. Chloe discreetly allowed her eyes to wander over his well-defined chest and biceps. She felt her heart begin to race as small beads of perspiration suddenly appeared on her forehead; she could smell him. As if she had inhaled a cloud of pure ether, Chloe felt lightheaded and couldn't resist the urge to smile.

"What's with you?" he asked, taking a quick glance. "You're all flushed. You feeling all right?"

"Sure … I'm great," she fibbed, turning away from him. "I'm probably just overwhelmed with all that's happened today."

Chloe then fanned herself and partially lowered the zipper on her suit, revealing the plunging neckline of her undershirt. She then turned her head back toward Armada and noticed that one of the strips of medical tape on his shoulder had come off.

"Hey, hold on," she said, gently grasping his left arm. "The tape on your shoulder has come loose."

Unable to resist the urge and desire to touch him, Chloe firmly pressed her body against Armada while repairing the patch. They both closed their eyes as she tenderly wrapped her arms around his waist and laid her cheek on his back. He slowly raised his hands to meet hers and they silently, instinctively, interlaced their fingers.

'Is this what love is supposed to feel like?' she quietly and contentedly asked herself as she listened to his heart beating.

"I feel … like … a complete idiot!" Armada declared, shattering the mood.

"What?" she asked, withdrawing her body. "Why?"

"Something's missing."

"What? What's missing?"

"Correct me if I'm wrong here, but … did we, or did we not, open any cases of wine?"

He turned to face her and placed his hands on his hips.

"Um…," she began, turning toward one of the shelving units. "You know, I don't … no, no we didn't come across any wine."

"It's pretty warm in here, dontcha think?"

"Yeah, so?"

"This is all distilled alcohol. Even though it's boxed up, changes in light and temperature won't have a detrimental effect on this stuff, at least not like it does on beer, and even more so on wine."

"So you think we've overlooked something? Or not in the right place?"

"Oh, yeah. They'd put all that in something where they can control the temperature, like with the frozen food."

"Sooo…."

"Sooo … now we need to find another walk-in, but for wine."

"Ugh! I'm starving!" she gruffly stated. "Promise me we'll find something to eat after this."

"I promise," he answered sympathetically.

He draped his left arm across her neck and shoulder.

"You know that thing did this, don't you?" she asked, reaching up to play with his dangling fingers.

"Thing? What thing?"

"You know exactly what I'm talking about. That thing that brought us here in the first place. That thing you talk to. It did this … all of it."

"Oh, that thing."

She pinched his love handles as he drew her in and kissed her head.

"I don't believe it!" she bluntly stated, stopping in her tracks.

"Believe what?"

Chloe shrugged her shoulders and held out her arm. "Hello? We walked right past it!"

There, adjacent to the wrought iron gate to the warehouse, was a shiny, wide, stainless steel door with a large sign above it that simply read CELLAR in large red letters.

Chloe slowly twisted her head and offered Armada a snooty smirk.

"Shut up!" he said with a strong hip check that knocked her off balance.

"Oh, yeah?" she responded, and retaliated by again jumping on his back.

This time, Chloe didn't taunt or agitate him, nor did she tickle or pinch. She firmly encircled his neck, gently squeezed her legs around his hips, and relished the feel of his strong hands on her hamstrings as he carried her a la piggyback. The sensation of being enveloped by Chloe was intensely invigorating and stimulating. Armada began to sweat profusely; he could feel the pounding of his heart all the way up to his temples.

"Here we are," he jovially announced. "The wine cellar. What's the thermostat set for?"

He spun to his right, giving Chloe a better view of the gauge.

"Sixty-six degrees," she replied.

"Okay; now, grab the handle."

Chloe let go of his neck with her right arm and reached out and gripped the handle tightly before Armada backed away from the mammoth door.

"Ugh!" she grunted, straining against the weight and vacuumed seal of the door. "It's heavy!"

The rubber gasket finally gave way and the couple happily entered.

"Wow! That's cold!" Chloe declared after dismounting Armada and immediately pulled her zipper all the way up to the collar.

"Whoa! Temperature spike!" he stated and briskly put his suit on.

The temperature-controlled wine warehouse was every bit as impressive as the liquor house, but surpassed it in style and amenities.

"Do you smell anything unusual?" he asked as they approached the first rack of wooden crates.

"No, not yet."

Unlike the liquor warehouse, the wooden crates of wine were segregated by country, regions, appellation, and varietal.

"Okay, I'm smart, but foreign languages wasn't one of my applications," Chloe informed Armada as they diligently perused the boxes. "I can't tell you one thing about this stuff other than that one is from Chile…and that one…is from Argentina."

"Well, as of now I'm not so concerned with what's what and from where and who made it. What I'm looking for is evidence of our flameless, smokeless fire. And…thus far…I see no such evidence."

While they initially began their second investigation with an up close and thorough examination of each shelf of wooden crates, that process soon eroded into a brisk walk up each aisle with a mere glance at one or two selections.

"Okay, I don't see any reason to think that the wine cellar experienced the same phenomenon as the warehouse," Chloe confidently stated. "Do you concur?"

"Visually, on the exterior, yes, I agree. But just to confirm this hypothesis, let's pick out one crate, open it up, and see if any of the labeling is scorched. Okay?"

"Fine by me. Which one?"

"I don't care, doesn't matter to me. I've never had the stuff. You pick."

"All right," she agreed and turned the corner on the aisle with a nameplate of 'France' affixed to the frame.

She looked up and down the racks on both sides of the aisle and came to rest in front of a collection of wooden boxes.

"This one," she proudly stated, pointing at the near chest-high stack of crates.

"Chateau Margaux, 1999," Armada read aloud. "Why this one?"

"I don't know; I guess I just like the way the name and picture is burnt into the wood."

"Okay then. One side, please."

Armada removed the case of wine from the stack, then hefted it up to his shoulder.

"Let's go," he said as he took her hand.

Chloe grabbed a mallet and pry bar that hung from a wall near the door as they exited and headed for the bar.

Armada gently placed the case of Chateau Margaux on the end of the counter. Chloe rounded the end of the long, smooth, black granite topped bar and took a seat in the first chair. She curled her legs up underneath her and leaned over on her elbows to watch Armada open the case. He firmly pressed the tip of the pry bar under one corner of the cover, then grabbed the mallet and struck the end a couple of times. With the bar now adequately wedged under the lid, he pressed down on the opposite end.

The top of the case popped loose with the greatest of ease.

After a shifty stir of his eyes, Armada quickly removed the cover and announced, "Ta da!"

Inside the wooden box there lay six bottles of wine, individually wrapped in tissue paper adorned with the Chateau Margaux name and picture of the charming French landmark.

"Looks nice," Chloe commented as she reached in and grabbed a bottle. "Any smoke damage?"

He flipped the top of the crate over and inspected its underside. "Nope. Nothing here."

He, too, then grabbed a bottle of the rare and expensive wine. "Any damage to the tissue paper?"

"No ... not that I can tell."

Like impatient children at a birthday party, they ripped away the flimsy wrapper but afterwards paused for a moment to examine and appreciate the elegant and sophisticated design of the label.

"Wow. I don't even know what it is I'm looking at, but ... I like it. I mean ... it just looks ... good."

"I know," Chloe said, smiling, as she turned the bottle in her hands. "There's something about it I can't explain. I wonder if this tastes better than your hundred-fifty Dabarci bat stuff."

"I don't know, we...," Armada started to say, but stopped in midsentence.

Chloe watched him as he gazed intensely at the bottle.

"Come on! Bring the bottle!" he loudly commanded. "Hurry!"

He tightly gripped Chloe's wrist and tugged on her arm, nearly yanking her off the stool as he came out from behind the bar.

"Hurry where?"

"Don't ask questions, just come on!"

He pulled her back through the liquor warehouse gate to the 'Cellar' door.

"Okay, follow me on this! Oh, this is great!" he exclaimed, lunging forward to kiss her. "You said it! You said it!"

"Okay! I said it! Great! What? Tell me!"

"All right, all right," Armada stammered, trying to calm down. "Okay, a while ago you said that thing did this. All right. So we tried to drink that ... hundred bats stuff and it tasted like crap! It hurt! Right?"

"Yeah, so...?"

"Don't you get it? This stuff here in our hands and this stuff in the cellar, we haven't drank it yet!"

With her mouth agape, Chloe stared at him, impatiently waiting for a clearer explanation.

"Augh!" he grunted. "Let me explain it another way. This morning, right before we came down the hall to our room and the atrium, the orb thing blocked us from entering the other corridor by expanding itself. Remember? It was a warning to not use those elevators. Right? Remember?"

"Oh!" she exclaimed, hopping about. "I get it! It's burning the labels to warn us about the liquor!"

"Yeah!" he ecstatically replied, wrapping her in his arms.

He lifted Chloe off the floor with an exuberant bear hug and swung her from side to side as they laughed.

"Oooh! I wanna check something," he stated and promptly lowered her. "Follow me."

They exited the liquor warehouse, passed through the bar, dashed across the cocktail lounge, and sped down the wide hallway toward the atrium and commons.

"Hey!" Chloe hollered. "What's the rush? Where are we going?"

"You'll find out soon enough," Armada quipped as he turned to face her while jogging backwards. "I need to test my theory."

As soon as they arrived at the commons, Armada made a beeline for the kitchen and food services facilities. With Chloe hot on his heels, he barely opened the door that led to the dry goods storehouse. He paused, extended his arm, and felt the wall for the light switch.

"What're you doing? Just open the door."

"Okay," he said, blindly fishing for the light switch. "If I'm correct in my thinking, we should expect to see something amazing!"

"Ah. There it is," he said, landing his fingers on the control plate and flipped the switch.

"Oh, c'mon! Just open the stupid door already!" she demanded and began tugging on both Armada and the door.

She playfully wedged herself between him and the door frame and used her back and legs to force it open.

While Chloe was first to enter the dry goods storehouse, it was Armada who noticed the visible changes.

"Yes!" he shouted victoriously. "Yes! I knew it!"

CHAPTER 26

ENCOUNTER

Chloe stood in the middle of the walkway, mesmerized with their discovery and its ramifications.

"This is … this is…," Armada stuttered with glee. "I'm gonna check the freezers!"

He leaned in, gave her a peck on the lips, and set his bottle of wine on a nearby prep table.

"Wow! Man, oh man!" he bellowed before running in the direction of the walk-in freezers.

Chloe remained unmoved.

'How could this be?' she silently asked herself.

Row after row, shelf upon shelf, charred and blackened labels appeared. The truly astounding aspect of the sight was that the scorched boxes and cans were interspersed amongst containers that appeared to be in perfect condition.

"Yes!" Armada yelled as he exited the first freezer. "It's in the freezers! Chloe! Woo-hoo!"

She slightly sniffed the air and identified the same scent of burning rubber. Glancing up at the lights, she saw no signs of smoke. Backing away from the shelving units, she also placed her bottle of wine on the stainless steel prep table.

"It's in the second freezer, too!" she heard him shout.

He ran to Chloe, scooped her in his arms, and spun around and around.

"I was right!" he excitedly announced. "It's trying to communicate with us."

Chloe remained silent as he set her down.

"Let's check out a box!"

Armada darted to the closest shelving unit, one with a nameplate that read 'Breakfast, Cereals, and Grains.' He briskly scanned the fronts of the boxes, then hollered out, "Found one!"

After tearing away the plastic shrink-wrapping material, he pulled out one case and zipped back to the prep table. He carelessly plopped the cardboard box on the table and struggled to read the partially blackened label. "Kellogg's Pop ... Pop ... oh, well, doesn't necessarily matter anyhow."

Chloe stood at the end of the table with her head down and fixed her gaze on the floor.

"Hey, what's wrong?" Armada asked, stepping beside her.

Chloe buried her face in her hands and wept. He embraced her and stroked the back of her head and neck.

"Augh!" she sobbed into his chest. "I'm tired! I'm hungry! I'm confused! I don't understand what's happening and why! I don't understand what that ... thing wants from us!"

"Ssshhh," he softly hissed, patting her back. "We're gonna be just fine. You'll see. Maybe that thing is helping us to ... to ... learn more and help others like us. Mark my words, you and I are getting outta here."

He placed his finger under her chin and tenderly pulled her face up.

"I promise you," he reassured her, smiling, "I'm never leaving you, and we're gonna leave this place."

"Promise?" she squeaked with red, teary eyes.

"I promise. I won't ever make you a promise I can't keep."

He kissed her forehead and gave her one final squeeze.

"Now let's check out the box, grab some supplies, then we'll go back to the room. Deal?"

"Deal."

He broke his embrace and turned his attention to the cardboard box. Chloe wiped her eyes and joined him at his side. Armada peeled off one flap of the case and extracted a small box.

"Ah-ha!" he said, holding the box directly in front of her nose. "See? I told you. It's trying to communicate with us."

She laughed and pushed the blackened box of pastries away from her face.

"Thank you," he loudly stated, looking up. "I don't know if you're listening or not, but ... thank you ... whoever you are."

Chloe then tilted her head back at asked, "Are you there? It's us ... from this morning. Is Armada right? Did you do this?"

They waited and listened.

With their arms slightly raised to their side and knees bent a bit, the couple slowly spun in circles, looking for a sign of response.

"Hello?" Chloe again called out. "It's me, from this morning. Are you there? Did you do all this? Can you hear me?"

Without warning, the large, industrial-sized light above them surged with a brilliant, almost blinding flash of light.

Chloe twisted back toward Armada, reached out for his hand, and quickly smiled at him.

"You can hear us?" Armada asked and almost instantly received his answer in the form of another pulse.

"Can you hear us all the time? Anywhere we go?" Chloe inquired.

Again, a flash of light beamed from the bulb.

"So Armada was right? You're telling us what not to eat or drink?"

The bulb flashed once more.

"Whenever we come across something to eat or drink and it's charred on the outside, then you don't want us to consume it. But if we come across something that doesn't appear to be burnt or scorched, then that's what you're labeling as safe and good for us. Right? Did I interpret that correctly?"

This time, all of the overhead lightbulbs emitted a flash of dazzling light, but they also flickered briefly.

"Oh! What about Eden?" Chloe suddenly thought to ask. "What do you want us to eat from Eden?"

"You can't ask it like that," Armada chided. "What, is it gonna go through each and every fruit? Reword it ... make it into a 'yes' question."

"Augh! Okay! Is everything we grow and harvest in Eden safe to eat? Do you want us eating that, too?"

The bulbs flickered off and on sporadically.

"Wow!" he said, then loudly stated, "Thank you."

"Yeah. Thank you, thank you ... whatever, or ... whoever, you are."

"I was just about to tell Chloe that ... in a little more than three hours ... I will have been on the run for twenty-four hours. I left the only thing I've ever known because I felt like I could trust you ... so, since I decided to follow you yesterday morning, my life has drastically changed ... for the better ... and I no longer have a feeling of just existing ... I feel like we're really living now. I can't begin to thank you enough ... I feel like I don't deserve this though ... I mean why me, us, specifically? Out of all the thousands to choose from, you selected us and I don't understand why ... but we're grateful and thankful, and ... we'll both trust you and follow you, and ... we'll keep our eyes open for your signs. Thank you."

"Can we call you?" Chloe interrupted. "I just want to clarify with you. What if we need something, or we're unsure of what to do, or maybe there's something bothering us and we're confused ... do you want us to just call out to you?"

Suddenly, every light throughout the entire warehouse blazed and flickered off and on repeatedly. As if attending a rock concert, the young couple stood in disbelief at the beautiful, yet unexplainable light show.

Then, just as it had started, the amazing display of power came to an abrupt stop.

"Whoa!" Armada exclaimed, slapping his legs just above the knees, "That ... was ... so ... awesome!"

Chloe turned to face him and was speechless.

"Did you ever...," he began to ask, but Chloe interrupted him by throwing herself against his body. With arms intertwined, they kissed passionately and hungrily.

"Hey," he said, trying to speak without breaking away from her lips, "I have an idea."

"What?" she asked, breathing heavily.

"How about ... (kiss) ... you ... (kiss) ... go back to the bar ... (kiss) ... and take one of the bottles of wine ... (kiss) ... and find something to open it with?"

"But ... (kiss) ... what about you?"

"I'm gonna ... (kiss) ... find ... (kiss) ... something to eat."

"Okay, yeah ... (kiss) ... we need to eat."

"You ... (kiss) ... better ... (kiss) ... get going."

He tenderly pushed Chloe away from him, reached out and picked up a bottle, and placed it in her hand.

"By the time you return, I'll have gathered up a feast fit for a queen. It'll be our first meal together. We have a lot to celebrate tonight."

"Kinda like our first meal away from home, huh?"

"Yes, ma'am," he said, chuckling.

Chloe placed her free hand on his neck, reeled him in, and offered one last smooch.

"All right, I'll be right back," she informed her mate. "I expect to be amazed by an appetizing demonstration of your culinary skills when I return."

"Oh, yeah!" he snarkily agreed, with a gentle kick to her bottom. "I'll get right on it, Princess."

Chloe jubilantly skipped her way out of the kitchen, laughing.

CHAPTER 27

RESERVATIONS FOR TWO

"Honey, I'm home!" Chloe pleasantly hollered out as she entered the kitchen and dry goods storehouse.

"I'll be right there!" she heard him shout.

"Where are you?"

"I'm on the aisle with the disposables. Hold on."

Chloe approached the prep table and watched as Armada exited the aisle with one large cardboard box on top of his shoulder and another tucked up under his arm. He again had the upper half of his suit unzipped and dangling from his waist. He smiled broadly as he touted his cargo. She beamed with simple, girlish delight at the sight of his exposed body. It was more than obvious that he'd been laboring during her short absence.

"I have some surprises for you," she coyly stated and folded her arms behind her.

"Oooh, I like surprises," he responded as he passed in front of her. "I, too, just happen to have a surprise."

She visually devoured his torso, gazing intensely at his swollen biceps, chest, and shoulders.

Armada turned down the first row, carefully lowered the carton under his arm, then lifted the case from his shoulder up on to a higher shelf.

"What kind of surprises did you bring me?" he playfully inquired, scooting the box on the floor under the lowest shelf.

"You'll just have to get over here and find out," she quipped.

As he approached her, Chloe turned fidgety and attempted to hide something.

"Okay. Let me tell you what I've done," he began, stepping to her side, and leaned back against the table. "I've started separating boxes based on contents and burns. It'll take us several days to identify and organize everything, but for now we'll bring the supplies of greatest importance up here to the first few rows of shelves."

As he spoke and pointed to the shelving units, Chloe scooted closer and closer, oblivious to what he was saying; she couldn't keep herself from admiring his physique.

"So, are you ready for your surprises?" he spryly asked, turning to face the table.

"Oh, yeah. But why did you cover everything?" she asked, noticing the cloth towels.

"Well, young lady, that's only part of the surprise. And for the first one, you'll have to close your eyes."

"I don't know if I trust you. What if...."

"Just shut up and close your eyes."

Chloe lowered her eyelids, smiling. Armada lifted the corner of a towel and pulled out his secret prize.

"Okay, now you gotta hold out your hands, but keep your eyes shut."

Chloe didn't resist his instructions and silently held up her hands. Armada laid the mysterious object in her palms.

"All right. You can look now."

Chloe opened her eyes to find a wide, thin, and flat item wrapped in shiny golden foil, lying in her hands. She turned it right side up, vertically, and mumbled as she quickly read its content.

"Chocolate?!" she yelled, jumping up and down. "You found chocolate? Oh, my gosh, Armada! I can't believe you found us some chocolate! I've never tasted it! Oh, thank you! Thank you!"

She leapt into his arms and squeezed him tightly. Armada couldn't resist laughing at her reaction.

"That's not all," he added. "Take a look at this."

She relaxed her stranglehold and backed away from him.

"Yay! Choco-choco-choco-chocolate!" she squealed, hopping up on her tiptoes.

One by one he lifted the cloth towels, revealing a collection of white ceramic portion bowls.

"Ta da!"

"Wow! Armada!"

After having removed the towels, Chloe was further blown away with the smorgasbord of food he'd gathered.

"How'd you find all these in such a short amount of time? I wasn't gone fifteen minutes."

"I've always been very efficient with my time and effort," he proudly stated before pointing out the selections.

"Tonight, madam, we have prepared a scrumptious meal. We have honey-roasted pecans, sea-salted almonds, dried blueberries...."

"And chocolate," she interjected, lifting the bar directly in front of his nose.

"Pitted black cherries, dried apricot and honey-crisp apple, apple sauce, dill pickles...."

"And chocolate."

"Black olives, canned peaches, mandarin orange, and pineapple. All of these, by the way, is certified organic and non-GMO."

"Uh, hello? We're walking GMOs."

"Well, we're different. We have gluten-free crackers from Israel. The box said it was kosher, although I don't know what that means, but they look and smell good."

"Don't forget we have CHOCOLATE!"

"We also have organic peanut butter, golden raisins, and something called craisins."

"I am impressed," she said, pecking him on his cheek. "I don't know what to try first. And none of these had a charred label on it?"

"No, ma'am," he replied, tossing a pecan in his mouth, then snapped, "And just where are my surprises?"

"Oh! I completely forgot. My mind was distracted with choco-choco-chocolate!" Chloe excitedly admitted.

"First...," she said, bending down, "I got the wine opened."

"Good girl" he announced as she stood and showed the bottle.

"There's a large lever-style bottle opener mounted on one of the bar cabinets. We walked right past it."

"Huh," he grunted, grabbing a handful of almonds.

"Next," she said, reaching for a large dill pickle, "one should only drink wine from ... a wine glass!"

Once more she knelt down, and when she rose, her hands were full. "Wine glasses, candles, lighters, candle bases ... everything was in the lounge and bar cabinets."

"Then let's do this properly and in style. You pour the wine and I'll light the candles."

Chloe removed the partially exposed cork from the neck of the bottle as Armada twisted the tapered candlesticks into their finely polished silver bases.

"Whoa! Look at that!" she exclaimed as she cautiously poured the aged fine French wine. "It's so dark. You can't even see through it."

"Wow," Armada commented as he lit the first candle. "It's like liquefied rubies."

After she poured them each a glass of wine, Armada dashed to the kitchen entrance and turned off the lights. Chloe stood next to the table, mesmerized by the soft glow of the candle.

"You know we were never allowed to have candles in our dormitories," she bellowed, waiting for Armada to return. "In fact, other than igniting our burners in the lab, I've never experienced lighting something on fire."

"Really?" he asked, emerging from the shadows. "We can fix that right now. Grab the lighter."

He came up behind her, wrapped his arms around her waist, leaned over, and blew out the flame.

"You're on," he whispered. "Just squeeze the trigger."

Chloe placed her left hand on his, pulled the trigger on the lighter, and lit both candles.

"Instant ambience," he declared, kissing her neck. "Let's eat."

"Wait a minute. This is a very special occasion; we can't begin without a toast. Make a toast."

Armada quietly retrieved his glass, held it up, and paused for a moment.

He gazed lovingly upon Chloe.

"To … a new beginning with, my best friend … and living out the rest of our lives together."

He watched her raise her hand to wipe away a tear, but she didn't break eye contact, and the smile never left her lips.

"So, I think now is when we're supposed to clink our glasses together," he then said.

After a timid touching of the rims, Chloe asked, "Do we drink it like water? Or do we sip on it?"

"Heck if I know," he confessed, sniffing the deep garnet-hued intoxicant. "Wow! That smells great!"

With broad smiles on their mouths, they watched each other take a sip.

Chloe hummed in approval as she swallowed, "Mmmm."

For an hour-and-a-half they sat on the edge of the cold, stainless steel prep table with their legs hanging off the side. The couple gorged themselves on nuts and fruits, olives and pickles, crackers with peanut butter, and washed it down with thirty-year-old Bordeaux. There couldn't be any better way to end their first candlelight dinner than by sharing a bar of dark chocolate for dessert.

Armada found it hard not to notice that over the course of the meal, he began to feel lightheaded. He also couldn't ignore the fact that Chloe was slightly slurring her words.

After downing the last few sips of Bordeaux, Armada glanced at the digital clock mounted above the kitchen entrance. In large, bright-red numbers it read 2:05 a.m.

"I think it's about time to turn in," he recommended, hopping down off the table.

"Oh, okay," Chloe agreed before guzzling the remainder of her wine.

Armada approached her from her left side and stated, "C'mon. We've had quite a day; we can both use a good night's sleep."

"Carry me," Chloe sheepishly requested, smiling at him.

"Carry you!? You all right? Wine gone to your head?"

"Yeah ... some ... but I just wanna know what it feels like to be held in someone's arms and be carried."

"All right," he agreed sympathetically.

He slid his left arm under her legs, supported her back with his right arm, cradled her, and picked her up. She felt almost weightless.

"Let's take the candles to the room," he said, leaning over the table.

Chloe draped her left arm behind his neck, stretched out her right arm, and grasped one of the candle bases and lighter. She brought it to her side and blew out the flame on the second.

"Now I know why normal people enjoy candles so much."

"Yeah, they're nice," Armada commented casually as he strode through the darkened warehouse and kitchen.

"Will you do one more thing for me?" she asked.

"Whatzat?"

"For the past couple of years, whenever I've had my evaluations, there's been this one physician's assistant that works for Engenechem in the Nursery. She never speaks to me directly 'cause she's rude and always on the phone talking to her boyfriend or whatever...."

"Okay? And?"

Chloe remained quiet as Armada slowly walked across the atrium.

"And what? What about her boyfriend?"

"I know you're gonna think it's weird, but...."

"Hey, just say it. What?"

"Well, they were constantly calling each other 'baby.' Baby this and baby that, and oh, baby."

"And?"

"Would ... would you mind ... calling me baby?"

"As in a term of endearment?"

"Well, yeah. I don't wanna say I'm Chloe Rover Seven anymore, or hear somebody yelling at me 'Hey! Rover Seven!' You know? I wanna be treated like, and feel like ... a woman. A real, live, human woman. And not looked at as just an ... an ... experiment!"

Her body began to tremble and her voice started to crack.

"I don't wanna have my blood drawn anymore. I'm sick of giving urine and stool samples! I'm tired of being poked and examined! I hate those interviews and taking their stupid psychological batteries!"

"Hey, calm down now. Just a few more steps...."

"And I can't stand being told what I'm gonna eat, how much, and when!"

He tried slightly bouncing her to calm her down, but the more she spoke, the more her legs and hands shook; she began sobbing and gasping.

"And ... I hate these ... stupid blue jumpsuits ... I've been ... wearing 'em ... my ... whole life! I hate ... being thought of ... as ... company property ... and ... I just want ... to be ... real ... and left alone!"

She turned her head into his chest and wept heavily.

"Hey, hey, now. Look. Here we are."

Armada carried Chloe into the room and headed straight for her bed.

"Hey, how about leaving the candle here on the table; okay?"

She lowered the burning candle on the four-seat table next to the compact refrigerator.

He then went to the far side of her bed and gently laid her down. Chloe rolled onto her right side, facing the nightstand and his bed. Armada retrieved the candle, walked between the beds, and set it on the nightstand next to the digital alarm clock.

"Here you go," he soothingly stated before sitting on her mattress. "Here's our special candle."

With her face now illuminated, he could see her red, swollen eyes. Tears streamed down her cheeks, her nose was running, and she couldn't seem to get her breathing under control.

"Ssshhh," he tenderly hissed as he slowly stroked her head.

"I'll be right back. Okay?"

With her eyes shut tightly, Chloe nodded her head.

Armada rose from her bed and went to the bathroom. He didn't turn on any lights, but felt his way to the sink and faucet. After twisting the hot water lever, he went back to the compact refrigerator and reached for the ice bucket. He then stuck it in the sink, adjusted the water temperature, and filled the bucket. Before exiting the bathroom, Armada groped the towel rack for a couple of washcloths.

"All right, all right, here we go," he softly announced as he approached Chloe.

Kneeling beside her bed, he set the bucket of water on the floor next to him. He submerged one of the washcloths in the warm water and swished it around. Although she was still upset, Chloe managed to slow down her breathing a bit.

"Okay now," he began as he wrung out the washcloth, "let's try this out and see how you like it."

He laid the cloth on her forehead and gently wiped her skin.

"Why don't you try lying flat?" he suggested.

With her eyes still closed, Chloe rolled onto her back.

"There you go."

He rubbed the washcloth across her skin from temple to temple. After a few minutes, he dunked the cloth and then turned his attention to the remainder of her face.

"Does this feel good, baby?" he playfully inquired.

Although he was sincere in his questioning, he wanted to lighten her mood.

Chloe's eyes remained closed, but she did manage to smile as she nodded.

He started wiping her cheeks and under her eyes when he asked, "I just wanna know, baby, if you're enjoying what I'm, baby, doing, baby?"

She reached up with her right hand and slapped kiddingly at his arm.

"I want you to know, baby, that I'm here for you, baby, baby, and that you'll always, baby, be my babety-baby-babe!"

That did it.

Chloe lurched to her left side, unable to contain her laughter, and covered her face.

"Well, baby?" he asked, poking her in the ribs. "What's wrong, baby? Huh? Where are you going, baby?"

He hopped on the bed and began tickling her, aggressively, as he intensified his verbal assault, "I just wanna talk to ya, baby. Don't turn your back on me, baby! Baby, I need you, baby! You're my babety-babe, baby, and don't ever babety, forbabyget it. Baby!"

Chloe squealed and shouted, "Augh! Stop it! Oh, my gosh, Armada! I'm gonna kill you!"

He at last ceased his intense tickling.

"You're such an idiot! Ugh!"

"All right," he said, climbing off the bed, "It's 2:32. Time for all good little girls to get to bed."

"Hey, no complaints here," she declared, panting heavily as she lay sprawled out on the mattress.

"We've had quite a day," he said, removing her boots.

"I know. I still can't believe it."

After having removed her socks, Chloe rolled to her right side and extended her left arm.

"Hey, c'mere," she instructed.

Armada took her hand and sat on the bed.

She looked lovingly and deep into his eyes.

"Thank you. Thank you for everything; for the whole day, for the meal... for keeping your promise and coming back to rescue me."

Armada spoke not one word. He placed his right hand on her head and gently ran his fingers through her hair.

Within seconds, Chloe was fast asleep.

Armada stood, walked around the bed, pulled up the comforter, and covered the sleeping beauty.

CHAPTER 28

I Do

Who could he possibly be talking to? Chloe asked herself.

She heard Armada speaking, albeit quietly, but was unable to understand what was being said.

Why am I not hearing another voice?

She was still lying on her right side when she opened her eyes.

Chloe looked at Armada's bed and noticed that not only was he not there, but it appeared that he had yet to lie down.

Where's that light coming from? she wondered.

A kaleidoscope of swirling and bleeding colors shone on the wall. The blue, purple, and green hues faded and blended into one another.

That's not coming from the ceiling lights or the bathroom, she thought.

Chloe slowly sat up in bed and propped herself up with her right arm.

She twisted back to her left and found Armada kneeling on the floor with his back turned to her. In the corner of the room was the orb. While it continually changed colors, just as it had the day before, she recognized that it had somewhat altered its appearance. When she first encountered the ethereal cloud, it was more or less the size of a basketball and semi-transparent. But now it was elongated, vertically, and measured roughly three feet in height. The apparition was much wider and seemed to taper off at the top.

"Armada?" she softly called out.

His name had no sooner escaped her lips when the beautiful mirage vanished, leaving the room as black as tar.

"Armada?"

"Whoa! Hold on, hold on," he quickly replied.

She heard him scurrying to his feet at the end of her bed.

"Hey, baby," he greeted as he squeezed the trigger on the lighter.

The tiny blue-and-yellow flame suddenly illuminated the nightstand and Chloe's face.

"What're you doing?" she asked as he lit the candle. "What time is it?"

"Uh ... four something."

He laid the lighter on the nightstand, stepped back, and sat on the edge of his mattress.

"How long have you been awake?"

"I haven't gone to bed yet."

"When did that thing get here?"

"I'd be willing to bet that you weren't asleep ten seconds before the power went out and he came into the room."

"You've been talking this entire time?"

"I asked him a few questions, but he did all the speaking."

"Well?" Chloe said, scooting up in bed. "What all did he say? What'd you talk about?"

Armada placed his hands on his knees, tilted his head back, and searched the ceiling. His mouth hung open in a half smile as he slowly shook his head.

"He ... told me so much, that ... I mean, there's a ton of information ... and ... I'm so overwhelmed my mind is absolutely flooded right now."

"Well, tell me what you can remember then."

"Chloe," he said, leveling his head, and stated, "I can't begin to express to you how good, and confident, and energized I feel at this very moment. I believe He came here tonight, to me, to this room, to give me some amazing advice ... about you and me."

"What?" she said with a cock of her head. "What kind of advice?"

Armada waddled over to Chloe's bed, got down on his knees, and took her hand.

"I think He came here tonight to tell me ... that you and I are to be, need to be, and should be ... husband and wife."

He gave Chloe an encouraging grin and tenderly squeezed her hand. She returned the smile and squeeze, but couldn't hide her quivering chin and trembling bottom lip.

"And just what did he say to make you assume this was his intent?" she smartly inquired, wiping her eyes.

"Okay, let me just say that while I believe what all He told me, He said a lot. So I'm gonna try to remember everything He spoke of, but I might accidentally chop it up a bit. Okay?"

"All right."

"Okay," Armada said prior to taking a deep breath. "About two thousand years ago, there was a man named Paul. Paul was kind of a leader back then and founded a church in Corinth. That's in Greece. So ... Paul stayed in Corinth for a few years to get everything organized and up and running. Okay? You with me so far?"

"Paul, church, Corinth, Greece, two thousand years ago."

"Great. Good. Okay, after a few years go by, Paul moves away and is gone from his people for another few years. So ... he decides to write them, the people in his church, and send them a letter. Now, this is why I think He came to talk to me ... to tell me what all Paul wrote, two thousand years ago ... He wants you and me ... to do what Paul told his people back in Corinth to do. Does that make sense?"

"Uh-huh," she answered and slid back down, scooting herself closer to Armada.

They subconsciously adjusted their fingers and laced them together.

"Tell me what Paul said. Oh, wait. Where'd he go? How long was he gone?"

"If I remember correctly, Paul went to Turkey to a town called ... um, uh, Ephes ... Ephu ... Ephuses ... Ephesus. That's it. Ephesus. He went to

Ephesus, Turkey, for three years, and that's when he wrote his letter to the Corinthians. Okay, I remember. So, Paul told the Corinthian people that … a man and a woman shouldn't … um, they shouldn't…."

"Shouldn't what?"

"You know…."

"What? Have sex?"

"Well, Paul said don't fornicate. He said it was wrong for a man and woman to just go and … go and have sex. Paul told them that if a man and woman are married, then … everything is okay. He said that when a man and woman are married, then … the man gives himself over to the woman. Conversely, after a man and woman are married, then the woman gives herself over to her husband. Does that sound right?"

"Mm-hm," she hummed, nodding. "If you and I were married … then, because you love me, you'd … give me everything of you … to make me happy. And if you and I were married … I would give you all of me to make sure you were happy and knew that … you'd know that I really loved you."

They both smiled at one another.

"What else did Paul write?"

"Um … love is … augh, this part was long. Love is … patient and kind. Love isn't jealous, boastful, proud or rude. It doesn't demand its own way. It's not irritable … and, it doesn't keep score of who did something wrong. Love is best whenever truth wins out. Love never gives up or loses faith. It's always hopeful and always endures … through every circumstance. The three things that Paul said would last forever are … faith, hope, and love … and the greatest of these is love."

Chloe smiled, drew Armada's hand close to her chest, and raised her left hand to play with his hair as he spoke.

"I can't remember everything He said … but … oh, okay … okay … there was another man named Moses, and he wrote a book called Genesis thousands of years before Paul wrote his letters. And in Genesis, Moses stated that it wasn't good for a man to be alone. He wrote that a man should have a mate. Paul also said that a man will leave his mother and father to be with his wife, and … and she'll leave her parents to be with him to be married. He included that in another letter he composed when he was in prison … I think in Rome, and sent it to the people back in Ephesus. He told the Ephesians when a man and woman are married … they're considered to be as one … as if they've become physiologically inseparable."

Chloe explored his face and eyes. She never felt so invigorated, so confident, yet completely relaxed. The sound of Armada's voice comforted her heart and calmed her spirit. The combination of his words, the tenderness of his touch, and the idea of freely living out her days with him seemed to deliver a much-needed dose of peace and tranquility to her psyche.

"Now, just how do we go about getting married? What are we supposed to do?"

"Well, seeing as how I didn't know He was coming here tonight to lay out his secret plans for us, I have nothing prepared."

"Isn't there something special we're supposed to say to each other that … that means we're married now?"

The confused couple thought of what they'd like to express to one another.

"This day! I'm telling you … man!" Armada commented nervously.

"All right, try this. I, Evan Armada Nine, want you, Chloe Rover Seven … to become my wife."

As the words escaped his mouth, he suddenly felt lightheaded. His stomach muscles started twitching and his lower lip tingled and buzzed.

"I promise you, Chloe, that I will never leave you … I'll never abandon you … no matter what happens to us."

He tightened his grasp on her fingers as he felt the saliva disappear from his mouth.

"I'll always do my absolute best to protect you. I'll try to always be honest and … tell you the truth."

Chloe sniffed deeply as she wiped a tear rolling down his cheek.

"I promise you that … one way or another, baby … I'm gonna find a way for us to get outta here. And wherever we go in this world, I will never, never, stop loving you. I marry you, Chloe, and will forever more be your husband."

They both attempted to stifle their sobs and sniffs, but were unsuccessful.

"Okay," Chloe squeaked, taking a deep breath. "I, Chloe Rover Seven, want you, Evan Armada Nine, to be my husband."

She couldn't manage to hold herself together and lost complete control of her emotions. Just the mere thought of the words she wanted to say was overpowering. It became impossible for her eyes to remain open as pure joy exploded in her heart and mind.

"And … I promise you … I promise I'll always love you … oh, Armada, I'll never stop loving you. I've been in love with you … for so long … it hurts."

Armada brushed the hair back and away from her forehead as she surged on with her vows and confessional.

"I … never want us … to be apart," she gurgled between breaths. "On Eden … on the SUBOS … anywhere … I give my life … over to you … and, I … marry you … Armada … and until the … day I die … I'll be your wife."

Armada leaned over his new bride and embraced her.

Chloe wrapped her arms around his back and neck and pulled with all of her might. How she longed and dreamed for someone to say those words to her, and she to them. The reality of the moment consumed her. The young bride grasped and clawed at Armada's body as she repeatedly called his name. As the newlyweds gently rocked from side to side, they declared their love to each other over and over again.

Armada raised his head and propped himself up on his elbows.

"Are you all right, baby?" he whispered, softly dragging his fingertips across her forehead.

Chloe smiled and nodded, still unable to speak.

"Here," he said, picking up the washcloth from the nightstand, "use this. I'll be back in a minute."

He placed the cool, damp cloth in her hand, kissed her delicately, and rose to his feet.

"I'll be right back."

Chloe started wiping her face as Armada slowly walked to the bathroom.

He closed the door and flipped the light switch. He had to squint his eyes as the brilliantly bright LED lights came to life.

"Ugh!" he grunted upon seeing his reflection.

His blue, one-piece jumpsuit was undeniably filthy. He turned on the water and pulled up on the rod for the plunger. While the sink was filling, Armada examined himself in front of the mirror. He had grown a considerable amount of coarse stubble in the last forty-eight hours. Unfortunately, as he quickly discovered, there were no means of shaving. He shut off the water and unzipped his suit, halfway down. After peeling back the shoulders and extracting his arms, he looked at the front of his undershirt. The ribbed tank top was stained with sweat, and had grey streaks on the straps from the dirty undersides of the boxes he'd been carrying.

He pulled the shirt over his head, wadded it up, and brought it up to his nostrils.

"Nope! Not wearing that tonight!" he mumbled, tossing it on the countertop.

Armada reached for a washcloth, dunked it in the hot water, and wrung out the excess.

"Thank you, thank you," he whispered as he began to wash himself.

He peered up at the ceiling, looking about as he spoke, and scrubbed his skin.

"Thank you for calling me. Thank you for the blackout. Thank you leading me to Chloe."

Armada felt his chin quivering the more he spoke.

"Thank you for knocking out the cameras the day before yesterday. Thanks for getting me outta the Arena and over to the SPUDs. Thank you for guiding me to a CARBEL. Thanks for getting me onto the SUBOS and into the Nursery."

X^N

Armada suddenly realized all of the impossible, inexplicable, and amazing miracles he had experienced.

"Thank you for making yourself visible to us. Thank you for guiding me to Chloe's dormitory. Thank you for leading us to this room and the Atrium and kitchen."

He stopped wiping, slumped to his knees, and wept as he continued to recall his experiences.

"And thank you for showing us your signs on the food. Thank you for coming here tonight to teach me. Thank you for Chloe. Thank you for bringing us together. I love her so much! Thank you! Thank you! I promise you that we'll do what you tell us to do, and we'll follow you and trust you wherever you lead us! Thank you, thank you!"

Armada placed his hands on the countertop and pulled himself up.

He again dunked the washcloth and proceeded to complete his sponge bath. After tossing the used cloth in the bathtub, Armada submerged his undershirt in the sink. Looking in the cabinet under the sink, he gathered up a bottle of mouthwash, a bottle of liquid hand soap, and a small tube of antibacterial hand sanitizer. He squirted generous amounts of soap and sanitizer in with his soiled undershirt. Once he swished the water around, Armada grabbed the shirt and scrubbed it against itself.

I'm married, he thought, proudly grinning to himself. *I'm a husband! I have a wife!*

The young groom stopped agitating his undershirt, wiped his hands dry, and reached for the mouthwash. After removing the cap and seal, he poured the bright-green liquid into his mouth and thoroughly circulated it. He spat out into the toilet, dragged a towel across his lips, and smiled at his reflection.

"I'm married," he repeated.

"Here I come!" Armada confidently announced as he turned off the lights and opened the bathroom door.

It took a moment for his eyes to adjust to the candlelight.

He took a few steps toward his bed and saw that Chloe's blue jumpsuit was laid out on top of the comforter.

"What were you doing in there?" Chloe asked. "I thought you'd never come out."

While he was administering his wipe down, Chloe removed her jumpsuit, used the damp washcloth to briskly scrub her own body, and climbed into bed.

With her right hand supporting her head, she gazed lovingly upon her husband and patted the mattress with her left hand.

"C'mere," she playfully demanded.

Armada inched his way to the nightstand and stood at the edge of the bed. Without so much as one word, he pulled the zipper all the way down the front of his suit and let it fall to the floor.

"Hey!" she exclaimed, pulling back the top sheet and comforter. "We have the same kind of shorts."

Armada was immediately intoxicated from the sight of Chloe's exposed flesh. Although she wore her undershirt and shorts to bed, just as he and his brothers had always done, this was their first physical, intimate encounter. Feeling his eyes roaming her body, she quickly drew up the covers, pulling them to her chin.

"Well?" she began, examining her half-naked husband. "Aren't you coming to bed?"

Armada couldn't move his feet; he stared at the floor.

Suddenly, with an incredible burst of energy, Armada sprang up onto the bed.

"We're married! We're married!" he shouted victoriously as he jumped up and down and back and forth from the other bed.

Chloe laughed out loud as he hollered, "I have a wife! I'm a husband! Baby, baby, baby! I'm your husband! Woo-hoo!"

"Shut up, you idiot!" she giggled as he bounced her across the bed. "Armada!"

She sat up and yanked his legs out from underneath him, making him fall backwards off the bed.

"Oh!" she squealed, then covered her mouth to hide her laughter.

"Oh, so that's how you wanna play?"

Like a lion stalking its prey, Armada slowly crawled onto the foot of the bed.

"I'm gonna getcha!"

Chloe pulled the sheet right up to her nose and did a poor job of containing her giggling.

"Rah!" he roared as he pounced on his bride.

He straddled her and tickled through the sheet while gnawing at her neck, growling as he teasingly devoured her.

Their juvenile wrestling act briskly transitioned into one of deep, passionate kissing, accompanied by curious roaming hands and heavy breathing.

Armada rose up off Chloe, drew down the covers, and climbed in bed. They lay next to each other and neither spoke or touched for a few minutes.

The newlyweds stared up at the ceiling.

Armada leaned to his right and blew out the candle, turning the room completely dark.

Chloe slid her right hand under the sheet 'til her fingers found his. She gradually scooted her body towards him and pressed herself against his left arm.

Silently, he raised his arm. Chloe rolled onto her right side and gently laid her head on his chest. She relished the simple pleasure of feeling his strong arm wrapped around her as she brought her left hand up to rest on his sternum.

In both her cheek and hand she felt the beating of his heart. Chloe was overjoyed with the sensation of feeling her head rise and fall with each and every breath he took.

Armada bowed and kissed his wife on her head.

"Goodnight, Mrs. Armada."

"Goodnight, Mr. Armada."

CHAPTER 29

SPECIAL DELIVERY

Armada abruptly woke up.

Why is it so hot? he thought to himself.

With his right arm wrapped around Chloe's waist, he opened his eyes and blinked several times. She faced away from him on her left side, and had spooned herself up against his body. He felt the heat radiating from her shoulders and back while listening closely to her breathing; it sounded heavy, congested, and labored. After cautiously removing his right arm, Armada slowly rolled away from his bride and sat up on the edge of their bed.

The digital clock read 7:40 a.m.

'Three hours?' he silently complained. 'I've slept for only three hours?'

He picked up the candle and lighter and tiptoed around the foot of the bed to the other side. Armada squeezed the trigger on the lighter and touched it to the candle wick. The concerned groom got down on his knees and brought the brightly burning candle to Chloe's face.

Armada's heart sunk as fear and panic ripped through his brain.

Chloe's chest was bright red. She had beads of perspiration on her upper lip and cheeks, and her hair stuck to her forehead.

He placed the back of his hand against her cheek; she was burning up.

"No, no, no, no!" he whispered.

X^N

He sat the candle on the ground and rose to his feet.

As he quickly stepped to the bathroom, Armada's mind shifted to the last time he saw Titan, his symptoms and appearance.

"Don't leave me!" he remembered Titan shouting to him.

As he held a clean washcloth under the faucet, Armada could still see Titan standing there in the Nursery Medical Services Facilities. His eyes were red and puffy, his skin was clammy and blotchy, and he had an incredibly high fever.

"I'll be okay, won't I? Tell 'em, Armada! Don't let 'em take me!"

The young groom dashed to his wife and crouched down beside her.

He raised the candle with one hand as he tenderly patted the cool cloth on Chloe's skin. She stirred a bit and rolled over onto her right side. Armada went around the bed, placed the candle on the nightstand, and proceeded to slowly wipe the moist rag across her forehead.

"Hey, baby," he lowly stated.

Chloe wrinkled up her nose, frowned, and pulled the sheet to her chin.

"Chloe? Baby? How do feel? Can you talk?"

"Mmm!" she moaned, then lethargically mumbled, "Why's it so hot, baby? I don't feel good."

"I know you don't. I'm gonna go get something for you to eat. Okay?"

Chloe again grunted and scooted closer to him.

"Armada, don't leave me," she whined.

"I'm just going to the kitchen. I'll be back before you know it. But I'm gonna need you to drink some water first."

Armada stood, hopped to the miniature refrigerator, and grabbed a cold bottle of water.

"C'mon now, just a few small swallows and you can go back to sleep."

Chloe could hardly sit up on her own.

Armada reached behind her and gently pulled her forward.

"There you go," he said as he twisted off the cap.

He brought the lip of the bottle to Chloe's mouth and tipped it back. She struggled to breathe while ingesting the water.

"That's my girl," he complimented as he eased her back on the mattress.

Chloe pushed her hand toward the mattress edge and spread her fingers. Armada lightly squeezed her hand and leaned in close.

"Oh, Armada," she groaned. "Not now. I can't get sick now. I've waited so long for us to be together … this can't be how it ends."

Tiny tears began rolling down her cheeks as she spoke. While she was talking, Armada couldn't stop his mind from flashing back to his best friend's face.

"That's why I gotta go find something good for you to eat. We need to figure out how to…."

Unable to finish his last statement, Armada gazed upon his sick bride while forcing himself to hide his fear and quivering chin.

"Do you think it's my end of cycle?" she asked, peeking up at him.

"No, no," he fibbed. "We're just … overwhelmed and tired. So much has happened in the last forty-eight hours that … well, think about it … we haven't even been married four hours. So … no, I don't believe it's your end of cycle. That's years and years away."

Chloe reached up and brushed his face with the tips of her fingers, trying desperately to keep a smile on her lips.

"Hurry back, okay? I don't wanna be alone."

"Ah, baby. Nothing will ever keep me away from you."

He leaned over and kissed Chloe's head.

"Now, try to sleep and I'll be right back."

Armada stood, watched Chloe make herself comfortable, and pulled the sheet up over her shoulder. Once she was settled and still, he blew out the candle then took his jumpsuit into the bathroom.

After closing the door, he turned on the lights and pushed down on the sink plunger. He stared at himself in the mirror as he wrung out his undershirt and rinsed it under the cold running water. With his shirt now relatively clean, he flung it over the shower rod to air and drip dry. Armada hurriedly donned his jumpsuit and slipped on his boots without first putting on his socks. Realizing that nobody was going to be seeing

him, he determined that it didn't really matter what he looked like or if his uniform was in order.

He turned off the light, opened the bathroom door, and glanced back at Chloe. Although the room was dark, he could barely see her head from the glowing numbers of the digital clock. After listening to her breathing for a moment, Armada delicately pushed down on the door handle and swung it open. Once out of earshot and in the corridor, he jogged briskly to the atrium and food services facilities.

Titan haunted his memories.

The more he thought about Chloe, her symptoms and sudden decline, the more Titan could be heard. As Armada turned on the lights and entered the dry goods storehouse, he remembered how fearful his best friend had become that fateful day. How similar, he observed, were both Chloe and Titan in their request that they not be left alone. The two had high fevers and sweated profusely, were weak and had pasty skin. Whereas Titan deteriorated rapidly over the course of several days, Chloe had only experienced one or two hours of ill-health.

"Hello?" Armada shouted, peering up into the lights. "Are you there? It's me!"

His eyes darted from light to light in hopes of receiving a visual response to the open call.

"I really need your help!" he loudly stated. "Chloe's back in our room ... I don't know if you're aware of it or if you're listening ... but she got sick all of a sudden ... she has a bad fever."

Not one bulb flickered.

"Please ... I'm begging you ... please don't let this be her end of cycle!"

Armada knelt down in the aisle with his head tilted back.

"She's afraid," he said with a trembling lip. "I'm afraid. We've gone through so much ... I don't know how to go on without her. Please ... please, help her ... I love her ... I need her."

Armada bowed his head and pressed his fingers firmly against his mouth to suppress his cries. With no acknowledgement to his call and sorrow in his heart, he wiped his eyes and slowly rose up.

He found a rolling three-shelf kitchen cart and swiftly browsed the rows of shelves. The inexperienced shopper gathered a few cans each of different fruits, a few bags of golden raisins, and some jars of apple sauce. After loading a case of bottled water on the bottom shelf of the cart, he went to the aisle with the disposable goods and pulled out plastic utensils, plates, bowls and cups, along with napkins and straws.

As he wheeled the cart to the kitchen entrance, he noticed the clock above the door.

"Eight twenty," he said.

While crossing the Atrium, he scanned his selections and thought to himself, *I gotta figure out a way to submit a request to Eden. I'll work on that while she's sleeping.*

He left the cart in the hallway to go in and check on his sickly bride. Other than her breathing, Chloe didn't make a peep.

Fresh from his first solo venture to the grocery store, Armada stealthily rolled the cart into their room and parked it between the chest of drawers and table.

He then sat on the other bed, pulled off his boots, and removed his jumpsuit.

Without a sound, Armada crept to their bed and deftly lowered himself onto the mattress. He pressed the back of his hand to Chloe's forehead once more and determined she was hotter than a half hour earlier.

Before he had an opportunity to reach for the damp washcloth, the room suddenly burst in bright orange and yellow light. Armada was overjoyed as the orb presented itself again and felt a sense of calm come over him.

The sphere approached Armada and crossed over the bed from the corner.

"I was calling you a few minutes ago," he whispered as he wiped his wife's forehead.

The orb passed to his right and hovered between the two beds, but offered no response.

For what felt like an hour, Armada quietly gazed at the apparition until at last he heard the voice confidently declare, "He will show you wonders and perform miracles."

"He? He who?"

"He has heard you and your desire to have Chloe healed."

As the orb spoke, it grew and stretched. No longer a miniature, opaque cloud of swirling colors, it now took on a form that appeared almost human.

"Thank you! Thank you!" he excitedly stated, "I just thought...."

"Let not your heart be troubled," it said, soothingly, "for she is not ill. She is with child. He is changing Chloe and at the end of three days she will be healed."

Armada's chin nearly fell to the mattress.

"What? She's...she's pregnant?" he exclaimed, "How? We've been married less than six hours?"

The glowing mirage continued to expand and grow as it spoke.

"In five months, Chloe will deliver a very special child...a boy...of His design."

"Five months? Five months?" Armada repeated in amazement. "A natural childbirth in almost half the normal time? That's impossible!"

"Through Him all things are possible."

Armada's mind was awhirl with questions and confusion.

"You will name your son Abdiel, and he will grow to be a powerful leader. He will be a blessing unto you, Chloe, and the world."

Armada gently combed his fingers through his wife's hair. He felt himself shaking as his heart beat faster and the saliva in his mouth evaporated. The apparition continued to levitate beside him as he processed the prophetic information.

Not knowing what questions he should be asking, the astonished father-to-be blurted, "What do we do now?"

"Be patient and love one another. He will be watching you, always, and will send me unto you again, soon."

With that, the shiny mirage disappeared.

By only the light of the alarm clock, Armada slowly and delicately laid himself back in bed and softly wrapped his left arm around Chloe. She was still breathing heavily and her temperature had not gone down. As he maneuvered his legs under the top sheet, her left hand curled up on his chest while he lightly ran his across her shoulder and upper arm.

The questions, confusion, and doubt swirling about in his mind soon gave way to happiness and excitement.

Just prior to closing his eyes to sleep, Armada chuckled, smiled to himself, and whispered, "A boy!"

CHAPTER 30

THE FOUR HORSEMEN

"Does this increase of debris entering Earth's atmosphere have anything to do with the disappearance of all the satellites?" the reporter shouted.

"What we discovered is that the debris entering our atmosphere is in fact bits and pieces of the missing satellites," said Goddard Senior Project Manager Chad Sagesur, "and not meteors or asteroids disintegrating and burning up as originally theorized."

The brood of fact-starved journalists and reporters clamored to capture the attention of the accomplished scientist.

"Dr. Sagesur!" one man yelled mightily. "Does this statement mean that the more than three thousand eyewitness reports and accompanying video clips are all recordings of damaged satellites reentering our atmosphere?"

"That's exactly what we're saying."

"How can that be?" another reporter hollered, waving her hand. "These sightings have occurred for nearly four months all over the world. And none of those are meteors or asteroids?"

"I know it sounds fantastic, but we've had teams scattered throughout the country and across the globe analyzing these videos. We've successfully determined that where the individuals were, geographically speaking, at what time, on which day, in what direction they were look-ing...they all correlate, exactly, to the last recorded position of all one hundred sixty-seven missing satellites."

"How? How did you verify this?" shouted one woman.

"Well, for one thing, we've been sifting through thousands of hours of recorded video footage and tens of thousands of still images from observatories...."

"Which observatories?" she again called out.

"Um...all of them," Dr. Sagesur proudly stated with a giggle. "For almost four months we've been reviewing, examining, and analyzing everything we can get our hands on from more than three hundred observatories. Air-based, space-based, ground-based, subterranean...all of 'em...we're receiving mountains of raw data every day. So we have to go through the daily and hourly records for each observatory, down to the minute and second, what direction was each telescope pointed in, what degree, what time, and so on. We're looking for a speck of dust on a needle in a haystack, and the needle is in constant motion."

"What evidence did you uncover that brought you to the conclusion that this phenomenon is damaged satellites reentering our atmosphere and not meteors, asteroids, or organic matter?" asked a man seated in front of the podium.

"Yes, I was just about to get to that," Chad politely replied.

"To begin, with nearly 330 observatories scattered throughout the world, some on the ground, some underground, in space and in the air, we thought we should cross-reference where telescopes were looking at the time of the last recorded position of each satellite. When we did that, we came across four stunning series of pictures and video footage. I want to walk through these one by one and show you why we drew these conclusions."

The crowd of journalists and intellectuals turned their attention to a massively large video monitor.

"First off," Dr. Sagesur began, aiming his red laser pointer at the screen, "I'm going to provide you with some technical data, and will then transition to language and vocabulary everyone can relate to. All right … right here, near the center of the image … this large, orange-red star is called Aldebaran, and is the red eye for the bull of the Taurus constellation. This collection of stars, known as the Open Star Cluster of Hyades, is in Taurus, but isn't part of the constellation. Now, a little more than two months ago, on May ninth, the NASA IRTF at the Mauna Kea Observatory in Hawaii captured the following images at a rate of one every five seconds. Keep your eyes on Aldebaran…."

The curious crowd of spectators watched the slide show, anxious to witness a celestial exhibition.

"And … freeze," Chad called to his assistants running the video equipment.

"At exactly 2:18 a.m., Pacific-Standard time, something peculiar and of high interest occurred. Two objects collided directly in the line of focus of the IRTF, and remarkably, temporarily obscured the presence of Aldebaran. Now, you might be asking yourself 'What does the eye of Taurus have to with missing satellites?' May ninth, at 2:18 a.m., was the moment when contact was lost with this…."

The television switched from the looped film footage to a close-up picture of an artist's rendering of a satellite.

"The AsiaStar communication satellite. Launched from the ELA-3 in French Guyana in March of 2000, this 6,000-pound, American-owned communication satellite was constructed through a joint venture between Alcatel Space and Marconi Space, but was operated by One World Space before changes in ownership. For well over a decade, the AsiaStar provided broadband and internet support to Australia, India, and Southeast Asia for hundreds of thousands of people. It was placed in geostationary orbit, specifically at 105 degrees east. So, to make a long story short, on May ninth, a telescope in Hawaii just so happened to be aimed at the Taurus constellation, when the AsiaStar entered the telescope's line of vision. At that very moment, an unidentified object collided with the AsiaStar, and…."

"Doctor?" a man politely interrupted. "If you have pictures of the collision, can't you identify what it is that struck the satellite?"

"Well, yes and no. Because mostly all observatories and satellites use high-resolution and high-speed cameras and film, normally we're able to do just that. But in this particular case, and the three others, we've remained unsuccessful in correctly identifying the craft...."

"Craft?!" some of the reporters repeated, raising their hands. "Craft as in alien? A spacecraft? Do you mean a flying saucer?"

"No, no, no ... people, we're not implying a flying saucer is up there attacking our satellites. We're using the term loosely because when we watched the full video of the collision, this appeared...."

The television monitor resumed playing the images recorded by the Hawaiian observatory.

"Okay, now, look here ... here ... here ... and, here," Chad stated, pointing his laser at the screen as the still images scrolled by.

"It's changing course!" the man in front of the podium hollered.

"Exactly!" Dr. Sagesur replied, smiling at the man. "Not only is it altering its path, it's rapidly descending. Whatever this is, it was capable of positioning itself in a predetermined location, and, after surviving a direct impact, for all accounts an intentional, direct impact, it then reengaged its propulsion systems and moved to a new location."

The throng of reporters, journalists, and tech bloggers quickly hopped to their feet, shouting their questions over one another.

"Please, please...," Dr. Sagesur bellowed, holding his hands above his head. "I can't answer you all at once ... please, calm down and I'll ... yes, okay, you sir...."

"Don't we have penetrating radar that can see into these crafts?" a woman inquired.

"Yes, we have the technological know-how, as do many other nations, organizations, and agencies of foreign governments. However, from what we've learned, these four crafts have deflecting and cloaking technologies that, so far as we know, make it impossible to track their movements and view their internal structure. In addition, our resources are being depleted most rapidly."

"Doctor?" a man in the rear of the room shouted. "Can you tell us what kind of satellites have been destroyed?"

"Yes. Our teams identified a trend in satellite technological capabilities that are obviously the primary reason for their targeted destruction. The satellites have been grouped into five categories: first, defense support, which are those that monitor for and warn of an attack by detecting ballistic missile launches. Then nuclear explosion detection, photo surveillance, electronic reconnaissance, and lastly, radar imaging. These marauders are hunting down defense systems components. And I use the term 'hunt' specifically, because it can't be interpreted in any other way. It doesn't matter if they're in a low Earth orbit of a couple hundred miles or a geostationary orbit of 22,000 miles. The US isn't isolated in these attacks...the defense satellites of the world's governments are being systematically eliminated, thereby rendering each nation helpless. These attacks are being observed by our allies as well in Canada, England, Germany, Australia, Japan, and others. Israel has lost numerous Ofeq reconnaissance and Amos telecommunication satellites. The Russians have lost nearly twenty of their Cosmos, Luch, and GLONASS satellites. In fact, to let you know of the severity of our situation, just prior to this press conference, we were notified by the deputy prime minister of Germany that they had lost contact with their SAR-Lupe 5 satellite. That makes...."

***

"Turn it off," Cain drolly stated. "I've heard enough."

Dr. White reached out for the remote control and turned off the live, televised press conference.

The two men sat quietly on the couch in Dr. Wyczthack's private quarters, tapping on the screens of their tablet computers.

"That went well," Dr. White mumbled. "It appears Chad's usage of the word 'craft' shifted their focus. You were right."

"Yes," Cain robotically replied.

"Would you care for a drink?"

"Um...," Cain began, but was too distracted to complete his answer.

Dr. White set his tablet on the couch cushion and slowly rose. He sauntered across the spacious sitting room to the handsomely ornate and well-stocked private bar.

"What'll you have?" he called out while grabbing two glasses.

"Uh ... Four Roses ... neat," Cain answered as he, too, placed his tablet on the couch.

The aged scientist approached the bar, pulled out a chair, and plopped himself down.

"Ah, that's the stuff!" Cain commented as his partner poured a hefty amount of bourbon in a glass. "And you?"

"The Dimple," Dr. White answered with a smile. "One doesn't fix what's not broke."

After serving his own stout portion of Scotch, Dr. White set his glass on the countertop and walked around the bar to join his friend.

"What shall we drink to?"

"How about ... the destiny of mankind," Cain drably suggested, raising his glass.

"Destiny, eh?" Dr. White repeated, pulling out a bar stool. "I'll drink to that."

The two men nodded to each other and sipped their spirits.

"We need to talk," Cain flatly stated, loosening his necktie.

Dr. White sat motionless and silent.

"Chloe Rover Seven and Evan Armada Nine. They vanished two weeks ago. What's happening?"

"Well, one, we're still investigating. I have hundreds of our staff dedicated to tracking them down. Two, something tells me they're still on the SUBOS. They've either successfully located a defibrillator, or ... gained access to an MRI in one of our medical services facilities to knock out their RFID chips ... making it impossible to track their movements."

Without turning away from Dr. White, Cain slowly rose his glass to his lips and took another sip of his bourbon.

"Continue."

"I can't explain how, but both Chloe and Armada have devised a method of avoiding retinal scanners and motion detection cameras. We have some of our best employees from the design labs working on this."

Dr. Wyczthack stared intensely at Dr. White.

Cain swiveled away from the bar, with whiskey in hand, and ejected himself. After swaggering out into the middle of the expansive living room, he took another sip of his drink.

"I'll not have our plans railroaded by a couple of runaways. We have too much to lose to allow them to remain free and roaming about."

"Yes, sir."

"Find them!" Cain suddenly shrieked and threw the lead crystal highball glass across the room.

"Find them! Now! Kill them! Now!" he screamed, whirling around to face Dr. White. "We can't take delivery from Oak Ridge with them walking the halls! We can't proceed as planned with those two roaming from place to place, sticking their noses where they don't belong. The last thing we need is to have two computer-literate supergeniuses who can't be tracked delaying our plans!"

"No, sir."

"We can't control the world ... if we can't control Chloe and Armada!"

CHAPTER 31

RECESS

"Oh, you are so utterly and thoroughly doomed!" Armada declared as he prepared to serve, crouching slightly.

"Oooh!" Chloe taunted, wiggling her fingers. "I'm absolutely petrified! I don't know if I can handle the mental torture. Please… stop … it … I'm … gonna … start … crying … if.…"

Before she could finish her sarcastic rebuttal, Armada released the new, white ping-pong ball from his left hand and gave it a mighty whack. The ball zipped across the net to the farthest corner of the table. Chloe's reaction was swift, almost effortless: she backhanded the ball to the outermost edge, just behind the net, landing it perfectly inbounds before lightly bouncing off the table.

"Augh!" Armada loudly growled, flopping himself face down. "I don't believe it! Five games? You've never played ping-pong and yet you smoke me five games in a row?"

"Beginner's luck," she jokingly commented.

"Ugh!" he grumbled, rising off the table. "I'm not gonna go through this every day. We gotta find something else to play."

"Well, let's see what all they've got buried in there," she suggested as she wrapped her arms around Armada's waist.

The happy couple pecked their lips together and briefly hugged.

Armada took his wife by the hand and led her to a gargantuan stack of cardboard boxes and crates located at the furthest end of an open area they dubbed 'the playground.' Even though the collection of boxes appeared to have been sorted out with regards to content, with so many of the labels printed in foreign languages it was difficult to ascertain what they were looking at.

"Okay, what about these?" Armada asked, placing his hand on the end of a long, wide box lying on its side.

"Sure."

Armada began pulling on the end flap while Chloe used the small pry bar from the liquor warehouse to remove the heavy-duty staples.

"Man! They don't want anyone get'n into this, do they?" he grunted, struggling to tear away the cardboard. "Way too much glue!"

"Aw, it's not too bad, Princess."

"I'll make you think Princess!" he quipped and gave the box flap one final tug.

After having removed several staples, the cardboard finally yielded to Armada and sent him rolling backwards. Chloe couldn't suppress her laughter and failed miserably in trying to hide it.

"So, you think that's funny?" he gruffly asked.

"Oh, yeah!"

Armada chuckled to himself and crawled to the partially opened box.

"Pry the rest of these on the bottom," he requested, pointing at the staples near the corner.

Chloe leaned over and attempted to insert the tip of the pry bar under a staple, but Armada began gently poking her in her ribs, just below her armpit.

"C'mon! C'mon!" he playfully taunted. "Hurry up."

"Stop it! You know I'm ticklish!" she laughingly demanded. "I have a weapon!"

Chloe's veiled threat failed to discourage her husband from antagonizing her all the more.

"C'mon, do your job. Whatsamatter with you? You're jumpy all of a sudden."

While trying to stave off the tickle assault, Chloe managed to pry loose four more staples.

"Augh!" she growled, tossing the bar to her side. "You just don't know when to quit, do you?"

Chloe dove on top of Armada with her fingers outstretched like talons. She dug into his abdomen and love handles while simultaneously gnawing at his neck.

"Get it off me! Get it off me!" he squealed, pushing her away.

The more Armada squirmed and fought, the more Chloe ratcheted up her attack. The couple rolled over each other as they wrestled, goosed, pinched, and laughed.

"All right, all right!" she shouted, clutching her arms tightly against her sides.

Armada sat on his wife's rump, relentlessly poking her in her ribs.

"You win! You win! Knock it off!"

He stopped his assault, leaned down, and tenderly kissed his wife's neck.

"Showed you, didn't I?" he whispered.

"Oh, yeah. You sure showed me."

Armada rolled off his wife and lay beside her, then started running his hand through her hair. Chloe turned to face her husband and scooted closer, took his free hand, and clutched it tightly against her chest.

"How are you feeling?"

"I feel fine," she softly answered, kissing the end of his nose.

"Any more fevers? Are you still getting sick?"

"No, no more fevers, and I haven't been sick."

"Have you been experiencing any…."

"I'm fine," she reassured her overprotective beaux. "Don't worry so much. I'll be okay, Doctor Armada."

The father-to-be looked down, placed his palm against Chloe's belly, and proudly stated, "We love you, Abdiel."

Without saying a word, Armada crawled to his feet, extended a hand, and pulled Chloe to her feet.

"Now, let's find out what's in the box and, after that … we'll round us up something to eat."

Armada spun around and proceeded to tear away the remaining cardboard from the massive container.

"Do me a favor, please," he grunted. "Count out how many boxes there are."

Chloe stepped to his side and started calculating the quantity of crates and number of individual boxes in each.

"And, we're done," he declared as he threw a piece of corrugate on the floor.

"Twenty-five crates of four," she said.

Armada forced his hand through an outer layer of shrink wrap and an interior layer of bubble wrap. With his arm outstretched shoulder-deep into the long box, he blindly explored its contents, trying to discern what his fingers were touching.

"Well, whatever this is, it's flat and smooth, but feels kinda fuzzy. Wait a minute … I think I got something."

"What is it?" Chloe curiously inquired.

"Uh … it definitely feels like a possum carcass."

"Shut up!" she said with a light slap to his shoulder. "I'm serious."

"You shut up!" Armada demanded and lashed out at his wife's leg.

Finally, he withdrew his arm and pinched between his fingers was a clear, ziplock-style plastic bag.

"Warranty," he stated, reading aloud the printed wording on the outside of the bag.

After handing it to Chloe, she quickly separated the two flaps and extracted the paperwork.

"Here," she said, handing him an instruction manual as she examined a packing slip.

"What's Olhausen?" she asked. "It says here, contents, one, Americana series Excalibur, Mahogany, eight-foot, cherry finish, red felt…."

"No way!" Armada joyously exclaimed, flipping the pages. "It's a pool table! Sweet!"

"The packing slip says this thing cost forty-five hundred dollars."

"Wow!"

"Wyczthack and White forked out half a million bucks ... for pool tables?"

"Well?" Armada shrugged as he reviewed the assembly instructions. "I imagine they're concerned with how to keep thirty thousand people entertained and preoccupied."

"And just what do you know about playing pool?" she playfully asked, yanking the booklet out of his hands.

"I know nothing about pool, but have heard Garret mention on more than one occasion that he plays on some kind of team on the SUBOS. He told Euclid and me that he's quite a ... a, uh ... shark. He says he's a pool shark."

"Is that a good thing?"

"I don't know ... maybe you should ask him."

"Can we eat now? I'm starving!"

"Tell you what ... I'll run to the kitchen and scrounge around for something to eat while you, Mrs. Armada, count out everything. Okay?"

"I'm okay with that as long as you bring me back some chocolate."

"You know, you're gonna deplete our supply before everyone even gets here."

"Ha!" she mocked him and spun him around.

"Now ... go ... your child and I are famished!"

Chloe teasingly pushed him and gave his rear a gentle kick.

"Yes, thank you, Armada," he sarcastically stated as he shuffled away. "I love you, Armada. You're a good man, Armada. Thank you for providing for me, Armada. You're the best husband a woman could ever...."

"I'm not listening to you!" Chloe shouted and turned away.

***

X^N

"Okay, we know there's a hundred pool tables and two hundred ping-pong tables," she said before tossing a handful of cashews into her mouth.

"Add to that two hundred sets of paddle ball, five hundred dart boards, and one hundred sets of bocce ball."

"Right," she stated after guzzling half a bottle of water and hopped off the ping-pong table, pointing, "Those weigh a ton ... we've got two hundred fifty. We'll need to bust one open."

Chloe stepped to the section of boxes she was referring to and tapped on the top of one.

"Two hundred fifty of these. And ... over there ... in the corner ... there's another hundred boxes that are similar in shape to the pool tables but are longer and wider. Those weigh a ton as well."

Chloe had started walking back when Armada hollered out, "So, three different size boxes that we don't know what's in 'em? Is that right?"

"No, two. We don't know what's in two different sizes."

Armada dunked a cracker into a bowl of peanut butter as his wife strolled back to their ping-pong table, pointing as she called out.

"All of these boxes here are board games. Monopoly, traditional and Chinese checkers, Scrabble, chess, something called Risk, Yahtzee, dominoes ... and beside those are card games. Skip-Bo, Uno ... and I don't know how many decks of playing cards. I'd guess there's at least a thousand."

Chloe turned away from Armada and leaned back against him, standing between his legs. She reached beside her and plucked a large pickle from a glass jar.

"You know...," she said before chomping on the big dill, "with everything Wyczthack has stored here and at Strataca ... Engenechem has invested billions and billions of dollars."

Armada wrapped his arms around Chloe's waist and gently swayed from side to side.

"I mean, just look at all this!" she growled, taking another bite of her pickle. "All this junk ... for a few thousand people ... and the remaining six-and-a-half billion ... they just get erased!"

"That's something we still have to figure out. How's Wyczthack gonna do it?"

Armada took Chloe's wrist, pulled her arm up and back, and bit off a large chunk of her pickle.

"Chemical? Biological? Nuclear? Depletion of natural resources? We gotta get on that. His method of extermination."

Armada nudged Chloe forward, lowered himself off the table, and walked around her.

"He'll have to do it in an expedient manner," she commented as she, too, dipped a cracker in the bowl of peanut butter. "It wouldn't make sense to drag out a mass extinction. It'll be catastrophic, fast, and on a scale nobody has ever seen or imagined."

"Nobody except Wyczthack and White."

Armada approached the leaning stack of long, wide cardboard boxes and attempted to lift one up off the ground. He spread his stance, squatted slightly, and sandwiched the container between his hands. With the greatest of ease he lifted the box.

"This doesn't weigh much at all," he declared as he lowered it down.

"Well, it felt heavy to me," Chloe responded.

The end flaps on this box weren't stapled like the other, and the adhesive used to seal the flaps wasn't especially strong. Armada peeled back the cardboard with very little effort.

"Well, that was easy," he stated while pulling back the interior flap.

Chloe placed the rest of the cracker in her mouth and began walking toward her beaux.

"This is actually pretty light," he informed her while slowly removing the mystery object from its shell,

"Ugh! More plastic wrap," she said as the end of the parcel became visible.

Chloe began tugging on the opposite end of the box, allowing Armada to remove the wide object.

"Looks like a soccer field," she commented.

"Soccer?"

Chloe knelt and stuck her hand in the box and retrieved a booklet.

"Official Competition Air Hockey," she read aloud.

"Yes! Air hockey! I wanna play!"

"Hold on there, Turbo. Let's open up one of those others first."

"Pool, air hockey, ping-pong, cards…," Armada recited. "We're gonna be pretty busy."

Chloe led him to a section of the 'playground' with a couple hundred of heavy corrugated boxes measuring roughly six feet long, three feet wide, and three feet deep.

"Now, these are the ones that weigh a ton," she said, patting the side.

"We'll see 'bout that," Armada commented as he placed his hands on top.

He tried pushing the box out and away from the rest, but it wouldn't budge.

"Huh. Whadyaknow?" she mumbled to her husband. "See? Told you it was heavy."

"All right, all right. Help me get my hands behind it."

The couple managed to pull one end of the box out a bit, allowing Armada to step into the gap. As Chloe tugged on the corner, Armada pushed with his legs. They eventually succeeded in creating a two-foot wide perimeter around the box.

"Baby, go and get the pry bar, please."

"Aaawww," she moaned in approval.

"Yeah, yeah," he drably replied as she skipped to the section of crates containing the pool tables.

"Here you go," Chloe cheerfully chirped, placing the tool in his palm, "baby."

"Thanks, baby," he said.

Armada forced the angled and forked tip of the bar under the seam where the two flaps met and pushed it deep. He pulled up on the curved end, forcing the metal through the thick layers of sturdy cardboard.

"This thing better be extremely fragile and breakable with the way they pack it up."

Chloe watched her husband work up a sweat as he wrestled with the container. Finally, at long last, he reached the opposite end of the sarcophagus.

"Yay for you, baby," Chloe cheered, leaning out to pull back one side of the torn cardboard.

"Bonzini," she abruptly stated.

"Bon what?"

Armada bent the remainder of the box top backwards out of his way.

"Bonzini," he repeated, reading the manufacturer's name printed boldly on a legal-sized manila envelope.

Chloe picked up the envelope, ripped away one end, and turned it upside down. Armada tore at strips of packing tape holding a flat piece of cardboard in place.

"Ah ... White and Wyczthack are the proud owners of more than one hundred Bonzini official regulation, competition-size foosball tables."

"Foosball? What's that?"

"Well ... from what I gather ... it's soccer with little men."

Armada stepped up behind her, peered over her shoulder, and shrugged with disconcert.

"Pool sounds more interesting to me."

Chloe lackadaisically tossed the instruction manual on top of the semiexposed game table and walked away.

"What are these?" Armada asked, pointing at a sequestered stack of boxes.

"Don't know. Haven't gotten to 'em yet."

The duo pushed and shoved themselves a path to the collection of two-foot square boxes.

"I wonder what's inside," Chloe commented as she examined the exterior decals.

"Only one way to know for sure."

Armada peeled back the center strip of packing tape on top of one box and ripped away half of the folded flaps. Chloe read aloud the wording on the labels and stickers.

"Fragile. This side up. Warning … electrical components."

Armada reached into the box and retrieved a handful of Styrofoam packing peanuts and a layer of bubble wrap.

"No way!" he shouted after glancing in the carton. "No stinking way!"

He jumped up and down while hollering, "Woo-hoo!" from the top of his lungs.

"What?" Chloe excitedly asked. "What is it?"

"Woo-hoo!" Armada continued to squeal, bouncing about.

He rushed towards her, crouched low, and flung her wildly over his shoulder.

"Yes! Yes, yes, yes! This is exactly what we needed!"

"Tell me, you idiot!" Chloe laughingly demanded as her husband hopped, twirled, and spun around.

"Oh, baby!" Armada joyfully remarked, flinging her off his shoulder into his arms.

"This is so unbelievably incredible!"

He lowered Chloe to her feet, placed his hands on her cheeks, and kissed her passionately.

"Oh, my gosh, Chloe. This changes everything!" he breathlessly declared.

Armada took his wife by the hand and led her back to the partially opened box.

"Thank you! Thank you!" he shouted, glancing up at the ceiling.

They both knelt down and Armada began vigorously tearing away at the box top.

"Wow, oh wow, oh wow!" he stated.

After having torn the remainder of the cardboard flaps, he extracted a thin but long and wide carton.

"Tablets. We got tablets!"

"Oh, Armada!" she exclaimed, grasping the small container.

"We can communicate," he stated, removing the computers one by one. "We can look at WATCHER and EGGS any time we want. I can access any record, file, or camera. I can contact Euclid. We can…."

"Eden?" Chloe interrupted. "Can you create a manifest request to Eden?"

"I can create a thousand."

With tears in her eyes, she suddenly lunged at Armada and snuggly wrapped her arms around his neck. After a lengthy embrace, she released him and sat back on her haunches.

"Thank you, wherever you are. Thanks for this," Chloe called out, wiping her eyes. "This'll really help us."

"Twenty, twenty-one, twenty-two, twenty-three ... twenty-five. Twenty-five tablets per case. And we have how many cases?"

"Plenty."

"Exactly. Let's take these and one more box back to our room. I'll go get the cart."

CHAPTER 32

I Spy

"All right, let me tell you what I'm thinking."

The couple stood in front of their bedroom dresser with all fifty tablets stacked neatly on top.

"I wanna get two more tablets, one for each of us, and use them as our primary keyboards and points of entry."

"What about all of these?"

"These … will be our monitors," he said, stepping towards the dresser. "I'll create a program that will broadcast certain video surveillance cameras to specific tablets and run on a timer … just like closed circuit systems."

"How many cameras do you think we'll need to access?" she asked as she began unpacking the first carton.

"I figure five cameras per tablet on broadcast loops consisting of twelve seconds each."

Armada joined his wife in removing the contents of the boxes.

"Problem is…," he started saying, then paused, "how do we keep fifty-two of these fully charged, twenty-four seven? We don't have extension cords or power strips. And there's only three outlets in here, plus one in our bathroom."

"Leave the power supply to me. I'm the engineer, remember?"

Chloe then bonked Armada on the back of his head with an empty carton.

"And just how, pray tell, do you intend to monitor the monitors?" she snarkily inquired, bonking his head once more.

"Oh … I'm way ahead of you," he replied, smacking her on the forehead with his empty, lightweight box.

"First, we're gonna take the box the pool table came in, bring it in here, and lean it horizontally against the far wall. Second, we'll slice small openings that will fold out so the tablets have something to rest on to support their weight."

"It'll take at least two crates, using both front and backsides, to house all fifty tablets. That gives us four panels to set them up," Chloe commented.

After removing the tablet computers and accessories from their cartons, Armada piled the empty boxes on the cart and swiftly wheeled it to the trash receptacle at the back of the kitchen.

A few moments later, as he was leaving the warehouse, Chloe was passing him on her way in.

"Hey there, pretty lady," he taunted playfully, "where are you off to?"

"Forklift charging station. I need wire strippers and electrical tape."

"Good luck," he stated as she approached him and offered up a quick kiss.

Armada returned to their room, plugged in one of the new, pristine tablet computers, and immediately set to work on creating his monitor program. A few minutes later, Chloe entered the room laden with wire strippers, voltage meters, electrical tape, soldering gun and wire, and several other devices. While Armada diligently wrote out his coding and selected the video cameras he wished to view, Chloe focused on the daisy chain assembly of the fifty tablet power cords and modifying the condensers. Within a couple of hours, she successfully spliced and grafted a single, unique power cord capable of charging thirteen tablets simultaneously, while occupying only one outlet. For Armada's plans to work, she'd have to fabricate three additional power cords to power up the remaining thirty-seven tablets.

Working hours and hours on end was nothing new to Armada and Chloe. Be it EVA assignments on the Arenas or Clouds, maintaining and caring for the animals in the Arks, or paying meticulously close attention to the crops on Eden, the couple could push through twenty-four-hour work details unfettered.

After having completed the assembly of her four adapted power cords, Chloe left Armada to his coding and programming while she wheeled the kitchen cart to the recreation area. She took with her a utility knife and scissors she found earlier in the forklift service bay. With one end of the box containing the first pool table already opened, Chloe cut along the edges of the cardboard panel, leaving a sheet of rigid corrugate measuring roughly four feet by eight feet. She leaned the panel against another box, then scooted two of the crates containing the tablets in front of the pool table. She gingerly pulled the ornately decorated billiard table toward her and slowly lowered it down to rest on the two smaller boxes. It took no time at all to cut out another panel from the backside of the mammoth carton. After repeating the process on the second pool table, Chloe had the four sheets of cardboard ready to go.

***

"Knock, knock!" Chloe stated as she dragged the sheets of corrugate into the room. "Special delivery."

"Wow!" Armada exclaimed, rising from his chair. "My, but aren't you the expedient one!"

"Hey, when you got a job to do...."

"What else you got?"

Chloe leaned the four sheets of cardboard against the wall on the far side of their bedroom, turned to face him, and held up her index finger. She silently brushed by her husband, entered the hallway, and before he could see her, began speaking.

"Breakfast is served," she said, rolling the cart into the room.

"Uh, miss, I don't recall ordering room service."

"No? Well, shut up and eat."

Chloe stood toe to toe with her beaux and entered his personal space.

"You shut up and eat," he sarcastically demanded.

"No … you shut up first, then eat."

The couple kissed and brought the cart up next to their table.

***

"All right, here we go," Chloe stated, but not with any confidence or enthusiasm.

She grasped the plug dangling at the end of the first power cord, leaned over, and pushed it into the top outlet. Chloe stood beside the first cardboard panel and waited.

"Well?" Armada said, facing the wall of powerless computers.

"Hold on…."

Chloe checked the ports on each tablet, pressing the adapters snuggly into place.

"What's wrong with it?"

"I don't know," she snapped, holding her hands in the air.

She reached behind the wall of tablets and jiggled the plug, just to make sure it was inserted completely.

Suddenly, a muted, high-pitched bell began chiming.

"Oooh!" Chloe squealed, jumping in place while clapping her hands.

"There's one," she proudly stated as the tablet's tiny green LED power bulb flickered to life.

"That's two," she proclaimed as the bell for the second computer started dinging.

Armada leapt at his bride, enveloped her in his arms, and spun them around and around.

"Woo-hoo! You did it, baby!" he joyously praised her.

He stopped spinning and held her up high, pulling her firmly into his chest.

While still suspended and pressed against him, Chloe laid her head on his shoulder. Her eyes suddenly felt heavy. Armada gently twisted from side to side, relishing the simple, tender moment, the blissful sensation of feeling her heart beating against his and the warmth of her breath on his skin.

They counted the chiming computers all the way to number thirteen.

"Job well done, Professor," Armada whispered.

Chloe giggled and nuzzled her face against his neck, as if preparing to go to sleep.

"All righty then, down you go."

"Mmmm," she hummed miserably and squeezed her arms tightly.

"Let's get you to bed. You've been a busy girl."

"Oh, baby, no," she moaned as her muscular husband bent over and tenderly laid her on their bed. "Armada?"

"Sorry," he commented as he dashed to the bathroom.

"I've got a ton to do," she heard him say just before he turned off the lights.

With her eyes already closed, Chloe rolled to her right side, away from the glare of the corner lampstand. She heard the clicking of the lighter and, through her eyelids, saw the bright orange flame of the candle on the nightstand.

"You had a long day," Armada commented as he squatted down beside her.

He unfolded and draped a wet, warm washcloth across Chloe's face and gently cleaned her skin.

"Aren't you coming to bed?"

"Soon."

"Okay ... just don't stay up too late," she groggily mumbled.

After wiping her face, Armada turned his attention to his wife's arms, hands, and fingers. He hadn't yet finished cleansing her bicep before she fell asleep.

The dedicated husband went to the foot of the bed, removed her boots and socks, and drew the comforter up over her.

***

Chloe's eyelids fluttered open to a display of lights and shadows dancing on the wall next to the vacant bed.

'What's that smell?' she asked herself.

She rolled to her back, stretched, and wiped away the matter in the corners of her eyes. Chloe then turned to face the cardboard panels and tablets, half of which were illuminated with live video streams. Armada was at the table, hunched over his computer.

"Have you been awake this entire time?" she asked, propping up her head in her left palm.

"Hey, you," Armada gleefully stated, turning to face her.

"What's that smell?" Chloe asked while her husband stood and extended his arms above his head.

"Coffee pods."

"Coffee pods? Where?"

"Found 'em in the dry goods. Here … taste this."

Armada grasped the mug on the table and walked around the bed to his wife.

"First things first," he commented, squatting on the mattress. "Good morning."

He smiled, leaned forward, and pecked Chloe on her forehead.

"Good morning back at you, baby."

Chloe grinned as Armada handed off his cup, "What is this?"

"Dark roast Colombian coffee, with one tiny melted square of dark chocolate."

After sitting up straight and crossing her legs, she brought the steaming cup of coffee to her nose.

"Wow! That smells good!"

Armada smiled as she took a sip of his coffee.

"Oh, my gosh!" she exclaimed. "This tastes incredible!"

"I know! I can't get enough."

Armada reached out to take back the mug, but Chloe pulled away from him.

"Oh, no you don't, mister!" she playfully teased. "This one's mine now."

She took another sip and darted her eyes. "This is so tasty! Sure wish you had one of your own to enjoy."

"It's all right. I've already had four of 'em," he admitted, then stepped to the miniature coffeemaker.

"So...," Chloe announced, crawling across the bed, "explain to me what's going on with this, thus far."

Armada began elaborating on his creation as he plopped a fresh pod into the brewer.

"All right. I've created a program for the first thirteen tablets whereby live video surveillance from five different cameras each will be streamed in twelve-second intervals."

"Every sixty seconds, sixty-five cameras."

"Correct."

"So, once all fifty tablets are up and functional, every sixty seconds we'll have two hundred fifty separate video feeds."

"Correct again."

Armada removed his mug from under the brewer nozzle, tossed in a chocolate square, and joined his bride. Chloe held out her mug and the couple clinked their cups in a toast to each other.

"That's gonna take up a lot of storage space," she commented with a negative tone. "That much data being recorded is bound to draw attention."

"Way ahead of you. We're not recording and storing. You're absolutely right; someone's bound to get suspicious with that kind of volume of data suddenly being stored. But this is untraceable and undetectable. All we're doing is watching. White and Wyczthack, on the other hand, are recording ... EVERYTHING. All we're doing is seeing what they see. If we find something of interest, we can access the camera history and investigate.

With this many video cameras being activated automatically and all of the different security departments monitoring those recordings, nobody will ever know who's watching."

They stood close to the bank of computers and stared intensely at the images as they shuffled by. Chloe leaned into her husband and nursed her 'cup o' Joe.'

"How many video cameras do you estimate Cain has?"

"Total? Everything?" he asked, draping his arm over her shoulder. "Well, you figure at a minimum … a hundred fifty for the Arenas. There's four of those."

"That's six hundred."

"Then we got the Halos, the three Arks, Eden, eight of ten Clouds, so far. My guess is with all that combined, along with the SUBOS, the WES, CARBELs and Aerie … maybe in the ballpark of fifteen to twenty thousand. Give or take."

Armada tilted his head down and kissed his wife's head. After taking another sip of his coffee, he set his mug on the table, then reached around Chloe and gently placed his hands on her belly.

Chloe laid her fingers on the back of his hand as he tenderly rubbed her protruding stomach.

***

"Are you ready?" she asked enthusiastically. "I'm about to plug 'em both in."

Without saying a word, Armada spun around to witness the final stage of power generation for the second half of the tablet computers.

"Here we go!"

Chloe knelt and inserted the plugs for the two newly fabricated power cords into the outlet. Almost immediately the green LED power lights lit up on all twenty-five tablets.

"Wow! Those reacted faster than the first set," he pointed out.

"I know."

Armada yawned and rubbed his eyes.

"Baby, you need to go to bed. You've been at this for more than thirty-six hours. You're gonna make yourself sick."

She approached him, pulled his head into her chest, and slowly ran her fingers through his hair, slightly scratching his scalp.

"Okay," he mumbled and tilted his head back.

They briefly gazed into each other's eyes before Armada rose from his chair.

"You can sleep as late as you want," she commented, walking behind him. "I got the power cords assembled, we got the tablets mounted, you wrote out the program for the cameras … so, now you get to sleep with nooo worries."

Like a lumberjack chopping down a tree, Armada flung himself on their bed, face down. Chloe got on her knees, removed his boots, and pulled off his socks. Within seconds of hitting the pillow he was asleep.

✳✳✳

"Baby?" he heard her whisper softly. "Baby, time to get up."

Armada slowly flipped onto his right side.

"C'mon, baby, I need you to look at something."

He felt the tender caress of her fingers on his cheeks. Upon opening his eyes, Armada was pleased to find his wife kneeling beside their bed with her face mere inches away.

"You said I could sleep as long as I wanted," he mumbled, grinning ever so slightly.

"I know, but that was last night."

Armada shut his eyes and didn't say another word.

"Okay, I tried being polite," she stated.

"Wake up! Wake up! Wake up!" Chloe suddenly shouted, jumping on the bed.

She straddled his hips and mashed down on his left arm and shoulder, making the whole bed jiggle. With her right hand, she reached behind her and began pinching his rear end while simultaneously tickling his ribs with her left.

"Stop it!" he laughingly warned her, brushing her hands away. "You're gonna get in trouble!"

"Oh, the tough guy's back, huh?" she taunted, pinching harder on his bottom.

Armada rolled onto his back, grabbed her left wrist, and with one mighty pulse of his hips, succeeded in bucking her off.

"Whoa!" she wailed as he overpowered her, climbed on top of her, and pinned her arms under his knees.

"Baby! Stop!" she screamed as he poked her rib cage with his thumbs.

Chloe laughed uncontrollably, writhing and kicking helplessly under the weight of her husband.

"You're gonna stop next time I tell you. Right?"

"YES!"

"I warned you. Didn't I?"

"YES!"

Armada removed his knees from Chloe's wrists and dismounted her. Totally spent and exhausted she remained in bed, laughing, while he sauntered to the small countertop above their refrigerator.

"So what's your justification for disrupting my much-needed and well-earned rest?" he sternly inquired.

"My reasons are many," she confidently stated, catching her breath. "However, as the saying goes 'A picture is worth a thousand words' . . . you should see this before I say anything."

"Oooh, I'm intrigued," Armada drably admitted, inserting a fresh pod of coffee in the brewer.

After placing his mug under the nozzle, he asked, "And just when exactly did you make your discoveries?"

"Augh, last night, Rip Van Winkle!"

Frustrated with Armada's lack of enthusiasm, Chloe quickly climbed out of bed, grabbed him by the wrist, and led him to the table.

"I'll make the coffee. You listen," she ordered and pushed him down into the chair.

"Right after you passed out, I opened your monitor program and numbered the tablets on the panels, just as you did in the program."

Armada spun around in the chair to inspect the cardboard panels.

"I had to move most of them around to get 'em in order," she said as she dropped a chunk of dark chocolate in his fresh coffee.

"So, starting in the top left corner and going down from left to right, the tablets are in sequential order and correspond to the sequence in your program. Tablet numbers are written above the top left corner and camera numbers are written above the top right."

"Wow! Thanks, baby," he exclaimed as she handed him his cup of coffee.

"My pleasure," she replied with a kiss.

"All right, that's more like surprise number one," Chloe said, pulling a chair up beside him.

"Now, moving on to my discoveries. I want you to look at a specific camera."

Chloe rolled herself backwards and sat in front of the wall of tablets and their dizzying display of alternating images.

"Okay, there it is. Twenty-three. Go to the program file for tablet twenty-three."

She wheeled herself next to Armada as he opened his monitor program and accessed the file for tablet twenty-three.

"Okay, now what, Detective?" he asked, sipping his hot java.

Chloe leaned over and reviewed the numbered files for the five different cameras Armada selected to monitor.

"I'm pretty sure it's this one: 08-GT10-43," she stated, pointing at the file.

Armada silently did as requested and brought up thousands upon thousands of subfolders.

"Open one of today's recordings."

Armada clicked a folder and a fifteen-second video clip began playing on his tablet screen.

"Watch closely," she said.

The footage showed what appeared to be a large white tarp rising up and down in the breeze, thereby activating the motion sensor in the video camera.

"Okay. So?"

"So? So?!" she repeated with incredulity. "None of that looked familiar to you?"

"No, not particularly."

"Augh!" she groaned, slapping his arm. "Are you blind?"

Chloe grabbed the tablet and replayed the short video.

"Okay...," she began, pausing the clip and zoomed in, "how about this?"

She set the tablet and its frozen image in front of Armada.

"Ring any bells?"

Armada held the tablet and concentrated on the magnified picture.

"Well, to me it looks like an ... oh, I don't know ... one of those picnic table umbrellas flapping around in the wind."

"No, baby, I don't think so. Look closer at the fabric seam."

After zooming in more and holding the computer a few inches away from his face, the light went off in his brain.

"No! Way!" Armada shouted, lowering the tablet. "No... stinking... way!"

Chloe quietly and slowly turned away from Armada, pulled her long hair off her left shoulder, and leaned slightly back. He gazed at the SPUD radar-deflecting fabric taped over her RFID chip, then at the paused image on the tablet.

"SHUT... UP!" he exclaimed and hugged his wife from behind. "White and Wyczthack are using SPUD shield to hide something!"

"I know!" Chloe agreed, spinning around.

"Cain doesn't want anybody to see what he's bringing into the SUBOS!" he surmised. "That tells me it's something big."

"And that brings me to my next point."

Chloe stood and positioned herself in front of the wall of tablets while Armada replayed the video.

"Okay," she began. "Open a new window for each of the tablet numbers I call out."

Armada swiveled his chair to face her.

"Twenty-two … we just looked at twenty-three … eleven … nine … and … two. Pull up each one in a separate tab."

One by one Armada opened the folders for the tablets Chloe selected. She retrieved her own cup of coffee and sat down beside him.

"Prepare to be amazed!" she announced, then sipped her coffee. "So, last night, as you lay snoring away…."

"I don't snore," Armada smugly interrupted.

"Uh … yeah, baby … ya do!"

"Any way…."

"Any way," she snarkily repeated, slapping his arm, "so I'd watch one tablet for a couple of minutes to get a sense of what all was being monitored."

"Good. My intention was—is—to gain a working knowledge of what's occurring in certain areas in real time."

"I kind of assumed that. Like with tablets one, two, and three, it's everything having to do with the docks, railways, off-loading, SUBOS elevators, and so on. Right?"

"Correct."

"Now, let's look at … tablet two."

Armada expanded the window for tablet two to reveal the list of camera numbers.

"First," she said, "open camera folder 09-CLT05-47. That one, I believe, is located at the very end of the staging area for waste capsules … it faces north, and think it shows the whole line of rail cars."

Chloe took another sip of her coffee as her husband investigated the stored video files.

Just as Chloe described, the latest recorded video indeed showed several Engenechem employees unloading a rail car of four nuclear waste capsules.

"Okay. So they're off-loading the WES capsules for ejection. And?"

"And? Just look at 'em. They're all walking around in their cute Engenechem uniforms with the matching caps. They're driving the big telehandlers and got their gloves and sunglasses on. It's all bright and sunny, skies are clear … everybody's happy. Right?"

Armada twisted his head and gawked at his wife.

"What's with you all of a sudden?"

"Nothing. I'm just asking you to look carefully and think about what you're seeing. It's important."

"Okay, okay. I got it."

"Now, go to tablet eleven," Chloe grumbled.

Armada expanded the window for tablet eleven and list of numbered camera subfolders.

"Keep in mind what you just saw and open 06-EAT99-22."

Armada opened the folder to find hundreds, if not thousands, of stored video files. He pulled up a recording that wasn't more than two hours old.

"This camera is mounted on a pole at the front of switchback one on the far west side."

"You're just full of all kinds of information," he commented as the video footage played.

"Pause it," she stated. "Now just take a long, good look at that sky."

"What?!" he blurted. "The whole train is under a SPUD canopy! Oh, my gosh! There's gotta be at least … thirty rail cars!"

"I know!"

"And even the cars are covered! Wow! Chloe! This is huge! We were right! Wyczthack's bringing something into the SUBOS he doesn't want anyone to see."

"Just wait a second, it gets better."

As if watching a movie in a theatre, Chloe leaned in close to her husband. While sipping her coffee, Armada raised his left arm, laid it on her shoulders, and gave a firm squeeze.

"All right, this is where it gets interesting," Chloe alerted him, pointing at the corner of the screen. "Coming down the lane … we have two telehandlers, aaaand … two personnel trucks."

The couple observed the two personnel trucks drive around and ahead of the telescoping forklifts and come to a stop at the switchback, just behind the second rail car.

Armada's jaw nearly came unhinged at the sight of the men as they exited their vehicles. He removed his left arm from Chloe's shoulder and stared at her, completely dumbfounded.

"I told you," she declared.

With a slight smile of disbelief, he stated, "They're wearing hazmat suits!"

CHAPTER 33

THE MAN UPSTAIRS

"**W**hatever you do, don't show any reaction to this message," Armada typed as he observed his friend's face via the internal helmet camera. "Remember, they're watching and listening. Always."

He clicked the 'send' icon, watched, and waited.

Armada held his breath as Euclid read the instructions on his holographic visor.

"I hope he doesn't say or do anything to draw attention," Armada commented, focusing on the live video feed from Euclid's helmet camera. "Garret, Mercury, Poseidon, and the others are seeing the same exact video."

"Like what?" Chloe loudly inquired from the bathroom.

"I don't know ... anything."

"Euclid's smart!" she hollered as she turned to admire her profile in the mirror and rubbed her belly. "He won't give it away."

'Euclid, this is Armada,' the next note stated. 'I'm alive and well.'

"Yes!" Euclid suddenly shouted, smiling broadly.

"Augh!" Garret moaned, quickly removing his earpiece.

"Crap!" Armada grunted, slapping the table.

"Mercury, bring Euclid Eleven to full screen on monitor one," Garret ordered.

"Euclid!" he barked. "Are ya tryin' to blow my eardrums? What was that?"

"Crap! Crap! Crap!" Armada roared, watching and listening to the conversation between Garret and Euclid. "He's busted!"

"I just got a little excited, sir," Euclid began. "What with us finishing Cloud Ten ahead of schedule, I felt a bit exuberant at the thought of going back to the SUBOS."

"Sir," Poseidon whispered, turning around, "Euclid's heart rate has increased and his suit's internal temperature just went up by two degrees."

"And that was reason enough to make me go deaf?" Garret sarcastically grilled.

"No. No, sir. I'm sorry. It won't happen again."

Armada nervously scratched his scalp as he listened in on Garret's interrogation.

"Euclid?" Garret called out, reinserting his earpiece, "You feeling all right? Shows here that your heart rate and core body temperature have both gone up. Anything you need?"

"No, no... I'm fine. Like I said, I'm just excited about... you know, doing a good job and all and completing Cloud Ten ahead of projection."

From the privacy of his room, Armada nervously awaited Garret's response.

"Sir?" Poseidon again whispered. "Internal suit temperature and heart rate are both stabilizing."

"All right," Garret bluntly announced. "You can resume your duties now, but in the future, do us all a favor and save the celebrating 'til you're on the Arena."

"Yes, sir," Euclid stated.

'Idiot!' Armada quickly typed and sent to Euclid's helmet.

Euclid chuckled to himself upon receipt of his brother's insult.

"Ugh! He's killing me!" Armada bellowed as he typed.

Chloe exited the bathroom, grabbed a handful of dried fruit from a bowl on the kitchen cart, and approached her husband sitting at the table.

"He's just excited and happy to know you're alive."

"Happy or not, he's gonna get all of us in trouble. Once you're synchronized with the Nest and POG, anything you say will be heard and recorded."

"Well, don't build him a clock, just tell him the time … give him the basics of what's happened. You tend to go a little overboard on details."

"Do not!" he argued while typing.

"Hate to break it to you, baby, but yeah … you do."

Chloe bent forward and offered up a small smooch on his neck.

"Where are you off to?" he asked, not at all concerned.

"I'm going to the receiving docks at the back of the warehouse. I need to devise a means of raising the door without an elevator access authorization code. If we can…."

"Okay. I love you," Armada stated, oblivious to what she just said.

"Because, as you know, the crocodile infestation in the bowling alley is getting way out of hand," Chloe snarkily commented, "especially after they've been drinking."

"Uh-huh," he mumbled.

"You're absolutely pathetic."

"Okay, be careful."

Once again she kissed him, turned, and exited their bedroom.

Armada sent instructions to Euclid on how to get from his dorm to the Arena activity room undetected. He also sent false identity credentials for logging onto the communication kiosk to contact him. Armada informed Euclid that a letter would be waiting for him, explaining all that had transpired over the past six weeks. Included in his lengthy communique were details on how to get to the SPUD station to obtain a swatch of the radar-deflecting material. While he felt it necessary to make Euclid aware of his encounters with the orb and union with Chloe, he elected to broach those topics whenever engaged in a real-time conversation.

***

'As soon as you disappeared, we were all suddenly confined to the Arenas,' Euclid's note stated. 'With exception to the Clouds, the staging zones, and our assigned Arenas, we were restricted from all other EVA projects, responsibilities, and assignments. Garret went nuts and temporarily suspended evaluations on the SUBOS. Wyczthack's army of 'doctors' have been coming here ever since.'

'Did Garret ever offer a reason for the changes?' Armada wrote in response.

He glanced back at the digital clock and Chloe as she lay sleeping, and snoring, in bed: 2:45 a.m.

'Nope. Just "Don't go here,"' the incoming message read.

'So, right after I left Cloud Eight was completed, and shortly thereafter Cloud Nine. Correct?'

'Yes,' Euclid swiftly replied. 'However, once we all focused on the assembly of Cloud Ten, something strange occurred. One morning, right after linking up my comm-line with the Nest and our unit's POG, I deployed to the staging area for Cloud Ten. I was about to assign work zones when something caught my attention. Off in the distance, underneath Cloud One, I noticed stacks and stacks of ten-foot tunnel frames. However, unlike those we used for creating the transfer corridors on the Arenas, these were black.'

'Are you positive they were tunnel sections for personnel? Did you see any wiring conduit for radiant heat? That's usually a telltale sign.'

'Couldn't tell you; I was too far away.'

'Who delivered them? When did they arrive?'

'Don't know and don't know. However, I can tell you without a doubt that it wasn't any of us. Stacks have appeared for each Cloud, but none so far for Cloud Ten.'

Armada quickly scribbled 'CARBEL' on his pad.

'Speaking of strange,' Euclid continued, 'last week, after our EVA projects and after I had accounted for everybody, it occurred to me that the Clouds are being moved away from the Arenas. I hadn't noticed it before, but as I activated my coil, the distance to Cloud Nine was noticeably farther away.'

'So what's been happening with the tunnel sections?'

'Two days ago, again, after our assigned EVA projects, I looked out at Cloud Nine, and underneath was an active POG, but I couldn't see anyone attached to the comm-links, even though the lines were extended and floating about. I could barely make out the internal lighting of helmets, but whoever's assembling the tubes, they're wearing black EVA suits. Furthermore, we're unable to synch-up with their POG. I brought it to Garret's attention, but he avoids discussing it. Plus, the tunnel sections are being assembled on the Cloud bellies, on end, aiming down. The whole thing gives me the creeps! Black suits, black tunnel sections, restricted movements, limited time out of our Arenas, and mystery contractors. I fear something nefarious is taking place right before our eyes.'

'I'm afraid you're correct, my friend. It'll take a considerable amount of time to go through everything with you, but rest assured I'm working diligently to stop Wyczthack and White from accomplishing their goals. I'll be in touch again soon.'

CHAPTER 34

PAPER OR PLASTIC

"If we can disconnect the drive motor," Chloe stated, pointing at the top of the roll-up overhead door, "then technically speaking, we should be able to place the fork tips under the door, raise the forks, and have enough room to retrieve the orders from Eden."

Armada bit his lip as he pondered her proposal.

"Or...," he said, raising his index finger, "we keep the drive motor intact, disengage the kiosk, disable the magnetic inhibitor, and you figure out how to reconfigure or rewire the manual open and close switch."

The couple traded contemplative stares and gazed intensely at the electric drive motor mounted high above.

"As soon as we force that door up without releasing that magnetic lock, the panels will buckle. Whoever's coming down, or ascending, is gonna notice it. We can't take that kind of chance. All we need is for someone to say 'Hey! Did you know...?' and suddenly there's an Engenechem response team dispatched to investigate the problem."

"Okay, I concede," Chloe declared, raising her hands. "I can see your point. So what should we do first?"

Armada thought for a moment, then said, "Baby, go back to our room and bring me my tablet. Also bring all your electrical tools."

"Be right back," she replied, swatting his bottom as she passed behind him.

"Thaaaanks, baaaaby," he sarcastically stated, "loving you!"

"Uh-huh," she mumbled, walking away.

Armada stepped around the corner into the charging station for the three electric forklifts. He hopped on one, turned the key, tilted back the three-stage mast, and slowly pulled forward. After clearing the battery chargers, he steered the lift directly at the overhead door, stopping just inches away from piercing the lowest panel with the fork tips.

Armada dismounted the forklift and directed his attention to the receiving kiosk at the far right of the overhead door.

Upon close examination, he discovered that the communication and power supply for the kiosk flowed through its connection to the bay door.

'If we disrupt the power…,' he theorized, *'then Eden can't confirm, or deny, whether or not a distribution request originated from here.'*

Armada peered upwards at the glowing green light above the door spool and spring.

"I'm back!" he heard Chloe holler.

She rounded the corner and unloaded her tools on top of the forklift counterweight.

"Whenever you'd receive a request for a distribution, would it show any specifics about who created the order?"

"No," she answered and stepped to the front of the forklift. "We only know when the requisition was generated, the terminal number, where it's to be delivered, and the content. It's never known as to who, individually, placed the order."

"So, if I create a request, I'm not gonna be forced to submit personal identity credentials. It'll just need to include the kiosk terminal number. Correct?"

"Correct. But if we fail to register a receipt authorization code, that'll send up a red flag with Eden. Remember, everything is tracked and monitored. If produce goes out but there's no supporting data to justify the disbursement, they'll send someone to investigate. I know Cassandra ... she'd track down a pea."

"Well, we don't want to upset Cassandra now, do we? Let's get the kiosk terminal number before we disconnect anything."

Armada approached the freestanding terminal and powered it up. In a few moments the screen flashed the sequence '16M-711KLT-65' in bright-red characters.

"All righty then, enter this sequence on my tablet."

After saving the kiosk identity number, Armada walked back to the forklift and instructed Chloe on what to do.

"I want you to get in the seat, pull the middle lever toward you, and raise the forks up to the bottom of the spool. Once I'm in place, I'll have you toss me the tools I need."

"Okey-dokey."

Chloe climbed up into the seat of the forklift and turned the key. "Hang on, baby. Going up."

Armada gripped the steel backrest as the carriage lifted him nearly twenty feet high. In no time at all he successfully disconnected the magnetic inhibitor and junction box that led to both the kiosk and manual switch for raising and lowering the overhead door. With the junction box removed, they would no longer be reliant on authorization codes to open and close the roll-up door.

"Done and done," he proudly announced. "You can bring me down now."

"Oh, may I, please?" she taunted and slowly lowered the forks.

"All right. All you gotta do is rewire the switch and we'll be in business."

Armada jumped off the descending forks, landing with a thud.

Converting the switch proved to be no challenge whatsoever to Chloe. Within seconds of removing the back plate, she reconfigured the wiring, bypassing the junction box, and reattached the cover.

"Hold on to your hats," she announced, placing her finger on the green open button.

"Fire away," Armada ordered as he stepped in front of the overhead door.

Chloe pressed the button and the heavy metal partition began to rise up off the floor.

"Good for you, baby."

"Yay for me!"

The couple then walked to the edge of the dock landing, leaned over the steel safety rails and gate, and peered down into the abyss.

"So this is what a 17-mile-high elevator shaft looks like," she commented, then gazed upwards.

"Yep, yep."

"You know, I must admit that from the perspective of an engineer, this truly is an impressive and awesome structure. Just the sheer size of it is intimidating, let alone the design and creation aspects of the internal systems and components, and their cohesiveness and interconnectivity. I would've loved to have been part of it from the beginning."

"Well," Armada began, scooting closer to her, "in a way we both have. Our being alive is part of the whole point of the SUBOS."

He curled his arm around her waist.

Looking down again, he noticed the flashing yellow safety beacon lights of the elevator. "Uh-oh. Platform's coming. Better get inside."

Armada removed his hand from her hip and turned away. "C'mon. It'll be here before we know it."

"Wow! That thing is really moving!" she exclaimed.

"How fast do those travel?" she loudly inquired as she jogged back to the safety of the receiving dock.

"You do the math," he replied, lowering the door behind her. "Eight 75-horsepower planetary drive motors. That platform can start at ground level and reach the Aerie in an hour."

"That's like three minutes a mile! Dang!"

In a break from traditional wire ropes, pulleys, and counterweights, the Engenechem freight elevators employed the use of eight electric, heavy-duty planetary drive motors, two on each corner, stacked one on top of the other. Each pair of motors turned two massive gears whose teeth dug into imbedded vertical strips of ribbed metal, with an electrified contact guide running parallel to, and in between, the panels of teeth. Operating much like a subway, the motors received a constant source of power via contact with the middle rail, thus allowing the elevator to 'drive' up or down.

"Okay, so now what?" Chloe asked.

"Now? You mean right now at this very moment? Well, I for one am...."

Armada stopped in midsentence as vibrations from the powerful drive motors rumbled through the bay walls and metal overhead door.

"Wow!" Chloe barked, covering her ears.

For a brief moment, the bay door shook and brilliant amber light shone through a tiny slit between the door and concrete dock.

"As I was saying," he continued once the vibrations subsided, "for now I think we should make a grocery list and place an order ... to go."

***

"Okay, here goes nothing," Armada nervously stated and clicked the 'submit' tab. In a matter of seconds he received a requisition acknowledgement.

"Here we go, here we go!" he excitedly stated and opened the order response from Eden.

Chloe stood behind him and reviewed the distribution receipt as he read aloud.

"Sixteen M ... estimated delivery ... requisition confirmation number ... strawberries, peaches, plums, oranges, bell peppers, red and yellow ... looks like everything we ordered was approved."

"Yay!" Chloe hollered and patted his shoulders. "Oh, Armada, you won't hardly believe how incredibly delicious these fresh fruits and vegetables taste!"

She came out from behind him and took a seat in the empty chair to his left at the end of the table.

"It's all organic. No fertilizers, pesticides, herbicides, or fungicides ... everything is grown by way of hydroponics and aeroponics. It's not like it is below with monoculture farming. I mean, everything interacts and works together: the bees, the plants, the trees, us, the workers ... I wish there was a way I could get you into Eden."

"What's the shelf life on this stuff?"

"Oh, gosh, weeks ... nearly a month. A requisition of this size, for two ... say seventy-five to eighty pounds ... that'll easily last two weeks at a minimum. That all depends on our portioning and how often we eat. But mark my words, as soon as you see and taste a twelve-ounce strawberry, a pound-and-a-half peach or ten-pound cantaloupe, you won't wanna stop."

"Well," he said, glancing at the clock, "it's 5:45 now, and our requisition confirmation says order delivery will be by 12:00 a.m. Sooo...."

"Sooo...," she mocked, lowering her voice.

"So, in the meanwhile, why don't we see what we can see on the Clouds?"

Chloe nudged her husband with her foot.

"Why don't I see what I can see on the Clouds, and you see what you can see with Euclid?"

"Deal," he replied, and spun his chair away from her. "Coffee?"

"You know it!" she exclaimed, pulling her tablet in front of her.

Armada rinsed out their mugs, tossed in a section of dark chocolate in each, and started the brewer.

CHAPTER 35

DISCOVERY

After logging on the Engenechem Master Server, Chloe made it her primary objective to identify the video cameras on the Clouds. Whereas everyone was aware of the surveillance systems on the SUBOS and orbiting Arenas, Arks, and Eden, details on the viewing capabilities of the Clouds were intentionally kept under wraps. What kind, how many, where, recording parameters and sensitivity, all information pertaining to Cain's 'electric eyes' was top secret.

"Going through the Master Server program by program is gonna take forever," she complained. "I don't know how we'll have enough time to inspect each and every file."

"How about this," Armada stated, walking to the table with their cups of coffee. "Let's review the Master Server history and identify the most recently added operational programs. After that, we'll go through each one of 'em and run a scan of what files are taking up the biggest amount of bandwidth space. Several hundred video cameras constantly downloading data isn't exactly easy to hide."

As Armada hacked his way into the active POGs for Arena One in search of Euclid, Chloe launched her investigation into the historical activity of the Engenechem data storage system.

"How long have we been in hiding?"

"Oh, in my estimation … eight weeks or so. Maybe nine."

After scouring the server's hard drives for an hour, Chloe located a new Master Server program titled 'CYCLOPS,' whose creation date was several months old. When she performed a scan to identity what features of the program were running in the background, hundreds of file numbers appeared.

"Baby, I think I found something," she said, poking his arm.

Armada leaned over as she turned her tablet screen toward him.

"Uh-huh. Now find out the file location, open the parent folders, and explore the individual subfolders. If there's that much data being downloaded to that many files in one program, odds are pretty good you've located the Cloud surveillance system."

Armada pulled her hand to his lips and kissed her fingers. "Good for you, baby."

"Thanks!"

Chloe smiled and began the arduous task of opening and examining every subfolder in the CYCLOPS program file.

***

"Augh!" Armada growled, rubbing his eyes. "I can't locate Euclid. I've gone through every comm-link on all active POGs and his identity number isn't registering."

"What about WATCHER?" Chloe asked. "Does his RFID chip show up?"

"No. I can only assume he made it safely and undetected to the SPUDs and got a piece of radar fabric."

Chloe reached over and scratched her husband's back. "Hey. Take a look at this. I think I found 'em."

Armada rolled up beside her and watched as a three-minute video clip played.

"What is this? What are we looking at?"

Although the recorded footage came from a helmet camera belonging to an unidentified worker, it didn't take long for him to correctly identify the content of the video.

"This is the underside of Cloud One. Right there...," he said, pausing the clip. "That's one of six vertical ascension ports for receiving all incoming craft. Inbound vessels will make their approach and connection upside down, belly to belly, for loading and unloading of materials and personnel. Instead of having all docks sequestered on one end and one level, side by side, this method allows for independent operations to occur simultaneously. On the Arenas, we have one humongous open docking station. If we were to experience an equipment failure, a loss of power, or have an accident like the Russians did in ninety-seven on the Mir, then all docking operations could come to a screeching halt. By incorporating separate, independent stations, we increase the overall functionality of the Clouds."

Chloe quietly nodded her head.

They watched the shaky film footage for a few more minutes, but saw no evidence of Euclid's stacked tunnel sections. With less than twenty seconds remaining in the video clip, Armada stood and stretched.

"Hold on," Chloe said, bumping his leg with her forearm, "I just saw something."

Reversing the video, she paused it on one particular image and asked, "Does this look anything like what Euclid described to you?"

Armada leaned on the table with his elbows and stared at the paused black-and-white image "Can you magnify that?"

Chloe expanded and zoomed in on the frozen video, then increased the resolution to decrease the grainy pixilation.

"How 'bout now?"

"Mmm...," he hummed, "it doesn't show enough detail and it's too close to get a good sense of proportion. What's the file path?"

Chloe told him the Master Server location for the CYCLOPS program as she began selecting another video file to review.

"Wow!" he exclaimed upon viewing the content of the parent folder.

"Okay. I have a couple of thoughts on how to go about finding the evidence we need."

Armada spent the next few minutes giving Chloe specifics on what he was in search of. With subfolders numbering in the thousands containing hundreds and hundreds of hours of captured video footage and only two of them to inspect the contents, time was their enemy.

After another two hours of nonstop investigation and nothing to show for her efforts, Chloe's tolerance level maxed out.

"Augh!" she suddenly shouted, slamming her palms on the table.

Slumping back in the chair, Chloe buried her face in her hands and growled again in frustration, "Augh!"

"Here we go, here we go!" Armada excitedly replied. "Look, baby!"

Disgruntled, Chloe flopped her arms on her lap and released a deep sigh.

"Oh, c'mon now … cheer up. Look, this is exactly what we were in search of."

Chloe reluctantly steered her chair beside him and leaned on the table, propping her head in the palm of her hand.

"Okay, let me play this from the beginning," Armada suggested, then started the clip. "This is what Euclid was referring to. Obviously, this footage was shot after those first few videos. Look at the surface of Cloud One."

Armada paused the video and pointed at a vast network of conduit measuring roughly three inches in diameter. The pipelines branched off a central manifold that was considerably larger. At the end of each tube was a ring that, in Armada's estimation, was ten feet across, and had multiple plugs and connection ports located near the rims. The rings were lined up in rows of ten, with one row staggered against the other, similar to a honeycomb.

"We did not build that," he defiantly stated, crossing his arms.

"You didn't?"

"No, ma'am!"

"Can you play the entire video in quarter time?" she asked.

"You mean like time lapse … in fast motion? Yep, yep."

Armada restarted the video, but this time played it in fast forward. The couple watched the digital film repeatedly, in its entirety, looking for any additional clues.

"What do those numbers in the lower left-hand corner signify? What do they mean?" Chloe asked, tapping at the screen.

"The top one is the helmet transponder, under that is the worker's identity number, then the POG comm-link coupler port, and at the bottom is the division or company name. So my recorded videos would have my transponder, then Evan Armada Nine, my POG comm-link port number, and Arena One A would be at the very bottom. Why?"

Without saying a word, Chloe sat up and retrieved her tablet. She quickly pecked at the digital keyboard and brought up a video she had seen earlier.

"Look at the identifiers in your video and this one I saw a while ago."

Armada glanced back and forth between the two screens, comparing the information.

"They're different companies!" he boldly declared. "Pull up another one. Any file. It doesn't matter, just open a new video."

Chloe skipped ahead, bypassing several weeks' worth of stored footage, and randomly selected a video file.

"Okay, pause it," Armada requested.

They again compared the identity credentials of the older video to those of the new one.

"This company name is different, too," she blurted. "But let's go ahead and finish this video before we…."

"Whoa!" Armada suddenly hollered, jumping in his seat. "Go back! Go back!"

Chloe silently did as instructed and replayed the clip.

"Stop!" he ordered, patting her arm.

"What? What's wrong?"

Armada tilted his head back, covered his face, and moaned with a halfhearted laugh.

"Oh, my gosh! I'm such an idiot!" he loudly complained.

"I know you're an idiot."

"I knew this looked familiar. It's a WES."

Chloe closely scrutinized the image on her screen.

"Are you kidding? A waste ejection system? On the surface of a Cloud? That makes absolutely zero sense!"

"Hey, I'm not saying I know what they're planning to do with it. I'm merely stating what it is."

"Are you mad? How would that work? Think about it. If one end of the tube is permanently affixed to the Cloud surface, how would they insert the canisters?"

"Baby, I'm not arguing with you. I'm just saying what they built has all the earmarks of a waste ejection system."

"This is ludicrous!" she loudly exclaimed, slapping the arms of her chair.

"Why create a means of launching nuclear waste into deep space, then turn right around and deploy the capsules for reentry into Earth's atmosphere?"

Armada watched his wife pace about nervously as she continued her rant.

"Why install ten separate systems and place them in orbit around the world? Engenechem would be forced to deliver the canisters to all ten Clouds, individually, and insert one in each...."

Chloe froze in midsentence with her jaw hanging low.

"Armada!" she squeaked, then covered her mouth.

"Hey," he said tenderly and rose from his seat. "What is it, baby? What's got you so upset?"

Armada gently squeezed and rubbed her arms before drawing her into him. Chloe pressed herself heavily into his chest and wept. Her body tensed and lurched forward with her soundless crying. Armada nestled his wife's head in one hand as he slowly ran the other in wide circles on her back and shoulders.

"Don't you see it?" Chloe suddenly and loudly asked, pushing him away from her. "They're constructing missile silos! Silos for launching nuclear missiles! That's how Wyczthack's gonna do it! He's constructing ten mobile platforms for nuclear missile deployment that can be positioned anywhere he wants!"

Chloe began walking in a circle as Armada stepped back to the table to reexamine the paused video.

"Baby, are you sure about this? Are you positive?"

"Whadyamean 'Am I positive'? Look! See for yourself! I'm not stupid…I know what I'm talking about! Cain's built ten maneuverable missile silos, and there's nobody and no government that can stop him."

Chloe brushed past him, stepped to the bathroom, and slammed the door shut.

Flabbergasted by Chloe's remarks and emotional outburst, Armada took his seat and slouched back.

If Cain has been installing nuclear missiles, he thought, staring at the tablet screen and its frozen, captured video footage, *then there should be recorded video showing the missiles being loaded on the SUBOS.*

He sat up straight and began typing on his tablet.

If there's camera footage showing the missiles, he further surmised, *then we should be able to identify the contractors.*

Chloe exited the bathroom in a huff, carrying a wet washcloth. She passed in front of the table without so much as a glance at her husband. Still visibly upset, she marched to their bed and flopped herself on the mattress.

Armada kept his eyes glued to the tablet screen.

"All I need to do is track one of the missiles from off-loading at the switchbacks to its point of installation on one of the Clouds," he mumbled lowly, but loud enough for Chloe to hear.

Armada reopened one of the video files Chloe had found and located the digital time and date stamp and camera number. He watched closely as the personnel raised the shrouded nuclear weapon from its moorings on the rail car. The bomb was then lowered and gingerly placed in a wheeled, hydraulic cradle that slowly crept to the SUBOS. A small army of Engenechem employees wearing yellow suits then escorted the cargo to the tower.

However, once the cradle arrived at the staging zone for the SUBOS elevators, the video suddenly stopped.

"What!?" Armada amazedly stated.

He backed up the video and replayed it, but once again the footage was cut short. There was zero evidence of a nuclear missile. The only images the video surveillance system recorded were those of an extremely large and cloaked object arriving at the SUBOS loading dock.

The video camera's parent folder contained a multitude of individual recordings. Armada randomly selected a new video to examine, and, after watching the first few seconds, went to the end of the footage. It, too, was suspiciously cut short.

With the newest video's time and date stamp still visible on his tablet screen, Armada searched the Master Server parent folders of every SUBOS elevator for a video file whose creation date and time were similar to that of the switchback camera. For all of his efforts, Armada found no data to support Chloe's theory.

No visual confirmation of a missile being loaded in the SUBOS, he thought. *In fact, no evidence of a missile even existing.*

Scratching his head, he gave pause to consider his last mental comment.

"No missiles. No evidence of missiles. No evidence."

At that instant an idea struck him: *There should be a trail of overlapping videos, starting with the SUBOS cameras and ending with the Clouds.*

Once he filtered the Engenechem Master Server hard drive for video files only, it became visibly clear that a massive amount of data was missing.

Deliberately.

The libraries for the switchbacks, the SUBOS elevator system, the Aerie, CARBELs, HALOs, and Clouds, had glaring gaps in their files. The file's creation times should, technically speaking, bleed into one another by at least a few seconds, but by no more than half a minute. These folders weren't off by ten seconds here or seven seconds there; absent were hours and hours of film footage. For some of the Clouds, entire days were missing.

'Cain's erasing the evidence,' Armada quietly told himself. 'He's having all video files showing missiles and personnel deleted. Chloe was right. Wyczthack's built himself maneuverable missile silos, and nobody knows it.'

Disgusted and disheartened with his findings, he again slumped back in his chair.

Armada twisted his head and silently stared at his wife as she lay in bed.

"Tell me how this works," he requested, knowing full well that Chloe's analytical personality would emerge, thereby distracting her emotionally. "If Cain's plan is to launch all these missiles, won't the heat damage and weaken the integrity of the Cloud's outer hull?"

"He doesn't necessarily need to fire the missiles from the Clouds in order to launch them," she commented from her horizontal position.

Armada's idea on how to calm Chloe down worked like a charm. He had barely finished asking his question when he noticed a complete change in her countenance.

"That's what the conduit is there for," she said as she stood and walked to the table. "They're going to quickly release a burst of compressed gas in the base of each missile silo. Just like they do on a submarine for an SLBM, the gas will rapidly expand at the bottom and propel the missile upward, ejecting it from the launch tube. Once the internal operating systems on the missiles kick in, sensors will let the onboard computers know when it's far away enough from the Clouds to activate the propulsion system."

"So, how soon could one of these hit its target?"

"Well...that's all relative depending on a couple of factors," she replied. "What's the elevation from the Earth's surface at the time of launch? Are they deploying Poseidon missiles? Tridents? Peacekeepers?

Minutemen? Decommissioned Polaris missiles? Some of these travel four to seven kilometers per second. If Cain were to fire the missiles from an orbit as close as one hundred miles, technically speaking … less than three minutes."

Armada gazed sternly at his wife as she continued her lecture.

"On top of that, there can be as few as six or as many as twelve independent warheads in every missile. At a minimum, each one can deliver a payload equivalent to three hundred kilotons of TNT. That's roughly twenty times the destructive force of the bomb dropped on Hiroshima. Little Boy vaporized tens of thousands instantly using a little uranium with a blast yield of fifteen kilotons of TNT. And that was a ground detonation. Imagine what just one warhead detonating a mile or half mile over Manhattan, Houston, or Seattle would do."

Armada turned around and stared at the grainy image on his tablet.

"So … every missile is programmed to launch to a specific area, then all the independent warheads are jettisoned, and those are pre-programmed to detonate at a predetermined altitude over a preset destination. And each warhead is basically twenty times more powerful than the Hiroshima A-Bomb. Correct? Do I have that right?"

He remained focused on the video as he waited for Chloe's answer.

"Yes, you're correct," she firmly replied.

Armada ran his fingers through his hair and briskly scratched his scalp in frustration.

"For the sake of arguing," he began, "let's hypothetically assume that Cain has installed, and is currently loading, one hundred individual missile silos on each Cloud. That means once completed, he'll have at least one thousand missiles at the ready. Right?"

"Yes," she said.

"And you stated there can be six to twelve individual warheads per missile. Yes?"

"Yes."

He hesitated before completing his thought process.

"That's six to twelve thousand warheads."

Armada twisted back to look at Chloe. Tears had once again filled her eyes.

With a crack in her voice she weakly asked, "Do you think he'll save us?"

CHAPTER 36

TRACED AND ERASED

'I don't understand his request,' the message read. 'It's illogical. If we're already gathered together, why have us break and reassemble in a new spot? He's never done this.'

'Can you tell me anything else?' Armada typed, and sent his question to Euclid.

"What all did he say?" Chloe called out from behind the partially closed bathroom door.

"He said Garret came to the Arena and told them all to be in EVA Dock in half an hour," Armada hollered back.

"And?" she loudly asked.

"And what? That's it."

"That's Euclid's idea of an emergency?"

"Well, it's more Garret's demeanor and delivery that's got Euclid's brain going."

"Euclid is unnerved because Garret wants to talk to everyone in a different location?"

Chloe closed the door, finished undressing, and stepped into the shower.

The word 'hello' suddenly appeared on the screen of Armada's tablet, followed by several question marks.

'What do I do now?' Euclid's next message asked, followed by, 'Don't ask me why, but I got a bad feeling about this.'

Armada read and reread his friend's note.

'Do you have the swatch of SPUD fabric with you?' Armada typed and pressed 'send.'

***

"And you're absolutely positive these transmission records are correct?" Cain inquired with his signature raised eyebrow. "Without a doubt?"

The young man quickly transferred his gaze from Dr. Wyczthack to Bianca Doyle, then to Dr. White and Riggs Woodburn, and back again to Cain.

"Yes," he nervously and sheepishly replied. "Yes sir, absolutely positive, one hundred percent without a doubt. The dates line up accordingly."

Cain casually reviewed the report once more, briefly skimming through its content. Riggs, Bianca, and Dr. White held their tongues as Cain contemplated the findings of the digital forensic investigator.

"That'll do," Cain stated without so much as a glance at the man standing before him.

"Sir?" he meekly asked.

"That … will … do," Cain bellowed, still unwilling to look the man in the eye.

Dr. White silently stood and motioned his head to the side. The investigator, taking the visual cue from Dr. White, backed away from the table, bowed slightly, and abruptly exited the room.

"Get Garret for me," Cain ordered, tossing the report on the table. "I want this matter resolved now."

***

'I just put the radar fabric on my shoulder. What now?' Euclid wrote.

"Chloe, locate and identify the cameras for the Nest on Arena One," Armada coolly instructed his wife. "Also, we'll need the camera feeds from the Arena, EVA Dock, and both of the dormitory corridors. Once you've opened live feeds, put them on the monitors."

Chloe diligently perused the extensive list of surveillance camera numbers and their locations as Armada contemplated the most effective defense strategy for his friend.

'Stay next to the terminal but don't move,' he typed. 'Wedge your right foot between the kiosk frame and the wall. You must remain perfectly still and totally silent for thirty seconds. After half a minute has passed, the lights and surveillance cameras will automatically go into temporary hibernation. Just stay put and watch the terminal screen. I'll keep you posted.'

"I got the Nest and Arena," Chloe alerted her beaux as he dispatched the instructions to his brother.

Armada spun his chair around and watched the real-time broadcast of Euclid hovering in front of the Arena communication kiosk.

"Activate the microphone," Armada requested.

Both Chloe and Armada observed Euclid reading the message, then glance up to his left at the motion-sensitive video camera. Just as he was ordered, Euclid sandwiched his right foot between the inner wall of the communication station and the Arena shell.

The statements 'We can see you' and 'Don't move a muscle' suddenly appeared on the screen in front of Euclid.

"Armada, look," Chloe anxiously stated.

Armada turned back to the wall of tablets just in time to watch Garret dart into the Nest. It was more than obvious that he was speaking with someone on his headset.

"Activate the camera mic."

The action in the silent video footage took on a whole new meaning once Chloe accessed the embedded microphone in the video camera.

"Yes, sir, I already did that," Garret shouted as he buckled himself into his command seat. "Yes, I'm pretty sure they're all in there. A WATCHER scan? No, but ... yes ... yes, yes, sir, right now ... hold on for a moment."

Armada quickly typed a note to Euclid, warning him, 'Garret's running an RFID scan right now. Stay still,' and clicked 'send.'

Through the infrared capability of the camera, Chloe watched Euclid as he read Armada's warning.

"He got it," she said.

"Do you have the EVA Dock yet?" Armada impatiently inquired.

"Putting it up now, baby," she calmly answered.

Armada turned around to see one of the tablet screens make the switch from an exterior shot of a CARBEL platform to an overhead interior look at the EVA Dock. There they were, Armada's brethren, all one hundred ninety-eight of them. Huddled together in multiple hovering clumps, the clones behaved as if nothing irregular had occurred.

"Turn on the camera mic."

Armada faced his computer tablet and pecked away as he and Chloe listened to the chatter of the unassuming men.

"What're you doing?" Chloe asked.

"Almost done, sir," they then heard Garret announce.

"I want to see the results of Garret's scan," Armada informed Chloe.

Armada hurriedly opened the WATCHER program files on the Master Server and retrieved the scan history.

"Here we go," he said confidently as he accessed the report.

Chloe stood and leaned over the table to see where WATCHER had placed the RFID chips on Arena One. Much to their pleasure, the scan recognized the clone's implanted tracking devices as being located in the EVA Dock. Euclid's RFID chip wasn't acknowledged.

"Okay, scan complete," they heard Garret declare. "I was right, they're all in there as we speak. No, they're fine, uh ... well, you know ... normal, everyday behavior, I guess. You want me to what? Would you repeat that, please? You're joking ... right? With all due respect, sir, I ... I don't understand this. But ... yes, but ... no, sir."

"He's gotta be talking to Wyczthack or White," Chloe theorized, then asked, "Would Garret authorize or initiate a scan on his own?"

"Not likely," said Armada, adding, "He'd only do it if ordered."

'Scan over. Nobody knows. You're safe,' Armada typed, sent to Euclid, and resumed watching the monitors.

"Gentlemen, gentlemen…," a voice suddenly echoed throughout the enormous EVA chamber. "Good morning. This is Dr. Cain Wyczthack, CEO of the Engenechem Corporation."

The brothers in the docking bay abruptly halted their conversations and looked about as they listened to their commander and creator.

"On behalf of Dr. White and the Engenechem global family, I want to extend to each and every one of you a sincere and well-deserved thank you."

'Cain's addressing everyone in the docking bay. Hold on,' Armada informed Euclid.

As Cain continued his speech, Chloe noticed something peculiar.

"Baby, look at Garret," she suggested, and asked, "Is it just me, or does something seem wrong with him."

Armada shifted his attention to the tablet streaming the live feed from the Nest. Although he was securely buckled into his chair, Garret was fidgety and restless. He repeatedly crossed and uncrossed his legs and gripped at both armrests. From their vantage point, it looked as if Garret was intentionally trying not to look at the Nest's video monitors; like there was something he didn't want to see or acknowledge.

"Yeah…," Armada agreed. "Cain probably jumped him pretty good for something he didn't do or did incorrectly. From what I've heard, Wyczthack can be brutal with his critiques."

"I don't know…looks to me like he got more than just a verbal lashing. That's not your typical 'Oh, I'm in trouble with my boss' body language. He's acting more like 'Uh-oh, my boss came unglued.'"

"Maybe, but if Wyczthack were going to…."

Armada stopped short of completing his thought when Cain's tone made an abrupt and noticeable change.

"And now we come to the real reason for this little gathering," Cain commented. "As you're all well aware, roughly four months ago, whilst you were entering the first stage of construction on Cloud Eight, your brother, Evan Armada Nine, disappeared…vanished…without a trace."

Chloe stood close to Armada, wrapped her fingers around her husband's bicep, and gently squeezed.

"He, along with an accomplice, managed to evade detection, and have, thus far, eluded our surveillance systems. But I'm proud to inform you all today that we've made a discovery…one of great importance and significance."

Armada and Chloe exchanged a brief but worried glance.

"It has been brought to my attention that one of you…has come in direct contact with Armada Nine. Five weeks ago, one of you received multiple messages on your holographic visor…."

Armada turned back to his tablet computer and frantically typed, 'Cain knows we've been communicating. He's interrogating everyone. Did you tell anybody?'

"Oh, my gosh, Armada!" Chloe exclaimed and began pacing. "He knows! He knows! He knows! Wyczthack knows we've been talking to Euclid! He's gonna…."

"Sshh!" Armada hissed and wrapped his arms around her, "Sshh. Listen…."

"…didn't identify a specific helmet transponder," Dr. Wyczthack continued, "But did record several messages relayed to one of you via the POG. So, effective immediately, all EVA endeavors will have designated, assigned, specific POG comm-links that are to be considered permanent identification markers, along with transponders."

Without warning, the sound of Cain's voice was suddenly absent from the audio feed. However, Armada and Chloe could still hear the clones speaking with one another.

***

"Call Garret back and tell him I said 'now,'" Dr. Wyczthack firmly ordered Riggs.

Riggs picked up the phone resting in the middle of the conference table and did as commanded as he, Bianca, and Dr. White traded uncomfortable stares.

Garret raised his right hand and pressed the tiny button on his earpiece, connecting the incoming call.

"Now," Riggs flatly stated.

***

"Look at Garret," Chloe nervously peeped, watching him closely. "He's talking to somebody."

"But...," they heard Garret mumble, "but ... there's gotta be another...."

He began crying and breathing heavily.

"Please!" he begged and blubbered. "Please, Riggs, not that. I can't ... I ... I just can't!"

"Ooohhh, Armada!" Chloe whined, unable to stop shaking. "Baby ... baby ... what's happening?"

Just listening to Garret weep was enough to make her begin to cry as well.

Armada looked at Euclid on the other screen and saw him staring up at the camera, obviously concerned with not knowing what was occurring a few meters away.

'Hold on, buddy,' Armada pecked out on his tablet keyboard. 'Just be still and patient.'

"So ... I will be most appreciative to know who it is among you that sought to assist Armada Nine with his escape," Cain coldly commented.

The confused brood of identical brothers turned to one another and started whispering.

"Riggs!" Garret painfully shouted. "Riggs! Please tell Cain … tell him … tell him I can't.... Oh, my God...."

"You have sixty seconds to surrender the traitor's identity," Cain added.

"Baby?" Chloe squeaked and covered her mouth.

"Aauugghh!" Garret screamed, lurching up and forward, and slapped at a control panel above his head.

"Oh, no!" Armada muttered and fell to his knees as he watched the video stream from the EVA Dock.

Chloe sunk down next to her husband and watched in helpless horror as the enormous interior steel door connecting the EVA docking bay to the Arena personnel corridor began closing.

"No, no, no, no!" Armada repeatedly roared at the tablet screens.

Garret's sorrowful moans nearly drowned out the cries and shouts of panic and fear from the clones once they realized they were being locked in.

Armada quickly stood and walked in a small circle, clutching his fists up behind his head.

"Aauugghh!" he painfully shrieked. "Cain! Cain!"

"Thirty seconds," Dr. Wyczthack was heard to say.

Cain, Bianca, Riggs, and Dr. White sat in complete silence while listening to the panic-stricken pod of clones.

"Use your ID lanyards!" the sequestered brothers shouted at one another as they attempted to open the thick, metal door. Try and try as they might, the security panel repeatedly rejected their credentials.

"Garret! Garret!" the brothers cried. "Help! In here! Open the EVA door!"

Garret sat in his chair, twitching and sobbing uncontrollably as the screams penetrated his brain and soul. He struggled to keep his eyes closed in order to not witness the clone's impending demise on the video monitors.

"Help them, Armada!" Chloe pleaded, still on her knees.

"I can't, Chloe!" he angrily shouted, raising his hands. "The moment

I generate an emergency override to release the magnetic locks on the doors, Cain will trace it. They'll find us ... they'll kill us."

"Warn Euclid then!" she yelled, twisting to look at him.

"Then they'll figure out it was him that's been communicating with us and they'll kill him as well."

"Put on your suits!" one of the clones hollered.

Armada collapsed beside Chloe.

They gazed upon the tragic madness unfolding in the Arena One EVA Dock thirty miles above them.

"Time's up, gentlemen," Dr. Wyczthack sarcastically declared. "Who ... helped ... Armada?"

"We don't know!" and "Nobody's spoken to him!" the brothers screeched, peering up at the cameras.

Several of them had managed to swiftly don their EVA suits, while others continued to fiddle with the security panel in hopes of opening the door.

"Well?" Cain sternly called out.

Dr. White caught a glimpse of Bianca wiping her eyes. He stared at Cain until his glare was acknowledged. Riggs watched Dr. Wyczthack as Dr. White discreetly darted his eyes toward Bianca. Sensing she was being watched, and in an effort to hide her tears, Bianca turned her chair away from the conference table, ever so slowly.

Cain leaned forward to ensure that she could still see him, albeit peripherally.

He focused on Bianca and spoke at her while gruffly instructing Riggs, "Get Garret on the line!"

Bianca clenched her eyes shut and quickly cupped her fingers over her lips.

"Help them! Please!" Chloe begged, peering up at the ceiling. "Can you hear me? Please, please! Do something!"

Armada crouched down in front of their wall of tablets and scoured the shifting timed images.

"What're you doing?" Chloe sobbed.

"The Aerie … I need to see the Aerie. I need the Aerie, CARBEL, and Halo cameras," Armada barked.

"Very well then," Cain drably commented to his captives.

"Tablets seventeen, eighteen, and nineteen," Chloe gurgled, pointing at the top far left corner of the tablet grid.

"Ten," Cain said, devoid of all emotion.

"Cain!" Garret painfully shouted.

"They need a POG!" Armada snapped. "That's their only chance! Without a POG to connect to, they'll suffocate!"

"Nine."

"A POG?" Chloe confusedly asked. "How can they get a POG in the Arena? I mean, they'd have to open the…."

"Eight"

Then, like a ton of bricks, it hit her.

"Cain's gonna make Garret open the outer doors. Isn't he?"

"Seven."

Armada couldn't force his voice to speak. In utter dismay and bewilderment, he gazed at his wife with his mouth agape.

"Six."

"Wait! Wait!" Armada's brothers screamed. "Cain! Please! No!"

"Without a charged POG close by to connect to, they'll die," Armada informed Chloe.

He then saw a shot of the Aerie suddenly appear on tablet nineteen.

"Platforms one and two are equipped with a POG!" he excitedly commented, pointing at the screen. "Three, four, and five are in dock-lock. That means one and two are either on the way up, or they're descending."

"Five."

"What about a POG on a Cloud?" Chloe inquired, wiping her nose. "Can't they attach themselves to one of those?"

"Crap!" Armada grunted as the Halo video camera streamed a live feed of Platform One pulling away from the massive frames. "The Clouds are too far away. They won't make it in time."

"Garret! Help! Help!" the trapped men pleaded.

"Four."

Bianca couldn't stifle her tears or whimpering.

Dr. White and Riggs watched Cain as he squinted his eyes into angry, narrow slits. He furrowed his brow as he watched his trusted assistant succumb to her feelings.

"Bianca," Dr. Wyczthack said calmly and softly, then patronizingly asked, "Why are you crying?"

She was incapable of facing Cain, let alone to look him in the eye.

"Three!" he blasted, slapping the table.

Bianca jumped in her seat and let out a frightened squeal.

"Can't they hold on to something?" Chloe suggested. "Use the tether cords or…."

"Comm-link tether lines are used in conjunction with a POG," Armada interrupted.

Bianca rose from her chair and briskly walked toward the conference room door.

Cain turned to Riggs and nodded his head. Riggs sprang to his feet and dashed after Bianca, catching her just as she pushed down on the conference room door handle.

"Two!" Cain bellowed.

Riggs placed his palm on the door and leaned into it with all of his weight.

"Where ever are you going, Bianca?" Dr. White casually inquired, rising from his seat.

Armada scurried to his tablet and frantically searched for the Arena One camera numbers, specifically, the exterior EVA cameras.

"Forty and forty-one," he snapped and crawled back next to Chloe.

"One!" Cain yelled.

From within the EVA Dock, everything became instantly still and eerily silent.

Chloe raised both hands and shielded her eyes.

Armada's brothers hovered about the bay, nervously anticipating Garret's and Dr. Wyczthack's next move.

Armada watched Garret unfasten his seat restraint and pull himself to the Nest's central operations control panel. Still whimpering and trembling, Garret reluctantly looked up at the video monitor. He placed his shaking fingers on the button to disengage the magnetic locks on the EVA Dock's external doors.

"I'm sorry," he whined before pressing the button.

The computer system immediately disabled the locking mechanisms, thereby allowing the vacuum of space to pry open the five gargantuan bay doors.

"No!" Armada howled, springing at the wall of tablets.

The suction and depressurization forces were so tremendous and sudden that the clones were flung across the cavernous holding bay like rag dolls. Their bodies collided with the thick metal walls and doors before being hurled into the frigid void. Within seconds, Armada's brothers turned into lifeless, frozen mannequins. It would be only a matter of minutes before inertia and the planet's gravitational force would draw the icy cadavers into a violent collision with Earth's dense atmosphere.

Cain extended his right arm above his head and snapped his fingers. Riggs reached down and forcibly removed Bianca's hand from the door handle. He firmly grasped her wrist, and in one swift move, twisted her arm and folded it up high behind her back. She grunted and winced from the blinding shot of pain that radiated through her shoulder.

Chloe slowly peeled her fingers away from her face, saw the empty EVA hangar, and turned away from the tablets.

Garret sank back in his chair, vigorously shaking his head.

As she approached Cain and Dr. White, Bianca began trembling and her breathing became short and heavy. She felt nauseated and weak as she struggled to kick free of her muscular captor.

"You can't leave us now, my dear," Cain coldly commented, spinning his chair away from the conference table to address her, "We've come so far!"

The well-groomed sociopath continued his lecture, rising from his chair at the head of the table, "There's too much at risk, Bianca. If we go soft now, well … it causes problems. Doesn't it? You, of all people, can appreciate that. And we don't want problems, do we?"

Cain took one step forward and sandwiched the young woman between him and Riggs. He cautiously reached behind Bianca and took hold of her wrist. Riggs relaxed his grip and Dr. Wyczthack aggressively pulled her body against his. He silently stared her down; his soulless and evil glare penetrated her heart. Shivers of despair rippled up and down her spine; her chin quivered as his warm breath danced across her cheek.

"This is something that, quite simply, I can't afford for you to miss. You were, after all, instrumental in bringing us to this point."

Chloe collapsed in a heap on the floor, pulled her knees in, and wept heavily.

Armada kept his eyes on the tablet streaming the live footage from the EVA Dock's external video surveillance cameras. Tears streamed down his cheeks as he watched his brothers' bodies drift away. Like flickering fireflies playing in the breeze on a warm summer evening, one by one the corpses burned briefly and brightly as they entered Earth's atmosphere and disintegrated.

"Why didn't you do something?" Armada barked, rising from his knees. "Why didn't you help them? Why? Where are you?"

He searched the room, looking for a sign, any sign, of acknowledgement.

"Are you even listening to me?"

Dr. White stepped beside Riggs and tenderly ran his long, bony fingers through Bianca's thick and luxurious blonde hair. A devilish smile gradually spread across his thin lips. He suddenly grasped a handful of Bianca's flowing locks and yanked her head backwards. From the corner of her eye, she saw Dr. White reach into his coat breast pocket.

Cain leaned forward slightly, shortening the gap between his and Bianca's faces.

"Please…," she sputtered, as saliva freely dripped from her mouth.

"Sshh!" Cain interrupted. With his left hand, he quickly reached up and squeezed Bianca's cheeks, forcing her mouth to pucker slightly.

Her heart sunk when she felt the familiar sting of a needle entering her arm.

As Bianca started to wilt, Cain frowned and stated, "I think we need to reassess your dedication to this project."

CHAPTER 37

A PREEMPTIVE STRIKE

"The final switchback has been completely off-loaded, sir," Light Huddleston politely shouted over the noise. "They're in the process of stacking quadracles."

"How long do you anticipate that to take?" Cain inquired.

"Quads require around an hour-and-a-half to two hours to assemble, sir. So ... maybe thirty hours, thereabouts."

Light stared up into the video camera as he answered his employer's questions.

"We'll stage the quadracles upon completion and begin our dispatch as soon as I receive word from you."

From the comfort of his private office one mile above the Earth's surface, Cain monitored the movements of his precious cargo. With a multitude of high-definition video screens in front of him, Cain Wyczthack, like Armada and Chloe, had unlimited access to the SUBOS surveillance system. The mad scientist dedicated hours and hours of his day to watching and eavesdropping on the tower's populace.

"What's happening now? There, right behind you," he snapped at the portly dock supervisor.

Light twisted back to look at what Cain was referring to.

"That's one of our portable gantry cranes," Light happily replied, thumbing over his shoulder. "We use two of 'em to stack the top layer of the quadracles. We bring the missile cradles right up to the dock and assembly area, lift 'em a few inches to roll away the cradle, and lower the rocket into the frames. Once we construct a four-pack, we cover it up 'til we deploy to the Aerie."

"Pantex says their team will be here in forty-eight hours," Dr. White whispered from his seat on the couch.

"How long to deliver all one hundred?"

Dr. White sat up straight on the cushion front to get a better view of the video monitors.

"Oh," Light began, folding his arms, "load in, lift to the Aerie, transfer to the CARBEL, lift to the Halo … four hours. One way."

"Per quadracle?" Dr. White questioned loudly, rising from the sofa.

"Yes, sir," Light confirmed, rocking back and forth on his boot heels.

"So, in total, you estimate each four-pack to take a minimum of six hours to assemble and deliver. Am I correct?" Dr. Wyczthack asked.

"Yes, sir, you're correct."

Dr. White sauntered to the wet bar and held a crystal highball glass up high for Cain to see. He pointed at the glass and raised his eyebrows, as if to ask him, *Wanna drink?*

"Can't we expedite these loads a bit more efficiently?" Dr. Wyczthack growled, pinching an inch of his thumb and index finger at Dr. White.

"Well, in all honesty, I could, technically speaking, have all twenty-five quadracles up to the Aerie in about eighteen hours," Light admitted, scratching at his neck. "But that would mean no load outs or returns for the entire SUBOS freight system."

Light allowed his statement to sink in for a few seconds as Cain looked over his shoulder to catch Dr. White shrug with indifference.

"In addition," Light continued, "twenty-five four-packs are gonna put the Aerie in a proverbial logjam for several days. How much time do your boys from Oak Ridge and Pantex require for each installation?"

Dr. White raised the glass of Scotch to his lips and held up three fingers to Cain.

"Three hours," Dr. Wyczthack snarled, rubbing his temples.

"If you don't mind me saying, sir," Light humbly began, "I can keep your boys well stocked until they're done. I personally don't see the necessity to clog the elevators and stuff the Aerie with cargo that won't be used...at least not immediately. It's your decision...but I'd send up one quad at a time."

Dr. White handed Cain his glass of Woodford Reserve, winked once, and nodded his head in approval at Light.

"Very well then," Cain blurted, obviously disappointed. "Assemble the missile quadracles, stage for deployment, and wait 'til I give you the go-ahead."

"Yes, sir!" Light proudly replied, smiling broadly. "I'll have my...."

Mr. Huddleston's words were cut short as Cain disconnected the live video and audio feed.

"Three hours?" Cain blasted, emptying the contents of the highball in one massive mouthful.

"Well, these take time," Dr. White consoled his friend and business partner as he stepped to the bar.

"Don't patronize me, Alan," Dr. Wyczthack quipped. "I know it takes time! I know! I know! I know!"

Cain wrestled with his hair in frustration as Dr. White retrieved the bottle of whiskey.

"What's got you all worked up?"

"You have to ask?" Cain snapped as he watched the caramel-colored spirit flow from the bottle into his glass.

"I just ejected nearly two hundred clones, we don't know the identity of Armada's contact, and we have yet to locate and capture two runaways!"

Dr. White gave pause, recognized the stress on Cain's face, and proceeded to pour more whiskey.

"Cloud Ten construction has slowed, and missile installation can't occur until that's completed. And all the while, our A-list test subject and his girlfriend are running around while we got our heads crammed up our rear ends! And you wonder what's got me 'all worked up'?!"

X^N

***

"Ooh, did you feel that one?" Chloe asked, rubbing her husband's hand on her swollen belly.

"Nah," Armada grunted as he toyed with his tablet keyboard.

"Here, try this."

Pulling his left hand across her protruding midsection, she pressed his palm down and away from her bellybutton.

"Wow!" he exclaimed, twisting to face her. "He's really kicking!"

"I know! He's been like this for almost two days."

Armada tossed the computer to the end of the bed and curled his arms around his entombed son.

"Hey! You in there!" Armada playfully shouted. "Abdiel! What's going on? What's all the fuss for?"

Chloe laughed and slapped his shoulder before combing her fingers through his thick and slightly curly hair.

"Only a few weeks to go, buddy. We love you so much and are ready to meet you. And your momma's getting fat."

"Oh!" she laughingly cried, hitting him with her pillow. "You're such a butt! You ruined a beautiful moment with a fat joke!"

Chloe gruffly pushed Armada away from her side and kicked at him while attempting to scoot out from the far side of the bed.

"Help me, Abdiel!" he yelled. "She's killing me! She's crazy!"

"Nobody's killing no one, Abdiel!" Chloe shouted at her belly. "Your father just can't keep from saying something stupid!"

As she briskly strode to the closet and refrigerator, she snapped, "Have you devised a doable plan to get Euclid out of the Arena?"

"Augh!" Armada loudly groaned, still lying on the bed.

"I'll take that to mean no."

Chloe leaned back against the counter after retrieving a gargantuan red apple from their refrigerator.

"Baby! He's been up there, alone, for nearly five days!"

She bit into the firm, crisp meat of the apple.

"I know," her beaux finally and drolly commented.

Armada sat up, grabbed his tablet, and resumed his work.

"Can't you just generate an authorization to get on the CARBEL?" she mumbled while chewing.

Without looking at the mother-to-be, Armada drably stated, "With Wyczthack's newly implemented guidelines and operational procedures for attaching to a POG, comm-links are to automatically synchronize with a helmet transponder and RFID chip. As soon as Euclid comes within fifteen feet of any active POG, his identity will be compromised."

"Well, how about an internal transfer to another Arena?"

"Baby, that won't work. All RFID recipients from the Euclid batch were on Arena One and disintegrated five days ago. If I create a false directive for reassignment, say to Arena Two, and we somehow manage to sneak him out of Arena One, the first retinal scanner on Two will pick him up. He won't even make it past EVA. He'll be singled out, Wyczthack will be called in … and then they'll kill him."

Although she stood not more than ten feet away from their bed, Chloe's glazed stare told Armada she was in a completely different place.

"I'm thinking it'll be easier to bring him down after Cloud Ten is complete."

"After?!"

"It's the only way to get Euclid back without creating an artificial reason or occasion. When Wyczthack and Riggs are ready, they'll schedule the return of all personnel to the SUBOS. They'll empty the Arenas. I can easily hide Euclid among six hundred twins, that's not a problem. The most challenging and dangerous method would be to move him, independently, without an accompanying event for a distraction."

"What about evaluations? The next time Euclid is scheduled for…."

"Nope!" he loudly and sarcastically interrupted. "The doc's temporarily suspended all evals. Until further notice, all vertical movement of Arena personnel is strictly prohibited. If we so much as…."

Armada failed to complete his statement, as a bright sounding 'ping' emanated from his computer.

"Speaking of…," Armada commented, pointing to his tablet. "He just sent me a message."

"What'd he say?" Chloe asked as she awkwardly crawled up the bed.

"'When am I getting out of here?' and 'How long will this fruit last?'" he recited.

"Ask him if he remembers when they received their distribution."

'Soon, buddy. I'm working on it. I want you safe. Chloe wants to know when you received the distribution,' he speedily typed and pressed 'send.'

"How long will it last?" Armada inquired of his wife.

"We determined that all produce is safe to consume up to three weeks after delivery. Three-and-a-half at most. I mean he won't die or get sick, but texture and flavor decline quickly after that. Tell him not to cut or portion anything, keep everything refrigerated, and only take out what he knows for sure he'll eat. Changes in temperature and light shorten the shelf life."

"So…," Armada began and folded his arms, "I have approximately two weeks to get Euclid off the Arena."

Chloe lightly and silently scratched at his forearm.

"In a little more than fourteen days, his food supply will become inedible," he added.

He quietly shook his head as he pondered what words to say to his stranded brother. After contemplating what information he should share, he assembled and dispatched a list of instructions for maximizing the longevity of his fresh produce.

'Can you see any of the Clouds from the Arena?' his follow-up letter asked.

A few moments later, Euclid's response appeared on Armada's tablet, 'Yes. Cloud Ten is close by. And I believe it's Cloud Nine that has been brought next to the Island. There's been plenty of activity with personnel loading materials on Nine ever since the tubes were installed.'

'What materials?'

'Couldn't tell you. All I know is more and more pods are being off-loaded from the CARBELs and being held at the Island. The Cloud was repositioned not two days ago, and they've connected a hard line to the Halos."

"Wow!" Armada blurted.

"Wow what?" Chloe asked, startled.

"Euclid says there's a tether line between the Halo and a Cloud that's been moved."

"What does that mean?"

"Well," he said, taking a short glance at the panel of tablet monitors, "it tells me that Wyczthack and White are about to populate the Clouds."

"But Ten hasn't been completely assembled yet. Has it? Last thing you told me was it hadn't gone through pressurization certification."

"You are correct, woman. I did say that."

He anxiously hopped to his knees and faced his wall of tablet screens.

"Ah-ha!" he exclaimed, pointing at one computer and scrambled out of bed.

"Ah-ha what, baby?"

"Look at the Halo. Up here on the left."

He crouched down and placed his index finger at the top corner of the tablet.

"Clouds," he excitedly stated. "Two of 'em, just like he said. Cain's getting ready to notify his inhabitants that it's time to come in."

"Are you sure? He's relocated all of 'em at one time or another, so what makes you think that this is 'it'?"

"Wyczthack, White, and Riggs wouldn't tether anything unless there's people involved."

"But what about Cloud Ten?"

"That's irrelevant. He's prepping the first nine for boarding, now."

"Okay," Chloe smartly agreed, lumbering out of bed. "Let's say you're right and Cain's trying to expedite his agenda. And let's also say that today, right now, Engenechem puts out the call for everybody to get here ASAP. How long do you estimate it'll take for thirty thousand people to travel to Las Vegas from all over the world? Secondly, if the Clouds aren't ready, where do they go after they arrive?"

"All right, I'll play along. First, the people Cain's chosen for this little gathering have more than likely prearranged their travel plans. All they need to know is 'when' and boom, they're on a plane. Shortest time? I'd say a couple of hours for those already in Nevada. Several hours for people in California, Utah, Arizona, and Colorado. Maybe half a day for East Coast, Canada, and Mexico. All things considered ... I imagine the entire populace can be here, at the SUBOS ... in ninety-six hours."

"And?" Chloe asked with a high lilt in her voice.

"And ... if the Clouds are uninhabitable...."

Armada held his arms out to his sides, palms up, and shrugged.

"Honey, let's go meet the new next-door neighbors. Cain'll fill this place up in a heartbeat."

"Ask Euclid how many launch tubes have been installed on Ten," Chloe suddenly requested. "Also, how long did it take for each to be constructed."

She watched her husband gruffly peck at his keyboard.

"I'm running outta time!" he snapped before sending his questions to Euclid.

"Well, baby? If Cain ... OOHH!"

Chloe winced from a burst of pain, leaned forward, and grasped her belly with both hands.

"What? What happened? Are you all right?"

The adoring father-to-be lightly placed his fingers on his wife's shoulder.

"Wow!" she grunted, slightly stooping. "He's got a killer kick!"

"Here, lie back down."

At that moment, the incoming message chimed.

"Euclid's calling you."

"You want anything?" he concernedly inquired as Chloe eased herself on the mattress, still cradling her bulging stomach.

"Nah, I'm fine. Oooh! Actually, baby, will you get me some of those fire 'n ice pickles? That sounds really, OH! ... good right now."

"Sure, sure," he gleefully replied, kissing her forehead.

After reaching for his tablet, Armada opened the note.

"He says 'Three tubes, and two hours for each tube.'"

Chloe closed her eyes and began breathing deeply through her nose. She grimaced as her unborn son wrestled in her womb.

"I'll be right back, baby. We finished off the jar of pickles so I need to go to the kitchen."

"Okay. I'll be … AUGH!"

Chloe clutched at the sheets, raised her head off the pillow, and slightly bent her knees as another jolt of pain ripped through her.

"Now?" Armada loudly called out, looking up at the ceiling. "You're joking, right? You're gonna make her go through this now?"

"It's okay, baby. He's not coming now. Go get my pickles."

***

"Are you outta your mind?" Armada exclaimed, nearly choking on a mouthful of pickle chips. "What good would that do?"

"It'll interfere with Cain's schedule," Chloe curtly answered.

"So what? That won't stop a missile launch."

"Look," she stated, placing her bowl on the nightstand, "Cain needs his missile silos to remain secret. Right?"

"Right."

"Okay. So, point number one: when it's made publicly known that Engenechem has been constructing, and is currently stocking, ten orbital nuclear missile silos, Cain will be forced to comply with an investigation. Two: while Wycz and White are entangled with meetings, press conferences, and inspections, that's a prime opportunity to bring down Euclid. You'll have more time to figure out how to stop the missile launch."

Armada chewed his pickles and washed it down with several gulps of Shiraz.

"All right. Let me see if I understand your logic. You want me to locate the deleted video footage of the missiles being loaded in the SUBOS cargo elevators, and then send the video files to the network news organizations, newspapers, and governmental agencies. Correct?"

"Yes."

"And you believe that by making the world aware of a thousand nuclear missiles floating above everybody's head, that will be enough of a distraction and hindrance to Cain's itinerary that he'll be significantly delayed in completing his Clouds. Right?"

"Right."

"Wrong!" Armada grunted, pouring himself another glass of wine.

"What a video clip making its way to the media WILL do is make Wyczthack mad, first, and then he'll speed up his schedule. Cain's a genius, but he's a nut! He's a sociopath, guaranteed! He won't be stopped by a few questions coming from reporters and agency heads. He laughs at that stuff. Mark my words. If we expose Cain and Engenechem we'll lose days, maybe even weeks, of precious time. Remember, there's six-and-a-half billion people depending on us."

***

As he lay next to his sleeping wife, Armada repeatedly reviewed Chloe's reasons for supporting the proposed 'first strike.' He mentally played out the 'If we … then Cain will …' chess game over and over again, until he eventually agreed to Chloe's battle plans.

'If I find recorded video showing nuclear missiles arriving at the Aerie,' he quietly theorized, 'and I create a mass dispatch … that will be enough reason for the UN and IAEA to send in their inspectors.'

A smile appeared on his lips while contemplating the potential results of their endeavor.

'They're not aware of Cain's EC program, so he'll have to move everyone from the Arenas to the Nurseries. Without them, Wyczthack can't get Cloud Ten assembled for pressurization certification, which means he won't be able to hide his remaining rockets.'

"This could actually work," he whispered.

With a sudden surge of optimism, Armada sat up, retrieved his tablet, and began investigating the video files in the CYCLOPS program. After an hour of examining the folder history with nothing to show for his efforts, a thought occurred to him: *Does CYCLOPS record transaction content?*

"Microsoft does it with their programs, why not Engenechem?" he muttered.

The stored Cloud video clips occupied a massive amount of space on the Master Server, with individual files numbering in the hundreds of thousands. Just as he predicted, Armada identified and opened a special tracking aspect of the CYCLOPS surveillance system. This little-known capability of the program kept a running record of not only when the original video clips were generated and file size, but if and when they were edited. In addition, the history displayed who did the editing, from what terminal and when, and, much to his surprise, an exact display of how much data was removed ... and where it saved.

"YES!" he shouted, thrusting his fists high above his head.

Chloe hummed disapprovingly and rolled away from him.

Armada highlighted the most recently edited video file, opened its properties, and read the location for a separate storage folder on the Master Server.

"Visitors? It's in an Engenechem visitor's registration log?" he asked himself with a chuckle while accessing the folder.

It took all but maybe two seconds for CYCLOPS to list out the entries in its humongous digital library. Armada couldn't contain his excitement as hundreds upon hundreds of secret video files populated his computer screen. With a creation date not more than five minutes old, the very last entry in the library was an eleven-minute video recording of a quadracle of nuclear missiles. The snippet clearly showed them being unloaded from a SUBOS elevator, rolled across the Aerie deck and onto the platform of CARBEL Three. He watched it again and again and again; he and Chloe were vindicated.

His brain and heart raced with exuberant joy, but at the same time had reservations about who to send the videos to, how many, and what content should be disseminated. Thousands of edited video files required viewing, but in his mind, Armada knew they had little time to spare. He would have to choose video clips at random and do so quickly.

First, he hacked the Engenechem personal e-mail account for Dr. White and typed the words 'Very Interesting' in the subject bar of a new e-mail. Secondly, after much self-deliberation, Armada selected and previewed ten video files to accompany his message. Third, he scoured through thousands of personal and professional e-mail addresses and phone numbers in both Dr. White's contact list and address book. Fox News, CNN, the Huffington Post, the US Senate Oversight Committee, MI5, the Department of Defense, the Joint Chiefs of Staff, Secretary of State, the UN Security Council, the IAEA, and hundreds more were included in his diabolical e-mail blast.

"I highly recommend you give close scrutiny to the enclosed attachments," Armada proudly typed.

He checked and rechecked the video files, made sure the recipient addresses were complete and correct, and gazed lovingly at his slumbering wife.

"Please, let this work," he whispered.

Armada dragged the cursor across the screen to the bottom corner of his open letter, drew in a deep breath, and lightly tapped 'send.'

CHAPTER 38

SACRIFICE

"How can it be that the most heavily fortified and powerful corporation on the planet gets hacked?" a reporter shouted and quickly stood, raising his hand.

"This is the work of a foreign government, no doubt about it!" Dr. White boldly proclaimed. "Iran, Russia, China, North Korea…one of them is behind this."

"But the e-mail blast was generated from your personal address!" a woman declared.

"You're correct, but it wasn't from me. Ladies and gentlemen, I know you have many questions that need answering, just as we do. But given that this mass e-mail was sent only a few hours ago, there's been very little investigation into the security breach. Rest assured that we here at Engenechem are doing everything we can to identify the culprits and are being most cooperative with federal investigators. Please be patient and we'll keep you apprised of our progress."

The throng of aggressive journalists rose to their feet while trying to outshout one another.

"What about the videos?" a man squealed from in front of the podium. "Was the content of the ten video files genuine?"

"You're being whipped into a frenzied mob of conspiracy theorists.

As I stated before, this is the work of a dangerous, rogue, foreign government, probably in conjunction with a terrorist organization to...."

"Are the videos real?" a woman angrily shouted, interrupting Dr. White.

"Digital animation, blue screens, layering and rendering, a bunch of CGI hacks have successfully broken into our system and made it appear that we...."

"C'mon! Is Engenechem deploying nuclear missiles?" she again rudely interrupted.

"I believe I've already explained our situation," Dr. White snarkily replied.

"Doctor White! Doctor White!" a man enthusiastically yelled. "Where are Dr. Wyczthack and Bianca Doyle? It's been nearly four weeks since Miss Doyle's last appearance at a press conference. Why aren't they here?"

"Dr. Wyczthack isn't feeling well, and Miss Doyle has been ... shall we say, relocated."

"Isn't it odd," the man continued, "that Cain's personal, professional assistant of more than ten years hasn't made contact with the outside world in twenty-seven days, and hasn't been seen?"

"No comment," Dr. White smugly stated.

The SUBOS atrium erupted as hundreds of suspicious reporters, bloggers, and journalists sprung from their seats. They shouted and screamed at Dr. White, hungry for information.

"Thank you all," he insincerely offered. "Now, if you'll please excuse me."

Armed security guards had to rush the stage to protect Dr. White as he exited from behind the podium. The rabid horde yelled obscenities and hurled insults at him for ending the public inquiry so abruptly.

Dr. White briskly walked to the elevators with his staff and bodyguards following close behind. As he stood waiting for the doors to open, he felt his phone vibrate in his coat's left breast pocket.

"White," he flatly answered.

The elevator doors separated and Dr. White quickly entered the spacious, empty cab. He held his palm out to the armed security detail and assistants and shook his head.

"Not well," he remarked. "I don't know how long we can keep 'em pacified without divulging any substantial information."

"Don't let them bother you," Cain casually stated. "We did the right thing by me not attending today. Keep deflecting. Keep distracting. Give them information they don't need and can't use. You'll have them chasing shadows instead of catching rabbits. Remember what Hillary Clinton said in 2009: 'Don't let a good crisis go to waste.' We can capitalize on our current state of affairs."

"So what do we do now?"

"Riggs and his aquatic EVA trainers are with me on the Aerie deck. They're going with me to finish stocking the Clouds and will conduct their sessions after Cloud population."

"After? I'm assuming then you want me to make the call right away?"

"Yes. Afterwards, send CARBEL transfer authorization codes to the Arenas, Arks, and Eden. The IAEA will want to look at those first, and the last thing we need now is a UN human rights violation investigation. So I want the Arenas, Arks, and Eden emptied, now. Get 'em back to the Nurseries."

"What's your deadline for our inhabitants?"

"Give them a five-day window to be on the SUBOS—no, make it four days."

"Cain, don't you think ninety-six hours is cutting it a tad too close?" Dr. White delicately inquired.

Dr. Wyczthack calmly answered, "No. We have a most opportune situation. Make an announcement that Engenechem will schedule more open press conferences and that a special crisis response team is being assembled to address our predicament, but don't go. Don't give interviews and don't answer questions. You stay out of the spotlight and send someone different each time. Change up the team members, alter their positions and authority, and switch their titles around. If we can keep 'em at bay for four days, that's enough time to bring in the clones, raise the quadracles, and prepare the Clouds."

Dr. White was hesitant to interrupt.

"Light told us he can deliver all quads in eighteen hours, and the clones can make their descent to the Nurseries at the same time. Once the twins are safe in their Nurseries, and after the missiles have been deployed to the Island, then we can begin boarding the Clouds. It's perfect! An additional thirty thousand people coming up to the Aerie will be a magnificent disruption to any inspection team. They'll interfere with the elevators and registration center, clog the Aerie, and interrupt the load outs on the CARBEL. There'll be so much confusion with everyone coming and going; this is going to work to our advantage."

The elevator came to a stop and bounced slightly before the doors parted. Dr. White exited and listened intensely to Cain's directions while walking to his office.

"Give the media everything we have. Elevator schedules, SUBOS surveillance camera videos, container manifests, packing slips, landings and departures, anything to keep them from conducting 'hands on' inspections. After we've populated the Clouds and reconfigured their orbital patterns, then we'll graciously grant open access to the Aerie, the CARBELs and Halos, and all remaining Engenechem facilities."

"And you're positive ninety-six hours will be enough time."

"Oh, yes. Ample."

As Dr. White entered his office, he stated, "Okay. Let me consolidate this conversation. You, Riggs, and the entire EVA team are making the lift to Cloud Nine. They will complete the load-in and stocking of the Clouds."

"Yes."

"Pantex will be here tomorrow to install tubes and missiles on Cloud Ten, and you want Huddleston to deploy all quadracles to the Aerie. A task he estimates can be accomplished in eighteen hours."

"Yes."

"You want to summon our inhabitants now and set a ninety-six hour deadline for their arrival."

"Yes."

"We're to empty the Arenas, Arks, and Eden, of all clone test subjects and return them to the Nurseries."

"Yes."

"And I'm to arrange for additional press conferences while assembling a crisis response team, but you don't want me to attend the meetings."

"Yes. Perfect!"

"And once I've set these wheels in motion, I'll back out all programs for PIN CUSHION and…."

"No!" Cain suddenly interjected. "Bring the Pantex hard drives with you but do not, under any circumstance, remove, relocate, delete, or alter one program. If the IAEA sends in an investigation team and they catch us suppressing or withholding information or changing the structure of programming support for our Master Server, it's bound to create suspicion. Bring all of the hard drives for the missiles and we'll do a remote install from Ten once we've colonized the Clouds. After the successful download of PIN CUSHION to our new server, then we can back it out from the Master Server. Retrieve your computer, grab the faraday case with the drives, and head to the Aerie. You'll join Riggs and me on Cloud Nine whenever a POG-equipped platform becomes available."

"This is happening, isn't it? Everything we've talked about and planned for … it's really happening."

"We're almost there, Alan. In one week … we'll recreate the world."

***

"Well, something's going on," Chloe commented out of frustration. "There's no reason for the Master Server to be taking so much time to confirm my access."

"Have you looked at what's running in the background?" Armada countered as he sipped his coffee.

Rather than answer his question, she opened the hard drive monitor to find a handful of familiar programs occupying a sizeable amount of bandwidth space.

"Baby, look at this," she suggested, scooting her tablet toward him.

Armada scrolled through the program names, announcing them one by one: "EGGS, CYCLOPS, ARENAS, CARBEL...."

His voice faded away as he started recognizing each program's content and interactive properties.

"He's doing it!" Armada blurted. "Cain's initiated the call to the Cloud inhabitants!"

Chloe sat back in her chair, slack-jawed, and stared at her husband in shocked disbelief.

"What? Are you sure?"

Armada's head hung low.

"I don't believe it," she confessed. "This isn't...I mean, he can't just.... Now?"

Emotions suddenly stole her ability to speak. She folded her hands on her belly and firmly grasped at her flesh and wept.

Armada turned to his wife, slid out of the chair onto his knees, and laid his head on her lap.

How can I tell her we'll be okay and everything will be all right? he thought. *This can't possibly be how it ends!*

For reasons unknown to him at that moment, Armada wasn't upset at all.

"Hey," he said, erecting himself, "we're gonna be just fine. You'll see."

Chloe shook her head vigorously and cried all the more.

"No we're not! We're gonna die!"

"Sshh, we aren't dying. At least not soon, and definitely not this way."

He leaned over, removed a tissue from a box on the table, and proceeded to wipe her eyes and nose. Knowing Chloe was somewhat easily distracted, emotionally, Armada made the decision to ask her questions about what she found on the Master Server hard drive monitor.

"Baby, I know it's an awkward moment to be asking this, but do you remember ever hearing of a program called PIN CUSHION?"

Amazingly, Chloe immediately stopped crying and opened her eyes. Although short on breath and slightly congested, she spoke clearly while answering, "No, I don't believe so. It doesn't sound familiar at all. What's its activation date?"

"I don't know; will you check on that for me? I just noticed it's on that list."

Through suppressed tears she managed to crack a tiny grin and nod.

Armada smiled lovingly at his wife, wiped her eyes once again, and took his seat.

Within seconds, Chloe retrieved the information he requested.

Armada suddenly rose from his chair, stepped in front of the panel of tablet monitors, and hurriedly scanned the transitioning images.

"If they're calling the Cloud participants.... Baby? Will you get the EVA video feeds from Arenas Two, Three, and Four? Quickly, please?"

Chloe smeared away the remnants of her tears and did as instructed.

Tablet screens one, two, and three briefly flickered, then began streaming live footage from within the EVA docks on the Arenas. All three cameras broadcasted a similar image: hundreds of clones dressing for deployment.

"Ha! I knew it! I knew it!" Armada declared, hopping and pointing at the wall of tablets. "Cain's bringing 'em down!"

He pounced on Chloe, held her face in his hands, and repeatedly kissed her.

"See? I told you! We needed a distraction to get Euclid back. Oh, man, this is good!"

"Baby?" she peeped, as he began typing a letter to his stranded brother. "I have the stats on PIN CUSHION."

"Lay it on me!" he gleefully commanded.

"Okay, to begin with, this program was created about four months ago. Right around the time you and I escaped."

"Okay."

"Second, there's exactly one thousand subfiles, and they each contain around the same amount of data."

"All righty."

"Third, the folder titles are alphanumerical and sequential."

Armada stopped typing and focused on Chloe's words.

"You wanna know what number four is?" she teased.

"Yes!"

"The folder titles are sequestered into two groupings. Nine hundred of them have titles that end with a capital A. The other hundred have alphanumerical titles that end with a capital I."

Armada leapt from his seat, shouting and clapping.

"Yes! Yes! Chloe! Chloe, Chloe, Chloe, baby!"

He grabbed her by the wrists and pulled her out of the desk chair.

"What?" she giggled as they stepped up on the mattress.

"Don't you get it?" he hollered, jumping back and forth between their beds.

"Get what?"

"Augh! Chloe! Think! A thousand folders, all the same size, sequential file numbers ... ACTIVE and IN-active?"

"Eee!" she squealed, bouncing slightly. "Armada! We've located the Cloud missiles! We know where Cain hid the program!"

"Woo-hoo!" they bellowed in unison, and, "Thank you, wherever you are! Thank you! Thank you!"

Armada abruptly stopped jumping on the bed and his smile disappeared.

"What's wrong, baby?" she happily asked, still bouncing.

"They're gonna begin arriving in hours," he factually stated, frowning. "They'll be sent up here for holding 'til time to board the Clouds. And as soon as Euclid steps foot on the Aerie, retinal scanners will single him out."

Armada stepped off the mattress and slowly strode to the refrigerator.

"How can we bypass the cameras?" she asked, partially winded, before collapsing on the bed. "Can't you simply delete his file?"

Her frustrated husband picked up the bottle of wine resting on top of the refrigerator.

"I can't just up and delete his creation records. It's not as simple as that," he grumbled as he poured himself a glass. "Everyone who enters the SUBOS receives an assigned retinal scan identification number. If you're not recognized, you get detained. Remember, Euclid should have died days ago. He's not supposed to exist. Sooner or later his retinas and RFID chip will expose him, whether or not his file exists."

Chloe sat on the bed and listened as Armada continued to point out the negatives.

"We need to get to the kitchen and stock up on our food supply. I'd imagine Wycz and White are about to flood this place. We've got to secure enough food and water to sustain us for several days."

Chloe's heart sank as she watched Armada gulp down the first goblet of wine, then pour himself another.

"We'll have to isolate ourselves for at least twenty-four hours … maybe thirty-six, until there's enough people to blend in with."

She could feel her heart beating and the veins in her temples throbbing.

"How do we hide? What's to keep the Engenechem staff out of our room?" she meekly asked.

Armada guzzled the second glass of wine and sauntered to the door. While scrutinizing the handle and card-reading mechanism, Chloe silently waddled across the room to join him.

"Well, since you're the electronics expert, I'll leave it up to you to devise a method of cutting the power to the lock, but in a manner where you and I can still go in and out. And ensure against Cain's newcomers from gaining access."

"Don't you think you should notify Euclid about what's going on before going to the kitchen? He needs to get suited up and prepared to move to the Halo. Right?"

***

"I'm on the Aerie, waiting for Halo One to complete its descent," said Dr. White, speaking into the microphone embedded within his helmet. "It's getting close; I think another fifteen minutes or so and we'll begin our ascension."

"Excellent," Dr. Wyczthack stated loudly, listening on the phone's speaker. "What about the Arenas and such? Have they been cleared yet?"

"Eden and the Arks will take longer than we originally anticipated, but I can assure you that they'll be vacated by tomorrow evening. The second half from Arena Four is on CARBEL One. When it touches down, all Evan subjects will have been accounted for."

"Good, good. What's the deck looking like?"

"Well, Mr. Huddleston's a man to be taken at his word. There's nine quadracles blocking traffic down here, so when he said we'd have ourselves a bit of a logjam, he wasn't kidding. Two are in the CARBEL right now, and all five SUBOS elevators are swapping rockets for personnel."

"That's what I want to hear! Clouds One through Seven will come out of orbit within six hours. Riggs and his teams will set the tether cables as soon as they arrive."

As he listened to Dr. Wyczthack, Dr. White observed CARBEL One gently come to a rest on the Aerie with a dense thud. The vibrations resonated throughout the concrete and steel structure.

"All right, good to know. Cain, CARBEL One just touched down and they're filing out already. I'll just plan to see you on Nine in about an hour."

"Fine. See you then."

Dr. White disconnected the Aerie Communications Console commlink from his suit, picked up his satchel and the case containing the hard drives, and walked into the path of the oncoming clones. As he passed through the disembarking brood, very few of his synthetic subjects looked him directly in the eye.

While approaching the CARBEL One platform, he noticed a red flashing light on the front panel of the deck-mounted POG. Standing next to the POG was the Aerie load master and one of the Arena Four clones. Dr. White stepped on the elevator, secured his tether strap to an eyelet in the deck, and connected a POG comm-link to the coupler in his suit. Within seconds, the transponder in his helmet registered with the POG and a tiny green LED bulb began blinking steadily.

"Good evening, sir. May I please see your CARBEL access authorization codes?" the load master politely requested.

"Here you go," Dr. White replied, handing off his cards.

"What have we here?" he then inquired, pointing at the lone clone.

"Thank you, sir," said the man after scanning Dr. White's authorization cards. "Well, something just doesn't add up with this one."

The man motioned for the clone to join him and Dr. White.

"We loaded the second half of the remaining personnel from Arena Four, and after everybody secured their tether straps and comm-links, only his transponder and RFID chip failed to synchronize with the POG."

The clone approached Dr. White and the man as he elaborated, "He's receiving oxygen, but due to the identification snag, the POG won't engage the communication aspect of his comm-link."

Dr. White gave the clone a swift look over and focused on his face.

"I think it's showing signs of 'end of cycle.' Whenever we tried speaking to him he'd just stare at us and wouldn't say a word."

Dr. White inspected the coupler in the clone's suit, as well as the connector to the POG comm-link. Both appeared to be functioning properly and the POG showed no signs of operations failure. He detached his line, reached over and disconnected the clone, then hooked himself to the same comm-link. In no time at all, the POG synchronized with Dr. White's transponder and the green light started flickering.

"See?" the man announced. "Something's wrong with this one."

Just when Dr. White placed his fingers on his suit's coupler, he suddenly noticed an irregularity of the clone's EVA suit: there were no exterior nameplates.

Dr. White reconnected both his and the clone's suit couplers to the POG comm-link and glared at the clone.

"Identity credentials and primary and secondary applications," he loudly inquired, resting his hands on his hips.

"Sir, I don't think he understands you," the man commented.

The clone stood silently before them, shifting his focus between the two.

"Oh no, he understands me just fine," Dr. White said grinning widely, extended his arm, and tapped his index finger at the location for the missing nameplate.

"Identity credentials and primary and secondary applications," Dr. White repeated gruffly, but received no response.

"I agree with your statement that there's a problem with this one, and it's right here, look...," he ordered, poking the clone aggressively in his chest, "directly below the location for the identification plate. The missing identification plate. That's problem number one."

The clone's eyes widened as fear and panic set in.

"We have yet an additional problem," Dr. White continued, "Because not only is there an absence of an identification plate, but this uniform should have an A4 on it, signifying that he was stationed on Arena Four. But seeing as how I can plainly make out an A1 ... I have to wonder how that's possible."

Euclid was trapped.

The load master hesitated to speak for a moment, but finally said "Sir, if you like, I'm more than happy to personally escort this individual to the Nursery."

"Oh, no. No, no, no," Dr. White dramatically replied. "That won't be necessary. This fine specimen ... is coming with me to Cloud Nine."

As he spoke, a devilish smile spread across his thin lips.

"And I'm sure Dr. Wyczthack will want to interview our walking anomaly, personally."

"Yes, sir."

Although unable to hear every word in the men's conversation, Euclid felt his stomach tighten as beads of sweat began to appear on his forehead.

The man disconnected himself from the POG, walked a few paces to the edge of the platform, and dismounted. He immediately waved his hand in front of a scanner on the CARBEL One control panel and typed in his security credentials and authorization for the elevator to depart. Euclid watched the man as he communicated with the Aerie personnel. The red warning lights started flashing, and soon thereafter, the deck slowly ascended from its base.

Dr. White carefully scooted the faraday case with his foot to the side of the POG. He pushed it up against the frame of the oxygen generator and stuck his briefcase in between, unfastened his tether strap, and reconnected it to one of the eyelets in front of the POG.

Euclid monitored Dr. White from several feet away as he unfolded the generator's keyboard. He then glanced at Euclid and the blinking red light at the port of his comm-link. After a few keystrokes, the LED bulb stopped flashing and switched to a steady green.

"Can you hear me now?" a voice resonated throughout Euclid's helmet.

"Yes, sir," he plainly answered.

"You and I have a lengthy journey ahead of us," Dr. White casually stated, folding the keyboard back in place. "And Dr. Wyczthack is bound to have a plethora of questions he'll need answers to, so . . . lets you and I first conduct our part of the conversation. Identification credentials and primary and secondary applications."

Dr. White stepped toward his copassenger.

"Evan Euclid Four. Aeronautics and metallurgy."

"A Euclid?" Dr. White amazedly repeated. "There are no more Euclid series specimens. You do know they're all dead, don't you?"

Euclid's demeanor suddenly transitioned from one of fear and despair to stifled rage. He elected to stare at his captor rather than answer.

"So, you've been hiding on Arena One this entire time? Knowing you won't. . . ."

"You're not going to get away with this!" Euclid forcefully interjected.

"Away with what?"

"You know. Don't play your mind games with me. We know about the missiles."

"Oh . . . that's what you're referring to. I can't begin to explain to you the myriad of projects and plans we've laid out for the benefit of mankind and survival of our dying planet. And you couldn't possibly imagine or understand the unfortunate necessity for...."

"Spare me your pathetic and perverted justifications," Euclid again interrupted, and with both hands pushed Dr. White with considerable force.

The men began to experience a small degree of weightlessness and Dr. White was momentarily airborne. The tether strap kept him from falling completely backwards.

"Stay away from me!" Dr. White demanded as Euclid knelt down and unclipped his tether strap.

Even though he outweighed Euclid and stood nearly a foot taller, the aged doctor lacked the agility, overall body strength, and familiarity of functioning in zero gravity to entangle himself in a row with the clone.

In an act of fear and haste, Dr. White unfastened his own tether strap and slowly backed away from Euclid.

"You ejected my brothers!" Euclid angrily shouted.

Dr. White took tiny baby steps and looked about the deck. Other than the POG, there was nothing and no one to aid the lone scientist.

"You must understand, Euclid, even I have my orders and instructions, and must be held accountable by those more powerful than me. They, they ... he, I mean, him, Dr. Wyczthack ... he ordered Riggs to...."

"Shut up, White!" Euclid growled and lunged with all his might, knocking him off his feet.

"Help! Help!" Dr. White screamed. "I'm being...."

Before he could finish his plea for assistance, Euclid disconnected the doctor's comm-link at the base of the POG.

Euclid stood defiantly in front of Dr. White as he struggled to erect himself. Not knowing exactly what he should do with his flailing prisoner, Euclid cautiously approached Dr. White. Like a caged animal, the demented scientist backed away, all the while searching desperately for any means of escape. He peered off into the dark, cold vacuum of space and at the Earth's surface more than twenty miles below.

When he neared the end of the POG, Euclid disconnected the comm-link from his own suit. Now both men had no means of communicating and would likely die from carbon dioxide poisoning before reaching the Halo and the safety of Cloud Nine.

Euclid turned his head down to the right and spied Dr. White's faraday briefcase.

"Stay away from that!" Dr. White roared, vigorously pointing at Euclid. "Don't touch it!"

Although his words were muffled and muted, Euclid knew that Dr. White didn't want him inspecting the contents of the box.

The interior of Dr. White's helmet was already showing signs of oxygen depletion. His rapid, shallow breathing caused ice crystals to begin forming on the outermost edges of his visor.

Euclid picked up the case and held it in his arms.

"I said leave that alone!" Dr. White shrieked and lurched toward Euclid.

Euclid easily out maneuvered his attacker by stepping to the side, and, by using the man's inertia against himself, pushed Dr. White past him.

With the doctor sprawled out several feet away, Euclid was safe and free to examine the faraday briefcase. He unclasped the three locks and lifted the lid.

Dr. White sat on the deck and watched Euclid as he removed one of the ten hard drives.

Euclid held the sandwich-sized drive up close to his visor to get a better look. Without a word, he twisted to face Dr. White and extended his arm. He suddenly coiled back and flung the hard drive over the side of the elevator deck.

"No!" Dr. White screamed. "Stop! You don't know what you're doing!"

Euclid removed a second hard drive from the case, showed it off to the deranged physician, and threw it, too, into the void.

Like a little girl having her favorite doll pulled apart, Dr. White helplessly squealed, "Stop it! Stop it!"

The maniacal scientist managed to regain his footing and slowly pursued Euclid as he removed the data cartridges, one by one, and hurled them from the deck.

"Augh!" Euclid faintly heard the man wheezily wail as he pitched the hard drives.

He could barely see through the thick layer of condensation on the interior of Dr. White's visor, but heard him shouting, begging, coughing, and crying.

After throwing the tenth data cartridge overboard, Euclid showed the empty case to Dr. White before tossing it to him.

Delirious from overexertion, unbridled emotions, and lack of fresh oxygen, Dr. White strained to control his balance, maintain focus, and keep his eyes open. Euclid watched as the doctor's torso heaved upwards in desperation for fresh, filtered air.

The two men shivered from having disconnected their suits from the POG. Not only were they losing precious oxygen and cut off from all communication, the POG was the sole power source for the EVA suit's radiant heat.

Dr. White staggered to the oxygen generator's frame, laid his hand against the side, and gazed down at the Earth. Euclid momentarily stared up at the Halo and the collection of orbital stations.

The isolated clone turned his attention to Dr. White and approached him stealthily from behind. He quickly and quietly wrapped his arms around the doctor's waist, pulled him in close, and jumped out into the darkness.

CHAPTER 39

OBSTACLES

"Then you tell me where he is!" Cain roared. "'Cause he sure as the devil isn't up here!"

"That's what I'm trying to tell you, sir," the flustered Aerie deck officer repeated, "We don't know where Dr. White went. No one has visually laid eyes on him, nobody's physically had a run in with…."

"For three hours? In three hours' time none of you have located Dr. White? One individual?"

"We're doing our best, sir. There's been such an influx of…."

"Have you checked the video records?" Cain rudely and impatiently interrupted.

"Sir, we have no surveillance camera videos to review, as me and my staff were given a specific directive, issued by you, Dr. White, and Riggs Woodburn, that all SUBOS surveillance systems, including those of the Aerie, CARBEL, Halos, and Clouds were to be deactivated until further notice."

In their haste to deliver the quadracles of nuclear missiles to the Clouds and depopulate the Arenas, Arks, and Eden, the three men decided it best that the video surveillance systems be temporarily shut down. The lack of recorded visual confirmation of armed atomic weapons would provide Cain with a certain level of deniability of their existence.

X^N

"Have you interviewed the load master on duty yet? Did you check the CARBEL manifests?" Dr. Wyczthack snapped.

"Yes, sir," the man answered as Riggs floated through the portal into Cain's private chambers on Cloud Nine. "He said he and Dr. White had a conversation regarding an inhabitant from Arena Four. Something about a transponder in the clone's helmet and RFID chip not being recognized by the POG."

Riggs and Dr. Wyczthack looked at each other in wide-eyed amazement.

"Are you sure about that?" Cain excitedly asked, giving Riggs a wink and thumbs-up.

"Yes, sir. He informed me that the individual, even though departing from Arena Four, wore the uniform of an inhabitant from Arena One. In addition, he said the clone's EVA suit was missing the nameplates on the chest and helmet."

"Armada!" Riggs joyously whispered, shaking his fist.

"Tell me, what did he do with the clone? Where did he take him?" Cain asked.

"He told me that while he extended an offer to personally escort the subject to the nursery, Dr. White politely refused and insisted on delivering the clone to you on the Cloud, adding that you'd probably want to interrogate him yourself."

Cain and Riggs glanced at one another, confused.

"So, is the load master saying that Dr. White and the clone made the ascension together? Just the two of them?" Riggs inquired as he hovered next to Cain.

"Yes, sir."

"Then they're on one of the Clouds," Dr. Wyczthack surmised. "You've checked all access points for Dr. White's identification credentials, yes?"

"Yes, sir. SUBOS elevators, Eden, the Arks, both Nurseries, Arenas, the Aerie cafeteria, and emergency room ... he's nowhere to be found."

"Keep looking," Cain demanded and disconnected the call.

"This is all of Armada's doing!" he then hissed, pushing away from his seat.

"How's that?" Riggs asked.

"C'mon! Don't you get it? He's toying with us! Armada's devised a means of avoiding the retinal scanners and disabling his RFID chip. He knew we weren't recording the lifts because of the missile quadracles. Armada's up here somewhere on one of the Clouds, and he's got Alan and the hard drives with him."

"Why would Armada risk escape from the Arena, only to turn around and go to a different station … with a hostage?"

"Are you blind or just stupid?" Dr. Wyczthack fumed, brushing past Riggs into the Cloud Nine communication center. "It's a delay tactic! He's trying to stall us! By holding onto Alan and the hard drives, Armada thinks he's buying himself some time and will derail our plans."

"Can he?" Riggs asked, floating close behind.

"No. Is it an inconvenience? Yes. But we still have the capability of arming and firing the missiles remotely."

"So what do you want me to do?"

The two men clung to the computer consoles as Dr. Wyczthack contemplated his next move.

"Take a break from preparing the Clouds and split up the EVA trainers into several groups. Let the boys from Pantex handle the missiles; just get the quadracles to the Island and let them do the rest. You, in the meanwhile, will inspect every inch on all ten Clouds. We'll flush 'em out!"

***

"Baby, I hate to tell you, but … this is going to be darn near impossible to monitor," Chloe lamented, shaking her head. "There's too many of 'em arriving at one time to track where they're being taken."

Armada reclined in his chair, drew in a deep breath, and rubbed his eyes.

"I'm keeping a watch on the BASKET folders, and they're being accessed too quickly for me to maintain any...."

"All right!" Armada grumbled, interrupting her. "Where are they arriving?"

"Vegas International, Edwards, Nellis, Homey, LAX ... everywhere. A few have even flown in here direct and are at the hangars as we speak."

"When you say 'too many' are arriving at one time, what kinda numbers are we talking about?"

Chloe backed out of a folder and gave a brief skimming of the parent file.

"So far? I don't know ... twelve hundred, maybe thirteen."

"Man! They're getting here sooner than I thought."

Armada allowed his arms to dangle as he stared up at the ceiling.

"Baby, c'mon. Tell me how you wanna handle this. You and I can't possibly keep an eye on every single one of 'em. It's not realistic."

She turned away from her husband and resumed monitoring the subfolders of BASKET.

"Ten more ... there's five ... here's another ten or so. I'm telling you, Engenechem is everywhere! Cain's got his people at...."

"Okay! New game plan!" Armada declared.

He suddenly jumped up out of his chair and began sliding his palms back and forth together.

"Tell me what you think. We stop with monitoring who's arriving where and when and focus instead on the SUBOS. It doesn't matter if they get here all at once or one at a time. What does matter ... is how they ascend to the Aerie and beyond."

Chloe swiveled from side to side as she listened.

"Elevators," she then stated, rising from her seat.

She approached Armada and offered a congratulatory kiss on his cheek.

"Think about it ... there's no room for 'em at the visitor's center. Right? They gotta go up," Armada announced and poured himself a glass of wine. "Thirty thousand people stuck on the ground floor should make for an interesting conversation."

"Oh … my … gosh! Wouldn't that just be delicious?" she asked and reached for the bag of ground coffee. "I'd absolutely love to see the faces of Wycz and White when they realize their Guinea pigs can't move. Baby, that's purely diabolical! It's perfect!"

"Now all we need to do is disable the elevator systems. That should give me more time to work on PIN CUSHION."

Chloe emptied a bottle of water into the reservoir of the coffee machine while Armada sipped his wine. As the freshly brewed coffee started dripping into the pot, Chloe commented, "With the access authorization codes you created for Euclid, I thought he would have been here by now, or at least attempted to contact us. It's been several hours. I sure hope nothing's happened to him."

CHAPTER 40

WORDS OF ENCOURAGEMENT

"And you're expecting me to do what?" Dr. Wyczthack queried. "Are you aware that I'm presently on Cloud Nine?"

"No, sir, I wasn't informed of...," the man nervously attempted to reply.

"I'm on Cloud Nine!" Cain blasted. "And I'm to remain on Cloud Nine for an extended period of time to conduct a series of long-term projects and experiments. Furthermore, I don't understand why you elected to contact me about a malfunctioning elevator."

"I'm sorry, Dr. Wyczthack. I apologize for not explaining myself correctly," the technician humbly offered. "It's not just one elevator we're having troubles with, it's the entire system. None of them are operating properly. The cabs don't go to the desired floors, doors are opening in midtransit, they're stopping in between floors, the alarms go off without warning, we can't even...."

"Okay!" Cain shouted, strapping himself into his chair. "Have you been in contact with IT Services yet? Or SUBOS Power Management Services? They're the ones to be communicating with, not me. I'm nearly thirty miles above you."

"Yes, sir, we've been working with them, but every time we get connected to one of...."

The conversation came to a sudden halt when Cain's ears were painfully pierced by a digital, high-pitched buzz. He slapped angrily at his keyboard to disconnect the call. A few seconds later, his computer screen showed multiple phone lines ringing simultaneously. Each time Cain acknowledged one of the blinking red lights, his ears were immediately bombarded with agonizing ring tones of various frequencies.

"Augh!" he shrieked and muted the computer speaker.

"Armada!" he lowly growled.

Dr. Wyczthack placed the computer keyboard on his lap and opened the CYCLOPS program. He selected the POG affiliated with Cloud Nine and entered the transponder number for Riggs' helmet.

"Woodburn," Riggs flatly stated.

"Where are you?" Cain rudely asked. "Have you found them?"

"Cloud Eight, sir. And no, we've yet to locate Armada and Dr. White."

As Riggs was speaking, Cain opened the surveillance camera system for Cloud Eight.

"Where on Eight?"

"I'm near the air filtration compartment."

"Stay there," Cain demanded.

Riggs clutched at the portal frame separating the oxygen purifiers from the transit corridor and waited.

"Look above you," he then heard Cain say.

Riggs spun his body backwards until he looked squarely at the tiny video camera.

"It's imperative that you find them, now!" Cain growled, looking at Riggs through the video surveillance camera.

"Sir, we're moving as expeditiously as possible."

"Well, it's not fast enough!"

"Dr. Wyczthack, we've already cleared Clouds Five, Six, and Seven, and are about to complete our sweep of Cloud Eight. There's a hundred fifty of us and only four Clouds remaining. We'll have this...."

"You don't understand, Woodburn. Nothing happens until you apprehend Armada! He's now screwing with the elevators! Whichever Cloud they're on, he's hacked our Master Server remotely! The inhabitants are arriving in droves, and we can't populate the Clouds with the lift systems out of commission! Find them! D'you hear me, Riggs? Find them!"

***

"You gotta be kidding me!" Armada remarked and repeatedly bonked his forehead on the table.

"Kidding about what, baby?" Chloe inquired from the comfort of their bed.

"Forget it! Game over!" he sarcastically blurted out, rising quickly. "This is impossible!"

"What? Talk to me."

She watched as he grabbed a fresh bottle of wine from the counter. It was more than obvious that he'd encountered an obstacle of great importance and significance.

"When I was in the process of acquiring my first certification," he began, searching for their corkscrew, "I had an instructor, Reese Williams. He was a theoretical physicist and mathematician."

Chloe snapped her fingers at her husband and thumbed him toward the bathroom.

"One day we were discussing stuff like artificial intelligence, automated reasoning…codes, sequencing, deterministic and randomized algorithms, encryption…," he continued after emerging from the bathroom and locating the wine opener, "and the conversation turned to the Enigma machine, cyphers, and…."

"Enigma…," Chloe said, "the World War II Nazi Enigma machine. Right?"

"Right."

"Wasn't it Alan Turing that broke the German's codes?"

"Right again."

Armada extracted the cork, filled his glass to the rim, and immediately guzzled more than half.

"All right. So we're sitting there and Reese gets this weird look on his face. He then asks for my opinion on an idea of his. A professor of Theoretical Mathematics at the Planck Institute is asking me ... his pupil ... to help him with his project."

Armada leaned against the countertop, shook his head, and gulped down more wine.

"So what was his project, Einstein?"

"He called it transitional encryption."

"What?"

"Transitional...."

"I heard that. What is it?"

"If we use the Enigma machine as a reference point," he started to say while refilling his glass, "to decode the German's messages, the Allies would have had to know the rotor order and positioning of an Enigma ... to decode the rotor positioning and order of another Enigma machine to decode a message."

"In essence then, one has to crack a code to crack a code to learn what's being said. Double redundancy. Right?"

"Right. And upon close examination of PIN CUSHION, it appears that Cain and Engenechem put Reese's idea to good use."

"It's that tough?"

"Are you kidding? Transitional encryption makes the Enigma machine look like ... like a game of tic-tac-toe."

"Wow! How does it work?"

"For PIN CUSHION, Wyczthack and White would have already determined their targets, the elevation for warhead detonation, location and position of the Clouds, and so on. Whenever they're ready to arm and fire the missiles, they'll have to enter an access or authorization code or password in order to gain access to the system to enter an access or authorization code to launch."

Chloe bit the inside of her lip as Armada further detailed the inner workings of the security program.

"The engineers probably registered two pass codes for each missile.

Wycz and White know 'em, maybe even Riggs. But it's the most important player that knows the two pass codes: the missiles. They know, they acknowledge, grant access, or deny access. Get it?"

"Yeah, I get it," she answered, nodding in agreement.

"So if I'm trying to hack the missile's programming and I enter an incorrect character, or if I take too long to enter the entire code…the missile's self-defense protocol will automatically create a brand-new access code."

"Which means you have to start all over."

Armada blankly stared at her, nodding.

"Isn't there another way to…."

"Yes, Chloe!" he snarkily snapped. "If I simply knew who did the programming and which servers and hard drives were used to store the data, then yeah, I guess there'd be a different method of neutralizing a thousand nuclear missiles!"

"Hey!" she shouted. "Don't take it out on me! I'm just asking a question to…."

Armada cupped his hands to his face.

Chloe helplessly watched as the toll of psychological stress consumed her husband. Without warning, he collapsed to his knees, curled in on himself, and began weeping.

"Oh, baby," she sweetly purred and clumsily scooted to the edge of the mattress.

She gently lowered her hips to the floor and crawled up beside him. Chloe adoringly laid across his back and placed her cheek between his shoulders at the base of his neck. Armada shook and twitched as grief, frustration, and anger seared his heart.

"I can't stop it," he muttered lowly.

"What baby?"

"I said I can't stop it!" he bellowed, rising up. "I can't stop Cain! There, I said it! He wins! Nothing I've thought of works, Chloe! Wyczthack, White, Engenechem…they got us trapped! We're all trapped! And there's not one thing I can do about it!"

Like a deer looking into a set of headlights, Chloe stared at her husband in shocked confusion.

"Can you hear me?" she boldly called out and closed her eyes. "Can you see me? Us? Can you see us? Do you see him?"

She turned her head upwards and peered up at the textured ceiling.

"Help him!" she angrily demanded. "He's been working day and night to stop Cain, and … and he's…."

Armada draped his left arm over her shoulder as she struggled to put her feelings into words.

"Why show me and Armada where to go, why say 'eat this, don't drink that,' why place life in my womb, and why alert us of our impending extinction … if you just plan on abandoning…."

Her words were cut short by a flickering of their bedroom lights and loss of video feeds to the tablet monitors.

"Uh…," Armada sheepishly moaned, drawing Chloe closer to his side.

The bulbs in the lamps experienced a power surge and glowed brilliantly as the fifty computers began shutting down, randomly, one by one. When the last monitor ceased functioning, the table and floor lamps started going dim. Within seconds, the couple was sitting in complete and total darkness.

"What was that?" Chloe asked and blindly encircled her husband's midsection.

Before Armada had an opportunity to reply, a blazingly bright light seeped into the room via the gap at the bottom of the door.

The orb entered their domain, passing from the corridor through the door as if it were standing wide open.

"Fear not, children," a man's voice reassuringly stated while floating past the bathroom and closet.

Armada and Chloe felt a wave of calm and peace envelope them, as if being wrapped in a thick, warm blanket.

They noticed that the vaporous mirage was altering its shape while it spoke.

"He has heard your cries and has not forsaken you," the voice confidently announced.

The ethereal cloud settled directly in front of Armada and Chloe, bathing them in pure white energy. Upon entering their bedroom, the apparition was a round, hazy mass of swirling colors, comparable to the size of a basketball. But now the mesmerized duo were focused on the definite, specific outline of a man with long hair, measuring more than six feet in height, levitating a few inches above the floor.

"With Him, all things are possible," he factually stated, adding, "He will soon reveal His plans for you and your unborn son. Be strong and of good courage; be not afraid, neither be you dismayed, for the Lord thy God is with you wherever you go."

Just as the apparition completed his statement, a lightning bolt of dazzling purple penetrated the room noiselessly.

The transparent man vanished.

Armada and Chloe were still clutching hands when the lamps came on. They glanced at their wall of tablet monitors and watched as the screens immediately resumed broadcasting the video feeds.

"Oh, my gosh!" Armada blurted, looking up. "Thank you! Thank you! I … I haven't known what to do. I've been so stressed…."

"He has," Chloe interrupted, squeezing his fingers. "He's not sleeping, he's been moody and irritable … well, you know how he is, you've seen him. He's been afraid. I'm afraid."

"I wanna make sure you're telling me what I think you're telling me. If I'm understanding correctly … you're saying … don't worry about when and how to stop Cain, because … you'll tell me what to do and when to do it. Is that it?"

They rose from their knees and waited for some display of acknowledgement.

"Is he right?" Chloe loudly inquired, but nothing happened.

Armada lightly nudged her and nodded his head in the direction of the bathroom.

"Ooh," she peeped, stepped to the doorway, and flipped the switch.

"Are you listening?" Armada again asked. "Did I understand you correctly? You don't want us to...."

Before he could complete his question, the lamps in their room pulsed with a surge of light. The expectant parents quickly joined hands.

"So, we don't need to ask you...," Chloe began, "you'll just ... tell us?"

The lights again flickered.

"And you'll determine when?" Armada further probed.

For the third and final time, the lamps, entryway, and bathroom lights glowed with the entity's response.

Armada and Chloe turned to face each other and collapsed in a strong embrace. They reveled in the security of their intimate hug and slowly rocked back and forth.

"Thank you for helping us," and "Thank you for listening," they whispered.

He slid his hands down her arms until their fingers met. With their eyes firmly shut, the two stood between the beds and spoke openly.

"Just tell us what you want us to do," Armada said.

"We'll follow you, wherever you lead us," Chloe added.

"We're here to listen to you."

"We believe in you. Thank you for helping us and the child growing inside of me."

After a brief and silent pause, they opened their eyes.

Armada leaned forward and kissed his wife on her forehead.

"I don't want to look at any more files or folders," he playfully demanded, shaking his head. "I don't need to examine any videos, and I refuse to inspect any program coding."

"Well, baby," she started to say, looking at the clock, "seeing as how it's nearly midnight, how about we call it quits for the evening and just go to bed."

Before she could kiss him, a sudden burst of pain emanated from deep inside her.

"Oh!" she winced and stooped over, resting her head on his chest.

"You okay?"

"Yeah." she groaned, erecting herself, "Abdiel's really been rooting around lately."

Armada led Chloe to the other side of the bed and gently eased her down. She puckered her lips and inhaled deeply when another flash of pain resonated throughout her womb.

He turned off the floor lamp in the corner, flipped the switch to power down the panel of tablets, then crossed the room and turned off both the bathroom and entryway lights.

"We won't need this tonight," he announced as he neared their bed.

"Need what?" she asked and rolled to her right.

Without a word, he stuck his hand down behind the nightstand and gruffly unplugged the alarm clock.

"Yay!" she cheered, lightly clapping, as he held it up for display.

He carelessly tossed the digital clock over his shoulder before turning off the table lamp.

In total darkness he slid under the sheet. Chloe rolled to her left, away from him, while he nestled up close and spooned her backside. She felt his right arm wrap around her waist and give a firm squeeze.

"Thank you for my wife," he whispered into her neck. "Thank you for my son. Thank you for saving us."

Chloe laced her fingers through his and closed her eyes.

CHAPTER 41

Saboteurs

"It's obvious you didn't look hard enough!" Cain scolded, adding, "Have them make another sweep!"

"Sir?!" Riggs retorted with incredulity, "We spent the last twelve hours looking in every conceivable…."

"No, you didn't! Had you and your crew conducted a thorough and complete inspection of each Cloud, then Dr. White and Armada would be standing in front of me right now, and I'd have the hard drives in my hand."

Riggs held his tongue while Cain carried on with his tirade. He grasped at a rung of an external ladder on the belly of Cloud One and punched at the hull with his free hand.

"Now," Cain continued, shouting into his headset, "I want you to split your team; half of you finish the supply load out from the Island, and the second half will search the Clouds … again!"

"Dr. Wyczthack, with all due respect, it's after one in the morning. My crew has been at it for almost sixteen hours straight. They need to rest for a while. By the time we get back to Cloud Nine and strip down, it'll be well after two. Four hours, that's all I'm asking for. Give me that and I'll have them out at seven."

"I want … Armada … now!" Cain shrieked.

"Yes, sir. I promise you that...."

Blinded by anger and a lust for vengeance, Cain ripped the earpiece from his head and sat in his chair, screaming.

***

Chloe kicked Armada's shinbone again, waking him from a deep sleep. She rolled away from him and kicked free of the top sheet.

"What's wrong, baby?" he asked. "Can't get comfortable again?"

"No!" she grunted in a fluster.

A few moments later, she flopped to her other side and let out a long, heavy sigh directly in his face.

"Aren't you hot?" she quipped.

"Chloe," he mumbled, "you're growing another human inside you so no, I'm not hot."

"I just can't seem to get in the right position. I swear, I'm about to burn up!"

Armada flung his arm to the side and laid his hand on top of hers. He made sure to remain very still while listening to her breathe.

He quickly sat up in bed.

"Was that you?" he enthusiastically called out and turned on the lamp.

"Was that me what, baby?" Chloe groggily replied.

"Not you, baby. Hold on."

He excitedly lurched towards Chloe and offered up a peck on her cheek, exclaiming, "Good morning!"

She sluggishly propped herself on her elbows and watched her husband through drooping eyelids.

"Was that you?" he repeated, standing up between the beds. "Did you do that?"

The lightbulb in the lamp briefly flickered off and on.

"Yes! Yes!" Armada screamed, leaping on the vacant bed.

"Are you gonna bounce around like an idiot, or do you plan on letting me...."

"You! It was you, Chloe! You said it! Whoo! Well, you said the words, but it was really...."

"Augh!" she growled, slapping the mattress. "What? Just tell me!"

Armada leapt to their bed, laughing, and jumped beside her, causing her to rock slightly.

"You said what we're supposed to do!"

Chloe stared at the ceiling, not at all following her husband's logic and explanation.

He hopped over her, bounced off the bed, and flipped the switch to turn on the tablets.

"Okay... there's ten Clouds. Right?"

"Yes."

"And each Cloud has approximately one hundred nuclear missiles."

As he spoke, he repeatedly clapped his hands.

"Yes, Armada! Please! Quit building me clocks and just tell me the time!"

"Position and burn up!" he energetically stated, holding his arms out to his side. "Isn't that great?"

He continued to laugh as he sprang to the countertop above their refrigerator and started scooping ground coffee out of a bag.

"It's so simple! I don't know why neither one of us thought about it, it's...."

"Armada!" she howled, trying desperately to sit up straight against the headboard. "Get over here and elaborate! Please! You're not making sense."

"Okay, Mrs. Armada! Right away!" he jovially bellowed

He overexaggerated his animated leaps to their bed and delicately eased his rear end on the mattress.

"You are so weird!" she jokingly insulted. "Now. Please explain yourself."

"All right. When NASA developed the shuttle program, there was a contractor called Morton Thiokol, or just plain Thiokol, that produced the shuttle's SRBs."

"Solid rocket boosters."

"Correct. Thiokol worked with Pratt and Whitney and Boeing Lockheed for years, then Thiokol was absorbed by ATK. They then became Orbital ATK. You know, they created the Cygnus cargo craft for the ISS."

"Cygnus. Got it. And?"

"The SRBs were huge, like forty feet tall, and generated nearly three million pounds of thrust force each. For fuel, the two rockets used a combination of ammonium perchlorate, atomized aluminum powder, iron oxide, PBAN, or polybutadiene acrylonitrile, and an epoxy curing agent. It's officially known as ammonium perchlorate composite propellant, or APCP."

"Put me out of my misery and tell me there's a point to all of this."

"I'm getting there, baby. The SRBs burned for two minutes and were the primary means of raising the shuttle stack to an elevation of twenty-eight miles above the Earth's surface."

Chloe gazed blankly at him and shrugged her shoulders.

"What does a cancelled shuttle program have to do with us and nuclear missiles?"

"Baby," he said, stroking the back of her hand, "those Clouds have ten miniature SRBs. Each. That equates to a ballpark capacity of ten million pounds of thrust force, per Cloud ... in a vacuum."

The wheels started turning in Chloe's brain.

"Oh! Armada!" she squealed and threw herself into his arms.

"Hey, you did it. Not me," he commented, rubbing his hands across her back.

Like water flowing through a collapsing dam, a flood wall of emotion consumed Chloe. She clung tightly to his neck and dug her fingers into his shoulders.

"How?" she croaked.

"It'll sound complicated, but I'll try to break it down into simple terms," he said and gently broke their embrace.

"I'm just now realizing this concept, so … gimme a minute," he admitted, rising to his feet.

Armada walked to the countertop, removed the pot of freshly brewed coffee, and held it up for his bride to see. Chloe gave him a nod of approval while reaching for a tissue.

"Within every Cloud SRB, there are three rate gyro assemblies. Better known as RGAs," he informed her as he poured the coffee, "each RGA contains two gyroscopes: one for pitch and one for yaw. These provide data about the axes to the orbiter's guidance, navigation, and positional control systems. We'll have to disable those. All of 'em."

Armada dropped a few tiny chunks of dark chocolate in both mugs, gave them a slight stir, and passed one off to Chloe.

"Additionally," he said, dragging the swiveling desk chair beside the bed, "each SRB has two hydraulic gimbal servoactuators. They're responsible for directing the nozzle fans up and down and side-to-side, and provide thrust vectoring to propel and direct the Clouds. We gotta disengage those as well."

He sipped his coffee, lost in thought, as he vocally identified more and more components and systems that required sabotage.

"Flight control system, guidance and positioning system, altitude and trajectory control, all telecommunications and server synchronization with Engenechem…."

"You can do all of that? From here?" she interrupted.

"We. Yes, we can do all this, and more. We don't have a choice."

"Sounds like a lot."

"Well, yeah, it is. But it's what we're supposed to do. Basically, we're trying to steal a car with the driver still inside … but don't want him to know … until it's too late to do anything about it."

Chloe took a large swallow of coffee and focused on her swollen belly. She rubbed slow, wide circles with her fingertips.

"All right. What do you need from me?"

***

Riggs floated through the open airlock that separated Dormitory C from the transit corridor on Cloud Two. He entered the tunnel, turned to his left, and was preparing to inspect Dormitory D when, from the corner of his eye, he thought he noticed something moving.

"Who's there? Identify yourself," he asked, but received no response on the speaker in his helmet.

"I'm here, sir," a female crew member finally answered, gliding out from Dormitory E behind him.

Riggs pulled himself to the tunnel wall and turned around to face her. "Who else is in tunnel three?" he asked. "I didn't think anybody was...."

"Sir?" she quizzically asked. "Should that be happening?"

She pointed past him and began pulling herself forward.

Riggs twisted himself in the opposite direction to see what she was referring to. He was right: something indeed was moving.

"No, that's not supposed to happen," he anxiously stated.

What Riggs saw moving wasn't a person; it was sunlight pouring through an oval window on the corridor outer shell.

Cloud Two was rotating.

"Get back to the EVA Hangar, now!" Riggs ordered, spinning around.

The duo hurriedly grasped at the center rung line that ran the entire length of the transit tunnel.

"This is Woodburn!" Riggs announced as they floated through the tube. "Are there any personnel currently at the Cloud Two operations center?"

"Negative," "No, sir," and "Not that we're aware of" filled his ears.

"I want everybody outta Cloud Two, immediately! We're experiencing orbital decay!"

"Riggs!" a voice suddenly rang in his ears. "Riggs! This is Cain! Where are you? Cloud Two is pitching...."

"Yes, sir! I'm aware of it! We're evacuating Cloud Two right now!"

"Evacuating?" Cain roared. "Armada's probably on Cloud Two hiding somewhere, and he's got Alan and the hard drives with him. Get over to the operations center and reestablish control! That's an order! Armada's trying to distract us by disabling our SRBs."

"Cain, I can practically guarantee you neither Dr. White nor Arma…."

Riggs's voice and comm-link signal suddenly disappeared from Dr. Wyczthack's video monitor and headset.

***

"I'd love to see his face right now," Chloe happily announced, pecking at her tablet computer. "I bet he's so angry he can't get up to the Clouds. Ooh! He's probably cursing us both."

"Oh, yeah!" Armada laughingly agreed. "And it's about to get even more interesting."

With his pinky held high, he daintily tapped the tablet screen.

"There went Cloud Two's air filtration and purification systems."

"So, what's next?" she casually inquired, laying her legs across his lap.

"I want you, dear woman, to cut all current video feeds to the tablets and find me every camera aimed in the direction of the supply island and the Clouds. I wanna see as much as possible. If it's on an Arena, an Ark, Eden, a Halo, I don't care. It's imperative that we have visual access to the Clouds."

Chloe quickly drew her legs back under her.

"What's on your immediate agenda?" she asked.

"Me? Oh, nothing really. I'm just about to override the data encryption capabilities on all Engenechem communication satellites," Armada responded in a blasé tone. "Other than that, not much."

***

"Riggs!" Cain angrily shouted. "Riggs! Are you listening?"

The enraged scientist toggled between multiple screens and program windows in a desperate attempt to reestablish a stable line of communication.

"Riggs! Anybody! This is Dr. Cain Wyczthack!" he repeatedly barked into his headset. "Can anyone hear me?"

A shadow passed over the window on the outer shell of his private chambers, temporarily distracting him. He unstrapped himself, pushed against the desk, and launched up and back. Once he came in contact with the wall, Cain pressed his face to the thick glass to get a better look at the Clouds.

Cloud Two had pitched to its side by ninety degrees, thereby momentarily blocking the sun.

"No, no, no!" Cain blasted, slamming his hand on the wall. "Armada!"

A series of tiny dings, bells, and alarms began sounding off.

Dr. Wyczthack spun around to find his video monitors in a state of disarray. Message windows and alerts started flashing and blinking on every screen, reading 'Loss of signal,' 'Connection terminated,' 'Terminal client unavailable,' and 'Host server not found.'

"Augh!" he wailed as he tried in vain to close out the warning notifications. "Damn you, Armada!"

CHAPTER 42

THREE, TWO, ONE ... FIRE

"Can you retract the door manually?" Riggs asked, hovering next to the EVA external personnel access portal. "If we force it open wide enough, I can pass you the power cord."

"Sir," the woman anxiously stated, "that's a hydraulic lock. It's a fail-safe. When there's a loss of power, the hydraulic locking mechanism automatically engages because the electromagnetic system is down."

"I know. I'm aware of how this works. Just...gimme a minute to think."

Aggravation and fear quickly settled in on Riggs.

There, near the hinge for the port's outer door, was the pinched power line that led to the hovering portable POG...on the outside of Cloud Two. Next to the crimped power cord was Riggs' comm-link, which was still attached to the POG. Unbeknownst to Armada and Chloe, Riggs' EVA training team was in the process of evacuating Cloud Two when they remotely disabled the energy supply. The team had already safely reached the floating oxygen generator and were retracting their comm-links when the power was cut. Riggs, however, had yet to reach the dock or detach the POG from the Cloud when the massive steel door suddenly closed, trapping him inside.

"How much reserve power is left in the battery?" Riggs asked.

"Sir, right now we're showing less than sixty percent," a team member answered, drifting next to the POG.

"Can you establish a connection with one of the other Clouds?"

"Negative, sir. We aren't picking up any signals to synchronize with."

"What about Cloud Ten? Can you see the Pantex crew? Are they still installing launch tubes?"

"Yes, sir, Team Pantex is currently on Cloud Ten, but no, we can't piggyback their POG."

"Can you connect to the Aerie or SUBOS?"

"No, sir. We're dead in the water."

The pod of cosmonauts was stranded.

Riggs mentally sifted through several rescue scenarios, but ultimately saw no viable means of escape for himself or the crew.

If he disconnected the comm-link from his own suit's coupler, he'd run out of oxygen more quickly. Even though the airflow from the POG was at a reduced rate, Riggs' oxygen was still being filtered and recirculated through the partially crushed umbilical. He could go back to the bridge and command center, but wouldn't know where to begin with the restoration of power. Plus, with the door closed so tightly on the charging cable, it was impossible to transfer the POG to another Cloud; the enormous coaxial was hardwired internally.

The EVA training team members couldn't disconnect their couplers from the generator due to the fact that the closest source for power and oxygen was CARBEL One, three quarters of a mile away. Unless that specific POG-equipped elevator just happened to be docked when they arrived, the trainers would asphyxiate on their own carbon dioxide.

Stay or go—either way, Riggs and his companions were doomed to die.

***

"And … forty-one," Chloe perkily stated. "Forty-two, forty-three…."

"Beautiful! Excellent!" Armada proudly praised his wife. "This is exactly what I need!"

He positioned himself in front of their wall of tablets and watched as Chloe populated the blackened video monitors with live feeds from the newly selected cameras.

"Forty-nine. And … ta-dah … fifty!"

"Thanks, baby!"

"Yay for me!"

She slowly rose from her chair and stepped in front of Armada. He wrapped his arms around her and kissed her neck as they viewed the new images.

"Wow!" she exclaimed, pointing at one of the computers. "Cloud Two has really shifted."

"Yeah, I know. Since it's in a low-Earth orbit and its SRBs have been disengaged, the orbital decay will be greater. Now, if the Cloud were in geocentric orbit, it'd take forever for the planet's gravitational force to pull it down."

The couple closely scrutinized each monitor, hungrily absorbing the new and crucial visual information from a fresh perspective.

"So why is Cloud Two not descending?" she quizzically asked.

"I imagine they're all tethered…."

"Did you see that?" Chloe interrupted, aiming her index finger at one of the screens. "Something's moving on the belly of Cloud Two."

Armada stepped out from behind her and leaned in close to the tablet.

"You're right," he said after staring intensely at the video. "Something's out there."

Chloe returned to her seat and began pecking at her computer. Within a few keystrokes the camera zoomed in and the images on the tablet grew sharper in detail. Armada tilted his head from one side to the other as he examined the video feed.

"It's a POG," he exclaimed. "It's a portable POG … and there's people attached."

"What're they doing?"

"Can't tell. From this angle, it looks like they're just ... sitting there, like they're waiting for something."

"Can we listen to them?"

"I guess so, but at this point I'd rather continue with the original plan. It's irrelevant who's saying what to whom. It's a nonfactor."

Armada turned away from the panel and took his seat next to Chloe.

"I wanna alter our attack strategy," he announced, turning to face her. "Instead of bringing down each individual system and component one by one for every Cloud, I think it best if we simply delete all guidance and positioning references and initiate a full burn on all of 'em ... at the same time."

"Ooohhh!" Chloe squeaked, clasping her hands together, "Cain won't know what hit him!"

"Exactly! We gotta overwhelm their operations centers! They might have a chance dealing with one problematic Cloud, maybe two. But trying to control ten thrusters on ten separate orbital stations? Impossible!"

"Oh, baby! I love this plan! You'll be ... OH!"

Chloe stopped praising her husband when their unborn son let loose with a series of kicks. She grimaced and bit on her lower lip.

"Abdiel?" Armada lovingly asked.

"Oh, yeah!" she blared, breathing deeply. "Go ahead. Finish what you were saying."

"Let's pull up the rate gyroscopes and the stabilizing and positioning coordinates, zero out everything, and engage a full burn out manually."

"Will that be enough?" she asked between respirations. "I mean, how long can it last?"

"Oh, twelve to fifteen minutes. There'll be no way for Wyczthack, White, and Engenechem to stop us or salvage the Clouds. They'll be hurling away from our solar system at tens of thousands of miles per hour."

"How?" she inquired, through closed eyes. "Just ... show me; don't tell me."

Armada dragged her tablet beside his and exited from their home-made surveillance program.

"First," he said, raising his left index finger, "I'm locking up access to all geospatial position controls by using the transitional encryption we were discussing."

After a few silent minutes he informed her, "Done. As of this moment, no one can regain control of the SRBs except us."

"Good for you, baby," Chloe mumbled, rubbing her belly.

"Next, we pull up both the rate gyroscopes and thruster levels for each Cloud."

Armada speedily rifled through the Engenechem Master Server and expanded the properties windows for the gyroscopes and thrusters for all ten Clouds. He then drew half of the tabs to Chloe's tablet and layered them in sequential order.

"When I back out the parameters for pitch and yaw on the X and Y axes and engage the thrusters, the Clouds would normally look like balloons with the air escaping. But in our case, the gyroscopes will auto-matically return all thrust vector dynamics to neutral and place the rockets in a perfectly perpendicular, 90-degree position. So when we hit 'OK and Apply,' we're gonna be in for quite a show."

"What do you need me to do?"

"Let me delete the pitch and yaw first and max out the thruster levels. When I'm ready, I'll tap 'apply' for both property screens and I'll have you exit each as soon as I do. Apply, apply, exit. Apply, apply, exit. This needs to happen boom, boom, boom, like dominoes tipping over one right after the other."

"Just tell me when."

Armada robotically tabbed through the SRB property windows, entering 'one hundred percent' in each field for the level of thrust force, and one thousand two hundred seconds for the burn duration period, but waited to apply the new parameters. Once the changes were made for each Cloud, he stacked the windows in numerical order.

"Oh!" Chloe grunted, tilting her head back.

"Okay, baby," he soothingly stated, standing up. "I wanna scoot you over here, so we can catch all the action."

Armada grasped the chair back and pulled her in reverse to the end of the panel. Next, he dragged the table toward the wall of tablets, along with his chair.

***

"Riggs! Riggs!" Cain shouted as he zipped through the corridor. "Can you hear me? This is Cain! Are you there?"

Dr. Wyczthack sped along the transit tunnel that led to the docking ports and receiving bay for Cloud Nine.

When he was approaching the docking stations, he again shouted, "Riggs! Anybody! Can you hear me? This is Dr. Wyczthack. I'm preparing to enter the EVA staging area on Cloud Nine for an emergency departure. All Cloud communication systems have malfunctioned. I'm about to suit up and will immediately cross over to CARBEL One. Can you hear me?"

Cain flew through the dual air lock that separated the transit tunnel from the individual docking ports and receiving bay. He slapped the actuator to close off the corridor and pushed against the door frame with his legs.

As he soared through the cavernous storage hangar, he again called out, "This is Cain Wyczthack. I'm preparing for emergency EVA departure from Cloud Nine to the Halos and CARBEL One. Can anyone hear me?"

Still, he received no reply.

"Augh!" he roared, breathing heavily.

Cain dragged himself past the five port doors to the EVA staging zone. He glided into the chamber, grabbed a handle beside the second door frame, and shut himself in.

Once inside, he reached for one of the folded and stacked EVA suits, yanked it off the shelf, and unzipped his one-piece jumper.

***

"All right. Here we go," Armada gleefully announced. "No turning back now."

"Mm-hmm," Chloe hummed, trying to regulate her breathing.

"Now, take a good look at Cloud Ten. Keep an eye on the front left."

Chloe massaged her stomach as she monitored the craft.

"And ... go," he stated, pressing 'enter' on his tablet.

The thrusters for Cloud Ten abruptly returned to their neutral position and ceased firing.

"Yes! Yes! Yes!" he proudly chanted, clapping his hands. "Isn't that a beautiful sight?"

"What's truly beautiful is the idea of getting this mule out of me in two weeks!"

He diligently disabled the rocket engines for each Cloud and rattled off a slew of praises for himself in the process.

"Cloud Nine ... done ... and then, because I'm so talented and really know what I'm doing...."

***

As he was pulling up the leg of his EVA suit, Cain glanced out the air lock window just as one of the Cloud Nine thrusters began rotating and locked in its default, vertical position.

"Augh! No!" he shrieked. "No! Riggs! Riggs!"

***

"And when I press this button...," Armada began. "Well, whadyaknow ... Cloud Eight ... off-line."

"You're absolutely pathetic."

"Thank you, dear woman!" he jokingly blurted. "Get ready, I'm gonna need you in a minute."

***

Dr. Wyczthack attempted repeatedly to stuff himself into the tight-fitting EVA suit, but was only successful in losing his temper. He shouted and screamed, helplessly, as he watched the neighboring space stations suffer the same fate as Cloud Nine.

***

Armada triumphantly called out each Cloud by number after successfully sabotaging its propulsion system.

"Cloud Seven … TOAST!"

"Cloud Six … history."

"Cloud Five … what Cloud Five? I know no Cloud Five."

***

"What? All of them?" Riggs hotly inquired. "Are you positive?"

"Yes, sir!" the man anxiously answered. "It started with Cloud Ten, and a couple of seconds later, Cloud Nine. The SRB's just … stopped. They appear to be in hibernation, like when we're replacing the fuel clods."

"What're they doing on Cloud Ten? Is the Pantex…."

"I'm assuming the crew's evacuating to CARBEL One," the man interrupted. "Cause from here, it looks as if they've disconnected from their POG.

"What's the battery life on ours?"

"Less than thirty percent."

"Here's what I'm thinking," Riggs said, and gave pause. "You all must release your comm-links, immediately, and hightail it over to the CARBEL."

"And leave you?" one female team member asked. "We can't abandon you, sir. That's not an option."

"I'm not asking for your opinion on the subject. This is an order. You need to…."

"I'm sorry, sir," another man sternly interjected. "She's right. We're not abandoning you."

***

"Okay! Here we go!" Armada excitedly stated, patting out a drum roll on the table with his hands. "Moment of truth!"

"Please tell me that this is really 'it,'" Chloe groaned, barely moving. "I just want to be done with the whole thing."

"I promise you, baby," he confessed, leaning to kiss her forehead, "a couple of keystrokes and Cain and Doc White are a thing of the past."

"Just ... tell me what to push and when."

Armada layered the windows displaying the fields for the Clouds' default positioning and stabilizing values. He maxed out the input levels for thrust force, zeroed the trajectory and vector angle, and extended the burn duration period of each rocket.

"The only thing you gotta do ... is tap 'exit' after I okay and apply the settings. All right?"

"Okay."

"But I need you next to me, here on my right."

"Ugh!" Chloe sighed and forced herself to stand.

"As soon as I press 'apply,' watch the monitors. This should take no more than two or three seconds."

His index finger hovered over the two command options.

"And ... go," he said, and quickly pressed the two buttons.

The couple's eyes were glued to the tablets streaming the live video of Cloud One. Suddenly, all ten rocket engines ignited in near perfect unison.

"Yes! Yes! Whoo!" they shouted as the massive steel vessel began ascending.

"Exit, baby, exit!" Armada crowed.

***

"Sir, Cloud One's thrust engines just engaged!" the man shouted to Riggs.

"Detach! Detach! Now!" Riggs screamed. "Disconnect from the…."

Before he could complete his order, Armada and Chloe sent the new parameters to the Cloud Two propulsion system.

The Cloud's SRBs sprang to life with such power that the floating EVA crew didn't have adequate time to react. The ten rocket engines, capable of generating a million horsepower each, provided a force so tremendous that the comm-link couplers were ripped from their suits as the craft accelerated away from them. The gaping holes allowed the frigid vacuum of space to suck the lifesaving oxygen and heat from their suits. Within seconds, the clan of cosmonauts was frozen stiff.

***

"Cloud Three … apply, apply, exit," Armada coolly recited.

Chloe gently pressed the red 'x' in the top right corner of the command boxes as he instructed.

"Cloud Four … apply, apply, exit."

"Cloud Five … apply, apply, exit."

They watched the monitors as the artificial environments noiselessly rushed away from them. Chloe wept almost uncontrollably, lurching forward with every breath and surge of emotion.

***

"This is Dr. Wyczthack!" Cain shouted, panic-stricken, fidgeting with his earpiece. "Can anyone hear me? The propulsion systems have malfunctioned on all Clouds! I'm about to eject from Cloud Nine EVA."

He put on his helmet, twisted it in place, and locked the clasp. After entering his identification credentials on the kiosk for the first air lock, Cain entered the chamber and quickly closed the inner door behind him.

He punched at the large red button to initiate the decompression process and an amber warning light began flashing.

***

"Cloud Six ... apply, apply, exit."
"Cloud Seven ... apply, apply, exit."

***

"C'mon, c'mon!" he muttered, peering through the window in the outer door.

He could plainly see the hard tether line securing Cloud Nine to Cloud Ten and Halo One. The twelve-inch diameter cord lay no more than thirty feet away. With one solid push of his legs, Cain could easily sail to the safety cable and drag himself to the Halo and CARBEL.

Finally, the amber strobe light stopped blinking and a solid green light shone on the panel, signifying that it was then safe to raise the outer door to the air lock.

Cain tapped the green button and the door slowly swung open.

***

"Cloud Eight ... apply, apply, exit."
"Cloud Nine ... apply, apply, exit."
"Cloud Ten ... apply, apply, exit."

***

Cain had yet to clear the path of the outer steel door when Armada and Chloe engaged the propulsion systems for Cloud Nine. Because the SRBs had been activated, the Cloud's safety features were automatically triggered to ensure that all external points of entry were closed.

The retracting, hinged slab of metal caught Cain just below his shoulder blades, dragged him down and back, and pinched him against the EVA portal frame. Powerful hydraulic pumps sent thousands of pounds of pressure to the air lock door cylinders, slowly crushing his chest.

Unbearable pain cauterized Dr. Wyczthack's nervous system as his lungs filled with blood. The weight of the EVA outer door, combined with the power of the hydraulic pumps, folded Cain in half, backwards, like an inverted V, squeezing the life out of him.

***

Armada stood and edged closer to his wife.

The awestruck couple was mesmerized by the images that flashed across the panel of tablets.

With all ten Clouds tethered together and secured to the frame of Halo One, the rapidly ascending orbital stations easily ripped the metal grid from the moorings of its four carbon braids.

In thankful shock and disbelief, they observed the quartet of nine-mile long cables slowly begin to collapse in on themselves.

Armada firmly embraced his wife and stroked her hair as she buried her face in his shoulder.

They silently swayed from side to side until Armada felt something grazing the top of his bare feet. He backed away from Chloe and looked down just in time to watch a torrent of clear fluid gush from her shorts, drip down her leg, and begin forming a small puddle between her feet.

CHAPTER 43

Exodus

"How about this one?" Armada asked and held up his tablet for Chloe to see. "I like it."

"Mm-hmm," she hummed and nodded in approval.

"We gotta make up our minds on the pictures we want to upload for the passports."

"Okay, I don't care, just pick one," she hissed and pulled Abdiel close as she breast-fed him, "Keep your voice down."

When Cain Wyczthack officially introduced the world to the SUBOS some twelve years earlier, the United States was still experiencing an influx of illegal immigrants, particularly in the southwest. The State Department, in conjunction with the Departments of Homeland Security, Customs and Border Protection, and Immigration, Citizenship and Naturalization, opened offices in the tower to facilitate the vetting of the incoming throng. In addition, the federal government thought it best to offer passport services to accommodate the growing number of foreign contractors whose involvement with Engenechem and the SUBOS required them to travel to the US.

Moreover, the relocation of the United Nations to the Nevada desert sparked a sudden need to increase the efficiency of the approval and authorization processes of foreign dignitaries wishing to enter the country.

"And you're positive this will work?" Chloe whispered while nursing her son. "You can create new passport identification credentials? No one will know it's us?"

"No, baby, I told you," Armada softly said and sat on the bed next to her. "We—you and I—don't officially exist. Nobody's looking for us. There won't be any Nursery attendants monitoring the entrances or visitors center. We'll go down the elevator to passport services, swipe our cards, and boom ... Chloe Holbrook and Evan Cierly will pop up."

"You can put everything on our cards? You're sure?"

"They've already got our pictures on 'em, so when we walk in we'll simply hold up our lanyards and swipe the reader. If we behave as if we know what we're doing, nobody will pay attention to us. Someone will look at our faces and compare us with the pictures I'm entering in their system, print a new passport right then and there, and stamp it. All we gotta do is act like normal, happy parents who've gone to Vegas to see the planet's largest man-made structure."

"And then we go to the airport. Right?"

"Right-O. We check in at a terminal, show 'em our passports ... and we never ... come ... back."

Armada pulled Chloe's hand to his lips and kissed her skin.

"Don't worry. This is what He told us to do. We'll be all right."

"And everything is already taken care of with the money. Right?" she asked as he stepped back to the table.

"Oh, yeah! Dr. White's accounts were pretty easy to get into. We'll have a sizeable cash advancement waiting for us when we land at JFK, courtesy of Engenechem and Dr. White."

"How much did you take?" Chloe inquired, giggling.

Armada didn't respond.

"Armada. How much did...."

"Ah-ah-ah ... Evan," he interrupted, raising his finger. "Can't call me

Armada anymore. You gotta call me Evan, or Mr. Cierly, or Mr. Genius, or…."

"Or pathetic idiot."

"Well, now let's…."

"Augh! EEVVAANN! How much did you get?"

"Enough," he stated loftily.

"Just say it, baby."

Evan twisted to face Chloe, grinned, and said, "In New York… twenty-five thousand."

"What do you mean 'in New York'? Is there more waiting for us after the second landing?"

"Maybe," he commented and resumed his work.

Chloe gingerly lay her infant son on the upper left side of her chest and began gently patting his back.

"Ah, good boy," she cooed, bouncing him slightly. "You were hungry! Yes, you were!"

"All right, he's done," Chloe then announced.

"And… so am I," Evan triumphantly declared, tapping on his tablet.

"What about the elevators?" she asked, inching to the mattress edge. "Did you reinstall the program coding?"

"Not entirely," Evan replied, rising from his chair. "I'll initiate a full download in just a minute."

After standing and raising his arms over his head, Evan stretched, grunted, and leaned from side to side.

"Are you ready?" he asked his wife.

"Well…," Chloe started to say as she began gazing about the room, "I think so."

"Passport photos and identification?" she called out as she stood.

"Done," Evan replied.

"Elevators?"

"As soon as we call Him, they're ready to go."

"Airline tickets?"

"Yep, yep."

The couple stepped through the room while Chloe ran down their 'to do list.'

"Hotel reservations?"

"Yes, ma'am."

"Maps, directions, contacts, phone numbers…."

"Got it all right here," Evan announced, holding up his tablet.

"Money?"

"We got cash waiting, and I set up a couple of overseas accounts for when we find out where we're supposed to live. There won't be any worries when it comes to money… ever. Trust me when I say… we're set."

"Transportation?"

"A shuttle leaves for Las Vegas every half hour," Evan informed her, taking a sip of his coffee. "We won't need anything in New York 'cause we'll be boarding a connecting flight."

"What about when we arrive? How are…."

"Baby, we'll be fine."

He reached out and tenderly stroked his son's back.

"Everything's going to be okay. After what all you and I have gone through, this will be a breeze."

Chloe leaned into her husband and wrapped her free arm around his waist. Evan firmly squeezed his wife, sandwiching their baby boy.

"I still don't understand why we can't just make arrangements to fly out from here."

"I explained that already. We can't take any chances with the SUBOS, Engenechem, the air base … there's too many opportunities for somebody to recognize us. The sooner we get out into the public and blend in, the sooner we ensure our safety and survival."

Evan and Chloe stood at the foot of their bed and took one last, long, good look at their domain.

"I still can't believe what we've accomplished … all from this room," she admitted.

"I know. It's amazing what can happen in just five months. If you told me three years ago what I … we … were going to do, I would have laughed in your face."

"I'm married, I gave birth to a son … we stopped a launch of nuclear missiles … we…."

Chloe choked on her words and took several breaths in an attempt to control her emotions. Evan rubbed her arms as he, too, tried to stifle his feelings.

"Is this it? Are we done?" Chloe asked and looked at her husband.

"Yeah," he answered, kissing her head, "I think so."

Evan peered up at the ceiling and proudly said, "Okay, we're ready to go now."

***

"I feel like everyone is staring at me," Chloe whispered in Evan's ear. "It's as if someone from Engenechem is watching and following us."

"Nah," he replied and glanced back over his left shoulder. "Cain still probably assumes we're hiding in the SUBOS."

As they neared the passenger drop-off zone, Chloe sat up straight and tilted her head to get a better view through the shuttle's front windshield.

"Why are there armed military at the airport?" she nervously questioned as the bus started slowing down.

"Well," Evan began, gazing out the windows, "I imagine they're here to guard against someone doing to the planes and terminals what we just did to Cain and the Clouds."

As soon as the bus came to a halt, the two side doors opened and four men equipped with automatic weapons quickly boarded. Dressed all in black with helmets, sunglasses, gloves, and bulletproof vests, the quartet of security personnel spread themselves out in the center aisle. The four men had lanyards with badges that hung around their necks, along with multiple patches and insignia representing various divisions of law enforcement.

"Ladies and gentlemen, please have all of your identification credentials open and ready for inspection," the officer at the front of the bus shouted. "If you will please keep your speaking to a minimum and cooperate with us, we can conduct our screenings much more effectively and efficiently, which means you make it to your gates on time. Let's go."

Abdiel made a faint whimper as Evan, Chloe, and forty passengers stood and rifled through their belongings in search of driver's licenses, travel visas, and passports.

"Just remain calm," Evan cautiously muttered. "Don't look at any of 'em 'til we're off the shuttle."

The line of jittery and agitated travelers slowly advanced to the exits and, one by one, had their identification documents scrutinized. Chloe's mind was set awhirl when her thoughts suddenly turned to the years of Gestapo-style interrogations and evaluations she and her sisters endured at the hands of Cain and Dr. White. Her heart started racing as she shuffled closer and closer to the open bus door and the waiting officers.

"C'mon, folks," she heard one of the armed agents call out. "Let's step it up a bit. Move, move!"

Looking down from the bus, Evan saw hundreds upon hundreds of people standing in lines awaiting verification of their identification and validation of airline ticket purchases.

"They don't have time to mess around," Evan mumbled in her ear from behind. "If they get suspicious, we'll be flagged and pulled out of line. So if he asks you anything, just answer the question as quickly as you can with the least amount of words."

Chloe nodded silently, draped the blanket over Abdiel's face, and reached behind her for Evan's hand. He discreetly pressed up against Chloe's backside and laced his fingers with hers.

"All right, next," the grim-faced officer stated and glanced up at Chloe. "Identification, tickets, and destination."

Chloe clutched at her baby boy and stepped off the shuttle stairs. She quietly handed the security agent her passport and the ticket Evan printed just a few hours earlier.

"Destination?" he gruffly inquired and shone a fluorescent flashlight at the passport.

"New York," she meekly replied, looking down and away from him.

The second armed officer took a step toward Chloe and gave her a slow going over.

"Ma'am?" he said. "Are you okay? I mean is everything all right with you?"

Taken aback, she stammered and didn't know how to respond.

"What? Am I okay? Am I … yes, yes. Everything is fine. Yes, yes … whu, whu, why? Why do you…?"

"Well, I'm standing here lookin' at you and all these other folks in front of the Las Vegas International Airport…," the man started to say and moved closer to Chloe. "And I got to thinkin' 'cause I couldn't help but notice that you appear to have no luggage, no purse, no handbag, no backpack … not even a diaper bag or bottle for your kid … but you're about to get on a jet to whisk you off to … New York City?"

"That is a bit odd," the first agent declared with a nod, folding his arms.

He and his partner stared at Chloe and her stained, tattered, and discolored one-piece jumper.

"The ensemble you've elected to wear today … uh…," the first officer commented sarcastically, shaking his head. "Would you mind explaining…."

"Our hotel room was broken into yesterday afternoon," Evan sharply interjected, stepping off the bus.

Chloe immediately clammed up and started bouncing Abdiel in her arms as her husband assumed control of the situation.

After handing off his passport to the officer on his right and his ticket to the agent on the left, Evan calmly elaborated on his impromptu alibi.

"We came to participate in the Spartan Run this weekend," he declared, pointing to a large banner advertising the cross-country race and obstacle course. "While we were gone, somebody stole everything. All we have left are our suits."

"You wore matching outfits for a thirteen-mile, high-endurance competition in the Nevada desert?" the first officer snarkily asked with a chuckle and handed Evan his passport.

"Yeah, well, you know … gotta do the whole husband-and-wife team thing."

"My wife wouldn't wear identical clothes to save her life," the other man commented and gave Evan and Chloe their tickets.

"How'd y'all do?" he then inquired.

Evan looked at Chloe and replied, "All I know is … we survived and made it out alive."

"I recommend you stop off at one of the gift shops once you've reached the concourse," the agent on his right suggested with a smile. "They got all kinds of shorts and shirts for sale. It's always more expensive in an airport, but at least you can get some decent clothes to wear."

"So we can go now?" Chloe sweetly asked.

"Yes, ma'am, you're free to go."

"Thank you," Evan offered, wrapping his arm around Chloe's waist.

The tiny family gently pushed their way through the congestion to the airport entrance.

"That was close!" Chloe confessed and forced herself to smile. "A cross-country race? Really?"

"It was the only thing I could think of that would account for our appearance," Evan countered as they briskly walked past the airline ticket counters. "Hey, it worked, didn't it?"

***

"Okay, we made it through the body scanners and inspections," Evan mumbled as they entered the terminal. "All that's left to do is present our passports and tickets to an attendant at the gate … and walk on the plane."

"We're not buying clothes before we board?"

"No way!" he whispered. "It's a perfect excuse! Staying in these suits and explaining our situation … it'll be a sympathy story … a couple with a newborn baby gets robbed … trust me, this is ideal. Nobody will question us, watch and see."

"Augh!" she growled lowly and pinched his hip.

Evan and Chloe walked through the terminal's main corridor, taking in the new environment and the ocean of people. Finally, as they approached their designated gate, Chloe felt a bit elated; in less than an hour the trio would be airborne.

Evan placed his wife in front of him at the end of the line to check in and firmly grasped her hips.

"We're gonna be just fine," he confidently stated and placed his chin on her shoulder. "He's delivered us, just like He promised. This is the start of a whole new life for you, me … Abdiel…."

Chloe closed her eyes, leaned back, and reveled in the warmth and comfort of his words and the sound of his voice. Her chin started quivering as memories of her life in the SUBOS flooded her heart and brain.

"Just a few minutes more, baby."

"I can help who's next," Chloe heard a woman cheerfully call out and opened her eyes.

She saw three beautiful young women standing behind the gate service counter, and all were wearing similar uniforms.

"That door to your right is the one we'll use to get on the plane," Evan commented as Chloe wiped away some tears.

As their line grew shorter, Chloe had a better field of vision and watched the girls as they performed their duties.

Look at how happy they are, she thought to herself as the ladies smiled, laughed, and engaged in conversation while they worked. She gently bounced her son from side to side while trying to read the girls' name tags: Vicki, Tori, and April.

"Next!" Vicki politely hollered.

"C'mon," Evan said and nudged Chloe on her bottom, "that's us."

"Hi! How are you today?" Vicki asked, smiling broadly.

"Hi," Chloe sheepishly answered as she and Evan nervously approached the counter and quietly presented their passports and tickets.

"Flying to New York today?" Vicki jovially inquired.

"Yes," said Evan.

Abdiel suddenly stirred and grunted a few times.

"How old is your baby?" Tori asked while handing a customer their boarding passes.

"He's ten days old," Chloe answered and turned toward her.

"Oh, I love baby boys!" April chimed in with a chuckle. "Actually, I just love babies, period."

"What happened to y'all's clothes?" Tori asked, and stepped next to Vicki as she pecked away at her keyboard.

"We...," Evan started to say.

"Our hotel room was broken into yesterday afternoon while we were out," Chloe interrupted.

"No!" the women exclaimed, along with, "Oh, my gosh!" and "I don't believe it!"

The three ladies converged on Chloe as she gave them the rundown on what happened and the seriousness of their plight.

"We have nothing 'til we get to New York," Chloe complained and laid it on thick with the woe and misery. "No luggage, no purse, no handbag, no backpack, no diaper bag ... I don't even have a bottle for my son."

Evan puckered his lips and focused on a television screen in order to not laugh out loud.

"Well, we'll fix you up good, starting right now!" Vicki angrily declared as Tori and April came out from behind the service counter and began hugging and consoling Chloe and Evan.

"What are you doing?" Evan asked Vicki.

"We're upgrading you from coach to first class!" she replied and speedily typed on her computer.

"You can do that?"

"Ooohhh, can we see your baby?" Tori asked and crouched slightly with excitement.

"Oh, yeah, let's get a good look at that boy of yours," April added and daintily clapped her hands.

"Well, I uh, we…," Chloe mumbled, unassured.

"Hold it, hold it… hold it right there!" Vicki demanded and joined her coworkers in front of the counter. "I'm not missing out on this."

Chloe looked up at Evan and shrugged her shoulders.

"It's okay," Evan said, "Let 'em see."

The three women, giddy with anticipation, watched Chloe while she adjusted Abdiel to a reclined, almost upright position in her left arm. Ever so carefully and slowly, she peeled back the makeshift blanket from her son's face.

"We haven't really exposed him to other people yet," Chloe admitted, "so I don't know how he'll respond to you."

The proud mother revealed her son to the anxious ladies.

Abdiel was already awake with his big brown-green eyes wide open.

Evan watched the women's facial expressions undergo an immediate and dramatic transformation. Moments ago, the gaggle of ladies were smiling broadly and all a twitter to see the infant. As soon as they gazed upon the child, the women started to tear up. The smiles never left their faces, but were somehow different now. Tori had to cover her mouth, whereas April removed a tissue from her pants' pocket and wiped her eyes and nose. Vicki's jaw hung down and her neck and chest turned bright red.

They were near hypnotized at the mere sight of the boy.

"What's his name?" Vicki asked as tears began trickling down her cheeks.

"Abdiel," Chloe answered softly, confused by their reactions. "We were told to name…."

"We were told his name means 'servant of God,'" Evan quickly interjected and placed his hands on Chloe's shoulders.

"Abdiel," Tori and April repeated in unison as they wiped their eyes.

"Abdiel. Precious Abdiel. You're a special boy, yes you are. I can tell just by looking at you," Vicki stated, then asked, "Can I touch him?"

Chloe grinned and nodded in approval.

Vicki slowly reached out to Abdiel, never breaking eye contact. The boy grasped at her index finger with both hands and jostled his legs.

"Oh!" Vicki gasped lowly at the sensation of the baby's touch.

She peered up at Chloe and Evan, smiled, mouthed to them a silent 'Thank you,' and pulled her hand away from Abdiel.

Vicki, Tori, and April stepped silently and slowly around the end of the service counter while keeping baby Abdiel in their sights. They continued to sniff and wipe at the last of their tears as they resumed their duties.

"Now," Vicki began after turning her attention to the computer screen in front of her, "I see you're to make a connecting flight a couple of hours after you land at JFK. What's your final destination?"

Chloe and Evan replied, "Jerusalem."

X^n
by Clint Townsend
[X to the Nth]

Titan clicked the blinking 'mail' icon and a small window opened on his monit·

'Don't go!' the note read.

He stared at the computer screen and quietly reread the message.

'I can't not go.' he typed nervously in response, then turned to look about t·
work station.

After a brief and eerily silent moment, the mail icon again blinked and pinged

Titan took another jittery glance around the room before opening and readi·
the new message:

'You know what happens when someone complains.'

A native Texan and much-traveled writer, Clint Townsend has also made his hor·
in New Mexico, Arizona, and Oklahoma. God continues to open doors for Cli·
despite receiving a diagnosis of ALS (Lou Gehrig's Disease) in 2006. Clin·
faith in Jesus Christ has empowered him to rise above the many obstacles a·
challenges he faces on a daily basis. He typed the entirety of this book with ·
eyes by using eye gaze tracking technology on a digital keyboard. Clint has·
daughter and granddaughter and currently lives in the Dallas area.

ELM HILL
A Division of
HarperCollins Christian Publishing

For information on getting your book published
visit www.elmhillbooks.com

CPSIA information can be obtained
at www.ICGtesting.com
Printed in the USA
LVHW011540250119
605274LV00007B/19